The Women on Platform Two

The Women on Platform Two

LAURA ANTHONY

G

GALLERY BOOKS

New York   Amsterdam/Antwerp   London
Toronto   Sydney   New Delhi

G

Gallery Books
An Imprint of Simon & Schuster, LLC
1230 Avenue of the Americas
New York, NY 10020

First Gallery Books hardcover edition March 2025

GALLERY BOOKS and colophon are registered trademarks of Simon & Schuster, LLC

For information about special discounts for bulk purchases, please contact Simon & Schuster Special Sales at 1-866-506-1949 or business@simonandschuster.com.

The Simon & Schuster Speakers Bureau can bring authors to your live event. For more information or to book an event, contact the Simon & Schuster Speakers Bureau at 1-866-248-3049 or visit our website at www.simonspeakers.com.

Interior design by Kathryn A. Kenney-Peterson

Manufactured in the United States of America

10 9 8 7 6 5 4 3 2 1

Library of Congress Control Number: 2024946266

ISBN 978-1-6680-4738-5
ISBN 978-1-6680-4740-8 (ebook)

To all the women on board—thank you!

Preface

The story that follows is based on a real-life event which occurred in the Republic of Ireland and Northern Ireland in the early 1970s. While the characters are entirely fictional, the story is loosely based on the fortitude and determination of real Irish women and their actions in bringing safe and legal contraception to the women of Ireland.

The Women on Platform Two

CHAPTER I

Dublin City, 22 May 2023

Saoirse

I have pee on my fingers. It's my own pee, but it makes me feel gross none-theless. I've never taken a pregnancy test before and I wasn't expecting it to be this fiddly. I set the test down on the back of the loo—face up, according to the instructions. I read them twice—front and back—hoping to calm my nerves. It didn't say anything about peeing on your own hand, but it did say to wait three minutes before reading the result. Three whole minutes. I think my heart might beat out of my chest by then.

"One line not pregnant. Two lines pregnant," I whisper out loud. *Oh God.*

I wash my hands, close my eyes, and take some deep breaths. Seconds seem to crawl by in slow motion and I hear the ticking of an imaginary clock inside my head.

Tick. Tock. You might be pregnant. Tick. Tock.

Finally, I open my eyes. I think I may be sick as I bring my gaze to the back of the loo. The small plastic test stares back at me, proudly displaying a single, bright blue line.

"One line not pregnant," I say again, louder this time.

My hand is shaking as I curl my fingers around the test, pick it up, and tuck it against my chest. Fat, salty tears trickle down my cheeks as relief washes over me.

The bathroom door creaks open behind me and I spin around. In my haste to test, I must have forgotten to lock the door. I find Miles, my fiancé, standing in the gap. His eyes are on the test in my clenched fist and his mouth drops open a little.

"Is that—"

"A pregnancy test. Yes," I say, wiping under my eyes with my free hand.

"Is it—"

"Negative."

Miles closes his mouth and his face fills with sadness.

"Negative," he echoes in a barely audible whisper.

"Yup."

I pass him the test so he can see the single blue line for himself.

"Be careful, there might be some pee on it."

"It's really negative," he says, shaking his head. "But you're two weeks late. I thought you must be pregnant for sure."

"You were hoping, you mean," I say, and I can't keep the frustration out of my tone. The swell of relief I felt at the negative test clashes with the disappointment in his voice and everything bubbles to the surface.

"Is that so wrong?"

"Yes. I've told you a million times that I'm not ready for a baby."

"But if it just happens . . ."

I raise my hand like a cop directing traffic. "Stop. Please. I can't have this argument again."

"It's not an argument. It's just . . ." Miles trails off.

His downheartedness whips around us like an icy breeze. I step back to avoid the freeze of it. I love Miles. He's my favorite person in the world. I love how his floppy brown hair falls into his eyes when he's overdue a haircut, like at the moment. I love his round-rimmed maroon glasses that he says are only for reading, which we both know is absolutely not true. He walked into a wall trying to prove how much he didn't need glasses when we first started dating. He still has the scar above his left eyebrow. I love that too. I love how he waits to eat dinner with me when I come home from a long shift at the hospital even though I know he's been starving for hours. Miles is wonderful. He would be a fantastic father. And the only, single thing I don't like about him is that he cannot accept that just because he's ready to be a dad doesn't mean I'm ready to be a mam.

"But you love children," Miles says, rehashing the same tired line I've heard more times than I can count. "And the kids at the hospital love you. You're their favorite nurse."

I puff out, "It's my job."

"But it's not your job to keep their artwork on our fridge or bake them cakes for their birthdays and stuff. It's not your job to care about them so much. But you do."

"Of course I care about them. They're sick and it breaks my heart. But making their day less crappy if I can is not the same as having a child of my own."

"We're not getting any younger, Saoirse . . ." Miles sighs. "Think about it. Our life could be so great."

"Our life is already great."

I'm not exaggerating. We have a great life. Careers we both love. A cozy one-bedroom apartment in the city center. It's small, but the perfect space for the two of us. A good group of friends. His and mine. Weekends away, dinners out, impromptu takeaways, and too much wine. A grown-up life with no room for a child.

Miles stares at me with longing eyes and my guilt is instant. As great as our life is, he needs more. I feel him cling to the hope that someday, for some reason that neither of us can put our finger on right now, I'll feel the same. I place my hand on my heart, take a deep breath, and try once again to explain.

"Most of the children at work won't make it past their tenth birthday," I say. "Last week we lost a seven-year-old who I really thought was going to beat the odds. I watched her fall into a forever sleep in her mother's arms and I watched her mother die inside too. I don't want that. I don't ever want to feel anything like that."

"But not all children get sick. Our baby would more than likely be perfectly healthy."

I shrug. "Yeah. Probably. But the 'what ifs' scare me. Christ, why can't you just accept that?"

"Because it's bloody selfish, Saoirse. That's why."

"See, this is why I didn't want to talk about this." I brush past him to make my way into the kitchen to pour myself a glass of water. "We just go round and round in circles. Over and over. It's pointless."

"It's not pointless. It's a baby. *Our* baby," he says, following me.

I fetch a glass from the cupboard and run the tap. I stare at the water flowing for a moment before I push the glass under and fill it. I drink some and feel better.

"Now who's being selfish?" I say. "Do you plan to keep arguing about this until I finally give in? I told you. I'm not ready."

"If you would just think about it," he says, as if I haven't already spent years agonizing over this. "I know as soon as you hold our baby in your arms you'll fall in love."

I slam the glass down on the countertop and water sloshes over the edge.

"How do you know that?" My voice is too loud for the confined space of our small kitchen. "How could you possibly bloody know that? Do you have a crystal ball?"

"Of course not," Miles snaps, his voice equally loud. "But all women love their babies."

"You mean, you *think* all women love their babies. But that is just not true. Sadly, for whatever reason, some women just can't. And besides, not all women are mothers. It's bloody insulting if you can't separate the two."

I march out of the kitchen and grab my favorite oversize cardigan from the coatrack in the hall.

"Where are you going?"

"Out."

"It's going to rain," he says.

"Then I'll get wet."

"Saoirse, stay. Please? Can't we talk about this?"

"No."

I slip my arms into my cardigan and open the door of our apartment. The lift creaks and groans as it lowers me two floors and spits me out at street level. I hurry outside and take a deep breath, inhaling as if I've just come up from underwater, and I start to walk, with absolutely no idea where I'm going.

CHAPTER 2

Saoirse

I wander around town aimlessly for a while. It's unusually cold for May, and without a coat, I'm shivering. I think about turning back, but instead I wrap one side of my cardigan over the other, fold my arms tightly across my chest, and lower my head into the wind.

The city is busy, just the way I like it. Solo shoppers dip in and out of shops on a mission to find the perfect bag or coat or shoes. Loved-up couples hold hands, window-shopping and enjoying a stroll. And of course, there are mothers and their children. Young women push buggies. Flustered mothers try to wrestle wiry toddlers while keeping an eye on fed-up older children. Pregnant women smile every time their hands brush against their round bellies.

One mother in particular catches my eye. She's about my age, mid-thirties, I'd guess. Her hair is red and curly like mine. She's petite too. No taller than five foot three. My height. I can't take my eyes off her and the little girl who holds her hand and skips alongside her so contentedly. The child is about four or maybe five. She's pretty. A miniature version of her mother. They look at each other every so often as they walk, and they both smile. They love each other very much and it's a beautiful thing. I try to imagine myself in the mother's shoes. I think about small fingers knitted between mine and round innocent eyes smiling up at me. I think about loving someone unconditionally and being loved all the same in return. I think about the responsibility that falls on every mother's shoulders the moment she brings a child into this world. A responsibility to put that child first, always. And I think that I could do it. I *know* I could. Miles is right. I know that the instant I held a baby of my own in my arms, that child would come above all else. But, more than that, my gut is telling me that I am not ready. I doubt I will ever be ready.

The mother and her daughter turn into Zara and I walk on. I pick up my pace, trying to keep warm as the sky darkens. I'm almost outside Connolly train station when there's a clap of thunder and angry clouds spit torrential rain. The street empties as people scatter, searching for cover. I race up the steps of the station and by the time I duck inside, my cardigan has turned from mint to dark teal.

"Summer my arse," someone says, as a handful of people huddle just inside the entrance. "It'd freeze the balls off a pool table out there today, so it would."

There's shared laughing and strangers engage in collective venting about turbulent Irish weather. Someone says something about the forecast looking better for next week. I break away from the small group of wet people and close my eyes. Rain pounds the roof like hundreds of tiny feet marching. I love that sound. Miles and I spend many lazy Saturday mornings in bed listening to the sound of stomping rain. I wonder if he's gone back to bed with a cup of coffee and one ear cocked toward the ceiling, listening. Or maybe he's pacing around our small apartment trying to walk off his frustration. Miles always paces when he's mad or hurt. This argument is going to have our carpets threadbare. I slide my phone out of my jeans pocket and think about calling him. But there's nothing I want to say over the phone. I decide to go home when the rain stops.

The station smells of engine oil and coffee. My stomach rumbles and I remember that I skipped breakfast and lunch. I pick up a bar of Cadbury Dairy Milk and a cup of machine coffee in the tuckshop and find a bench to sit down and wait the bad weather out. I sip bitter coffee and enjoy the soothing sounds of the busy station: the rumbling of a train coming to life and chugging away. The hum of commuters chatting, and the patter of their feet as they hurry down the platform and hop aboard. Finally, I realize the rain has stopped. But I sit a little longer, alone with my thoughts, an empty paper cup, and service announcements.

Please stand back behind the yellow line. The next train departing from platform two is the thirteen-fifty enterprise service to Belfast. Calling at Drogheda, Dundalk, Newry, Portadown, Belfast.

I've never been to Northern Ireland before but I've heard it's beautiful and the wine is cheaper, apparently. One of the girls in radiology travels across the border every Christmas to stock up on booze and chocolates. She says that even with the exchange rate from euros to pounds she saves a fortune. I wonder if Miles and I should take a trip. It's only a couple of hours from Dublin, and a long weekend away could be just what we need.

I'm googling hotels in Belfast when an elderly lady passes by. I catch her glossy silver hair and baby-pink raincoat from the corner of my eye and I hope I'm half as glamorous when I'm older. I watch her for a moment as she tries her best to hurry toward a waiting train. She carries a scrapbook by her side, the way a businessman might carry a briefcase. I smile as I'm reminded that before mobile phones and laptops, people used scrapbooks or photo albums to hold their memories. My heart pangs and I wish I was living in those simpler times. I sigh audibly and stand up to go home. I'm dropping my cup into the nearby bin when I notice an old black-and-white photograph on the ground nearby. *The lady must have dropped it from her scrapbook*, I think as I bend down to pick it up.

"Excuse me," I call out.

A teenager with a backpack slung over one shoulder turns around and makes eye contact.

"No. Sorry," I say, standing back up and pointing toward the lady gaining distance.

He nods, turns back, and continues walking.

"Sorry, excuse me," I call out again, louder this time.

My efforts are no match for the noisy station. The lady doesn't hear me. Instead, she gingerly steps over the gap and onto a waiting train.

I stare at the photo in my hand, hoping to find a clue about its owner. One corner is missing and another is fraying. Unsurprisingly, the gray image has adopted a yellowish hue over the years, but the bright smiles on the two young women looking back at me are no doubt as fresh as the day it was taken. The women stand each with one arm wrapped around the other's shoulders and with their other arm punch the air as if they are cheering. Their joy emanates from the delicate paper, and I wonder what they're celebrating.

I guess from their clothing the photo was taken in the sixties or maybe the early seventies. The taller of the two women is slim and stylish. Her hair is centered on the top of her head in a neat bun and she's wearing corduroy trousers with a flare at the bottom. The other lady is older, or perhaps just less fashion-conscious. She wears a box-pleated skirt and sensible shoes. There's a train in the background and it takes me a moment to realize the photo was taken here, in Connolly Station. The station has changed somewhat since then but certainly not enough to be unrecognizable. I turn the photograph over, hoping to find a name or an address, but unsurprisingly there isn't either. There is, however, a date handwritten in blue pen.

22 May 1971.

My breath catches when I realize the photograph is exactly fifty-two years old today. I sweep my eyes over the station, searching for the lost and found. I spot a small hatch with a sign above it exclaiming LOST. The FOUND seems to have peeled away. The irony makes me sigh. *The place where lost things go and are rarely found*, I think. I shake my head. It's obvious this photo is of great importance—why else would someone carry it in a scrapbook for more than fifty years? I'm not sure why, but I can't escape the sense that I owe it to the smiling women staring up at me to ensure that this photograph is returned safely to its owner.

A train horn honks, and there's no time to think before I instinctively start running toward platform two. I don't have a ticket and I balk when I reach the turnstile. I count backward from three and jump. My face stings and I'm certain I'll feel the hand of security on my shoulder at any moment, but I keep going.

"I'm not getting on. I'm just giving a woman her photo," I find myself announcing to no one in particular as I race down the platform.

I'm red-faced, mortified, and short of breath when I step onto the train. I shuffle down the aisle, scanning the seats on both sides until I come upon a lady with silky silver hair shaped into a neat bob that frames her face. The scrapbook is lying on the table in front of her and up close I can see it's fragile and dog-eared, just like the photo. The leather spine is cracked and has been hand-stitched with green and blue thread.

"Hi. Hello," I puff. "I think you might have dropped something."

I open my hand and show the lady the photograph.

Her hands cup her face and she lets out a distressed gasp. The skin on the back of her hands is thin, like tissue paper covering her bones. Her nails are painted a delicate pink and match the coat she has taken off and folded across her knees.

"Oh goodness yes. That *is* mine. How on earth did I drop it? I'm usually so careful." Her voice has the distinctive crackle that comes with age.

"Ah, it can easily happen," I say, trying to make light of the situation. "I left my phone in the cinema a few weeks ago." I pass her the photograph and smile, rather pleased with my good deed for the day.

"I was rushing, you see," she continues, noticeably swallowing an emotional lump. "I have to be in Belfast for dinner this evening and I couldn't miss this train. . . ." She trails off. "But if I lost this . . ." Her voice cracks. "Well, Bernie would never forgive me." She points to the shorter of the two women in the photograph. "That's Bernie there. And that's me beside her. We were best friends for over forty years. I still haven't forgiven her for dying and leaving me to take this train alone."

I'm not sure how to react to that.

"You can smile," she says, reading my discomfort. "Bernie would. She was always smiling and laughing. Oh, what fun we had."

I do smile, because I notice how she strokes her finger over the photo, gently caressing Bernie's image with such fondness.

"I'm so glad you got this back," I say. "Enjoy Belfast."

I turn to walk away when I feel her grab my hand. She's trembling slightly and I wonder if she could use a drink. I know I could do with one after the turnstile incident.

"Thank you," she says. "Thank you so very much."

She lets me go and reaches into her purse. She pulls fifty euros out and shoves it toward me.

"For helping me . . . eh . . ." She smiles at me with her head cocked slightly to one side, and it takes me a moment to realize that she's waiting for my name.

"Saoirse," I say.

"Thank you, Saoirse." She straightens her head once more. "I'm Maura. It's lovely to meet you."

"Maura and Bernie," I whisper, my eyes falling onto the photo again. "You look beautiful."

She presses the money against my palm. "It was a beautiful day."

I smile awkwardly, not sure what to do or say and certainly not sure if I should accept an elderly lady's money. But Maura doesn't give me time to overthink it. She guides my fingers to curl around the crisp note. Satisfied it's firmly in my grasp, she cups both my hands in hers and squeezes gently. My heart swells and I enjoy this unexpected moment.

Suddenly, I lose my footing and I grab the back of Maura's chair to steady myself. "Are we moving?"

"It seems so," Maura says.

"Oh God. Oh no."

"What is it? What's wrong?"

"I'm not supposed to be on board. I mean, I just got on for a minute to give you the photo. Feck, this is all I need today."

"Oh, love." Maura's face fills with concern as she pulls her shoulders toward her ears and holds them there. "Have you somewhere very important that you need to be?"

I shrug. "Actually, no. Not really. It's my day off."

Maura's shoulders fall back into their rightful place and she pats the seat beside her. "Oh well, that's all right, then," she says. "I think you should sit yourself down. Drogheda's the first stop. It's not too far. You'll be back where you started in less than an hour."

"I don't have a ticket," I say, flopping into the seat next to her.

"Don't worry, m'dear. I boarded this train for the first time on the twenty-second of May, nineteen seventy-one, so I can have a word if they ask. It's very hard to say no to a nice little old lady."

"That's the date on the back of the photograph," I say. "The twenty-second of May 1971. Was it your first time on a train?"

"Oh no." Maura scrunches her nose. "But it was my first time on *this* train. Bernie's too. It changed our lives forever." A rosy hue brushes across her cheeks and I think she's blushing. "But hey, I'm just an old lady now," she says. "I'm not sure anyone wants to listen to my ramblings."

"What happened on that train ride?" I ask.

There's a twinkle in Maura's eye and I've no doubt she's replaying the memory in her mind. She stretches her arm across the table and places her hand on the scrapbook, pausing for a moment as if it's a delicate, sleeping thing that she doesn't want to disturb. The skin on her hand highlights her age. Time has patiently embroidered lines and folds over the fifty-two years since the photograph was taken. *Fifty-two years*, I think, *and still, she clutches the scrapbook photo as if it's her most prized possession in the world*. I have no doubt that it is.

Finally, she flicks through the scrapbook and settles on a page somewhere in the middle. She pulls some sticky tape out of her handbag and attaches the photo with a firm press.

Then she flicks the scrapbook back to the first page and, keeping it open, guides it across the table toward me.

"Bernie always said a story is best told over tea and biscuits. Do you like tea?"

I glance over my shoulder toward the confectionery cart at the end of the carriage and back toward the scrapbook with a handwritten message on the first page that reads *Property of Mrs. Bernie McCarthy*.

I haven't had a cup of tea in years; I'm a coffee person—occupational habit, I guess. But suddenly there is nothing I'd like more than a cup of tea and a chance to hear Maura and Bernie's story.

"Tea sounds great," I say.

CHAPTER 3

Dublin, November 1968

Maura

It's a perfectly ordinary Saturday, mundane even, when a man walks into Switzers department store on Grafton Street and changes my life. I notice he is tall first. He is six foot if he is an inch. Next, I take in his clothes: an expensive trilby hat—the type my father wears, of that scratchy material that can't be comfortable—and a long tan trench coat. We stock that trench coat in our menswear section. It costs thirty-two pounds and fourteen shillings—more than a month's wages for me.

He walks up to the counter, looks me in the eye, and says, "Has anyone ever told you you are the spitting image of a young Doris Day?"

I blush, although I'm not sure why. People tell me I look like the famous Hollywood star all the time.

"Oh, Maureen, if she isn't a mini Doris," my aunt told my mother on my confirmation day.

"I know." Ma nodded. "With Maura's good looks she'll catch herself a fine husband someday."

I've made a conscious effort to style myself in Doris's image ever since. I visit the salon once a month and have my already fair hair dyed a little blonder. I keep it cropped above my shoulders with just enough length to tuck behind my ears. And I never leave the house without dark mascara and ruby red lipstick. My mother says it makes me look like a harlot.

"It's the sixties, Ma," I tell her. "Women want to look their best these days."

Besides, management insists all female staff wear makeup to complement our uniforms. Our emerald green pinafores must sit exactly above our knees—not an inch higher, and we must wear black shoes with a block heel. I spend almost half my wages on new shoes every month, and Ma says I'd better break the habit before I get married, because no man in his right mind would put up with that.

"Do you like Doris Day?" I ask the man in the trilby hat as he stares at me boldly.

"I think she's the most beautiful woman in the world," he says, with a confidence that makes my knees want to buckle.

My cheeks sting for a moment before I manage to spit out, "How can I help you today, sir?"

"A coat," he says matter-of-factly. "It's my darling mammy's birthday next week and I think a coat would be a fine thing."

"Yes, indeed. Especially in this weather." November has been particularly nasty so far. We had snow to start the month and there's been hail almost every day this week. "Wool?"

He shakes his head. "Fur, I think."

"Fantastic choice."

I walk around from behind the counter to lead him toward some of my favorite blond mink coats that arrived in stock for Christmas.

His eyes drop to my legs and he makes no secret of the fact that he is studying me. I try to ignore the heat in my face as I lead the way and fetch a heavy coat from the rack. I drape it across my arms and turn it toward him.

"It's wonderfully soft," I say.

He strokes it and nods. "This will do nicely."

He doesn't ask how much, and when I ring it up on the till he opens his wallet and hands over the cash without batting an eyelid. I can't help but imagine how wonderful it must be to have a life like that.

I fold the coat, wrap it up, and pass it to him, and wait for him to walk away. He doesn't. Instead, he says, "Do you like Doris Day?"

"I like her films very much," I say. "*Calamity Jane* is one of my favorites."

"Mine too," he says with a toothy grin, and I notice how straight his teeth are. "She has a new film just released. I saw the poster outside the Savoy today when I walked by. Oh, what was it called . . ." He strokes his chin, thinking. "*With Six You Get Eggroll*, that's it."

I'm smiling and I want to say something clever, or at least interesting, but before I have time to open my mouth, he says, "What do you say? Would you like to go to the pictures tonight?"

"Together?" I ask.

He laughs. "Well, yes."

"Tonight?"

"It's only playing for two nights. Last night and tonight. So . . . ?"

"I don't even know your name?"

"Christopher." He extends his hand. "Christopher Davenport."

I take his hand and shake it. "I'm Maura Flynn. And I *would* like to go to the pictures with you, Christopher."

"Christy, please," he says, with a charming smile. "Call me Christy. All my friends do."

"You'd like us to be friends?"

"I would. Yes. Very much."

There's devilment in his sea-gray eyes, a sparkle of mischief that catches under the light, and I suspect life with Christopher Davenport is never dull.

"The film starts at six o'clock. Where will I pick you up?"

"You drive?" I say, my eyes round like two pennies.

He nods. "Your folks' house? Is it here in town?"

"I couldn't expect you to drive all the way to Rathgar. I'll meet you under Clerys clock at five fifty," I say, and it comes out confident and assured.

I see couples meeting under Clerys clock most evenings when I'm walking home from work and I've often wanted to be one of them. My belly fizzes with bubbles of excitement that tonight I will be.

"Five fifty at Clerys," he says; then he takes my hand again, kisses the back of it, and walks away.

I've scarcely caught my breath when Geraldine, my colleague, appears from the stockroom shortly after.

"What has you smiling like the cat that got the cream?" she asks.

"I'm going on a date tonight."

"Ah, Maura." She jams her hands on her hips and shakes her head.

Geraldine, at twenty, is five and a half years younger than me. She's a tiny thing, built as if a puff of wind could blow her away like a cobweb, but I've seen her lift boxes men would struggle with. She has fiery red hair and a personality to match. She wore flat shoes to work when she started, and she told our manager she had a sore big toe and he could like it or lump it. I'd never heard a woman speak to a man like that before. I have to admit, I secretly enjoyed it. And besides, Dick, our manager, is aptly named. Geraldine has worn flat shoes since. It wouldn't surprise me if she turned up in a pair of trousers someday.

"Is he good looking?" she asks.

I nod.

"Tall?"

I nod.

"Rich?"

I nod.

"Marriage material?"

I laugh. "It's a first date, Ger. Marriage might be pushing it a stretch."

"That's what they all say and within six months they're giving up their jobs and moving in with their husbands. Next it's a baby on your hip and another in your belly."

I grin just thinking about it. I rub my empty stomach and try to imagine what it would be like to grow a baby inside me.

"Ah, Maura, there's no hope for you, I see it in you. You'll be married in no time and then you'll have to give up your job, and who will I talk to?"

"You have all the other girls."

Geraldine waves her hand as if she's swatting the idea out of the air. "With the amount of engagement announcements in the place? Ha. Soon there'll be no one left but me."

"Maybe you'll get married yourself someday."

"Never," she says, with firm determination. "Never ever. You couldn't pay me enough to take in a man."

I've heard the rumors, the whispers among the other girls behind Geraldine's back. I can't remember exactly what they called her, something beginning with *L*. It's not a word I'd ever heard before, but I think they were implying Geraldine would rather kiss a woman than a man. I've told them to hush up more times than I can count. Talk of illegal behavior like that could get Geraldine in a lot of trouble. Besides, what business is it of theirs who she wants to kiss?

"You could stand him up, you know," Geraldine says.

"Ger," I balk. "That's awful talk. He seems like a nice chap."

"I'm only pulling your leg, Maura. Go. Have a great date. Just don't get married too soon and leave me."

"I won't. I promise."

CHAPTER 4

Maura

I love Doris Day. I love her films. But I'm not paying attention to a single scene from *With Six You Get Eggroll*. Instead, I'm thinking about the moonlight shining on Christy's hair as he waited below Clerys' big old clock on O'Connell Street. I'm drinking in the sound of his laughter as he thoroughly enjoys the antics on-screen. I'm lost in his smell, like a walk in the forest mixed with warm spices. Without exaggerating, I am basking in the bliss of the most enjoyable evening of my life. All too soon the film is over. We file out of the cinema among other couples, some with their arms around each other, some holding hands. Some stopping for a kiss. I long to feel Christy's lips on mine, but of course I know he wouldn't dare. It's much too soon for that. Instead, we take a walk around the sleeping city streets. The wind is sharp, but I'm grateful for the icy air that cools my warm, excited blood. We talk and talk and it feels as if I've known him forever. I tell him about my job in Switzers and my love for fashion and cosmetics. He tries hard to show interest and I try even harder to suppress a giggle. He tells me about his job as a junior doctor and I don't have to fake my fascination. His career sounds exciting and rewarding.

"It must be wonderful to help people every day," I say. "You're amazing."

Christy's cheeks flush. It might be the cold night air, but I like to think he's blushing. We talk more and I lose all sense of time. I'm not sure why I'm compelled to glance at my watch, but my eyes almost fall out of my head when I do.

"What's the matter?" Christy asks, immediately attentive and concerned.

"It's almost eleven p.m. I've never dared stay out this late before."

"Say no more."

Christy insists on dropping me home and I don't protest. My father is waiting by the open front door. I don't want to think about how long he might have been standing there. Long enough to work up a face so sour it could turn milk.

I thank Christy for a wonderful evening, and I'm in such a hurry to get inside that Christy has to shout after me.

"I'll see you again tomorrow, won't I? Under the clock?"

I look back and nod. I can't think of anything I would like more.

"Maura," Da says in a commanding tone that stops me in my tracks as I walk up the garden path. "Where were you until this hour?"

"The pictures, Da," I say nervously. "Doris Day has a new film. It's very good. I think you and Ma would like it."

"The pictures with a chap?" He glances over my shoulder and his eyes narrow as he takes in the line of Christy's car.

I nod.

"Who is he? Do your mother and I know him?" Da begins squinting, trying to get a better look. "He's not one of the Lynches from the other side of town, is he? You know your mother doesn't get along with Mrs. Lynch."

"His name is Christopher Davenport."

My father makes a face as if he's searching his brain for a long-lost neighbor or acquaintance.

"Davenport. Davenport." He shakes his head. "No. Can't say I know them."

"He's a doctor, Da," I say.

A huge smile bursts across Da's face and he raises his arm and waves as if he's seeing royalty in the flesh.

He continues to wave until Christy's car rounds the corner at the end of our road. With Christy out of sight Da lowers his arm, shakes his head, and tuts, "A doctor, and you didn't ask him in. Oh, Maura, where are your manners?"

Inside, Ma plates up fresh apple tart and custard and Da sits at the table waiting.

"A spoon, love," he says, when Ma sets the heaped plate down in front of him. "And a cup of tea would go down nicely too."

"I'm just waiting for the kettle to boil." She smiles, already on the task.

"Did you hear our Maura is stepping out with a chap?" Da says.

Ma turns toward me, wide-eyed and unsure.

"A doctor, if you don't mind," he adds.

Ma's face lights up. "A doctor," she says, with a single clap of her hands. Then she tucks her clasped hands under her chin and rocks her head from side to side. "Oh, Maura, how wonderful. You've caught yourself a good one, haven't you?"

I see Christy almost every night after that. The only nights I don't see him are those in which something crops up at the hospital and he has to work late. He always apologizes with flowers or chocolates, no matter how often I tell him there's no need. When we're together, I feel happier and more content than I ever have before. There are walks in the Phoenix Park after work. Lazy Sunday drives in the Wicklow mountains. Dinners in fancy restaurants and talk of our perfect future. Sometimes, when I imagine our life filled with a beautiful home and a handful of children who look just like their father, I'm so full of happiness I think I might burst.

The happiest day of all comes on Sunday, 18 May 1969—six months after our first date. Christy joins my parents and me for a roast beef dinner. Da doesn't change out of his suit after mass. Ma keeps her Sunday best on too, and I wear my favorite red dress. It has a tulip collar and it sits just above my knee. Ma says it's a little short for her liking and when she turns her back, I roll my eyes.

My mother always keeps a pristine home, but today she outdoes herself. She shoves a cloth and some polish my way and tells me to shine the door handles as she sets to work washing the kitchen floor. Neither of my older brothers were given chores when they brought a lady friend home for the first time. Instead, Ma fussed over them like a clucking hen. *My darling boys*, she called them. We don't see them all that much since they got married and I can tell she misses them something terrible. I promise myself that when I get married, I will still see my parents all the time.

The smell of beef roasting in the oven wafts around the house. Da sits in the front room with his feet on the coffee table and the newspaper in his hands. Ma brings him a cup of tea.

"To keep the hunger out until dinner," she says.

Da kisses her cheek and says, "Thank you, my darling Maureen," and he watches her with adoration as she leaves the room.

I shine the door handles to perfection as I observe them both. I hope someday, after years and years of love, Christy will still look at me the way my father looks at my mother.

Christy arrives promptly at one minute before two o'clock.

"He's early," Ma says, instantly in a tizzy when the doorbell chimes. "Well, don't just stand there, Maura, open the door, for heaven's sake."

I do as I'm told. I find Christy looking more handsome than ever in a new navy suit and a sky blue tie that complements his blue-gray eyes.

Christy passes me a tin of Jacob's biscuits and winks. "For your folks," he says.

"Oh lovely, my favorites," I hear Ma's voice behind me. I try not to smirk. Ma never eats Jacob's biscuits. She says they're far too expensive. I turn around to pass her the large tin and find she's taken off her apron and applied some lipstick.

"Hello. Hello. Welcome, young man," Da says, joining us in the hallway. Suddenly the space feels far too small for four people.

"Dinner won't be long," Ma says. "You'll have a drink, won't you, Dr. Davenport? Sherry? A whiskey, perhaps?"

"Just water would be lovely. And it's Christy, please. Only my patients call me 'Doctor.'"

"Oh. Yes. Of course." Ma blushes.

Dinner is splendid. The table is set with my late grandmother's finest china—the china normally reserved for Christmas and Easter. The meat is tender and there is not a lump to be found in the mashed potatoes or gravy.

"Maura peeled the spuds," Ma announces, as if I should be proud.

Da rubs his belly, looks Christy in the eye, and adds, "The Flynn women can cook, I'll tell you that."

"There's nothing to it, really," I say.

Da's eyes narrow, reminding me that he hates to be interrupted.

"It really was a lovely meal, thank you," Christy says, and he seems unsure where to look. He settles on me and gives me a bright smile. "You're a lucky man with grub like this in your house, Mr. Flynn."

"The spuds are my grandmother's recipe," I jump in, chuffed with Ma's and my efforts.

"Maura!" Da says my name in a familiar clipped tone that insists I hush up. He reinforces his command with a furrowed brow and pinched lips. "Christopher was speaking." He turns toward Christy and shakes his head as if he's terribly disappointed in me.

After dinner Da and Christy retire to the front room and I overhear them discussing a headline from today's paper. Ma and I clear the table and set about the tidy-up. I wash while she dries.

Ma hums the chorus of an Elvis Presley song on repeat, stopping every so often to say, "Oh, he's a lovely boy. A lovely, lovely boy. Well done, Maura. Well done."

I know what my mother *really* means is, *he's a lovely doctor.*

She goes back to humming, but it's not long before she sets her tea towel down and reaches for my sudsy hands. She's rather serious looking, but there's a twinkle in her eyes.

"He's asking your father for your hand, Maura. You know that, don't you?"

I gasp. It takes me a moment to catch my breath. "Really? Do you really think he is?"

"I'd put money on it," she says, squeezing my wet hands.

Bubbles of excitement pop inside my belly.

"You'll say yes," she says, and I know it's not a question.

But it doesn't matter, because obeying her direct order is the one thing I want most in the world.

"Mrs. Davenport," I whisper. "Oh my goodness, Mrs. Maura Davenport."

I try the name on as if it's an expensive coat or a fine hat, and it makes me feel pretty and sophisticated.

Finally, I look up at my mother. "Oh, Ma."

Ma throws her arms around me and kisses the top of my head. "That's my girl."

CHAPTER 5

May 1969

Maura

"Good morning," I say as Geraldine arrives at work.

She's wearing slender-legged trousers that show off her ankles and she has a newspaper rolled like a telescope tucked under her arm.

"Well, do I have a bone to pick with you," she says.

I glance at the grandfather clock next to the rack of ladies' blouses. Geraldine is twenty minutes late for work for the second time this week. If anyone should be picking bones, it's me. "What is it, Ger?"

She sighs and joins me behind the counter. She's unrolling the newspaper and spreads it across the desk.

"What did I tell you about marriage?" she says. "I said it, didn't I? I warned you that dating leads to weddings."

I look down at the paper. Geraldine has circled the engagement announcement in blue pen. I let out an excited squeak and my feet pedal the ground as if I'm riding an imaginary bicycle.

"'It is with delight that Mr. and Mrs. Charles Flynn of Rathgar, Dublin, announce the engagement of their only daughter, Maura, to Dr. Christopher

Davenport of Rathmines, Dublin,'" Ger reads aloud in a most posh and proper accent.

It makes me belly laugh.

"Oh, Ger, isn't it wonderful?" I say.

"If you're happy, then yes. Yes it is."

"I *am* happy. I am so very, very happy."

My mother insisted on placing the announcement in the paper the moment Christy and my father returned to the kitchen.

"I'll call the *Irish Times* first thing in the morning," she said.

In all the excitement, Christy didn't have a chance to actually pop the question directly to me, but my parents' enthusiasm left no room for technicalities like an actual proposal. Luckily, Christy and I managed to steal a kiss and a hug alone in the garden later.

"I'm going to give you the most wonderful life, I promise," he said, between soft, warm kisses pressed onto my lips.

"I'll miss you something terrible," Geraldine says now, with a voice crack that cuts through my daydreaming. "You're nothing like the other girls here. You have a good head on your shoulders, Maura. Don't let becoming a doctor's wife knock it off."

I'm not sure what Geraldine means but I smile and promise not to change.

"When do you have to give up work?" she asks, closing the newspaper and shoving it under the desk.

"The wedding is the twenty-first of June."

"So soon." Her eyes widen as she counts dates on her fingers. "That's only five weeks away."

"I know," I say, as nervous excitement fills me to the brim. "But I can work right up until the big day."

"And then you can never work again. Can't even apply for a bloomin' job because you're someone's wife. It's ridiculous." Geraldine jams her hands on her hips and puffs out, "It makes my blood boil. Married women can work everywhere else, you know."

I shake my head. I've never heard of a married woman working, unless she was a teacher.

"They do," Ger says, indignant. "My cousin lives in England and lots of women with children and everything work over there. I bet they work in America too. I bet women can do whatever they want in America."

"I doubt any woman can do whatever she likes no matter where she lives, Ger," I say, not in the mood for another of her fanciful arguments about women's rights. "And besides, I don't mind. Christy says we'll probably have a baby by early next year. I'll have my hands full then."

"Then you'll be someone's wife *and* someone's mother."

I smile, proud as punch.

"Just promise me you won't forget you were Maura Flynn first?" she says.

"I promise."

"You'll come see me, won't you?"

"All the time."

I choke back sentiment and set myself the task of refolding the cashmere jumpers. There's a mustard one I quite fancy and I think about buying my first pair of trousers to pair with it. I envisage myself wearing the chic going-away outfit as I step into my new life and my new name. A tingle runs down my spine.

"I have something for you," Geraldine says.

"Oh?"

"It's a secret," she whispers. "When the other girls come in, we can take our break."

Intrigued, I'm about to ask what it is when a couple of older ladies come in looking for hats. The morning drags, and by the time two of the other girls arrive in, my tongue is hanging out for a cup of tea.

In the alleyway nearest the shoes and accessories entrance Geraldine and I share a cigarette, cups of tea, and half a packet of biscuits. The alley smells of the fishmongers nearby and I suggest stretching our legs with a walk, but Geraldine guides me into the doorway of a boarded-up shop. She reaches around her back, pulls a newspaper out, and shoves it into my hands.

"Another paper?" I say, surprised. I've never seen Ger read the newspaper before and yet today she's sharing two.

"Shh." Geraldine places her finger against her lips. "It's not the *Irish Times* this time," she says.

I unroll the paper and read the header. "The *News of the World*," I whisper.

Geraldine's smile grows wide and full of mischief as I open the paper and flick through the pages. I gasp when a large-breasted, topless woman on page three stares back at me. I slam the paper shut and, flabbergasted, accidentally drop it on the damp ground. Geraldine tuts and bends down to pick it up. She wipes the back of the grubby paper against the leg of her trousers and stands up again.

"Haven't you ever seen boobs before?" she asks.

"No! And certainly not in a newspaper. It's a bit . . . erm . . . a bit . . ."

"Liberating?"

"I was going to say shameful."

Geraldine shakes her head and sighs. "A woman should never be ashamed of her body."

"Where did you get this?" I ask.

"My cousin in Manchester sent me a copy. The one who works even with a husband and two children."

"You shouldn't have this," I say, concerned. "It's banned. You must know that, surely?"

"Of course I bloomin' know that. Why do you think I have to get my cousin to send it over?"

I cringe and feel the heat of embarrassment creep across my cheeks.

"Who do the government think they are, banning a newspaper, for Pete's sake? What do they think will happen; we'll see boobs and all go mad?" she puffs out, defeated. "They can read this in Northern Ireland." Ger jams a long nail against the paper, poking a small hole. "Did you know that?"

I assume her question is rhetorical, but nonetheless she glares at me as if she's waiting for an answer.

"Isn't that just the most ridiculous thing you've ever heard? Ireland is one island with completely different rules for the North. It's not fair."

"One island is geography. Two different governments is politics," I say as I glance over my shoulder, making sure there's no one in earshot, because the conversation makes me increasingly more uncomfortable. "Why would you even want to read this filth anyway?"

"Because who's to tell me what I can and can't read? Who, huh?"

"Oh, Ger. I love the bones of you, but this feisty temperament of yours is going to get you in trouble someday. I worry about that, you know?"

"Do you want the damn paper or not?" she says, pinching her brows.

I look at her, not entirely sure why I would. "You're about to become a married woman," she tells me. "And someone needs to open your eyes to the ways of the world."

"I'm five years older than you," I remind her.

"And none the wiser for it." She laughs. "There's articles in here you wouldn't believe."

"Like what?" I say, slightly concerned that we shouldn't be reading about such matters.

"Women in America are burning their bras because they're sick of being second-class citizens," Ger says, her eyes wide and almost wild with the thoughts of it. "They're sick of being expected to look pretty or dress a certain way. They're sick of listening to rules. They're protesting in the streets. They're fighting for their rights."

My mouth opens but no sound comes out.

"They're standing up to their government. Could you imagine something like that happening here? Wouldn't that be great?"

Geraldine is my friend. I like her very much. But she's young and full of colorful ideas about changing the country. I'm confident that when she grows up some more, she'll understand that life is about compromise. Women have compromised for centuries. It's just the way it is.

"I like to look my best," I say. "I like lipstick and nail varnish because it makes me feel good inside. When I am married, a beautiful wife will make my husband proud. This is the life I want. I don't want to see topless women or read about women burning their bras. Ger, I hope you understand."

Geraldine rolls the paper and lifts her blouse to tuck it between the waistband of her trousers and her back. "I *do* understand." She takes the last biscuit from the packet and bites into it. "But if you ever change your mind, you know where to come looking."

I inhale and nod, confident that contraband *anything* is not something I will ever actively seek out.

"Come on," Geraldine says. "We better go back inside before the girls start a rumor that I tried to have my wicked way with you."

"Ger!" My voice comes out an octave higher than usual.

She cackles. "Don't worry. You're not my type."

CHAPTER 6

2023

Saoirse

"We are now arriving at Drogheda. The next station is Dundalk."

The generic announcement interrupts Maura's story and I find myself resenting the prerecorded voice.

"Did you really marry a man you had only known six months?" I say, willing the train to slow down and give me time to hear more.

Maura smiles. "I did. But it was different back then. My mother warned me that when you meet a fella like Christopher Davenport you don't waste time. Besides, I knew Christy as well after six months as some women know their chaps after six years."

My chest tightens. Miles and I will have been together six years this summer and sometimes, like this morning, I wonder if we really know each other at all. I slide my phone out of my pocket and glance at the screen, checking for a text from him. I don't find any.

"Christy and I went to the pictures almost every night," Maura continues. "We met for lunch most days too."

"I can't remember the last time Miles and I went to the cinema. Or out for lunch. Or out at all, really," I confess. "Both of our jobs are shift work.

Sometimes we just pass like ships in the night. And when we *are* off together, we're usually so tired we stay in with a takeaway or something."

"Staying in sounds lovely," Maura says. "A night in front of the fire and a bit of telly can be better than any date."

I smile. I don't tell her that Miles and I live in an apartment and that we haven't watched anything that isn't streamed since we moved in. Once again, I find myself longing to live in a simpler time, a time with open fires and black-and-white television.

"We didn't have to deal with commuting in my day," Maura says suddenly, with a sigh of relief. "I know a chap who commutes from the Midlands to Dublin every day for work. Two hours on the train in the morning. And the same again home." She seems flabbergasted just thinking about it.

"At least he's not stuck in traffic," I say. "Miles can sit on the M50 for an hour some evenings barely moving an inch at a time. It drives him crazy."

"Well, no wonder he's tired," she says, and her kind eyes seem a little tired too. "The farthest Christy and I had to go to see each other was a stroll over the Ha'penny Bridge. He worked a short hop across town in Jervis Street Hospital—it's a shopping center now. Do you know it?"

I nod. Everyone knows the Jervis Street Shopping Center. But I wouldn't imagine a whole lot of young people know it was once a busy hospital. As a nurse, I can't imagine two places more different than a hospital and a supermarket.

"I spent a week there in nineteen seventy. Something to think about next time you pop in for some frozen peas." Maura laughs. Her chuckles are hearty and contagious and I find myself giggling too. "I could never have imagined how much would change in fifty years. But that's the beauty of time. You can't save it. You can only spend it wisely. I like to think I did."

The train creeps into the station and comes to a screechy stop.

"We are now arriving at Drogheda. Mind the gap."

The doors open and passengers filter off.

"This is you," Maura says, pointing out the window at the platform.

I glance at my phone again and at the blank screen with no messages. I'm surprised when the feeling that follows is relief. I'm not ready to talk to Miles. I'm not ready to go home and have a conversation that will inevitably end with raised voices and tears until finally one of us backs down and offers an apology that we don't mean just so we can move on.

"You know, maybe I could get off at the next stop," I say.

"Please stand back behind the yellow line. This is the thirteen-fifty enterprise service to Belfast. Calling at Dundalk, Newry, Portadown, Belfast."

Different people come aboard. The doors close and I'm relieved that we're moving again, as if once we keep chugging forward I won't have to think about going home.

"More tea?" I ask.

Maura checks her watch. "It's nearly two o'clock," she says. "What is it you young people call it these days? Oh yes, wine o'clock."

I let out a startled laugh.

"It's wine o'clock, Saoirse. Wouldn't you agree?"

I couldn't agree more.

CHAPTER 7

14 June 1969

Maura

I finish work on a Saturday, a week before my wedding day. Ger throws her arms around me and tells me that I'm the best friend she's ever had. She cries and so do I. Some of the other girls shed a tear or two. But one of them announced her own engagement last week and the other is going steady with a nice chap from Cork, so I suspect they will both be leaving soon enough too. Dick appears on the shop floor fifteen minutes before my shift ends. He gives me a small bouquet of pink carnations and passes me a letter. I know without opening it that it's from senior management. I've seen other girls receive the same crisp white envelope over the years.

"Goodbye and good luck," Dick says, shaking my hand.

"Thank you."

Dick walks away shaking his head and I've no doubt the headache of training my replacement is putting him in a bad mood.

One of our regulars is in buying a new hat for Sunday mass.

"Are you leaving?" she asks, sounding disappointed.

She glances at the flowers in my hand and the envelope tucked under my arm. I nod, past the point of pushing out words without tears.

"New job or getting married?" she asks.

"Married." I sniffle.

"Ah, isn't that nice."

I ring up her purchase of a maroon hat with a feather at the side and make my final sale with mixed feelings of nostalgia and dreamy excitement. When she leaves, I open the envelope Dick gave me.

Switzers Department Store
88 Grafton Street
Dublin 2
14th June 1969

Miss M. Flynn
12 Birch Road
Rathgar
Dublin 6

Dear Miss Flynn,

The management and staff of Switzers Department Store would like to take this opportunity to congratulate you on your marriage. It has been our pleasure working with you and we wish you well in the future.

Sincerely,
Mr. P. Wright,
Managing Director

"Hypocrites," Ger complains, snatching the letter from my hands and waving it above her head. I hold my breath as a vision of her burning it races through my mind.

"'Wish you well,'" she mimics. "Lies. Bloomin' lies. Wish you goodbye and good riddance. That's what they mean."

I jump up and take the letter back. I fold it and place it in the pocket of my pinafore. I think about how strange it will be to take this uniform off and never put it back on again. There is a sudden, sharp pang of regret. I press my hand to my chest and let silent tears trickle down my cheeks. I have loved working in Switzers. I love the fashion and the people, the staff and the customers. I will miss the thrill of ringing up a big sale or telling a customer that their chosen emerald jumper brings out the green in their eyes. I might even miss Dick, although I doubt that. I've put my heart and soul into this job for almost six years and it will be hard to walk out the door for the final time. But my heart belongs to Christy now. How lucky am I? I push the feelings aside and concentrate on the chapter ahead.

CHAPTER 8

Maura

The days leading up to the wedding crawl by in slow motion. On Sunday my parents and I walk to mass. I spot the lady from Switzers in her maroon hat three pews ahead of us. She notices me too and waves. I wonder if I should start wearing a hat to mass after the wedding. I decide hats are for older ladies and that women of my generation are free to make more liberal fashion choices. We walk home.

Da spends the afternoon reading the *Sunday Independent* and my mother spends the day roasting a leg of lamb. On Monday my mother asks me if I'd like to crochet with her. I would rather not, but she says, how else am I going to learn how to clothe a baby? We start with a pattern for booties. I'm not very good and my mother has to rip out my stitching and start me over several times. On Tuesday, we go to town to pick up some groceries. We pass by Switzers and my heart aches.

"That's not your life anymore," my mother says when she catches my turned-down lip from the corner of her eye. "You're about to become a doctor's wife, Maura."

On Wednesday she says there's great drying out. We wash clothes, hang them on the line, wash, and repeat. Thursday, we return to town because we've run out of spuds for the dinner. She walks into town the long way around and

I know her intention is to avoid passing by Switzers again. The large bag of potatoes is heavy and my arms hurt by the time we get home. That night, she comes into my room when I've gone to bed. She kisses my forehead the way she did when I was a little girl and she tells me that not all weeks of my new life will be as full of chores.

"But be assured, Maura, a woman's work is never done. Men might think they rule this world. But behind every good man is a great woman."

"Beside every man?" I question, assuming she misspoke.

"No," she says firmly. "I mean behind. A good wife knows her worth. A man values a woman who runs a smart house, keeps a pretty face, and gives him children. Do your best and you will have the wonderful life you deserve. I'm so proud of you, my darling. So very proud."

My eyes weigh shut with her words circling in my mind. I love my parents dearly and equally, but for the first time in my life I realize they are not equals under this roof. Under any roof. It saddens me.

Like most little girls, I started daydreaming about my wedding day from the moment I first knew what a wedding was. And like most little girls, I never offered consideration to the marriage that would inevitably follow. When I was five or six years old, one of the young women on our road got married. All the neighbors stepped onto the street to see her off with well wishes and a round of applause.

"Look at her, Maura," my mother said, pointing at the bride's long satin dress and the veil that ran from the tip of her head almost down to her toes. "That'll be you someday, my love. A woman's wedding day is the most wonderful day of her life."

On the morning of the wedding, sun shines through my curtains, casting oddly shaped shadows on the floor. I get up, draw the drapes back, and take in the beautiful day waiting outside.

Christy chose our wedding date.

"June twenty-first is the longest day of the year and I want our wedding day to last as long as possible," he said a few weeks back when we took a drive through the Dublin mountains in his brand-new Ford Capri.

It was the most romantic thing I'd ever heard. I made him pull over so I could kiss him. I kissed him long and hard and he kissed me right back with an intensity that made my cheeks burn. As his hands reached for me and I could feel we were heading for more, I gently pulled away and placed his hands back on the steering wheel, breathing hard.

"Dammit, Maura."

The blast of the horn as he brought a clenched fist down onto the steering wheel made me jump, and, instinctively, I pressed my back against the car door.

He turned toward me quickly and cupped my face in his trembling hands.

"I'm sorry, darling. I'm so sorry. Did I scare you?"

I nodded and struggled to catch my breath.

"You're just so pretty. Too pretty. It's hard to wait until our wedding night. But you're right. Of course you're right. We mustn't rush. It will be all the sweeter for waiting."

He leaned forward and kissed me once more. I relaxed at once and I was filled with a warm glow that lasted until we got home. I wonder if he knew it was just as difficult for me to wait until our wedding night. Maybe I'll tell him sometime when we're old and gray and he'll know how much I wanted to lie in his arms from the moment we met.

Now, in my childhood bedroom, my mother helps me into my dress. It was my cousin's. She got married last year and made it herself. It had to be altered for me, taken in and let down. It sits cinched at the waist, with a round neck, three-quarter-length sleeves, and an A-line skirt resting just below my knees.

Ma holds her face in her hands and cries when she tells me I'm the most beautiful bride she has ever seen. I wear a ring of white carnations in my hair and I slip my feet into stilettos with a heel as slender as a knitting needle. I have never felt more beautiful or more alive in my entire life.

The photographer is waiting when we arrive at Whitefriar Street Church in the center of the city. Passersby clap and cheer and wish me well. Da links his arm through mine and we stop in the door arch to have our photograph taken.

"Are you ready?" he asks.

My fingertips are tingling with nervous excitement as I curl my hand a little tighter around my bouquet. Certain and yet somehow still a little shaky, I take a deep breath and say, "I am."

Christy's younger sister, Agatha, is my bridesmaid—having no sisters of my own, I felt obliged to ask her. I don't know her well and it's all slightly awkward, but she smiles often and tells me we'll be close friends. I like to think so too.

When the organ begins to play, Agatha leads us into the church. My breath catches as Da and I follow.

Inside, a small smattering of my family and friends sit on one side. A larger gathering of Christy's family and friends sit on the other. Christy and his older brother, Declan, stand facing the altar. Declan is also a doctor, their mother, Grace, takes great pride in reminding me regularly. He married a nurse two years ago and Grace seems rather pleased about that. Today, Declan is Christy's best man. They wear matching black suits and smart top hats. Christy stands a fraction taller and I can see the rise and fall of his shoulders with each deep breath. I'm comforted to think he's as nervous as I am. Declan peeks over his shoulder, offers me a wide smile, and turns back to whisper something in his brother's ear. Christy's shoulders steady and so do my nerves. It's a long, slow walk to the top of the church as the organ bellows. At the top, Christy finally turns, looks at me with wide, almost starstruck eyes, and shakes my father's hand. And then Da hands me over.

The mass is long and my stomach is full of butterflies. I trip over my words as Christy and I say our vows and I hear Agatha stifle a giggle behind me. My hand shakes while I sign the register.

The priest stands behind us and places a hand on my shoulder and another on Christy's and he says, "Congratulations, Dr. and Mrs. Christopher Davenport. Christy, you may kiss the bride."

My face stings as the congregation applauds, but when Christy's lips press against mine and I kiss my new husband every feeling except euphoria melts away. *Ma was right*, I think.

The photographer lines us up outside the church with military precision. He takes snap after snap. Christy and me. His parents with us. My parents with us. Everyone. He repeats his efforts on the steps of The Shelbourne when we arrive to enjoy our wedding breakfast.

"Just one more," he says, as everyone is flagging.

The midday sun is blisteringly hot and Da is complaining about a hole in his stomach that needs filling.

"Last one, last one," the photographer says, and then he lowers the camera to look directly into my eyes as he adds, "Beautiful. Absolutely beautiful. You look like a young Doris Day."

"Keep your eyes off my wife," Christy says.

Everyone laughs. Even Da, who is as grumpy as a grizzly bear by now.

I laugh too until Christy's hand tightens around my back and his fingers dig into my waist. I try to pull away, just a fraction, but he pulls me back. That's when I realize what Ma meant. I belong to Christy now. A possession with a measured value. Like a pocket watch, or a pair of old gloves.

CHAPTER 9

Maura

June 21 is the summer solstice. Every year, on repeat, it is the day with the most hours of light and the fewest hours of darkness. The longest day and the shortest night. Yet, somehow, June 21, 1969, is the longest night of my life. Ma said a woman's wedding day is the most wonderful day of her life. She never said anything about the wedding night.

The Shelbourne has a reputation for punctuality, and it lives up to it when lunch is served at 1:00 p.m. sharp. Da says the turkey and ham is worth every penny. Ma says she's glad they have only one daughter because weddings are expensive. Christy's parents don't say much about any of it. My father and Christy's father make speeches. Declan is the last to say a few words.

"Congratulations to my brother. He's finally found a woman who will put up with him. Welcome to the family, Maura."

Declan's words wrap around me like a warm hug and my face aches from smiling. At 4:30 p.m., Agatha accompanies me to the ladies' bathroom on the second floor and helps me out of my dress. I slip on tan trousers and the mustard cashmere jumper that I selected with such vigor and excitement from Switzers. I pair them with a matching tan blazer. I saw Doris Day wearing a similar outfit on a film poster a few months back and everyone called it a bold fashion statement.

"A suit," Agatha says, goggle-eyed. "You look amazing."

"Thank you."

I reapply some ruby red lipstick and tuck a flyaway strand of hair behind my ear as I give myself the once-over in the mirror.

"Are you nervous?" she asks.

I look at her, unsure.

"About later. About tonight." She shuffles on the spot and makes a face. "About your wedding night."

I take a deep breath. "No. I'm not nervous."

"Wow. Have you . . ." Agatha pauses and looks at my trousers once more. She can't seem to take her eyes off them. "Have you, you know . . . have you already?"

I let my breath out with a rough huff. I don't answer that question. Frankly, I'm insulted that the answer isn't obvious.

"We should go," I say. "I don't want to keep Christy waiting."

In the lobby, Christy is standing by the front door. His mouth gapes just a fraction when he sees me. My going-away outfit cost me three weeks' wages but I decide it was a small price to pay when I see the look on his face. Staff and another bride compliment me on my outfit as we leave the hotel. And someone else, yet again, compares me to the legendary Hollywood actress.

Outside, the afternoon sun shines high. I rest my hand above my eyes like a visor and squint, trying to adjust to the light. Momentarily blinded, I don't see it coming.

Heat explodes across my face. Christy's hand catches my cheekbone and the side of my nose. The slap sets me spinning and I almost tumble down the steps. I grab the railing and steady myself just in time. Fire pulsates in my face, and my mouth is gaping as I look up at him. He doesn't meet my gaze.

"Stand up straight," he says. "The valet will be back with the car any moment."

Sure enough, within a few seconds Christy's Ford Capri pulls up at the bottom of the steps. A young man in uniform and cap hops out, hurries up the steps, and passes Christy his keys.

"Thank you," Christy says, handing the kid some money.

I don't see or ask how much. My feet are steadying now, but my mind is still spinning. Christy takes my hand, like a perfect gentleman, and guides me down the steps. He opens the passenger-side door and lets go of my hand. I look at him once more, but he still refuses to look back at me. He places his lips next to my ear and whispers through gritted teeth.

"Get in."

Cheering and clapping carry from the top of the steps. Our respective families have appeared there to see us on our way.

"Enjoy your honeymoon," my mother calls out.

"Drive safely," Christy's mother shouts.

Everyone waves and cheers. Christy places one hand on the small of my back and raises the other in the air, waving back at everyone as if butter wouldn't melt in his mouth.

"Get in," he grunts again.

I search for Ma's eyes at the top of the steps. She looks back at me with so much pride and joy. I look away, certain I won't be able to keep the tears from falling for much longer. Christy tells me to get into the car for a third time and follows his words with a shove. I don't want to. I want to run up the steps and into the safety of my mother's arms. I want to tell her that I've made a terrible mistake and ask her to fix everything for me. But of course I know life doesn't work that way. I'm a doctor's wife now, whether I like it or not.

I sit into the car. My tan, slim-legged trousers and mustard jumper that I had chosen with such joy as my going-away outfit suddenly feel tight and chafing. Christy lights up a cigarette and walks around the front of the car to slip in behind the wheel. He slams the door behind him and starts the engine.

"How dare you embarrass me like that?" he says, gripping the steering wheel so tightly his knuckles whiten.

"Christy, please, you're scaring me!"

"A suit."

Christy's face is puce. I choose my words carefully. "Don't you like it? It's new."

"It's a kick in the teeth, that's what it is. My father was horrified to see a woman, my woman, dressed like a man."

"I'm sorry," I say. "I thought you'd like it."

"I don't."

"I won't wear it again."

"No, Maura. No, you won't."

Silent tears trickle down my cheek when I stare out the window at our family and friends waving as we drive away. I replay Agatha's question in my mind. *Are you nervous?*

I'm not nervous. I am terrified.

CHAPTER 10

Maura

We take the ferry to the Isle of Man and I'm sick a couple of times shortly after we board. Christy gathers me into his arms and dots kisses on the top of my head as we stand on the deck, watching the coastline of Dublin fade out of view.

"Don't worry, darling. Everyone suffers a little seasickness from time to time."

The sea is calm and the ferry glides through the water like a swan on a lake. I want to scream at him. I want to tell him that the sight of *him* is making me ill.

Instead, I wrap my arms around myself, rubbing my hands up and down them as the sea breeze bites.

"I've never left Ireland before," I say, followed by some deep breaths.

"You see," he says, his voice as gentle as the sunlight kissing the sea. "It's just a touch of travel sickness. It will soon pass."

He takes off his suit jacket and drapes it over my shoulders.

"I love you, Maura. You know that, don't you?"

I nod.

"And I wouldn't ever do anything to hurt you. Not on purpose."

My mouth opens but no sound comes out. There are no words to fit this moment. I stare into the dark blue sea, watching as the bow of the ferry slices through the water like a knife. I push the thoughts of what happened on the steps of The Shelbourne deep down into my gut but they bubble back up like the churning waves.

There are many couples and families on board. Christy smiles at some children playing tag. The sound of their laughter in the air soothes me.

"You don't need to worry yourself with fashion anymore, darling," Christy says. "You're a married woman now—soon to be a mother, if the good Lord blesses us. You'll have to change the way you dress, it's as simple as that. You don't see women in trousers out pushing a pram. Oh darling, I can't wait until we have a baby. Lots of babies. You're going to be the most wonderful mother."

I let myself imagine it for a moment: small, chubby arms wrapped around my neck, bedtime stories and good-night kisses.

I want to be a mother so much. I want it more than I want anything in the world. I want it even more than I want to stay angry with my new husband.

"I can't wait too," I say, and then I let him kiss me.

We're the first car off the ferry and Christy entrusts me with reading the map as we navigate the sleepy island.

"There should be a lighthouse around here somewhere," he says. "And the B and B is just around the corner on the left."

Sure enough, as we round the next bend, a white-and-red-striped lighthouse comes into view. There's a small cream bungalow opposite. A woman stands waiting at the door. Her gray hair is pinned back. Her round-rimmed glasses take up most of her face, and there are baking stains on her floral apron.

There doesn't seem to be anywhere to park amid the lush green grass and the wild hedging that seems to punctuate the island. Christy settles on parking at the side of the road, but I can tell he's uncomfortable about it.

"You must be Dr. Davenport," the lady says, breaking into a wide smile as we get out of the car and walk toward her house. "I'm Rita. It's lovely to meet you."

Rita extends her hand and Christy shakes it. "Nice to meet you too. Will my car be all right parked there?"

"Oh, I should think so. We don't get many vehicles on the island if not for deliveries."

Christy's stiff shoulders relax.

"And this must be your lovely new wife," Rita says, smiling at me. "My goodness, if you're not the spitting image of that actress who plays Calamity Jane. Oh, I do love that film. Beautiful music."

Christy glares at me, once again sweeping his eyes over my trouser suit that he detests so much.

"Come in, come in," Rita says, ushering us inside.

She leads us down a narrow corridor to show us to our room and tells us her husband, Bert, will fetch our luggage. She stretches her arms out and opens her hand, waiting for Christy to pass her his car keys.

"We couldn't put him to that trouble," Christy says, clearly having no intention of parting with the keys to his pride and joy. "I'll fetch our things."

Rita retracts her hand.

"You'll be all right for a moment on your own, darling, won't you?" he asks, smiling at me like Prince Charming.

I nod again and close the bedroom door when Christy and Rita leave. Now that I'm alone for the first time all day, tears begin to fall. I catch them on my fingertip and flick them away. There's a small white dresser in the corner with a bottle of holy water and a mirror on top. I brace myself before I look at my reflection. To my surprise, there isn't a mark on me. I touch my face. I palpate my cheeks and the side of my nose with my fingers. It's tender to the touch but thankfully there is no redness or bruising. Christy mustn't have hit me as hard as I thought. *Maybe I'm making too much of it.*

The door creaks open again and Christy walks in with a bag hanging from each of his shoulders. His and mine. He sets them down next to the bed and places his hands on my waist.

"Are you ready?" he asks.

My breath catches and he looks at me, waiting for an answer. The answer, we both know, must be *yes*.

Last week, as Ma and I sat crocheting booties, I asked her what to expect on my wedding night. She set her crochet hook down, took me by the hands, and said, "Maura, m'dear, God has blessed you with a healthy body. That is as much as you need to know about it. Do you understand?"

I understood. My body and how it functioned were outside the realm of socially acceptable conversation.

Christy reaches for the button on my trousers and my legs tremble just a little. Undressing is slow and embarrassing. I have to fight the urge to cover up with my hands as my husband sheds my clothing. He's confident and critiques me with hungry eyes. I must admit, I can't take my eyes off him and the shape of a man's naked body. He smiles when he catches my eye and he guides me to lie on the bed. He climbs on top of me and kisses me. He tastes like cigarettes and desire. His skin is warm and soft and I can feel his eagerness to push. The pain is hot and sharp and I gasp out loud more than once as I squirm. I wonder if we should stop. Surely if there's pain then something must be wrong?

Christy groans and quickly I ask, "Does it hurt?"

He steadies himself.

"It's all right, Maura," he says between gentle kisses on my lips and cheeks. "It won't be as bad next time."

"Did you know it would be like this?"

"It's just the first time or two. You'll get used to it."

I stare at the ceiling. It doesn't surprise me that my doctor husband knows more about my body than I do, and yet I still feel like an uneducated fool. I let him continue, and I distract myself from the burn by thinking about the children I am so looking forward to having. I close my eyes and promise myself in this moment that if I have a daughter, I will not raise a fool. I will tell her anything she ever needs to know.

CHAPTER II

Maura

I wake to the sound of my belly rumbling. Christy and I skipped supper last night, and still I feel no hunger. I do, however, feel a headache. I didn't sleep much and when I did, I woke with a jolt as I remembered I wasn't in my own bed and never would be again.

Beside me, deep, gentle snores highlight my new husband's contentment as he lies belly down on the opposite side of the bed. I count backward from three in my head and peel back the sheets to take in the skin and curves of the man who has given me his name. I hold my breath and wait for desire to come. Last week, the thought of Christy displayed for me would have sent a hot ripple through my whole body. But this morning my thoughts and feelings are jumbled inside my head. Our "I dos." Our first kiss as husband and wife. The pride in my mother's eyes. The sting of his hand across my face. The woody smell of his cologne as he lay on top of me. The ache to feel more and at the same time the urge to push him away. The knowledge that I am Mrs. Maura Davenport now, no matter what.

There's a knock on the bedroom door and Rita's voice follows.

"Good morning, Doctor," she says, before clearing her throat to speak a little louder. "It's nine o'clock. Your breakfast is ready."

Christy tosses but he doesn't wake.

"Thank you," I call out. "We'll be there soon."

I hear Rita leave and I climb out of bed to get dressed. My trousers catch my eye, discarded on the tired wicker chair in the corner, where Christy threw them last night. I pick them up, fold them, and hold them against my chest as if they were a cuddly toy. I flick away the tear that trickles down my cheek and then I shove the trousers into the bottom of my travel bag before I leave the room to find the bathroom and freshen up.

Afterward, I try on several outfits before I settle on a pale blue pinafore that I wish were a little longer and a pink cardigan that doesn't match but covers me right up. Christy grunts and groans when I gently shake his shoulder. He smiles when his sleepy eyes focus on me.

"Good morning, darling." The rattle of morning in his voice makes me smile. "You look nice."

"Thank you."

He yawns and stretches, and when he reaches up to stroke his thumb across my cheek, I fight the urge to pull away from him.

"Rita has breakfast waiting for us," I say.

"Oh goodness." He sits up and rubs his eyes. "Is it nine o'clock already?"

I nod, realizing Christy arranged a wake-up call without discussion.

He stands and faces me, and it is as if I am seeing him without clothes for the first time all over again. He notices and smiles, oozing a confidence I imagine most men could only dream of.

In the dining room, Rita and Bert join us for breakfast. Christy smiles charmingly, but I can tell their presence bothers him.

"It's a full fry," Rita announces as she places plates of bacon, egg, sausage, and white and black pudding in front of us.

"Thank you," Christy says, eyeing the greasy food. "The morning paper?"

Rita's smile wavers. "Oh, but it's Sunday."

"No Sunday paper?" Christy cocks his head to one side.

"We get the evening press of a weekday. And that does us nicely, doesn't it, Bert?"

Bert nods with a mouthful of food and moves his teacup to make room for his wife to sit beside him. Christy picks up his knife and fork and tries to hide his frustration.

"Perhaps we could pop on the radio, then?" he suggests, jerking his knife back and forth through the tough bacon on his plate. The screech of stainless steel against porcelain makes the fine hair on the back of my neck stand on end.

"No radio neither," Rita says. She raises a single finger in the air and adds, "We don't get a very good signal here, I'm afraid."

Christy sets his knife down and exhales sharply. I close my eyes and hold my breath, only opening them again when I feel his hand take mine.

"Well, we really have come to the land of tranquility, haven't we, darling?"

I exhale and force a smile.

"I know what," Rita says, with an excited clap of her hands. "I'll pack you a picnic. You can take it with you when you go for a walk later."

The flash of disgust on Christy's face is so quick that if I had blinked, I'd have missed it. I've missed it before, I realize. He exhales and places a hand over Rita's. With a warm smile he says, "A picnic would be delightful. Thank you."

"Oh, Doctor." Rita blushes as she tucks a strand of short hair behind her ear. "It's no trouble."

Christy holds conversation with our hosts as effortlessly as if he had known them all his life. Their words float over me like bubbles, only popping when they've passed me by. But I lift my head when I hear my name.

"Is she always this quiet, your lovely Maura?" Rita asks.

Christy beams at me with round eyes, as if he has won a competition and I am his prize. "I think my wife might be a little tired this morning. Yesterday was the most wonderful day and we're still on cloud nine as we start this new life together."

"Yes, indeed." I sigh. "A new life."

CHAPTER 12

Maura

The remainder of our honeymoon passes blithely. Christy is his usual caring and attentive self once more. Dashing and charismatic. And mine. He is every inch the man I excitedly walked up the aisle to. He is the man who says, "I cannot wait to have a baby with you." And "I am the luckiest man in the world." And "Maura, my darling, I am going to make you so happy, just you wait." He is the man whose love fills me to the brim and he is the man who, I am certain, will never hurt me again.

By day, Christy and I explore the island on foot. The green fields stretch out for miles, and sometimes our feet hurt and we laugh about being city folk who look forward to the hustle and bustle of Dublin when we return.

He turns women's heads as he walks, and I tease him once they have passed.

"I only have eyes for one woman," he tells me, blushing.

We hold hands and talk about our future. We eat a simple picnic most days and time seems to pass without punctuation. One day is set apart from the next only by the beautiful sunsets that dip into the sea. The nights are long and full of intimacy. Christy was right; each time it gradually becomes more bearable, and by the time we are leaving there is almost no pain at all.

"See? What did I tell you?" he says as we pack our bags on the morning of checkout. "It's the same with having babies. The first one is a bit of a shock to the system and after that it'll be no bother to you. We'll have four or five at least, won't we?"

"More."

Christy dresses in the suit he wore to our wedding and on the ferry on the way here. I think about the trousers folded at the bottom of my bag and I squash the pang of sadness as I pull on a box-pleated skirt, tan nylons, and a blouse, and I marvel at how much I look like my mother. I spend time brushing my hair until it's as silky and shiny as Doris Day's and tuck it behind my ears on both sides.

"Don't do that," Christy says.

"Do what?"

"Don't wear your hair like that; it makes people stare."

"I thought you liked it," I say. "When we first met you said—"

"We're not just meeting." Christy cuts me off with a clipped tone. "You're not a single shopgirl anymore. You're my wife. And I can't bear you catching the eye of every red-blooded man who walks by."

"Christy, I—"

"Tie. It. Back!"

Tears gather in the corners of my eyes and if I dare to blink, they will spill. Christy shakes his head, as if he's trying to shake off a part of himself he doesn't recognize. A part we are both afraid of. My tears blur my vision as I wait for his next move. When he speaks again and softly says, "Tie it back, darling, won't you?" I realize I was holding my breath.

He reaches into my bag and pulls out a silk scarf.

"Your something blue," Grace said on our wedding morning when she gave it to me.

It's a beautiful scarf, royal blue silk with small white flowers embroidered around the edges. I wore it knotted around my thigh, under my dress, like a garter. It felt rebellious and cheeky. I thought Christy and I might laugh about it when I told him. I had forgotten about it until this very moment and suddenly I don't want to tell him anymore.

I snatch the scarf from his grip and tie it around my hair. I glimpse myself in the mirror and I am irritated to find that the vibrant colors look rather pretty against my fair skin.

He smiles and says, "That's my girl. Gosh, you're just too beautiful. Do you know that?" He gathers me into his arms and kisses me hard. "I love you, Maura. I love you so much."

I kiss him in return as my silent tears finally escape.

Christy settles our bill and we say our goodbyes to Rita and Bert and thank them for their hospitality.

"You'll have to come back and visit us," Rita says. "Once you have little ones running around. The island is a wonderful spot for a family trip."

Christy reaches for my hand and squeezes it gently. "Wouldn't that be wonderful?" he says.

My fingers curl around his and I truly *can't* think of anything more wonderful than becoming a mother.

Christy shakes Bert's hand and then Rita's, and he turns and walks toward the car. I follow him and once again slip my fingers between his.

"Lovely couple," he says.

"Yes. Lovely."

"How long do you reckon they're married?"

I shrug. "Thirty, maybe forty years."

"I'd say forty or more. That'll be us someday," he says zealously.

My mind wanders toward our distant future. I swallow a lump as I imagine forty years of being told how to dress and how to wear my hair.

Christy and I sit into the car and he leans across to kiss my cheek.

"Thank you for a very special honeymoon. I'm a lucky man," he says.

"Yes. And I'm a lucky woman," I say, although the words taste bitter leaving my mouth.

Christy is about to start the engine when we hear a female voice screeching.

"Doctor, Doctor!"

Rita races toward the car, waving her arms above her head. "Doctor, Doctor, come quick!"

Christy opens the car door and hops out.

"It's Bert," she says.

I glance back at the house. Bert is lying on the ground outside the front door. He's clutching his arm and his face is the color of barley water. Christy opens the boot and pulls out his black leather medicine bag. He runs toward the house, kicking up dirt behind him. He's on his knees at Bert's side while my mind is struggling to catch up. I drape my arm over Rita's shoulder. She blesses herself and begins to pray.

"Hail Mary full of grace . . ."

"Maura, water," Christy shouts, summoning me with a click of his fingers.

"Water?" I ask Rita.

"Holy Mary Mother of God pray for our sins. . . ."

She doesn't hear me above her own chaotic mumblings. Her focus seems solely on trying to save her husband with mere words. I let her go, afraid for a moment that she might fall to the ground, but she doesn't. I run through the open front door and into the kitchen. I pour a glass of water, and by the time I return, Bert is sitting up. He's wrung out, but a hint of color is returning to his cheeks.

"Angina, most likely," Christy says, taking the glass from me and helping Bert to sip some. "You had a lucky escape this time. But you need to contact your local practitioner. You might not get a second chance."

"Yes, Doctor." Bert is scarcely able to draw his breath but he answers obediently. "I will do just that."

Rita has snapped out of her trance and tears are trickling down her flushed cheeks.

"Thank you, Doctor. Thank you so much," she says.

Christy slips Bert's arm over his shoulder and helps him to stand. Rita flaps around them like a headless chicken and I feel for her—so helpless and frightened. Christy and Bert shuffle inside and Christy settles him in the fireside chair in the sitting room. Rita fetches a blanket and drapes it over her husband's knees despite the humid June weather.

"Can I make you something for the road?" she asks. "A tart, maybe? I make a fine apple tart."

"No, thank you," Christy says, dusting the garden dirt off his knees. "We'd best be on our way. Make that visit, Bert, won't you?"

"Oh, I'll see to it that he does," Rita says.

Christy smiles, but I don't miss the flash of annoyance in his eyes that Rita has answered for her husband.

"Let's go, Maura," he says.

"You're a lucky young lady," Rita says, catching my hand and squeezing it tighter than is comfortable. "You're married to a wonderful man. A wonderful, wonderful man."

Christy walks away and I follow him. I glance over my shoulder at Rita and Bert. Rita is crouched next to her husband. She is kissing his face and stroking his hair.

"Will he be okay?" I ask as we sit into the car once more.

"If he listens to his doctor and not his wife." Christy exhales, starting the engine. "She'll kill him with her greasy cooking."

CHAPTER 13

Maura

It's strange to get off the ferry and drive straight to Christy's house and not my parents'. But I remind myself that Rathmines is where I live now. My new home is mid-terrace, with a redbrick front and lacy net curtains hanging in all the windows.

Grace has already given me tips on how to keep them white.

"Bicarbonate of soda, love," she said, taking me aside just before the speeches at the wedding. "Bicarbonate of soda and some soapy water, that's what you want."

I promised to do my best. But the responsibility of keeping something white didn't hit until just now. Christy parks on the side of the road, in a spot clearly left for number 11. Our house. Each house from number 1 to 29 is identical to the one next to it, like concrete soldiers in smart red jackets and black top hats, standing to attention as they guard the cobblestone street outside. I imagine on sunny summer days the neighbors sit in their pristine front gardens and supervise their children playing hopscotch.

Da has been moving my stuff piecemeal over the past couple of weeks or so, and when Christy opens the front door, we are greeted by three milk crates. One full of my clothes, another of shoes, and the last one containing pots and pans and kitchen utensils that Ma must have gathered up for me.

I bend down, ready to rummage through my things, but Christy takes my hand, looks me in the eye, and leads me upstairs to the bedroom. I've been in Christy's house before. Once at Christmas for a singsong with his family, and once more recently, when he had a fever and I brought him some chicken soup. But I've never been up the stairs before. Walking into his bedroom for the first time takes my breath away. The walls are painted royal blue and the carpet is bottle green with a swirly lime pattern. There's a queen bed with a stripey blue and green duvet and matching pillows. The curtains are brown, no doubt expensive, and at odds with everything else.

Christy gives me a moment to survey the room and then he says, "Are you tired?"

"No," I say, instantly wishing I could change my answer as soon as I see the longing look in his eyes.

I'm in no mood, but Christy kisses my neck and helps me onto the bed.

"Welcome home," he says.

"Let's unpack," I suggest, remaining upright.

He shakes his head. "Tomorrow."

I inhale, defeated, and lie back. We make love for almost an hour and afterward Christy falls asleep. He's snoring loudly when I creep downstairs and sort through the crates. I fold clothes away in the empty drawers in the bedroom. I shove my shoes under the bed, taking care not to disturb him when I lift the edges of the blankets, and I find space in the already amply stocked kitchen for Ma's bits and pieces. With my possessions stowed away and feeling somewhat more settled in the house, I climb into bed next to my husband and try to sleep.

CHAPTER 14

December 1969

Maura

One morning follows another, and soon, Christy and I fall into a routine the way I imagine most married couples do. We both get up early when his alarm clock rings. He bathes and shaves, and when he comes downstairs dressed in one of his many dapper suits—that I know cost an arm and a leg in Switzers— I have his breakfast waiting. Rashers and eggs, mostly; they're his favorite. I learn the hard way that he does not enjoy porridge. The bowl he smashed in protest was my grandmother's and I couldn't hold back my tears when it lay in pieces on the floor, tangled among gloopy porridge. Christy left without a word that morning and I cleaned up my tears and then the mess. That same evening, he arrived home from work with a new set of fine bone china.

More than five months pass before I finally open the box and make room in the cupboard for the delicate white delft with hand-painted flowers. I am in an especially cheery mood this morning and fancy china seems like as good a way as any to start the day. Christy sits at the table, reading the paper, as he does every morning. Without conversation I place a plate in front of him. He sets the paper down and looks at me with satisfied eyes when he recognizes the floral pattern beneath his runny egg.

"You like the plates," he says.

"I do."

I keep the part about its inability to replace the sentimental value of my grandmother's china to myself.

"They have cups and saucers to match in the shop," he says.

I know. I worked in homeware for almost a year when I first started in Switzers.

"Would you like them?" His fork squeaks against his plate as he cuts the fat off his rasher.

"There's no need."

"If you like them, there is every need. Say the word, darling, and they're yours."

I join Christy at the table and we eat our breakfast in silence.

"I'll pop into Switzers after work and pick some out," he says.

"I'll go," I suggest gently. "It will give me a chance to catch up with some of my old colleagues. And I could meet you for lunch, perhaps?"

Christy makes a face. "I can't today, I'm afraid. But buy yourself something nice. A new coat, maybe? Something long to keep you warm. They say it might snow next week."

I hide my disappointment with a forced smile. Lunch with Christy used to be my favorite part of the day. He always had a compliment for the chef or a kind word about a waiter's uniform, openly admiring the décor and gushing over the delicious food. Christy had a knack for making people feel good just by being in his presence, and I was no exception. We'd share our news over tea and sandwiches and an hour was never enough. I have rather exciting news to share today, but as always, he's too busy. I take a deep breath and remind myself that he works hard and provides a wonderful standard. I should have no complaints.

Christy opens the front door and I follow him into the hall, still in my nightdress and housecoat. I stand next to him and wait for the kiss on my cheek that I've learned is coming.

"I love you, darling," he says.

"I love you too."

We say the same words every single morning. There is no deviation. No additions. And no exception. When he leaves, I bake soda bread for later and wash up. Once the kitchen is gleaming like a new penny, I bathe and get dressed. I choose my favorite shoes, black patent with a round toe and a block heel. Christy doesn't like them, and I will change into slippers before he returns home. Later, my feet will hurt from walking into town and back to pick up some bits and pieces for dinner. I did the same yesterday and the day before. My mother encourages me to appreciate the slow pace: "Once a baby comes, you won't have a minute to yourself. High heels will be the last thing on your mind then, m'dear."

I don't pretend to understand why motherhood would be synonymous with flat shoes, but nonetheless, I can't wait until every minute is filled with taking care of my baby. For the past six months I've crossed my fingers behind my back. And every month I've had to break the news to Christy that it hasn't happened. His heart has broken as much as mine and I can feel him losing patience. There have been many smashed plates to sweep away, slammed doors to open, and bruises to cover up. I've cried alone and often, and I always dry my tears before he gets home. I've cried for the busy life I left behind on Switzers' shop floor and yearned for the baby I left it all behind for. Finally, this month it might all be different. I haven't told Christy yet, but I'm two weeks late. My doctor's appointment is booked for 11:00 a.m. and I've said the rosary every day this week while I've waited.

I take a washed-out jam jar I have set aside into the bathroom. It takes me ten minutes of hovering over the toilet before I relax enough to fill the jar. Afterward, I screw the lid on and hope the answer to all my prayers is inside.

My stomach flutters with nervous anticipation as I pull on my heavy winter coat and choose a headscarf to wear today. I've a collection of scarves now, soft silks in beautiful colors. *Christy spoils me*, I remind myself as I tie a burnt orange scarf over my hair. My hair is longer than it has ever been before, and people rarely tell me I look like Doris Day, I guess because I don't anymore. I leave the house and face into the winter wind. It stings my cheeks and I hope it snows. It would be delightful to have something as exciting as snow to break up the mundane winter days.

I walk in the opposite direction from the one I usually take and get lost a couple of times before I find the quiet side street I'm searching for. I scan both sides of the street until I spot the doctor's office above a newsagent. A small plaque next to a blue door says DR. BUCKLEY'S FAMILY PRACTICE. It said in the Golden Pages that they had the fastest pregnancy testing service in Ireland. *Results in two weeks*, the ad said. I've no doubt the next fourteen days will be the longest of my life.

I push on the heavy old door and it creaks open. My legs quiver as I ascend the steps I find inside. Thankfully, upstairs is bright and airy. A woman about my age sits behind a desk and typewriter. She looks up and smiles when she sees me.

"Hello," she chirps.

"Hi. Erm. Hello. My name is Maura Davenport. I'm here to see Dr. Buckley."

Her smile widens.

"Oh yes," she says. "You can leave that here with me. Results will be back in a fortnight. Shall I put you in for a return visit on the nineteenth?"

"Erm."

"First time?" she asks me.

I nod.

"How exciting." She writes something in a large green ledger and adds, "Well, that's all booked in for you. We'll see you in two weeks, Mrs. Davenport."

She reaches her arm across her desk and I realize that's my cue to root in my bag and find my jam jar. I pass it over, blushing a little. She doesn't bat an eyelid as she places a sticker with my name on the front.

"See you on the nineteenth," she says again.

I leave, and the wait begins.

CHAPTER 15

Maura

I don't remember the walk back into town, but somehow I find myself on Talbot Street. It's thronged with enthusiastic Christmas shoppers. I think about how busy the staff in Switzers must be. I think about the large Christmas tree in the foyer that smells of pine cones and the complimentary mulled wine they dish out in the homeware section. I'm looking forward to a glass to warm my belly. Ma says alcohol isn't for ladies, but everyone knows a glass every now and then is good for the baby.

I settle on a visit to the butcher first. If I'm going to lose an afternoon to mulled wine and a catch-up with Geraldine I had best get my chores out of the way beforehand.

Inside smells of red meat and sawdust. I cover my nose and mouth with my hand and try to hide how the scent makes me heave.

"Any nice plans for the weekend?" the butcher asks. He's a block of a man with shoulders as wide as playing fields and hands like shovels that bag up my meat.

"The weekend? Golly, is it the weekend already?"

He laughs. "It's Friday. The week is nearly through."

"I thought it was Thursday," I say, trying to recall how the days have slipped away again this week.

I asked for two lamb chops and some liver, but he places a bag packed full of meat on the tall glass countertop. I look around, suspecting the bag is for someone else.

"To thank Dr. Davenport for taking such good care of my missus," he says.

It surprises me how often strangers recognize me as Christy's wife. People sometimes walk up to me on the street to ask how my husband is keeping. They tell me about their bad back, or shingles, or all manner of ailments. And they always, always end the encounter asking me if I'm aware how fantastic my husband is. I never roll my eyes, but sometimes I want to.

"There's some steak in there," the butcher says. "Filet. Only the best for the doc."

"Oh." I blush, realizing he wants me to take the bag of meat for free.

I roll onto my tiptoes and fetch the bag. It's heavy and my shoulder pops silently.

"This is very kind. Too kind," I say, thinking I won't be able to nip into Switzers with a giant bag of meat hanging off my arm. I can only imagine how annoyed Christy will be when he comes home and discovers I haven't picked out new delft after I promised that I would.

"You tell the doc if my missus has a wee boy this time there'll be a free turkey for him next Christmas. Big as he likes."

I've no idea what to say to a man who thinks my husband can arrange a baby's gender and would like to thank him with raw meat.

"I'm outnumbered, you see," he says. "I've three daughters already. Each one more like her mother than the last. I need a little chap to take over the business someday."

"Maybe your daughters could run the business in the future," I say, waiting for him to shoot me down.

He shakes his head. "My girls are smart as buttons. Each and every one of them. They'll want to finish school and maybe try their hand at college. They're meant for great things."

I'm momentarily lost for words. I've never met a man who values a woman's education before. My father is a wonderful man and a loving father, but from the time I was a child he made it crystal clear that a woman's place was in the home. In truth, I didn't know men who thought differently existed.

"You'll tell the doc I was asking for him, won't you, Mrs. Davenport?"

"Maura. Please call me Maura. Mrs. Davenport is my mother-in-law." I smile sheepishly.

"Maura," he says with a nod. "I'm Dan. Daniel McCarthy."

I nod. I know his last name already. It's above the door outside.

"Well, thank you, Dan," I say, tilting my head toward the heavy bag of meat dangling from my arm. "I'll be sure to let Christy know these come with your compliments. And I'll keep my fingers crossed for a son for you."

"Ah." Dan glides his hand through the air. "I don't mind, really. Once the wee one is healthy and the wife comes through it well, that's me counting myself a lucky man."

I thank Dan once more, kick off the sawdust from the floor that has stuck to my shoes, and walk back outside into the cool December air.

CHAPTER 16

2023

Saoirse

"How often did he hit you?" I ask, finding it hard to align the glamorous lady sipping white wine from a paper cup with her pinkie extended with the young woman in her story.

"Not often," she says. "Christy actually believed himself to be a good man."

"Good men don't hit their wives," I say.

"I know. But he saved lives every day. He was a good doctor if nothing else. I will always admire him for that."

"Were you afraid of him?"

"Sometimes," she says, raising the glass to her mouth, and her lips curl into a satisfied smile. "This is nice, especially for train wine."

I don't think train wine is a thing, but I sip from my cup and agree that the wine is lovely. If I'm honest, I don't overly notice what it tastes like, my mind still racing from the day's chain of events.

"You think I should have left him," Maura says, putting her cup down on the table in front of us.

"I would have."

"Would you? I don't think you realize how different times truly were. If I couldn't talk to my mother about something as simple as sex, I certainly couldn't open a conversation about domestic violence. Even if I had left my husband, even if my parents had fought the stigma it would have brought on our whole family and welcomed me back with open arms, I would still have been a married woman in the eyes of the law. All the restrictions that came attached would still have been there. I wouldn't have been allowed back to work. Much as it pains me to admit it, I needed Christy."

"I can't imagine how hard that must have been," I say.

"Without hardship, how can we ever know how strong we truly are?"

"S'pose. But wouldn't it be nice if every now and then we could raise our hand and take a break? Life is exhausting sometimes."

Maura's eyes burn into me as if she's searching for what I'm not saying. "You'll have plenty of time to slow things down when you're my age. But for now, enjoy being young. Trust me, it passes in a blink."

"Oh, I know." I sigh, deflated. "One of my colleagues told me last week that my biological clock is ticking."

Maura doesn't reply. She sips her wine and waits for me to say more.

"I'm thirty-five, so technically she's right. But the thing is, my fiancé is the same age as me and no one has said anything like that to him."

"Do you want a baby?" Maura asks.

"He does."

"But what about you?"

Her question shocks me. No one has ever asked me outright like that before.

"Everyone just sort of thinks I'll get around to it, you know? Like when I finish my exams, or get that promotion. Or when Miles and I get married. And I know he can have babies forever and I only have a window, but that's not why people say it. It's just the way people think. They assume I'll become a mam at some point, but they don't automatically assume he'll be a dad."

To my surprise, Maura's smile widens. "A baby isn't the right fit for everyone."

"I love Miles," I say. "It's breaking my heart that he wants a baby so badly and I keep denying him that."

"The women of Ireland fought hard for choice, Saoirse. But no one ever said choosing would be easy."

"Maybe I should just have a baby and be done with it."

"Oh, love," she says, lowering her wine. She places her hand on top of mine and a huge breathy sigh tumbles out of me. "You know someone who would tell this so much better than me?"

I shake my head.

"Bernie," she says with a warm smile. "My gosh, could my best friend tell a story. She could have been a writer, you know. It's all here. All here in her scrapbook. But don't take my word for it. See for yourself." Maura flicks to the second page of the scrapbook and slides it closer to me. There's a black-and-white picture of a young woman with her hands on a pram. A bundle that I can only guess is her baby is tucked away under some blankets. My eyes are drawn to the wheels of the pram. They are huge, almost like the tires on a toddler's bicycle, and I can just about make out the branding in the center of each wheel that says SILVER CROSS. There are two little girls in the photo, too, standing to each side of her. They wear their long hair in pigtails and they can't be much more than five or six.

"Bernie was a mother. And I was not," Maura says, with a soft exhale. "And yet it was no easier for either of us."

CHAPTER 17

December 1969

Bernie

I scrubbed our flat from top to bottom this morning but I can still get the stench of dead meat. The walls have soaked the scent up over the years and every so often they take pleasure in spitting it back out. I suppose that's to be expected when you live above a butcher's shop. It's not so bad now, but in summer, if I open the windows, the smell is rancid enough to knock a horse.

My doctor says a woman goes funny when she's expecting a baby. Smells things she normally wouldn't. Feels things she normally doesn't. I wonder how he knows, having never had a baby grow inside him.

"You'll be grand, Bernie," the chap with the glasses and posh accent said on my last visit to the hospital. "Stick your head out the window—for a bit of fresh air and whatnot."

I know where I'd like to stick him, I think, as another bout of morning sickness hits and I take his advice. I open the window and stick my head out. I observe the street below as I take deep breaths and count backward from ten.

It's my first experience of a hospital birth, and, if I'm honest, I'm regretting the decision. I won't tell Dan, of course. He's slaving all hours to pay for it.

"I think we need to come into the twenty-first century," I said. "Home births are gone with the flood."

Dan didn't argue. He said if it made me feel better, we'd find the money. He can't understand why I'm so sick this time around.

"You've had three already; shouldn't this be a breeze to you?"

None of my pregnancies were a breeze, but this one is particularly difficult.

"Ma, Ma, Ma, I need to pee," Elizabeth, my middle daughter, shouts, racing toward me with her dress pulled up to her belly button.

"All right, all right," I say, reluctantly pulling my head back inside.

We're too late and a yellowish puddle circulates on the floor tiles.

"I'm sorry, Ma. It sneaked up on me."

"S'all right," I say, worried she'll be twenty-one and still wetting her pants.

"Marie," I call out. "Fetch the mop."

My six-year-old knows the drill. She returns carrying a timber-handled mop twice her size.

"Oh no you didn't," she says, pointing at the puddle and then at her sister.

Marie begins to laugh. Elizabeth begins to cry. And, Alice, my youngest, loudly stirs from her nap.

I hurry into the one and only bedroom and pick my one-year-old up from her cot. I sit her on my middle, where her little brother or sister is growing.

"Shh, shh. It's all right, it's all right," I say, and I wish I believed my own words.

"Maaaaaa," Marie calls out. "She did it again."

I rejoin my older children in the remainder of our flat and observe the second, and growing, yellow puddle.

"Elizabeth," I scold in a tone sterner than I have energy to produce. "If you do this again, as Jesus is my guide, I will slap you. Do you hear me?"

"You're going to get your arse reddened." Marie laughs.

My hand flies and comes down on Marie's bottom. "Where did you hear that word?"

My eldest child stops in her tracks and tears fill her eyes as she reaches behind her to rub where I've just slapped. "A boy in school," she says, her bottom lip dropping. "I . . . I . . . I . . ."

I realize she doesn't know what she's said, and I want to take it back. I want to cuddle her and tell her how sorry I am.

"Well, don't ever let me hear you say it again. What would Father Matthews say if he heard you say something like that? And with your first Holy Communion just around the corner."

"I'm sorry, Ma," Marie says, beginning to mop up her sister's mess.

At just six years old, she already carries out responsibility greater than any child her age should. She helps me cook and clean, and although she teases Elizabeth from time to time, she is a caring older sister.

I sit the baby down on the tiles, and she protests at the cold. She cries and reaches her arms back out to me.

"Marie, play with your sisters, please," I say, taking the mop from her to finish cleaning.

Marie is relieved by her new chore and she joins the baby on the floor. Soon all three of my girls are playing and laughing. I finish mopping and turn my attention to the stove. A large pot full of Alice's cloth nappies is about to boil over. I kill the heat and lift the pot to the sink. It's heavy and I hear something in my back click before pain shoots down my legs. I yelp like a wounded animal. Marie is on her feet in an instant and the fear on her face is worse than the pain.

"I'm all right. I'm all right," I lie, taking deep breaths. "Nothing to worry about."

Marie doesn't believe me. "I'll get Da."

My eyes widen. "Noooo. Don't. I really am all right, love. Da is busy workin', best not to disturb him."

I'm not quite halfway through this pregnancy as yet, and I've never seen Dan so worried. He thinks he hides it well, but I can see through him as if he's made of glass.

"Never again," he said last week when I lost a day in bed with a blistering headache. "I'm never putting you through this again. No more babies. I'll sleep on the sawdust floor in the shop if I have to, but we can't share a bed anymore once this baby comes."

I laughed at first, but when I realized he was serious I didn't find it funny.

"Don't be daft," I said. "That's not a marriage."

"No more babies."

"Ma. What's the matter?" Marie says, dragging me back to the here and now. Her little face is contorted with worry. "Are you going to die?"

"I don't want Ma to die," Elizabeth begins to cry.

"Kate's ma is dead," Marie says. "She gots to live with her granny now. And her granny is cross and smells funny."

"That's very sad for Kate," I say, trying to picture the child from Marie's class in school in my mind.

A little girl with curly red hair and no coat in the depths of winter comes to mind. Kate O'Rourke is the youngest child in a family of seven or eight or so. With no mother in the house and a father working all hours of the day to put food on the table, those poor craythurs are left to fend for themselves all day. It's a wonder they're in school at all. I decide I'll pack an extra apple in Marie's school bag tomorrow—for Kate.

"Right, girls," I say, clapping my hands to command my daughters' attention. "Let's hang these up." I point toward the pot of freshly boiled nappies. "And then we'll go to the market."

Elizabeth's tears quickly turn to joy. A trip to the market and a lollipop is her favorite. Marie smiles and fetches a stool from the table so she can climb up and reach the washing line that stretches from one side of the kitchen to the other.

"Ready, Ma," she says, and I wring out the first spotless nappy and pass it to her.

She secures it with a wooden clothes peg. Elizabeth claps her hands sporadically and cheers. "Good girl. Good girl."

Marie and I make light work of hanging the washing. Then I take my eldest child's hand and she hops down from the chair.

"Coats, everyone," I say.

The girls gather their coats from the ends of their beds and put them on. Elizabeth's wrists poke out past the ends of her sleeves and the hem barely hangs below her bottom anymore. I muffle a groan. Her coat will need replacing before this winter is through and certainly before Marie has grown out of her coat to pass it down. I take the biscuit tin from the dresser, pop the lid, and count the money inside. There's enough for a Black Forest gâteau from the fancy bakery on the corner. Dan turns thirty next week and I've been saving for almost three months. I hoped to have enough change for candles and some balloons too. But Elizabeth needs a coat and Dan will understand. I take a bedspread from the dresser, a heavy red one that used to be my ma's and is one of the few items of hers that I have left now. I raise it to my face and inhale deeply. The smell reminds me of my childhood and carefree days. I savor the scent and the memory. It's a warm woolen material and it will make a fine coat. I'll leave it with the dressmaker in town and hopefully there will be enough material to get a coat for Marie out of it, too, while we're at it.

I put on my own coat, which doesn't close over my ever-growing belly. I notice a new hole in the left underarm. I'd leave it with the dressmaker, too, but I've nothing to wear in the meantime. I scoop the baby off the floor, pop on her coat, and the girls and I leave the flat.

"Be careful on them stairs," I call out as Marie and Elizabeth show little regard for the slippery concrete steps leading down onto the street. "Girls, walk! No running."

I sit the baby in the pram waiting at the bottom step. She grumbles and, as usual, reaches her arms up to me.

"Shh. Hush now," I say, and I cover her chubby little legs with a blanket. Elizabeth curls her fingers around the side of the push bar on the left. Marie does the same on the right and together we push the pram out the door and onto the bright, busy street.

CHAPTER 18

Maura

She pushes her pram right into me and I drop the heavy bag of meat. There's a broken spoke on one of the wheels and it nicks my ankles. I feel a little drop of blood stick to my nylons.

"Oh Jaysus, I'm sorry," she says.

I suck air in through clenched teeth and bend in the middle to rub my throbbing ankle.

"Did I hurt you with this damn thing?" She kicks the broken spoke back into place as best she can. "I can be a right klutz sometimes. I'm sorry."

"I'm fine."

"Here, let me help you," she says, letting go of the pram to pick up my bag.

I stop her from taking the weight of it when I notice she's heavily pregnant. I pick up the bag of meat and spot a rectangular, brownish-black book on the ground.

"Oh, that'll be mine," she says. "It must have tumbled out when I hit you."

I pass her the floppy, leather-bound book. The spine is cracking and I wonder if it could use a stitch or two to keep it going. She opens the book and flicks through. It's chock-a-block with children's drawings, shopping lists, and other pages I can't quite make out. Obviously satisfied it's in one piece, she wipes the front and back of it across her skirt before tossing it into the tray under the pram.

I notice her face for the first time. She's my age, give or take a year or two, I'd guess. She's petite, barely up to my shoulder. Her brown hair falls in curls around her face and shoulders as if she lets it grow any way it pleases, and I wonder if she's taken the time to brush it at all today. There's a baby in the pram. A little girl. She's sitting up and sucking on the edge of a blanket. And two girls not much older than each other stand on either side of the pram. They're pretty, with dark plaited hair and green eyes like their mother.

"Another baby," I say, and I want to shovel the words back into my mouth instantly. "I'm sorry, that was rude."

"We're blessed," she says. And then she adds, "A little too blessed, to be honest."

I smile, and I'm not quite sure what to say. But when she laughs, I decide it's okay to laugh too.

I pick up my bag of meat and say, "Well, it was nice to meet you."

"Where you goin' with that?"

"Excuse me?"

"I said, where you going? That looks heavy. I can carry it for you if we're heading in the same direction."

She points to the metal tray under the pram and then she points down the street toward Switzers.

"Thank you, but I'm going this way." I tilt my head and point my thumb over my shoulder.

I'm lying and I can sense she knows it.

"You buy that in McCarthy's?" she asks, glancing into the bag that's starting to pull painfully on my shoulder.

"Yes, McCarthy's butcher's. It was a gift, actually."

"Oh." Her eyes widen and I can sense she disapproves.

"Ma, can we get a lollipop now?" the tallest of the young girls says.

The woman looks at her daughter and places her finger on her lips. "Shh, Marie. I'm speaking to the nice lady who looks just like Doris Day."

It's the first time I've heard the comparison in a while, but she isn't complimenting me. Her clipped tone and cocked head make that much obvious. The little girl nods and doesn't say another word.

"A gift, you were saying . . ."

I regret speaking as much as the little girl does. "Um."

"McCarthy's are giving away free meat now, are they?" She stands with a hand on one hip and the other hip jutting out. "Can't afford a coat for my little 'un and he's in there giving out free chops. I'll bleedin' kill him, I will."

I'm not sure what I've said that has upset her so much. My ankle is throbbing and the bag is growing heavier by the second.

"Maaaaa," the smaller little girl calls out, losing patience.

"Hush," the woman says, crosser now. "I said I'm talkin'. I'm asking this lovely lady why your da is giving her free chops when we barely have enough on our own table."

"Oh, you're Dan's wife," I say, finally understanding. "Nice to meet you."

I extend my hand but she doesn't shake it. Her eyes narrow. I still haven't eased her concern.

"I'm Maura. Maura Davenport. I'm Dr. Davenport's wife. Dan says my husband is your doctor."

Her cheeks pinken and her stiff shoulders round. She takes my hand and nearly shakes it clean off my wrist.

"Oh," she says. "Oh."

I take my hand back and wait, but she can't seem to find any more words. I think I've made her as uncomfortable as she's made me.

"Well, as I said, it was nice meeting you, Mrs. McCarthy. I best be off."

"Bernie," she says, at last. "I'm Bernie. And this is Marie, Elizabeth, and Alice."

She places her hand on her daughters' heads in turn as if she is counting steps of stairs.

"Your coat is very loverly," Elizabeth says with a slight lisp.

"Thank you. Yours is lovely too."

I can't help but notice how snug her coat is and Bernie seems embarrassed when she catches my eye.

"Elizabeth is right. Your coat *is* very nice," Bernie says, pointing at me. "Is it from Switzers?"

"It is."

"Did your husband buy it?"

"No. It's an old coat. I bought it when I used to work there."

Her eyes widen. "You worked in Switzers? Wow." She seems as impressed as if I'd told her I was an astronaut or a celebrity.

"Yes. Up until June when I got married."

"And you had to give up your job to mind the kids," she finishes speaking for me.

"Well, no children yet," I say. "But we're hopeful."

I cross my fingers and hold up my hand.

"He's a doctor," she says, with longing. "I bet he knows all the tricks for having 'em. And for not having 'em."

"I don't think there's tricks for either, unfortunately. It's all in the hands of God."

Bernie rolls her eyes. "God's hands didn't have much to do with this." Her fingertips seem to instinctively touch her round belly.

I've never met anyone quite like Bernie before, and I wonder if she always says the thoughts in her head out loud.

"Right," she says, taking the bag from me and shoving it under her pram before my mind has time to catch up. "Jaysus, what does Dan have in here? Rocks."

"I . . . I . . . I . . ."

"I'm taking this before my husband is to blame for your arm falling off. No arguments. I'll go where you're going. Besides, the girls and I could do with stretching our legs and catching some fresh air."

"Doesn't get much fresher," I say, as sporadic flakes of snow begin to fall.

"Maaaaa," Elizabeth says again.

"I haven't forgotten your lollipops," Bernie tells her girls. "We just have to help Mrs. Davenport out first."

"Maura. Please?"

Bernie smiles. "Right, Maura. Where are we off to?"

"Rathmines," I say.

"Jaysus." Bernie's voice raises an octave. "You're even posher than I thought. C'mon, girls. Let's see how the other half live."

Bernie winks and knocks her shoulder against mine and I think I might like her. I might even want to *be like* her.

CHAPTER 19

Bernie

I've never been to Rathmines before. Not because I didn't want to, but because what would I ever be needing with a place like that? I hear everyone owns a car there and they go on holiday to fancy places like the seaside. Dan's bicycle does us just fine, and I've never owned swimming togs in my life.

"My legs are hurty," Elizabeth grumbles, after half an hour or so.

"Mine too." Marie nods.

We're about halfway, I think, measuring the route in landmarks. The GPO. Switzers. The Iveagh Gardens.

Elizabeth jams her hands on her hips and stomps a single foot. "I wants to go home."

I take a deep breath and try not to swear. I slide Alice to the top of the pram, taking care not to wake her. Then I lift Elizabeth and settle her in the empty space I've created.

"Don't wake your sister," I tell her.

Elizabeth nods, keeping her knees tucked under her chin, folding herself like an envelope to fit in the cramped space. Marie looks up at me with round, teary eyes.

"I'm sorry, love. I've no more room. But you're a big girl now."

"Just a minute," Maura says, and then she dashes out of sight.

She reappears from a corner shop with two red lollipops and offers one each to Elizabeth and Marie. Elizabeth snatches hers quickly and shoves it in her mouth.

"Yummy," she says, as a sugary dribble trickles down her chin.

Marie is less sure. She eyes Maura with trepidation.

"It's all right," I say. "You can take it."

"Thank you," Marie says at last.

We continue walking. Every so often I catch Maura watching the baby sleep. I wonder if she knows she touches her stomach each time.

"How far along are you?" I ask.

"Erm, another mile or so. I can carry it the rest of the way if you need to turn back."

She bends down ready to lift the meat off the tray under the pram. I've never met anyone like her before, so reserved and polite. I bet her manners got her places in life. And I wish I could be more like her. Better able to keep my gob shut when needs be.

"Another mile is fine," I say. "We're enjoying the walk, aren't we, girls?"

"Mm-hmm," the girls say in unison.

Tiredness is painted on Marie's face. Her cheeks are rosy and her feet clip-clop alongside me. But she sucks her lollipop contentedly and she doesn't complain. The sugary treat is a fraction of its original size and her tongue has turned bright red. She takes great satisfaction in sticking it out and pointing it toward her sister, who squeals with joy.

"It's red. It's red." Elizabeth giggles.

"Hush. Hush, don't wake the baby," I say.

"They're just wonderful," Maura says, beaming with happiness as she watches my daughters. I suspect she is trying to envisage her future child at Elizabeth's or Marie's age.

I ask my question again, this time looking directly at her stomach so there can be no confusion.

"How far along are you?"

"Oh." She blushes and stares at her feet. "How did you know?"

"I've been around the block a few times. You learn to spot these things."

"It's not for certain yet," she says.

There's so much longing in her voice, and I envy her soon-to-be baby. So wanted, with a prim-and-proper mother and a doctor father. A sharp pang of guilt stabs me like a physical pain. The poor baby growing inside me is much less wished for. I cried for three days when my monthlies were late, and Dan couldn't stomach a decent meal for a week when I told him.

"Another mouth to feed," I had said.

"We'll figure it out, my love. Don't you worry."

Dan would figure out the answers to all my problems if he could. Bless him. But some problems there's just no solving. Like two healthy adults making babies.

"I've been hoping for this for a long time," Maura says. "The days can be very long at home on my own. My mother says I should enjoy the peace and quiet but I'm ashamed to admit that I'm lonely."

Envy is the last thing Maura needs right now, but nonetheless, I can't keep the look off my face. I've never known a quiet home. I'm the eldest of seven. Some of my younger siblings were still children when I moved out to marry Dan. No sooner were Dan and I walked down the aisle than Marie was in my belly. The nine months when it was just the two of us as we waited for Marie were a gift that I will always cherish. I love the bones of my girls, but every so often I long for some peace and quiet.

"How late are your monthlies?" I ask.

Maura jolts upright as if I've hit her with a hot poker.

"Excuse me?"

I stare at her. I know she heard me.

"Look, I'm no doctor like your husband or nothing, but do you want to know the way I see it?"

Maura stares back at me with a look that tells me she's not so sure she wants to know. But I'm going to tell her anyway.

"You did what needs to be done with your husband, yes?"

She inhales sharply.

"Grand. That's step one. Now, your monthlies are nowhere to be seen. Step two. You don't need no fancy doctor to tell you step three. A baby is in there. That's just how it is."

"Do you really think?" she says, and I wonder how anyone can make it this far into life and still be so full of sweetness and innocence.

"How old are you?" I ask.

"Twenty-six, closer to twenty-seven."

"It's a little old to only be starting," I say. "But by the sounds of it, you're on your way. I've a friend who was married a year and nothing. Then all of a sudden, twins. She's been pregnant every year since. She has six kids now and she's my age. I'm twenty-six too, by the way. I'd say she'll have an even ten by the time she's thirty."

"Oh, I don't think I want ten," she says, with a girlish giggle. "One is just fine for now."

"Eh, I don't think that's how this works, love." It's my turn to laugh, and the way Maura looks at me tells me she doesn't find it funny anymore. "Sometimes there's just no choosing how many he puts in there. And I'm not talking about God, you know."

CHAPTER 20

Bernie

The baby wakes. It starts to snow. And we reach a row of the smartest, poshest houses I've ever seen. I bet folks pay top dollar just to breathe the air in a neighborhood like this.

"I need to do a wee-wee," Elizabeth announces loudly. "It's coming. It's coming."

"Don't pee in the pram," Marie shouts, sounding much older and wiser than her six years.

"Too late," Elizabeth says, almost triumphantly.

I glance at the blanket wrapped around the baby. The soft pink has turned a wet, dark cerise and I've no doubt it's soaked through to the bedding underneath. I lift Elizabeth out of the pram. She's drenched from the waist down. I could cry and I think Maura knows it.

"Why don't we all go inside out of the cold?" she says, untying her head-scarf to reveal a perfectly styled blonde bob. I'd give my right arm for hair so perfect, and I wonder why anyone with a gift of such beauty would want to cover it up.

"We can get Elizabeth cleaned up, and I've some freshly baked apple tart just waiting to be shared," Maura adds in a cheery singsong tone.

I've never had help with the kids. Not from anyone. Dan works all God's hours and my family live at the far side of the country. I'm lucky to see my ma and sisters twice a year. Maura's simple suggestion that she help me with a wet-knickered toddler is the kindest thing anyone has said to me in years, and try as I might, I can't hold the tears back.

"Thank you. Thank you so much." I sniffle.

Maura places her hand on my back and smiles. "Let's get inside, eh?" She pulls a key from her bag, which is even fancier than her coat, and opens the door. The girls charge inside first and Maura helps me with the pram.

"Are you rich?" Marie asks when Maura closes the door behind us.

"Marie," I scold, "don't be rude."

Maura's lips curl into a subtle smirk, but she ignores the question as she leads us into a kitchen so large I think I could fit my whole flat inside. The walls are painted cool white and the lime green cupboards pop like something from a magazine. There's even a fridge. Big and tall with some magnets stuck on the front. Maura opens it and places the bag of meat inside. Dan says you can keep all sorts fresh inside a refrigerator for days, even weeks. He says we'll buy one just as soon as we've saved up some.

"Would you like something to drink?" Maura asks the girls. "I think I have some Coca-Cola in the cupboard."

"What's Coza-Cola?" Elizabeth says.

She turns to me and shoves the chewed and soggy stick from her lollipop into my hand, then draws the sleeve of her coat across her mouth. Some fluff sticks to her sugary lips.

"It's fizzy pop," Marie tells her, with a superior smugness. "I love Coza-Cola."

"And where would you be drinking fizzy pop?" I ask, shoving the lollipop stick into my coat pocket and knowing I'll regret it later when I have to fish it back out.

"School."

I fold my arms and stare my daughter down. "Stick out your tongue."

Marie's confidence falters.

"Stick it out."

Marie opens her mouth just the tiniest bit and pokes the tip of her tongue out.

"There. See. Black as coal," I say. "That's what fibbin' gets you. A dirty black tongue."

"I wanna see, I wanna see," Elizabeth demands, tugging on Marie's coat to turn her around.

Marie pulls her tongue back and her bottom lip quivers. "I don't want a black tongue."

"Well, no more fibs, then," I say.

Maura covers her mouth and does a terrible job of hiding her amusement. "Is every day like this?" she asks.

"Like what?" I say, bending against a protesting round belly as I pull off Elizabeth's shoes and then her wet tights and knickers.

"So busy," she says, almost wistfully. "And so lovely."

Elizabeth almost slips as she stands with one leg on the floor and the other wriggling away from sopping tights. I catch her arm and steady her and she looks up at me with a loving grin and a wrinkled button nose.

"Oopsie." She giggles.

I lift Alice from the pram and sit her on the floor, telling Marie to watch her as usual. Then I rinse the wet clothes and the baby's bedsheets in the sink while Maura heats some apple tart in the stove. She adds log after log to the stove and I think soon her kitchen will be as warm as a summer's day.

"You can dry those here," she says, pulling a fancy white clotheshorse into view.

She opens it like an accordion filling its lungs and hangs the clothes. I imagine what it would be like to have a fancy contraption like that in my flat, instead of some twine tied from one side of the kitchen to the other.

Maura plates up generous slices of tart and fills some cups with Coca-Cola, and the girls and I sit to the table. I bounce the baby on my knees as we eat and drink.

"This is lovely," I say genuinely.

I've never tasted black fizzy pop before, but I don't admit that out loud.

"More, please," Elizabeth says, shoving her empty plate toward Maura.

"Elizabeth," I scold, so sternly it makes the baby jump.

"Oh, that's all right," Maura says, on her feet again to cut another slice. "Christy and I can't possibly manage all this on our own."

"You made a tart this big just for the two of you?" I say, chasing crumbs around my plate with my finger and popping them into the baby's mouth. She kicks her legs with approval.

Maura passes Elizabeth more tart and sits down. "I like baking," she says, seeming delighted that my little girl is enjoying the treat so much. "It fills the hours."

"You'll have to give me the recipe," I say, equally enjoying Elizabeth's delight, although my happiness is short-lived. Apples are expensive and I'm not sure how often I could afford to make such a fancy tart. Nonetheless, I click my fingers and Marie fetches my scrapbook from the bottom of the pram. I flick it open, quickly finding the middle, where there are pages from cookery books torn out and stuck in and several other recipes already jotted down. There isn't room for much more. When Maura passes me a pencil and begins to recite the recipe from memory, I make my writing as small as possible.

"Is it a recipe book?" Maura asks, pointing.

I smile. "Yes. And a photobook, and somewhere to keep my girls' artwork. All the scraps that make up life as a McCarthy girl, I suppose."

"That's lovely," Maura says with a longing sigh.

"Well, when your little one arrives you can start your own. A Davenport scrapbook. Although I'm sure you're probably much too busy," I say, glancing around her pristine kitchen with cupboards that gleam like shiny pennies.

A bright smile lights up her pretty face as she mulls the idea over and I wonder if she knows she's rubbing her tummy again.

"I just wish the wait wasn't so long," she says.

"Do you miss working?" I ask.

Maura forces down a lump of tart that she hasn't quite finished chewing and places her fork on the table, next to her plate. My question has upset or offended her, I can tell. I'm about to move on when she takes a deep breath and looks me in the eye.

"Yes," she whispers as if the walls have ears. "I miss it a lot, if the truth be told. But I'm hoping all that will change once the baby comes."

I take her hand and squeeze it gently as Alice squirms and demands I bounce her on my knees some more. Elizabeth is a half-dressed mess and Marie is not far behind as crumbs gather at the corners of her lips and on the collar of her coat, and yet their grubby faces, lit up with the joy of full bellies, fill my heart right up to the top.

"I can't promise every day will be wonderful," I say. "But there will be some wonderful moments in every day, that much I do know. It's enough for me. I hope it will be for you too."

"It will be, oh I just know it will be. I can't wait to fill a scrapbook of my own," Maura says, her eyes as bright and as full of innocence as my daughters'.

The girls become restless, beginning to fidget and spin and swing on their chairs.

"We should get going soon," I say.

"But Elizabeth's clothes aren't dry yet. Stay. Please. Have more cake? Christy won't be home for hours yet."

"I couldn't eat more if I tried," I say, itching to open the button on the side of my skirt.

Maura's face falls and my heart sinks. I look around the upmarket kitchen, out into the lush garden, and finally I bring my eyes back to settle on Maura's expensive clothes and fancy haircut. At first glance you'd assume Maura was a woman with everything you could possibly wish for, and maybe she is, but what good is snazzy bric-a-brac if you're full to the brim with loneliness?

"Girls, why don't you go play outside?" I say, realizing that my curious daughters are listening with cocked ears to every word we say.

Marie looks over her shoulder and out the window, noticing for the first time that the green space behind us is an enclosed garden. A safe place to skip and jump and run. A place we don't have outside our flat. She jumps down from her chair and grabs Elizabeth's hand, almost toppling her over as she pulls her to her feet.

Maura glances at Elizabeth's bare legs. "She'll catch her death out there."

"Ah, she'll be fine. Running around will keep her warm."

Maura doesn't seem convinced. "What about some television?" she says. "Would you like to watch some telly, girls?"

"What a telly?" Elizabeth asks.

I look at Marie and wait for another smug explanation, but she's stumped. Her eyes are wide and curious.

"What's a television, Ma?" she says.

"It's like a wireless, but you can see the people moving around inside the box."

"There's people in a box?" Marie's delight is contagious and Elizabeth begins to jump up and down on the spot.

"I wanna see a box of people. I wanna see."

Maura leads the girls out of the kitchen and soon I hear sound carrying through the walls, followed by the delighted squeals of my daughters.

"Thank you," I say when Maura returns. "I think this might be their best day ever."

Maura sits back down, picks up her fork, and takes a mouthful of tart. "I'm having a rather lovely day too."

CHAPTER 21

Bernie

Maura sets about cleaning up like a whirlwind. I offer to help, but she won't let me lift a finger. Soon, except for Elizabeth's pants drying, the kitchen is as good as new. Keeping the house tidy seems immensely important to her. I imagine cleaning is how she fills most of her days.

She makes a pot of tea and joins me at the table once more. Alice reaches for my cup every so often, and it's a balancing act not to spill hot tea on her chubby, giddy legs.

"Can I ask you something?" Maura says, tucking the legs of her chair under the table with a shrill squeak as if she needs to get closer to me to whisper. "Does it hurt?"

"Does what hurt?"

Maura inhales and holds her breath for a moment before she manages to puff it back out and say, "Bringing life into the world."

"The birth, you mean?"

Her eyes widen as if I've said something blasphemous. "I . . . I . . ."

"Didn't nobody ever tell you about this stuff? Your ma? A big sister?"

"Oh goodness no, my ma isn't a talker. And I've no sisters."

"So who told you about the birds and the bees, then?"

"No one. I just sort of worked it out over the years." Maura closes her eyes and shakes her head and when she opens them again, I see a flash of confusion and fear and I think, *Despite all her money, I wouldn't swap shoes with her for all the tea in China.*

"I thought I was dying," she says, and a subtle quiver creeps into her voice. "When I bled for the first time, I really thought that was it for me. I was twelve or thirteen, I think. Certainly no more. I was in school when it started. Sister Dymphna, the principal, asked me and one of the other girls to go outside to the bathroom and cut up some old newspapers. The toilet roll was for the nuns only. We were cutting the newspapers into squares, just like sheets of toilet roll, when the pain in my stomach hit. I thought it was a bug at first. My brother was sick the week before, and my da. I can still see the stain on my underwear now as clear as day. I sat there thinking my insides were falling out. I knew bleeding from the inside was bad. I remembered seeing my friend's da cough blood into his hand once. He was dead a few months later. I thought it'd be the same. I thought I'd done something terrible and the devil was out to get me. I stuffed my pants full of newspaper, went back to my classroom, and waited to die. But then, in a few days, it stopped. And the next month it came again. And so on and so on. Until I finally realized that it's just something that happens. When I was older, sixteen or seventeen maybe, I asked my ma why she never told me. She hit me over the back of the head with a tea towel and told me if she heard me talking like that again she'd wash my mouth out with soap and water."

"Jesus," I say, unable to find better words.

"Like I said, my ma's not a talker."

"I have four sisters," I say. "We talk a lot."

Her envy is palpable.

"I don't see them as much as I'd like to," I add.

She swallows again. This time there's no tart to choke down but the lump seems to get stuck regardless.

"I've learned a thing or two since then. How babies are made, for one thing," she says.

I smile. I don't doubt that was the first thing her new husband taught her.

"Christy says having babies is what women do," she says. "It's what their bodies are made to do."

"Doctors." I roll my eyes. "You can be the smartest man in the room, but you will never understand what it's like to push new life into this world."

"Christy doesn't know about the baby yet," she says. "I wanted to wait until I knew for sure. I didn't want to get his hopes up."

"Doesn't he know your monthlies are missing?"

"God no. Why would I tell him that?"

"Dan's no doctor," I say, laughing at the thought of it, "but he knows as soon as my monthlies are gone that we're having another baby. It's just nature."

"Christy and I don't talk about things like that."

"And you don't talk to your ma 'bout it neither."

"No."

"Who do you talk to?"

"Nobody. It's not really something you talk about, is it?"

"We're talking about it now, aren't we?"

Maura takes a deep breath and observes me.

"I'm sorry," she says. "Forget I said anything."

"You and me are going to be friends," I tell her, as matter-of-fact as if I'm saying birds fly or fish swim. "And we're going to talk about all sorts, all the time. Because that's what friends do. It's what women should do, eh?"

I take her hand and give it a gentle squeeze.

"Friends," she says. "I'd like that."

CHAPTER 22

Maura

Bernie and I fritter away hours, chatting like a pair of lifelong friends. Long enough for Elizabeth's clothes to dry, the baby to feed and nap, and the children to enjoy some fun and games in the back garden.

"They'll sleep tonight," Bernie says, watching her daughters play through the window.

I worry about their little legs growing tired on the walk home but Bernie assures me they're used to walking all over town. I call the girls inside and split the last slice of apple tart between them. I'll have to make another before Christy gets home or he won't be pleased. But baking anew is a small price to pay for the loveliest afternoon I've had in a long time.

"Fuel for the road," I say, and they rub their full tummies with satisfaction.

I help Bernie navigate the pram through the front door and back onto the street. And then I take my coat from the newel post at the bottom of the stairs and offer it to her.

She looks at me with curious eyes, but she doesn't take it. I noticed there's a hole under the arm of her coat and the material in the back is threadbare from years of repeated wear.

"This would look so much better on you," I say, edging my coat toward her. "I'm too tall. It does me no favors."

Bernie's eyes glass over and neither of us addresses the fact that I'm lying.

"I couldn't possibly," she says.

"Please. For all the meat your husband gave me. This way neither of us is getting something for nothing."

"So an exchange," Bernie says.

"Exactly."

Bernie takes the coat. She strokes the fur and her face lights up. She slips off her old coat and folds it into the tray under the pram, taking care not to squash her scrapbook, and then she slides her arms into my coat.

"Just as I thought. It suits you," I say.

Bernie twirls on the spot and giggles like a schoolgirl. "I love it. I really, really love it. Thank you."

"You'll come visit, won't you?" I say when Bernie stops twirling and grips the handle of the pram.

"I'm tired," Elizabeth complains.

"Me too," Marie adds.

"Today was a good day," Bernie says.

"The best," I say.

We share some mutual nodding and I watch as Bernie and her daughters walk away. And I wonder if I'll see them again.

I watch until they turn the corner at the end of the road and I'm about to close the door when Christy's car comes into view around the same corner. He's early. Panic rises in me in the shape of an acidy bubble that bursts in the back of my throat. I've no dinner on and with the apple tart all gone, I've nothing to offer him.

He parks his car under the old oak tree just down from our front gate. Most of our neighbors have cars and there is a silent understanding among residents about who parks where. Mr. O'Toole across the road parks next to the tall, green post box. Mrs. Sweeny in number 18 parks behind him. Her husband died recently and she's started driving his car. It's the talk of the road, and no one has a good word to say about a middle-aged woman finding independence behind the wheel.

Christy steps out and slams the car door behind him. He has a face like thunder and I think about charging inside and locking myself in the bathroom. I could pretend to have an upset stomach, but I used that excuse last week. Or I could lie down with a headache, but again, that excuse is worn thin. Bedsides, Christy left me medication to take to ease them.

Just last week he passed me a packet of round white pills. "To keep you on your feet," he said, making it clear that an afternoon of skipped chores was unacceptable, migraine or not.

At the door, Christy gathers me into his arms and kisses my cheek. His stubble is coming in and I want to pull away, but I don't.

"What a day," he huffs, and cigar breath hits me. "At least something smells good."

"You're early," I say, easing myself out of his grip. "I wasn't expecting you home for another hour or so."

"I'm tired. And hungry," he says. "Mrs. Cartwright had twins this afternoon and she screamed the bloody place down. Where are those headache pills?"

I search my brain trying to remember where I put them. I draw a blank.

"Why don't I run you a bath, eh?" I say.

Christy's tense shoulders relax. He kicks off his shoes inside the door and drags himself up the stairs without another word. I hurry into the bathroom and begin to fill the tub; then I race downstairs to make sure I have enough cooking apples for another tart. The relief when I find I have plenty is intense.

"Bring up the paper," Christy calls out.

I fetch the paper from the kitchen countertop and make my way upstairs again. Christy is half undressed when he takes the paper and reads the header.

"That's this morning's paper. What would I want with stale news?" He rolls his eyes. "Where's the evening press?"

"I didn't get a chance to pick up the paper today."

Christy's eyes narrow. He has one leg in his pants and one leg out, and if his eyes weren't thin like commas his appearance might be comical. Instead, it's a little scary.

"All right," he says, slipping the other leg off. He folds his trousers and places them neatly on the bed.

"I . . . eh . . . I got delayed in town," I say, beginning to stutter.

Christy laughs. "What is it with women and fine china? How many hours did you waste picking out delft?" He is soft-spoken. Relaxed, almost. But I've learned he is always most calm before a storm. My palms begin to sweat. *The damn delft.*

"I hope you didn't spare any pennies," he says. "My parents are coming for Christmas dinner and my mother will know if we're trying to be cheap."

Christy's family joining us for Christmas dinner is news to me, but it's the least of my concerns right now. I need to get his mind away from the delft I didn't buy. I step back, keeping the door in easy-to-reach distance.

"I popped into the butcher's on Talbot Street today."

Christy looks at me, wholly uninterested.

"Dan McCarthy insisted on giving me a bag of free meat and—"

"Dan?" he says, his attention suddenly piqued. "Since when are you on first-name terms with McCarthy's butcher's?"

"He asked me to call him Dan and I just—"

"You were just so busy obliging a stranger that you forgot to pick up the damn newspaper for your husband."

"I'm sorry, Christy. But he gave me this big bag of free meat and it was heavy and—"

"Free? What are we? Some sort of charity? We don't need free anything from anyone."

I take another step back. "I know. I know. But he said you look after his wife and I think he was just trying to show his gratitude."

"Money is the best way to say thank you. Money. You should have told him that. I should be paid double listening to that woman drone on and on about her swollen ankles and sick stomach. You'd swear she'd never had a baby before. It's her fourth, for pity's sake. Just get on with it."

"I think she's finding this pregnancy harder than the others," I say.

Christy folds his arms and stares at me as if I'm something he scraped off his shoe. "Are you a nurse now, Maura?"

"No, but—"

"Then how the hell would you know?" Christy laughs as if my stupidity amuses him. "I'm getting in the bath now. I'll have dinner in one hour, when I'm done."

"Okay," I say, trying to hide my relief that I have time to cook something up as I walk toward the door.

"Oh, and Maura . . ."

My chest tightens. The door feels so close and yet so far.

"Mm-hmm," I say, turning back.

"I'll have a slice of apple tart in the meantime. It smells good."

I swallow hard.

"I burned it," I say, blurting the first excuse that tumbles into my head.

"You burned it?"

I nod. Christy steps forward and begins sniffing like a dog. He's still a foot away from me, maybe two, and yet the heat from his body seems to fill the space between us until it feels as if it might singe me.

"It doesn't smell of burning," he says.

"I opened all the windows."

My palms begin to sweat as I back through the door and onto the landing.

"Really?" Christy follows me through the door. His strides are twice their usual size.

"I can make another tart. I have more apples, I checked."

It happens so suddenly that I don't remember seeing him raise his arm, or even feeling the punch as it comes crashing down against my skull. But I do remember the fear, the split second of horror that whips around inside like a whirlwind.

I find myself in darkness at the bottom of the stairs. It takes me a moment to realize my eyes are shut, and once I do, I decide not to open them. I'm too afraid of what I'll see. My legs are crumpled underneath me, like those of a rag doll. Christy is standing over me, I can tell. I hear his heavy breathing, feel his hot breaths against the top of my head. Seconds or minutes pass, I'm not sure.

"Maura, oh my God, my darling." Christy's voice carries toward me as if I'm under water. "Are you all right? Are you hurt? Talk to me, darling. Talk to me, please?" Each word pulls me closer to the surface until, finally, I am brave enough to open my eyes and look at the man crouched over me. The man who is supposed to love me more than anything else in the world. The man to whom I gave my heart. The father of my baby.

The man who someday, I worry, might kill me.

"Maura, Jesus," he says.

His face is blurry, hovering above me. I blink, but I can't focus. There's a pain in my chest and for a moment I think his foot might be stomping on me, crushing me into the floor. It's not. My focus sharpens and I notice he has tears in his eyes.

"You fell. Oh, Maura, you fell. You're so clumsy, my darling. But you're all right. That's all that matters. You're all right."

I search my brain for words. None come. Not even when I open my mouth and try to force something out. There's a wet patch beneath me, I realize. It's warm and collected in my underwear and on my skirt. At first I worry that I've wet myself with fear. Heat creeps into my cheeks thinking about it. But when cramping in my stomach starts, the slow realization that I'm losing the baby hits me harder than any punch from my husband.

"Maura, talk to me," Christy says. He's concerned and soft-spoken again, like the gentleman I thought I married. "Are you all right?"

I see him clearly now, standing in slightly off-white Y-fronts and navy socks with a brown polka dot. He looks ridiculous, and silently laughing at him inside my head gives me a guilty pleasure.

He reaches his hand out to me and I take it and allow him to help me to my shaky feet.

"There now," he says, almost whispering. "See, you're fine."

Blood begins to trickle down my leg and I wonder if he'll notice it spilled on the carpet.

"Why don't you get yourself into bed, eh? That was a nasty tumble. There's no need to worry about dinner for now. A sandwich will be fine later when you're feeling up to it."

I hate him in this moment. I really, truly despise him.

Christy helps me up the stairs and I let him tuck me into bed as if I were a small child.

"I'll fetch you some water," he says.

"No. No, thank you. I just need to sleep."

I'm desperate for him to leave me alone so I can check on the bleeding. Christy nods and closes the heavy curtains, instantly turning our bedroom dusk.

"I love you, darling," he says, and then he breezes out the door and closes it behind him.

I lie still and listen for his footsteps on the creaky stairs. I count each step, and when I'm confident that he's downstairs and in the sitting room or kitchen, I peel back the bedspread and stand up. To my relief, blood hasn't made its way onto the bed linen. I open the door slowly, concentrating so as not to make a sound, and hurry into the bathroom.

The bright red blood takes my breath away. There's more of it than I was expecting. Memories of my first period—when I thought I might die—rush back. Pain stabs my lower abdomen and bends me in the middle like a question mark as I yield to it. I hold the sink and try to catch my breath. In a moment of panic, I think about calling out to Christy. Not as a supportive husband, but as a doctor. I don't want to die. But I am not one of Christy's patients. I am his wife. He would find some way of making this my fault. He would blame me for losing our baby. *His baby.* I couldn't cope with another hit. Not now, of all times. I decide to take my chances with life and death. I made it through my first period on my own. So, too, I will make it through this. *I hope.*

A sudden knock on the door makes me yelp like a puppy.

"You all right in there?" Christy's voice calls through the door.

"Yes. Yes. I'm fine." My voice is strange as I push it out through gritted teeth when another cramp grips me.

"I thought you were going to rest."

There's a spark of irritation in his voice. I can tell he's furious to find me out of bed.

"I'm feeling much better," I call back.

"Good. Good. Listen, I'm going to the White Arms for a pint or two. I won't be more than an hour. We'll have the dinner when I get back."

I don't remind him that he suggested a sandwich. Clearly, some bread and ham is no longer going to satisfy him.

"There's steak in the fridge. The ones from McCarthy's," he says.

"All right."

The cramps ease and I stand up straight and catch my reflection in the mirror. My right eye is swollen and purple and the color is already attempting to drain down my cheek. By tomorrow the whole right side of my face will be black and blue. Just as it has been before.

"Right. I'm off," Christy says, and then I hear the stairs creak again and the front door open and close.

I slide to the floor, tuck my knees into my chest, and cry.

CHAPTER 23

Saoirse

I reach for Maura's hand as a tear trickles down her cheek. I shove my other hand in my pocket and pull out some tissues and offer them to her.

"It's clean, I promise," I say softly.

Maura nods and smiles and takes it. She dabs under her eyes and blows her nose.

"Oh, look at me being all silly," she says, swallowing a stubborn tear-soaked lump. "I haven't cried about all this in a long time. But every now and then the memories sting."

My chest feels tight. Suddenly Maura's story isn't the loveliest story I've ever heard. And, somehow, at the same time, it feels like an even greater honor to hear it.

I put that tissue in my pocket earlier, just before I stormed out the door of my apartment. I thought I'd walk around for a while and have a good cry. But tears didn't come. As much as I wanted to cry, I had no tears. But now, holding Maura's hand and feeling the gentle shaking of her body, tears gather in the corners of my eyes.

"I'm sorry you married such a bastard," I say.

Maura stops sobbing and bursts out laughing.

I'm so confused. But her laughter goes on and on, and then she snorts and laughs even louder. I find it's quite contagious. Soon tears are pouring down my face, but this time it's because I'm in hysterics.

"You know, I've been telling this story for fifty years. Every year on this exact train I make it my business to tell at least one person this story. And nobody, not one single person, has ever called my husband that before."

I take a deep breath, worried I've offended her. "I'm sorry. Sometimes I speak before I think."

"Like Bernie," she says.

"Yes. I s'pose."

I feel a ginormous sense of pride in being compared to her best friend.

"You know, you're a lot more receptive than that businessman last year. Poor chap. I thought he was going to jump out the window when I mentioned childbirth." The corners of her lips curl into a cheeky smile. "Thankfully, he settled for shoving some earphones in."

"His loss," I say, and Maura's smile widens. "More wine?" I ask, anxious to get back to the story, if she's ready. "My treat this time."

CHAPTER 24

Bernie

It has snowed for two days straight. What started as a beautiful, fluffy white blanket is now an ugly mess like churned butter as traffic and pedestrians slowly navigate their way through the slippery streets. I have a hospital appointment today, so despite the weather, the girls and I make our way into town. There are no complaints of tired legs as Marie and Elizabeth stop every so often to throw snowballs at each other. I learned quickly that dragging the pram is a lot easier than pushing it, and Alice finds the whole experience hilarious. She gurgles and coos. By the time we reach the main doors of the intimidating Georgian building I'm sweating despite the near freezing temperature. I fight with the pram as I try to guide it up the concrete steps and, exhausted, take a seat in the large communal waiting area.

It's my fourth or fifth visit to the hospital—I've lost track. I'll never understand why I need to visit so often. I wonder what they expect to find in there, if not a baby.

"He'll see you now, Mrs. McCarthy," says a young nurse. Her face is fresh and childlike, as if she would better belong in a school pinafore than in a starched white nurse's uniform.

I give Alice a bottle, which she immediately turns upside down and shakes. I ignore the mess and leave Marie in charge.

"Don't move off them seats," I say, kissing each of their heads in turn. Then I promise shepherd's pie for dinner. Their favorite. A heavily pregnant lady offers to keep an eye on them for me while I'm with the doc. I'll return the favor as soon as I'm done and watch her large brood of beautiful and immaculately kept children.

The nurse leads me behind a movable partition. She folds it around us as best she can and apologizes for its poor attempt to offer privacy.

"It's all right," I say, but I blush nonetheless when she asks me to take a seat and peel off layers of winter clothing so she can draw blood and measure the circumference of my stomach.

"Everything looks great," she says. "How are you feeling?"

I redress quickly and tell her about my swollen feet, tiredness, and general aches and pains. She listens and nods.

Dr. Davenport joins us after a while. His highly polished black shoes squeak against the tiled floor. He wears a long white coat over what I think is a navy suit, and his dark hair is gelled off his face. He's a particularly dapper man and I can only imagine how beautiful his and Maura's baby will be.

"Yes, yes, swollen ankles are quite normal for this stage of pregnancy," Dr. Davenport tells the nurse when she relays my ailments and asks if there's anything that can be done to ease the discomfort.

"Try to stay off your feet, eh?" he says, paying more attention to his pen and paper as he makes notes than he does to me.

"And I've been having some headaches," I say.

"Black tea before bed. Two cups. That will help."

"I think something might be wrong. I never had swollen feet or headaches before. Not on any of my pregnancies." I rub my stomach as if my baby needs comforting from my words.

Dr. Davenport glances at the nurse with an expression that tells me I'm pressing his patience.

"You're tired. As I said, you need to stay off your feet more."

I stop rubbing my stomach, fold my arms, and rest them on top of my belly, which seems to grow rounder by the day. "That's not altogether easy with three little ones under my belt already."

"Let the children out to play and sit down with the paper. You'll be all the better for it," he says.

I don't ask him if he's serious. I know he is. I also don't tell him that even if I had a garden for the children to play in, or the daily paper to read, it would not help how I'm feeling.

Dr. Davenport lowers his pen, puffs out, and looks me in the eye. "Mrs. McCarthy, I assure you, if I had a shilling for every woman who worried that something was wrong with her baby, I would be a very rich man indeed."

I think about Dr. Davenport's beautiful home and lush green garden and I doubt he needs a single penny from concerned mothers to make him any richer than he already is.

A baby begins to cry somewhere in the waiting area. It's not Alice, I can tell. But I'm anxious to get back to my children.

"I'll see you in six weeks," Dr. Davenport says, dismissing me with a wave of his hand. "And remember, black tea before bed."

I fight the urge to roll my eyes and stand up. My puffy ankles sting as they object to taking my weight once more.

"Thank you for your time," I say.

The nurse fiddles with the partition once again and it spits me out into a room full of voices and round bellies and fed-up children. I spy my children, sitting and playing hand-clapping games. My feet are on fire as I shuffle toward them.

The lady after me is a long time behind the partition. A half an hour, easy. And I begin to worry if everything is all right. When the stiff curtain finally creaks open, both the lady and Dr. Davenport appear. They're laughing and smiling.

"Do tell your ma I was asking for her, won't you, Christy?" she says.

"Of course, of course. And your parents too. Wish them all the best. We'll have lunch soon. You and all the children. Maura will be only too glad to cook."

The lady tosses her head back and laughs as if Dr. Davenport is the most charming man she's ever met.

"Goodbye now, Philomena," he says, and then he kisses each of her cheeks in turn before he disappears behind another partition.

"Wonderful man. Wonderful, wonderful man," she says when she rejoins me in the waiting area and sets about gathering up her children, who have been playing contentedly with mine.

"Yes, he's great," I say, looking down at my feet, which bulge over the sides of my shoes like a couple of cakes rising in the oven.

"Such a pity he has no children of his own. Married six months and no sign. It's sad, really. Christy would be a wonderful father."

"And Maura will be a great mother," I add.

"You know the Davenports?" She cocks her head as she surveys me from head to toe.

"My husband is their butcher," I say, and I've never wanted to clamp my hand over my big mouth more.

Her expression stiffens as if she's just been hit with a bad smell. I notice her elegant leather shoes and matching handbag for the first time. She smells of expensive perfume, the summer fruit kind that Dan says he'll buy for my birthday someday.

"That's nice," she says. "I'll be sure to call in to your husband for all my meat in future."

It's only when the last of her children follow her through the door that I realize she didn't ask Dan's name or where his butcher's shop is.

CHAPTER 25

Bernie

On the way home, the girls and I call into the dressmaker's. It's a little off the beaten track but it's considerably cheaper than any of the fancy places in town. There's no name above the door or elaborate shopwindow full of dresses or coats. It's simply a red door on the side of a gray building. I'd never have found Mrs. Stitch by myself—it was one of Dan's customers who recommended her years ago—and I've been mighty glad since then that she did. I've lost count of the number of bedspreads and tablecloths that Mrs. Stitch has turned into fine outfits for my growing girls over the years. Mrs. Stitch isn't her real name, obviously. But she was introduced to me as such and I've never questioned it.

As always, I knock three times on the door and wait for it to open. Mrs. Stitch is oddly insistent that it must be three knocks precisely. She won't answer to anything less or anything more. You can't enter from the outside. There's no handle, just a heavy chrome knocker in the shape of a lion's head. Seconds turn to minutes, and I knock three times again.

"Where is she?" Marie asks.

Marie's excitement is tangible. She's practically been bouncing on the spot all week since Mrs. Stitch measured her and Elizabeth up for new coats. With Maura's coat to keep me warm, I was able to save the bedspread and hand my old coat in to Mrs. Stitch instead.

"Oh, this will do nicely," she had said as she held a measuring tape around Marie's waist. "And there's lining too. That'll keep this pair nice and warm all winter. I need three days to work my magic. Come back on Thursday afternoon, please."

I check my watch. It's 11:45 a.m. Not quite noon yet. Maybe she doesn't open for another fifteen minutes.

"I need to go a wee-wee," Elizabeth announces.

"Can you hold it?"

Elizabeth closes her eyes and scrunches her face. "I don't think so."

My heart sinks. If Elizabeth wets her pants now she'll be frozen and probably catch cold on the walk home. I knock on the door again, banging harder this time.

"Mrs. Stitch, it's Bernie. Bernie McCarthy. Are you in there?"

There's no reply, but when I press my ear to the door I can hear voices inside.

I knock again, banging furiously now.

"Mrs. Stitch, please? I have the children with me and it's freezing out here."

Footsteps hurry toward the door and I pull my ear away and stand up straight. The door opens and Mrs. Stitch appears. Her short hair is more gray than brown and she wears thick-rimmed glasses; she blames years of threading needles for ruining her sight. She's wearing a bright red apron that she seems to use as a pincushion, with needles and pins threaded chaotically all over.

"Three times," she says, licking some blue thread and squinting as she tries to push it through the eye of a needle. "You're supposed to knock three times. It's not that complicated."

"The little 'un needs the toilet," I say.

Mrs. Stitch looks at Marie.

"Not me. Her," Marie says, pointing at her sister. "I can hold mine. I'm six."

Mrs. Stitch smiles. "Well, she's going to have to hold it too."

"Please," I say, shocked that Mrs. Stitch would deny a bursting child the loo. "It's just a wee. She'll be very quick."

"You're early," Mrs. Stitch says, and there's a spark of frustration about her. "I said afternoon. I don't do business before noon."

"I'm sorry. Normally we'd wait, but Elizabeth can't hold what's not in her hand."

Elizabeth has taken to hopping from one foot to the other. Alice laughs, thoroughly entertained by it all.

"Right. Fine. Just this once," Mrs. Stitch says.

I take Elizabeth by the hand, leave Marie with the baby, and walk toward the only door at the back of the small shop. The toilet flushes, and when the door opens, a young girl comes out. She's about sixteen or seventeen—certainly no more—and she's been crying. Her red-rimmed eyes look ready to fall out of her head. Seeing me, she jolts. Her mouth opens and I can see her swallow panicked breathing. It's as obvious as the nose on her face that she wasn't expecting anyone other than Mrs. Stitch to be out here. We brush past each other and I close the door behind Elizabeth and me.

"Ew, it smells funny in here," Elizabeth says, holding her nose.

"Hush, don't be rude," I say, and help her onto the toilet.

She grabs me tightly, afraid her tiny body might fall in. Elizabeth is right—the smell in here is unpleasant. Bleach and vomit. The acidity of both stenches makes my own stomach heave.

"Done," Elizabeth announces.

I sort her out, wash her hands, and turn to search for a towel or something to dry her hands. When I turn back, I find Elizabeth with a glass Lucozade bottle in her hand.

"Fizzy pop," she squeals, delighted.

I take the bottle quickly.

"Hey," Elizabeth moans, "give me a-back my pop."

I ignore her, grumbling as I examine the bottle. The label has been torn off and it's full of slightly murky water rather than amber Lucozade. I unscrew the lid and inhale, coughing immediately. I've clearly found the source of the potent bleach smell. I screw the lid back on and we leave the bathroom.

"What the hell are you doing with that?" Mrs. Stitch snaps so unexpectedly that my heart jumps.

She snatches the bottle from my hand and her long nail snags my wrist. I put my wrist to my mouth and look at her, lost for words.

Alice is growing fussy. Marie is trying her best to keep her calm by rocking the pram. I glance around the small shop for the teenage girl, but she's gone.

"I was going to put it in the bin," I say, picking up the baby and bouncing her on my hip. "I think someone poured something nasty in there. Bleach, is my best guess."

Mrs. Stitch doesn't reply. She takes the bottle and places it under the table where she keeps her sewing machine.

"Aren't you going to throw that out?" I say.

"Your coats are ready," Mrs. Stitch says, gathering two small coats from a nearby rack and passing them to me.

The coats are beautiful, and Marie and Elizabeth tug at them in my arms, trying to get a better look. I don't pay them much attention.

"I think the young girl left it in there," I say, struggling to gather my thoughts. "I think she might be in trouble or something. She was crying."

Mrs. Stitch ignores me. "There's enough material left over to get a coat for the baby too, if you like?"

"Why would she leave something like that where someone could find it? Could be very dangerous if a child got their hands on it. Elizabeth thought it was fizzy pop. Could you imagine if she drank it?"

"Do you want the coats or not?" Mrs. Stitch asks.

"I just think—"

"Mrs. McCarthy, please." Mrs. Stitch jams her hands on her hips. "This is not something you need to concern yourself with. You're married. You don't have to worry about the same things young girls do."

"What does marriage have to do with anything?"

Mrs. Stitch snorts and rolls her eyes as if my ignorance is exhausting her. My girls begin to dance and twirl, playing princesses or fairies. Marie hums a tune and Elizabeth smiles and giggles. Their childhood innocence snatches my breath away as the threads of Mrs. Stitch's words gather. I see the young girl's face, her teary eyes and shaky hands. I see the stinking Lucozade bottle that belongs in the bin, not hidden under a desk like a dirty, dangerous secret. I think about Mrs. Stitch's strange opening hours, how I've seen young women in here earlier than noon. Always young women. Always with the weight of the world on their shoulders.

"Is she pregnant?" I whisper, as if just asking out loud will bring the four walls crashing down around us.

Mrs. Stitch glares at me with narrow eyes, and she doesn't say no.

"Oh my God."

Mrs. Stitch turns her attention away from me and helps the girls peel off their old, too-small coats so they can slip into their new ones. They're a picture in petite royal blue coats that are as fine and dandy as the best ones Switzers has to offer.

"Look, Ma," Elizabeth says, stretching her arms out as wide as they go. "I'm a grown-up, like you."

My heart aches, and for a moment I wish my beautiful little girl never had to grow up, never had to become a woman.

"You didn't actually want her to drink that, did you?" I ask, my anger bubbling to the surface.

"That will be three shilling and sixteen pence, please." She puts out her hand and I know this conversation is over.

"You could kill her with poison like that. What even is it?"

"And I suppose you have a better solution, do you?"

"I . . ."

I exhale and let my tired shoulders round. There is no better solution, I know that. Every woman knows that. A baby outside of marriage is a death sentence. Families throw young women out on the street. Girls as young as sixteen are left with nowhere to go and nowhere to turn—and that's if they're lucky. The unlucky ones are sent to one of those homes. Dan says they're run by the church, but they are as far from a place of God as you can imagine. I didn't ask him how he knew. You'd be surprised the things a man will hear in a butcher's shop.

"Women gossip like clucking hens," he says. "Especially if it's their neighbor's business. Young girls go in, and haggard, broken women come back out. *If* they come out. Some don't, and I often wonder what happens to them."

I have my suspicions that they die in childbirth, but I don't dare tell Dan. He climbs the walls with worry every time I have a baby. It wouldn't do him well to land more worry at his feet.

Besides, I wonder more where the babies go. No baby has ever come out of one of those homes. Ever. I don't know much about them, I'll admit, but one thing I know for certain is no daughter of mine will ever set foot inside one, no matter what mistakes she makes.

"I hope she'll be all right," I say, making eye contact with Mrs. Stitch. "The girl, I mean. She must be so frightened."

"Oh, she'll be back," Mrs. Stitch says, with a confidence that makes me both sad and relieved. "They always come back."

I nod and swallow a lump that feels too cumbersome for my throat. I pass Mrs. Stitch some money and she counts it out loud.

"Come along, girls. It's time to go," I say.

Marie and Elizabeth thank the seamstress for their new coats and I push the pram out the door with the girls following behind me. I've never been so relieved to inhale fresh air in all my life.

CHAPTER 26

Bernie

I'm not quite sure why I find myself at Maura's door. I tell myself I'm here to show off Marie's and Elizabeth's coats, and to thank Maura again for giving me the warm fur coat that made it all possible. But that's a brazen lie. I'm here because I need to tell someone what I saw in the dressmaker's today. I need to talk it through and then maybe I'll get that poor young girl's face out of my mind. I need a friend. Maura said we're friends. I hope to God that's true.

I knock on her door and wait for an answer. The cool winter's sun peeks out from between some clouds and tries to melt the snow. It has its work cut out for it, but the gentle heat on the top of my head is wonderful nonetheless. My girls begin to play in the garden and I tell them to be careful and to keep their new coats clean. I knock on the door again and continue to wait. There's still no answer.

"Nobody's home." I sigh. "That's a pity." I place my hands on my daughters' shoulders. "Come on. Let's go."

I turn toward the road when I catch the curtain twitch from the corner of my eye, and I turn back in time to see Maura let it go and jump away.

"Maura, is that you?"

The curtain sways for a moment before it steadies.

"I saw you," I shout.

I watch the lacy curtain, white as the snow that's gathered on the window-sill beneath it.

"Maura," I call out.

The curtain doesn't move. The house is a sleeping thing once more. Disappointment hits first, followed by hurt. I really hoped we could be friends. But as I look up and down the road of fine cars and beautiful homes, sprinkled with snow like icing on a cake, I know I don't belong on this side of town. Even the snow is whiter here.

My feet throb and my ankles hurt. I haven't eaten yet today and I'm slightly lightheaded. Mostly, I'm embarrassed. Embarrassed that I'm standing outside another woman's house with her door closed in my face. I don't understand. She seemed so nice. Her coat is on my back. And she asked me to visit. Those were her exact words.

I decide to knock once more. If she doesn't want to be friends, I'd like to at least hear why she's changed her mind.

"I'm not going away." *Knock.* "I have all day." *Knock.* "I know you're in there." *Knock.*

The girls kick up snow and giggle heartily. The curtain twitches once again and I wave. Seconds later, the front door creaks open and Maura appears in the gap. She's wearing a headscarf. It's lilac with a swirly gold pattern running all over. It's beautiful, but an odd choice for indoors. The scarf is sitting awkwardly on her head, too far forward and almost completely covering her left eye.

"Hello," she says.

Now that the door is open and I'm face-to-face with her, my words seem to tumble out of my brain but not out of my mouth because I'm not sure what to say. It's Elizabeth who speaks first.

"I did a wee-wee in a smelly place."

Maura seems shorter today, if that's possible, and her skin is flushed and blotchy as if she's been crying. She is skittish and glances over her shoulder as if there's something inside her home that she is afraid to take her eyes off of.

Her appearance startles me and my words still won't come. I wait for her to invite us in but she seems equally as lost for words.

"It's cold," Marie says.

"My toes hurt," Elizabeth adds.

Elizabeth and Marie charge past me and Maura steps aside to let them into the house.

"Girls," I call out sternly, finally finding words.

"Oh, it's all right," Maura says at last. "Come in."

"Can we have more fizzy pop?" Marie asks.

"And tart?" Elizabeth adds.

I cringe, mortified that my girls have lost their manners, but Maura's lips curl into a half smile.

"I'm afraid I'm all out of pop and tart. But I have some tea and biscuits."

"I like tea," Marie says.

"And I like biscuits," Elizabeth adds.

Maura reaches forward to help me lift the pram up the doorstep. When she bends, her scarf slips, revealing a badly bruised eye. I gasp and she lets go of the pram to fix her scarf. In the kitchen Maura makes tea and opens a packet of Jacob's fig rolls. Elizabeth takes a bite, scrunches her nose, and spits it into her hand.

"Yuck."

Maura seems to find Elizabeth's antics charming.

"That's all right," she says, showing Elizabeth where the bin is. "I don't like them either."

Maura passes me a small white handkerchief with hand-embroidered flowers. I clean Elizabeth up and warn her to behave herself. When the girls finish their tea, I shoo them into the garden and tell them to enjoy the snow while it lasts. The clouds are parting and the sun is shining high and bright once more.

Maura makes small talk about my girls' lovely new coats, the weather, and even unpleasant biscuits. I listen and nod, until finally my concern bubbles to the surface and comes out as an accusation.

"Someone hurt you."

Maura jolts, spilling some tea. It pools on her saucer.

"Oh bother," she says, and she fetches a cloth to clean up.

"I saw your eye."

She lifts her cup and begins to dry the saucer.

"Earlier, when your scarf slipped. It's black and blue."

"I fell. I tumbled down the stairs. It's embarrassing, really."

I look at her, but she won't meet my gaze. The saucer is dry but she continues wiping.

"The baby?" I say.

She shakes her head.

"Oh no. Maura. Oh, Maura, I'm so sorry."

I place my hand on hers and she lets the cloth go and flops into the chair behind her.

"I wanted this baby. I wanted it so very much."

"What happened?"

She shrugs and I can see how painful the memory is for her.

"I'm silly. I'm so silly. Christy and I were talking. And I stepped back. The stairs were right behind me. I tumbled from top to bottom."

"Oh God. How awful. You must have got such a fright. And here I was almost accusing Dr. Davenport of . . . well . . . of the worst. You must think I'm horrible."

"How long does the bleeding last?" she asks.

"I'm not sure. I've never lost a baby."

"Oh."

Maura's pain breaks my heart. It's raw and recent and the sadness is written across every inch of her. No wonder she didn't feel like smiling.

"But you can try again."

"Yes. I suppose."

"What did Dr. Davenport say? He must be equally as upset. I met a lady just today who told me how wonderful a father he would be."

Maura exhales until I'm certain there is no air left inside her and I get the feeling I've said something to upset her even further.

"He *would* be a good father, wouldn't he?" I say.

"Do you think I could cover this with makeup?" She points to her eye, sidestepping my question.

"I think so. Do you have any purple or blue eye shadow?"

Maura shakes her head. "I haven't worn much makeup since I got married."

"I never wear makeup," I say. "I don't like the stuff much."

"Oh, I love it," she says.

I don't ask her why she doesn't wear it if she loves it so much. I have a feeling that would be another question she'd rather not answer. And I can't quite shake the suspicion that there is more to Maura's story than a simple tumble down the stairs.

"I need to go into town this week," she says. "I have to pick out delft. It's very important that I do."

"Very important delft," I say, as if I understand.

There's a sudden scream in the garden, followed by crying. The girls race inside and Marie points to a bloodied knee. I scoop her into my arms and cuddle her. I hold her until her crying turns to sobbing and once she's ready, I take a look. Maura fetches some cotton wool and hot water and Marie lets her wipe away some gravel and dirt. Maura is gentle and caring and it's obvious she'll be a fantastic mother.

"The girls and I could go to town with you tomorrow, if you like?" I say. "We could help you pick out some nice delft?"

Maura hesitates. She seems nervous.

"We could get some makeup too."

She nods and thanks me.

My girls and I leave with a promise to meet tomorrow outside Switzers at noon. I don't mention the young girl in the dressmaker's shop. But I think about her the whole walk home.

CHAPTER 27

Maura

"It looks worse than it feels," I say when Geraldine inquires about my face.

She leaves her position behind the cash desk on the men's floor and comes around to stand in front of me for a better look.

"What in the blue blazes happened to you?"

"I fell down the stairs, can you believe it?"

"Were you drinking?"

"Alcohol? No. Of course not."

Geraldine laughs. "I'm only pulling your leg, Maura. It's great to see you."

"It's wonderful to see you too."

Switzers is packed and Geraldine is run off her feet. Not unusual in the run-up to Christmas, but I wish there was more time to catch up with my old friend. There isn't time to introduce Bernie or reminisce about old times before Dick eyeballs Geraldine.

"I better get back to work. But I'm on my break in twenty minutes, can you wait?"

I look at Bernie and she doesn't seem to mind the idea. I nod and tell Geraldine we'll meet her outside the front doors at half past one.

"Perfect," she says, kissing the air on both sides of my cheeks. She's never done that before and I've no doubt it's something she's read about in one of her contraband magazines. A part of me, a big part, is glad to see that Geraldine O'Connell hasn't changed one iota.

While we wait, Bernie and I buy some dark purple eye shadow that I layer on in the bathroom with the tip of my finger. Bernie says it suits me but I despise it. Not so much the color, but more what it covers up. Next, we pick out some delft. I choose the most expensive set in the shop. Bernie's eyes are almost watering as I fork out the extortionate amount for fine china that I don't even like but that I know will satisfy both Christy and his mother this Christmas.

Bernie's girls are growing restless and they begin to whinge and bicker. It's been a long morning and they're tired.

"I know, how about a visit to Santy?" I suggest.

Marie and Elizabeth stop their arguing and look at me. Excitement sparkles in their green eyes.

"A little birdie told me that if you're very good girls, Santy would like to see you. He's waiting downstairs in his magic grotto."

Bernie's eyes widen like two shiny marbles that seem as if they might fall to the ground when she shakes her head.

"I really don't think . . ."

"Oh goody, goody, goody," Marie says, hopping from one leg to the other. "I can't wait to tell Santy I've been a good girl all year."

"Me too. Me too," Elizabeth says, and I'm not sure she fully understands what's happening.

Bernie tugs my arm and pulls my ear closer to her lips.

"Have you seen the prices?" she whispers. "A visit to Santy is expensive. My girls have never been before."

"My treat," I say.

Bernie straightens up and exhales. "No, that's really not—"

"Please," I say. "For the girls. And for me. You've been so good coming with me today. I don't think I'd have been brave enough to come alone."

"All right. Just this once. But no more charity. We don't need charity."

"I'm sorry, I didn't mean—"

"San-ty! San-ty! San-ty!" Marie and Elizabeth chant.

Geraldine is late and the girls are completely fed up by the time she meets us outside. I introduce Bernie and her daughters, in order of age. Geraldine gives the girls a lollipop each and they are instant best friends, and Bernie and Geraldine hit it off, too. I haven't seen Geraldine since my wedding, but we catch up now as if no time at all has passed.

"I must say, I really thought you came in today to tell me you were expecting," Geraldine says as we head back inside and make our way to the back of the store to find Santy. "But I'm glad you and Christy aren't rushing into it like most people do."

Bernie offers me an empathetic smile and tries to not so subtly change the subject.

"Have you worked here for long?" Bernie asks.

"I'm the longest-reigning female employee in the drapery department," Geraldine says with an unmissable sense of pride. "Everyone else keeps leaving to get married and have babies. That's why I'm glad you're not pregnant, Maura. Do it on your own terms, I say. You're dead right."

My heart sinks. Geraldine means well, but she's an expert at putting her foot in it.

Marie and Elizabeth squeal with joy as we reach the grotto and see Santy sitting on his throne in the middle of the floor. I recognize the face in the bright red costume as that of Gerry, the maintenance man, but today I wave and smile and say, "Hello, Santy. We have two very good little girls to see you."

I pay, and Marie and Elizabeth take turns sitting on Gerry's knee.

He listens to their tales of good behavior and asks them what they would like for Christmas.

"Fancy dresses for my dolly," Marie says. "Just like the dresses upstairs. They're the prettiest dresses I've ever seed."

Bernie's face is the color of Santy's beard as Elizabeth chirps, "Me too. Me too. Dresses for dolly."

Gerry asks the girls to be on their best behavior between now and Christmas and he promises to bring them a lovely surprise. The look on Bernie's face tells me she's worried that her girls might be disappointed on Christmas morning. I feel awful for suggesting a visit to Santy after all.

The girls are hyper after that. Geraldine seems to enjoy their loud voices and giggles immensely, and when I ask her if she's changed her mind about marriage and children in her future, I'm certain I know her answer.

But, as always, she jams her hands on her hips and shakes her head. "Never. Absolutely never."

We chat for the remainder of Geraldine's break. And when it's time to go she hugs us all.

"I miss you," she says. "Do me a favor and come back soon, eh?"

"I will. I promise."

Bernie is quiet as we walk across town and toward McCarthy's butcher's and her flat overhead. The town is packed with enthusiastic Christmas shoppers, arms laden with brightly colored bags. My own included. Bernie's hands are empty.

"I'm sorry," I say. "About Santy and the promises he made. If I had known—"

"Dan will figure something out," Bernie says. "He always does."

"You're a very lucky woman," I say.

Bernie looks at the bags of makeup and expensive fine bone china dangling from my hands. And she sighs. I wait for her to tell me that I'm the lucky one. People say it all the time. Patients of Christy's, mostly. Women envy me, married to a clever and handsome man. They wish they had a big house like mine with a south-facing kitchen and not one but two indoor bathrooms. They like Christy's fancy car and his expensive suits. And men want to be him. They want the status and respect that comes with the title of Doctor. There's not a man, woman, or child in Rathmines who doesn't adore Christy.

But Bernie doesn't say anything. She shifts her gaze toward my black eye that makeup attempts to cover up and shakes her head.

"My Dan is a good man. A great man," she says. "But I know not all men are. And if there's ever anything you need to tell me—anything at all—well, you know where my door is."

I almost begin to cry. I don't need to tell Bernie anything. Everything I want to say, I suspect she already knows.

CHAPTER 28

Maura

Bernie McCarthy makes me laugh. Her beautiful girls make me smile and her friendship is fast becoming a treasure. She shares amazing recipes from her scrapbook. Delicious stews and crubeens and colcannon. Christy raved about the latter and I was in his good books for days. I teach her how to apply makeup and we straighten her hair with the iron.

"Dan couldn't keep his hands off me," she says.

"Even with your growing belly?"

"Even more with a belly on me. The damage is already done."

She laughs and I think I've missed the joke.

The girls regularly enjoy television. There isn't a peep out of them while they watch *Wanderly Wagon*. Sometimes Bernie and I become accidentally invested in the lively stories of a man, his wagon, and his talking dog. These are the days I'm glad I have a stew brewing in the background, or there would be hell to pay. Bernie and the girls are always gone home before Christy arrives in from work. Bernie has never said anything, but I know she watches the clock as much as I do.

"Best get these little 'uns home and washed up for dinner," she always says. But I know that what she really means is, *Best keep out of your husband's way.*

This particular afternoon, a large log crackles on the open fire in the sitting room. I sit in the fireside chair and enjoy the flames warming my knees. It's five days until Christmas and I'm absentmindedly humming "Silent Night." I seem to be stuck on a verse, humming it over and over as I pull and tuck my crochet hook through pretty lilac yarn. I stop every so often to examine how the little doll's dress is coming along. Lilac is Marie's favorite color. I'll switch to yellow for Elizabeth. Bernie tried her hand at crochet, and although she's a fast learner, she doesn't have the time or skill to have two dolls' dresses prepared in time for Christmas. I'm more than happy to help.

"I can't wait until they wake up on Christmas morning and find these under the tree," Bernie said.

I wonder if I'll ever share the joy of a child's happiness on Christmas.

When I have two lilac and two yellow dresses complete, I set my crochet hook down and wrap each dress in shiny silver foil paper that I bought from the traders on Moore Street. I stick a hand-cut gift tag on each one, and I carefully write *Love from Santy* on each tag. I check my watch and, expecting Christy home soon, go upstairs and hide the parcels under the bed. Then I putter into the kitchen to check on the rice pudding in the oven.

I hear Christy before I see him. He's humming a Christmas carol too, "Good King Wenceslas," I think.

"Hello, my darling," he says as he dances his way into the kitchen. I can barely see him behind a huge bouquet of red roses. There are a dozen, at least.

"Are they for me?" I ask, and my voice is squeaky and high-pitched, as if I'm nervous. I think I might be.

Christy sets the bouquet down on the countertop beside me and scoops me into his arms. It's unexpected and my breath catches. He kisses my cheek and my neck. I go with it as I try to reach my arm behind me to twist the knob on the oven. The last thing I want is the rice pudding to burn.

"Oh, my darling, how are you?" Christy asks, between kisses dotted on my neck. His lips are warm and soft, and I close my eyes and try to relax.

His hands are in my hair and then cupping my face. His thumb strokes my cheek. He's tender and gentle and my heart races, unsure.

"I'm good," I say, at last, realizing I've kept him waiting for an answer. "I . . . eh . . . I got some new recipes to try out. I made—"

"Oh hush, hush, don't worry about that now. I mean, how are you feeling? Are you tired? Have you been sick? Your back isn't hurting, is it?"

I'm confused. And concerned. Finally, I reach the knob on the cooker and twist it until I feel it click off. I relax a fraction.

"I'm good," I reiterate. "Would you like dinner now? Or would you rather freshen up first? I've made rice pudding for after. I could make some custard, or would you rather have ice cream with it?"

"Oh, Maura, I love you," he says, hugging me tight. "I love you so much. Do you know that?"

"Yes, of course. Of course I know." I kiss him back, realizing I haven't yet. "I love you too."

"You're going to be the most wonderful mother; do you know that?"

The fine hairs on the back of my neck stand on end. "Someday that would be wonderful," I say, choosing each word carefully.

"In about seven and a half months, if my calculations are correct."

I swallow hard, trying to push rising panic down.

"Christy, I'm not—"

Christy lets me go and steps back to look me up and down. His eyes steady on my middle as if it's the most beautiful thing he's ever seen.

"I bumped into Dr. Buckley today. Lovely man. Lovely, lovely man," he says.

Oh God. Heat creeps across my face. I feel faint.

"He shook my hand and congratulated me. It was the most wonderful surprise, I'll tell you that."

"Christy, I—"

"Pregnant! Oh, Maura, a baby. I couldn't be happier, really, darling. I truly couldn't."

I have no words. I look at the beautiful bouquet of red roses beside me that Christy thinks he has bought for his pregnant wife and I think I might cry.

"Why didn't you tell me?" he asks, his smile so wide and bright that his teeth look too big for his mouth. "Were you afraid to get your hopes up? Dr. Buckley said your result came back yesterday, but you didn't return to get it. Oh, Maura, the news is good. It couldn't be better."

Christy embraces me again and this time I feel as if I'm suffocating.

"Leave dinner," he says, sniffing the air as the smell of rice pudding cooling in the oven wafts around us. "We're going to The Shelbourne. A man should treat his expecting wife, shouldn't he?"

My tongue feels huge and I think I might choke on it.

"Wear that red dress I like, yes?"

I hate that dress. It's tight and pinches under my arms and looks more like something an old spinster would wear than a dress for a woman who's not yet thirty. But Grace bought it for my birthday and Christy said I'd never looked more beautiful.

"Oh, Maura, do say something. Are you scared? There is no need to be. Really. I've told you. Having a baby is the most natural thing in the world. It won't knock a bother out of you."

"I lost the baby," I say quickly. As if the faster I say it, the less awful it will sound.

Christy pushes his shoulders back. "Excuse me?"

"I'm sorry. I'm so, so sorry."

"You're not expecting?"

"Not anymore."

The smell of the rice pudding is turning my stomach.

"How do you know, if you didn't go back to see Dr. Buckley?"

Christy's question catches me off guard. I want to ask him how he could possibly credit me with such little intelligence, but of course I don't dare.

He steps back and folds his arms.

"What happened—exactly?" he says. The tenderness in his tone is slipping.

"I bled." My face is hot with embarrassment.

"When? How long? How much? Jesus, Maura."

"I . . . I . . ." I can't bring myself to say. I can't discuss the intimate details of my body with this man.

"When?" he says again. This time, his tone makes it clear he expects an answer.

"Not long ago. It hasn't been two weeks yet."

"When *exactly*?"

"When you pushed—"

Christy's neck juts forward.

"When I fell down the stairs."

"Right. Upstairs. I want to see for myself."

"Christy. No. Please."

"Up. Stairs. Now."

"Please?" I say again, desperate to cling to my dignity. "I'm still bleeding."

"Fine," he says, grabbing my hand. He's hurting me but I don't say. "If not me, then one of my colleagues. At the hospital. I want a doctor to tell me my baby is lost, not some stupid woman."

"Christy, please. I don't want to. I just want to move on. We can try again. We can have another baby."

Christy doesn't reply. He drags me into the hall and picks up his car keys from the glass-topped table just inside the door.

"Get your coat," he says, letting my hand go.

My fingers part instinctively, pulsing where he crushed them.

"Let me freshen up first. I need a wash. I've been in town all day."

"Get your coat."

"Christy, please. I don't feel clean. If a doctor is going to look, eh, down there, I need to feel clean."

"Fine. Do without a coat. But get in the damn car now, Maura, or so help me God."

He snatches my hand again. I yelp and he opens the front door and drags me outside.

CHAPTER 29

Christmas Eve, 1969

Bernie

I remember some chilly Christmases growing up, but I'm hard pushed to remember a colder Christmas Eve ever. Our small flat feels as nippy as the meat fridges in Dan's shop below us. The girls wear their new coats indoors and I keep Alice wrapped in blankets, which, much to my frustration, she seems determined to kick off. Our breath dances like small clouds in the air every time we speak. Thankfully, the girls find it wonderfully entertaining as they puff out over and over. They're lying on their backs on the living area floor staring up at the ceiling, to which Dan has secured many multicolored decorations with thumbtacks. There's a yellow crepe paper bell, a silver paper star, and plenty of shiny foil garlands looping from one side of the room to the other. Every so often the girls jump up and try to touch one.

"Santy is coming tonight," Marie tells her sisters. "And he's bringing dresses for our dollies. He said so, didn't he?"

"I like Santy," Elizabeth says.

The children's excitement is electric and it should excite me too, but a weight sits in my chest. I look at the Christmas tree in the corner. It's tall, with a gold star on top and red, blue, and yellow fairy lights twinkling brightly. It's wrapped in chunky red tinsel, and every time the girls touch the tickly tinsel they squeal with joy. Under the tree an empty floor sits waiting for Santy's arrival. *Empty. Waiting.*

"What are we going to do?" I whisper when I pull Dan into the kitchen and out of earshot of the girls. "Maura promised she'd have dresses ready for the girls' dolls in time. But she's fallen off the face of the earth."

My girls and I have walked to Maura's house three times this week. We knock on the door as usual, but there is never an answer. Marie and Elizabeth have called out to her, but still, there is nothing. The curtains are open and hang perfect and gleaming. The grass is cut and the full milk bottles are brought in and empty ones are left out on the porch for collection. The house is the epitome of a blissful suburban life, just like all the other houses on the street. But behind closed doors, I fear it is a very different story indeed.

"I'm worried about her," I say. "Dr. Davenport has a temper."

"Bernie!" Dan says, shocked. "You can't say something like that."

"I can. And I just did. Because he has."

"Temper or not, he's a doctor. Folks don't appreciate talk like that about a doctor. He's a local hero, for God's sake."

"Hero, my foot."

"You'll think differently when he places a healthy baby in your arms."

I roll my eyes, but Dan is right. An end to this pregnancy and a healthy baby is the only gift I want this Christmas.

"Didn't Maura teach you how to crochet?" Dan says, pulling me toward more urgent worries. "Could you make something for our girls?"

"Not in time," I say, my heart aching as I imagine their disappointed faces as they stand under an empty tree in the morning. "And besides, I've no yarn."

"I could dash out. Pick some up. What colors?"

I shake my head. "I'm not good enough or fast enough."

"Mrs. Stitch," he says, and it's obvious he's grasping at straws. It unravels me even more.

I've tried hard not to think about Mrs. Stitch and the goings-on behind her closed doors. But I do know her little shop is not somewhere I want to visit ever again.

"Mrs. Stitch doesn't open before noon on a good day. I doubt she opens on Christmas Eve."

"Oh, Bernie, love, don't let this upset you. We'll think of something."

Dan gathers me into his arms and kisses me. I kiss him back, but my stomach is full of worry.

"I'll go out. I'll buy coloring pencils and paper; you know how Marie loves to draw."

He's right. She does.

"And, a pram, I'll buy Elizabeth a pram for her dolly. She'll be just like you. She'd like that, wouldn't she?"

Elizabeth would love that. But toy prams are expensive. We don't have that kind of money to spare.

"Dan—"

He kisses me again. Hard this time, and I can feel how determined he is to fix this. When he pulls away from me and looks into my eyes, I nod.

Dan will fix this. Even if we have to eat beans on toast until the summer. Dan will fix this. And I will be so grateful that he did.

"I love you," I say.

"I love you too."

"Now go. Quick. Before the shops close."

CHAPTER 30

Christmas Day, 1969

Maura

I wake to the smell of stale whiskey and cigars. I slide out of bed and the cold of the floor drives up through the soles of my bare feet as I make my way toward the bedroom window and open it wide. I take a deep breath of December air and it steadies me.

My face only hurts when I yawn or sneeze and so I'm careful not to. I freshen up in the bathroom, brush my teeth, and apply a thick layer of makeup before Christy wakes. I left two dresses out last night. A long black one and Christy's favorite red one. I'll ask him which one I should wear today.

When I return to the bedroom Christy is up and the curtains are open. He's kneeling at the side of the bed saying his morning prayers. I don't dare interrupt him. The room is filled with bright morning light and it stings my swollen eyes. I take a moment to adjust to the light and as I do, I notice my dresses are missing from the bedside chair. I wait until Christy stands up to ask about them.

"I thought I might wear the red dress today," I say. "I know how much you like it and red feels festive."

Christy doesn't speak.

"I'll make us some breakfast and then I'll get the turkey in the oven. It's a big bird, so it'll take most of the day to cook. But not to worry, that gives me plenty of time to concentrate on the trifle. I do hope your ma likes it. She told me trifle is her favorite, so . . ."

"Maura, stop." Christy raises his hand and I freeze. "No one is coming."

I wait until he lowers his hand before I speak. "I don't understand. You said . . . and I bought the delft your ma likes . . . and a huge turkey from McCarthy's and—"

"Maura, stop," he says again, but his hand remains by his side this time and he seems disappointed. Or sad. "Look at you." He points. "You're a mess."

"I'm sorry. I'll fix my hair. And with a nice dress . . ."

He shakes his head. "I've told my family you're poorly. They understand."

"But I feel fine, honestly. I—"

"Maura!"

I close my mouth.

"Where are the presents?" he says.

"Under the tree. There's one for everyone. Yours is there too."

"Thank you. Now. Get yourself back into bed and rest. I'll be back this evening."

"You're leaving?"

Christy chuckles. "Of course. I'm going to be with my family."

"But it's Christmas."

"Exactly. Family time."

I think about my own parents and how much I would love to see them today. For a moment, I think about going to them once Christy leaves. But I know I can't. I can't bring my problems to their door. They can't help me. No one can.

"Don't worry, I'll give your apologies to my mother. And to Agatha, of course. She'll be disappointed not to see you." He takes brown pin-striped trousers, a blue shirt, and a navy jumper from the wardrobe and begins to get dressed. "What did you get for Agatha, by the way?"

"A necklace."

"Gold?"

"Yes."

"Good. Good. She'll like that."

Christy slips on his highly polished black shoes and opens the drawer on his bedside table. He pulls out a small box wrapped in green paper and tied up with a gold bow. He offers it to me and kisses my cheek. His lips feel warm and moist and I want to pull away. I don't. I stand still and force my fingers to curl around the small gift.

"Happy Christmas, darling," he says with a wide smile. "Well, go on. Open it."

I tug at the edges of the bow and slide my nail under the paper. A small silver box appears. It opens with a click and inside are the most beautiful emerald earrings I have ever seen. They sparkle in the morning sunlight.

"Thank you," I say, and I promise myself I will never wear them.

He walks toward the door, turning back just before he opens it.

"Into bed, darling," he says, as if he's spilling over with concern. "You heard what the doctor at the hospital said."

Memories of the hospital flood back. The smell. The bright corridors. Cold hands. Indignity. No one said a word to me. But a male doctor, about the same age as my father, spoke at length to Christy when I was finally allowed to put my clothes back on.

"Six weeks. You'll be ready to try again in six weeks and I need you in tip-top shape," Christy says, as if he's already counting down the days. "Imagine next Christmas, when we have a little one of our own."

I climb into bed as he watches. I lie down and he closes the door. I listen as his footsteps descend the stairs. I listen as he rummages under the tree, picking up the presents I shopped for and lovingly wrapped. I listen as his car starts. And finally, I listen as he drives away.

I almost start to cry, but I decide on a better way to spend my time. I get out of bed and rummage in the tall chest of drawers under the window for my going-away outfit. I pull out blouses and headscarves until finally I spot the trousers I haven't seen since that day. I slip them on. They're a little snugger now. *Too much apple tart*, I think.

I find the matching jumper and wear that too. Then I kneel down and pull silver parcels out from under the bed. Downstairs, I remove the tags and replace them with new ones, which I sign with my name and a single kiss. I place the parcels in a plastic bag and get ready to leave the house. I stare at the warm fur coat Christy bought me, but I don't put it on. Instead, I find an older, lighter one. It won't keep me much warm but at least it's a coat I bought for myself before I was married.

The streets are almost empty. There's something serene and liberating about being alone with just the birds in the sky above me. Multicolored fairy lights shine brightly in the windows of houses I pass, and I can hear noise and laughter inside some. *The joys of family together on Christmas*, I think. It begins to rain as I reach the city center, and I enjoy the feeling of cool drops hitting my scarf-free head. Shutters are down and lights are off in all the shop fronts. McCarthy's butcher's comes into view. I've never seen it closed before. I knew it would be, of course, but nonetheless I feel delighted to see for myself that Dan McCarthy has taken a day off to enjoy time with his family. I imagine the little girls upstairs cuddling with their father or enjoying rides on his shoulders. I almost chicken out of knocking on their door—too ashamed to disturb them. But I look into the plastic bag and decide that little girls shouldn't be deprived of pretty dolls' dresses because of grown-up problems.

I knock on the door at the side of the shop. I have to knock louder and a couple of times more before I hear footsteps coming toward me. The door creaks open, and Dan's face is the picture of concern when he sees me.

"Jesus be blessed," he says, and clearly the rain has washed some of my makeup away and my battered face is peeking through. "Come in. Come in. It's wet out there."

I step inside and he closes the door behind us. In front is a set of concrete stairs.

"Mind your step," he says as he leads the way up, then calls out, "Bernie. Oh, Bernie, you'll never believe who's here."

I smell stuffing and gravy and my stomach rumbles. I haven't eaten properly since Christy dragged me to the hospital. I've prepared dinners as usual, but I couldn't bring myself to put a bite in my mouth.

Bernie opens the door at the top of the stairs and her hands cup her face when she sees me.

"Oh, Maura. I knew it. I knew it was bad. What did I tell you, Dan? Huh? Huh?"

Bernie elbows her husband's ribs. He doesn't say a word. But he agrees. I can see concern etched between the furrows of his brow.

"What happened, dare I ask?" Dan says.

I shake my head and Dan nods his, understanding.

"Right," he says, with a clap of his hands that startles everyone. "I'll take the girls for a walk. Give you two some time to talk."

Marie, Elizabeth, and Alice are playing contently on the sitting room floor. There are some coloring pencils scattered around them and Marie is trying her best to create a house, or possibly a car, on crisp white paper. Elizabeth is wheeling a small pram around in circles and Alice is chewing on some building blocks. It's a pleasure to observe the children enjoying Christmas.

"No, please, don't disturb the children. I won't stay. I just came to drop these off."

I open the bag and take out the silver paper parcels. The sound of shiny paper against plastic draws Marie's attention, and she's on her feet and eyeing me eagerly.

"I have something for you," I say.

She scurries toward me and wraps her arms around me and her head rests against my hip. My heart flutters. It's the warmest, most genuine hug I've felt since I left my childhood home. I bend and scoop her into my arms. "Happy Christmas."

I feel a hand on my back and Bernie says, "Oh, Maura, do be careful. You're not one hundred percent yet. You've been through a lot and Marie isn't light."

I lower Marie, letting go when I feel her feet touch the ground. I pass her one of the parcels and she tears it open.

"A dress," she squeals. "A pretty, pretty dress for my dolly." She hugs me again. "Thank you. Thank you."

Elizabeth appears at my side. She looks up at me with wide, expectant eyes that inquire whether I have a parcel for her too.

"And yours," I say, passing over her gift.

She struggles with the paper and Bernie has to help.

"Ellow," she exclaims, curling her chubby hand around the small yellow dress. "I love ellow."

I apologize that I don't have a gift for Alice and I promise to crochet some blankets for the new baby once he or she arrives. I wave goodbye to the girls, who have turned their attention back to their toys, and walk toward the door.

"And where do you think you're going?" Dan asks.

"Eh . . ."

"You'll sit down and have a bite to eat, won't you?"

"Eh . . ."

"Is Dr. Davenport waiting for you?" Bernie asks, and I can hear the concern in her tone.

I shake my head. "He's gone to his mother's."

"Jesus," Bernie says. "Right, well, good, because that bird in the stove is much, much too big. We'll need all the help we can get to finish it."

"C'mon, Maura, pull up a chair," Dan says. "You'll have a sherry, won't you?"

"Oh."

"Go on," Bernie says. "I'm having one. It's good for the baby."

"All right so. Yes. A sherry, please."

The sherry burns, but I have another. The turkey is delicious and I have seconds, and the conversation and laughter and joy fill me to the brim with happiness. I think I might just be full enough to last all year. Dan sits cross-legged on the floor next to his daughters. He colors with Marie and plays make-believe with Elizabeth and he cradles Alice in his arms as she falls asleep.

My father is a good man. A great man. He loves me, I know. But from the time I was very little—Elizabeth's age, perhaps—I've known that he values my brothers more. Dan McCarthy treasures his daughters as if they are precious rubies. It pains him to pulls his eyes away from them. Bernie doesn't say a word. She sits in the fireside chair and drifts in and out of relaxed sleep. My eyes seem to naturally fall on her large belly. I think about the child growing inside her. Such a lucky little baby with a wonderful family waiting to love him or her.

When it's time to go, I hug every member of the McCarthy family as if they are my own and I thank them for the most wonderful day I've had in a long time.

CHAPTER 31

February 1970

Maura

Christy and I learn how to better live with one another after Christmas. Or, more honestly, I learn how to better appease him. I know when to join in conversation and when to keep my mouth firmly shut. I know what meals to cook and not to cook. I know when to look my best and when to stay out of his sight.

Christy's thirtieth birthday falls on a Saturday. I've bought him a watch with a square face and a black leather strap. He says he'd prefer a brown strap. I tell him I'll change it in town next week, and I'm glad to have the chore and an excuse to visit Bernie. She hasn't been coming by as often lately. Her feet are badly swollen. She doesn't complain, but Dan confided in me that walking is causing her pain.

"This baby can't come soon enough," he said. "Her headaches are getting worse by the day."

I asked Christy if headaches in late pregnancy were normal and he told me I'd find out for myself someday.

Christy's birthday runs like a military operation. At 11:00 a.m. on the dot our doorbell rings and his family comes inside for brunch. We chat and eat and laugh. Declan says the house looks great. Agatha compliments my dress and Grace passes me a box of bread soda that she picked up in the market.

"For the net curtains," she says. "They're looking a little yellow."

I soaked every curtain in the house in boiled water and bread soda last week for the occasion. They've never looked whiter. But I smile and thank her nonetheless.

At 2:00 p.m. the Davenports leave and Christy heads for the pub with his colleagues.

"I won't be long," he says, pulling on his coat by the door. "We can celebrate, just the two of us, later. Wear those earrings I bought you for Christmas, eh?"

Christy opens the door and a gust of icy wind scurries inside, but it's a sense of dread that chills me to the bone. I watch him leave, then hurry upstairs and fetch the silver earring box. I sit on the bed and count backward from five before I muster the courage to open it. With shaking fingers, I lift out one of the earrings. My heart sinks. As I feared, the delicate emerald jewelry is not clip-on. It has a stem for pierced ears. My ears are not pierced. I spend much of the afternoon fighting panic. A couple of times I try to push the stem through my earlobe, but I fail each time the pain takes over.

At 6:00 p.m. the front door opens and song fills the hall. I creep onto the landing and view Christy sitting on the bottom step of the stairs trying to pull off his shoes while singing "Sweet Caroline." He isn't holding the melody correctly and the lyrics are off. I hope if I stay out of sight long enough he'll sing himself to sleep right there in the hallway. Unfortunately, my hopes are dashed when he pulls off his shoes and shouts, "Maura, what's for dinner?"

There's a stew waiting on the cooker, and by the time I fix my hair to cover my ears and make it downstairs he's helped himself to a bowl.

"There you are, my darling," he says. His eyes are glassy and unfocused. "This is delicious." A little gravy trickles down his chin.

"Glad you like it," I say.

Mouthful by mouthful, I watch as sustenance seems to sober him. His focus sharpens and begins to cut into me. My heart races as his eyes sweep over my face. If he touches my hair, I think I'll run.

I needn't worry—it's not my hair he wants to touch. He sets his bowl down and slides his arm around my waist, pulling my chest against his. Face-to-face, his breath smells of alcohol and carrots.

"Thirty," he says, as if his age shocks him. "Can you believe I'm thirty years old now?"

Christy has no lines in his face and there is only a hint of gray hair sprinkled at his temples.

"Thirty and still not a father. My father had all three of us by the time he was twenty-eight."

I don't speak. I can't guess what he wants to hear.

"Let's rectify that now," he says.

I stiffen. "But it's only been five weeks."

Christy laughs, but his face turns sour when he realizes I've been counting the days.

"The doctor said to wait six weeks, didn't he?" I say.

Christy taps his chest with his fingertip. "This doctor says five is fine."

My palms start to sweat. If we make love, Christy will almost certainly push my hair away from my ears.

"I have a terrible headache," I say.

"There are pills in the bathroom cabinet."

"They're all gone."

"There are more in my bag."

"But—"

"Maura, are you listening? My father had three children by my age. I have none. I am not asking."

"Christy, please?"

Christy says my name once more through clenched teeth, and when he grabs a fistful of my hair and drags me toward the bedroom, I know earrings are the least of my problems.

CHAPTER 32

Maura

I have long grown used to the bruises. A swollen eye or an aching jaw is just part and parcel of life as Mrs. Christy Davenport. But lying in bed, beside my snoring husband, I feel an ache like no other. It's not the hot, burning sensation between my legs. That's uncomfortable, of course, but I can bear it. I think, by now, I can bear most of the physical pain Christy dishes out. This ache is something else—something new, something I cannot bear. Shame sits inside me like a dirty thing. I want to take a kitchen knife to it and cut it out of me. I lost count of all the times I said no. I said no when he tore off my clothes and when he kissed me and when he pushed me onto the bed. I stopped speaking and closed my eyes when he forced inside me.

"Good girl," he said. "Good girl."

I am so tired of being a good girl. Christy has taken my consent, my choice, my dignity, and pulverized them. He has made it very clear that I do not own my own body.

I cannot sleep. I toss and turn all night, and at first light I finally go downstairs and make myself some cocoa. I'm stirring milk in a pot when Dan comes skidding into view through the front window. He hops off his bicycle before it comes to a stop and races up my garden path. I drop the spoon and meet him at the front door.

"What is it? What's wrong?" I say before he has time to open his mouth.

"It's Bernie. She's turning blue. We need Dr. Davenport. Oh Jesus. Oh suffering sweet Jesus."

"Christy," I yell over my shoulder. "Christy." The guttural sound comes from somewhere deep inside me. I'm racing up the stairs, taking the steps two at a time. "Christy, come quick."

Christy meets me on the landing. He's still in his checked pajamas and he's rubbing his eyes. He takes one look at me before he hurries back into the bedroom. He reappears seconds later with his shoes on and his medical bag in his hand.

"It's my wife, Doctor," Dan says as Christy runs down the stairs, with me hot on his heels.

Christy grabs his car keys from the hall table and says, "Come on."

Dan follows him outside; they hop into the car and drive away without another word.

I lean against the doorframe, my legs thinking about buckling, and I stare at the front wheel of Dan's bike, which hasn't yet stopped spinning.

"Oh, Bernie," I say. My eyes are wet.

I step outside, close the door behind me, and pick up Dan's bicycle. I pull my nightdress above my knees and hope I can remember how to keep my balance. Then I pedal hard and off I go. My floral nightdress is no match for February winds, and my teeth chatter. I whip past a sleeping Rathmines and pick up the pace as I head downhill into the city. The milk van passes, with bottles rattling. Cars begin to pull onto the road. Pedestrians appear and other cyclists too. Dublin is awakening. It's all very normal—habitual, even. I pedal faster, almost losing my footing and tumbling into the canal running alongside me.

Finally, I reach the city center. It's bustling with folks heading about their morning business. The back wheel skids as I turn onto Talbot Street. Shop shutters are rising and voices are carrying in the wind.

"Morning. Lovely day," I hear someone say.

"Sure is," someone else calls back.

The shutters of McCarthy's are firmly shut, but the windows in the flat above are open. I hop off Dan's bicycle and lean it against the wall. I listen. I expect to hear the sounds of a woman in labor. I hope for it. But the flat is silent.

I raise my hand to knock on the door when I hear voices inside. *Thank God.* The door swings open and it's Christy I see first.

"Maura, step aside," he says, calmly commanding me.

I move. Dan comes into view next, with Bernie in his arms. Her face is gray like the stonewashed building and her head and arms are dangling lifelessly.

"What is it? What's happened? Is she all right?"

No one answers me. They don't even look my way. Christy's car is waiting. He opens a door and Dan lays Bernie across the back seat.

"Should we call an ambulance?" I say.

Christy shakes his head. "There's no time. It's faster if I drive. Get in," he instructs Dan.

"The girls," I say. "Where are the girls?"

Dan looks at me blankly, and for a split second it feels as if he doesn't know.

"Where are the children?" I try again.

"Sleeping. They're still sleeping."

"Go. Go. I'll stay with them. Go."

Dan nods and squeezes into the back of the car with his wife. The engine purrs and they drive away, and I wonder if I will ever see Bernie McCarthy again.

CHAPTER 33

2023

Saoirse

"Did she make it? Bernie made it, right? You said you got the train to Belfast together, so Bernie survived, didn't she?"

My chest is tight and I'm as invested in Bernie McCarthy's well-being as if I had just witnessed her being bundled into the back of Christy's car right before my eyes. Maura sighs, remembering, and I can see that even after all these years this part of her story is still raw. Our train is stopped somewhere in the middle of nowhere. The service announcement said something about a fallen tree on the tracks—I couldn't make it out exactly over the sound of collective grumbling from passengers. Maura seems content to sit and wait, looking out the window at the pretty scenery of untouched countryside.

"She made it. Yes, she did. But her little boy, her beautiful little boy, did not."

"Oh." My heart sinks.

"Philip, they called him. He'd be fifty-three now. A man. With children of his own, perhaps."

"I'm sorry. I'm sure that must have been an awful time for you."

"It was an awful time for a lot of women," she says. "But thankfully there were men in the world like Dan McCarthy. Men who cared more about their wives and their daughters than anything else."

My phone rings and Miles's number appears on the screen.

"I'm sorry," I say. "I should take this."

"Is he a good man?" Maura asks, pointing at my phone.

I swallow. "He's a great man."

Maura smiles, and I stand up and put the phone to my ear. "Hi."

"Hey."

I walk toward the back of the carriage where it's quieter.

"Are you okay?" he asks.

"Not really. You?"

"Not really."

"Where are you? Are you coming home?"

"I'm on a train . . ." I take a breath.

"A train. To where?"

"Belfast."

Miles scoffs. "What's in Belfast?"

"I'm not sure, really. Answers, maybe."

"Answers?"

"I'm sorry. I know this is making no sense. I didn't even mean to get on a train. But I met this lady, and she's sort of telling me her life story from back in the day and it's helping, you know."

Miles takes a deep breath and puffs it out. "I'm not really following, to be honest."

"I know. I know. It's all a bit mad. I know. But, Miles?"

"Yeah?"

"You're a good man."

"Eh?"

"I just want to tell you that. I know I stormed out earlier and things are up in the air right now, and I'm on a train . . ." I giggle and hope he laughs too, but he doesn't seem to find any of this amusing.

"When are you coming home? *Are* you coming home?"

"I think I need to see this journey out."

"A journey to Belfast."

"It's a bit more than that, but yes, I need to go to Belfast. And then I'll come home. I'll get on the very next train back to Dublin."

"You're scaring me, Saoirse. Just come home, please? We need to talk."

"I'll text you when I get to Belfast," I say. "And when I'm on the train home, okay?"

Miles doesn't reply and I swear I can hear his heart aching. It hurts me.

"I love you," I say.

"I love you too. I'll see you later, yeah?" He sounds unsure.

"I'll see you later," I say. "Bye."

"Bye."

The train starts to move again without warning and I wobble and almost stumble. I slide my phone back into my pocket and return to my seat. Maura lets me have the first word.

"That was my fiancé," I say. "He was just checking where I am."

"And where are you?"

I look out the window at the countryside, whizzing by once more. But I know Maura is asking for more than my location. *Where am I? I'm where I want to be. Childless.* Maura might be okay with that answer, but I know in my heart that Miles will never be. I stare out the window at countless green fields and hay bales and cattle and I wonder if the Irish countryside has changed much in fifty-odd years.

"There's a stop coming up soon, if it's time to get off," Maura says, and I feel her hand on my knee.

"I don't think so. It's not time yet."

CHAPTER 34

February 1970

Bernie

"She's lucky to be alive," Dr. Davenport tells Dan.

Both men stand at the end of my hospital bed. Dan's arms are folded, as if he's protecting his heart, and he's nodding furiously, hanging on to the doctor's every word.

"Preeclampsia is not to be sniffed at. Bernie is lucky we caught her when we did," Dr. Davenport says.

"Lucky," I snort, thinking of the tiny little boy they whipped from my body.

My son. My baby. Gone.

"My advice?" Dr. Davenport says.

Dan nods more, lapping it up.

"No more babies. It's dangerous. This can and will happen again. Frankly, it's nothing short of a miracle that Bernie made it to a fourth pregnancy without this raising its head before. Bernie may not be so lucky next time."

"Lucky." That damn word.

"No more babies," Dan says obediently. He looks at me, waiting for me to agree. I don't move or speak.

All I can think about is my baby's face. His button nose. His powder blue eyes. His tiny, wrinkled hands. *Philip.* His name is Philip McCarthy, I decide.

"I'll leave you two alone now. Sister Lillian will be around soon to check on you," Dr. Davenport says.

Dan unfolds his arm and stretches out his hand. Dr. Davenport shakes it and they exchange a nod.

"Thank you, Doctor. Thank you so much. My Bernie. You saved my Bernie. There's free meat for you. Free meat for life. It's the least we can do."

"Thank you, but that really isn't necessary. I'm just doing my job." Dr. Davenport pulls his hand back and shoves it into his pocket. "Good luck," he says. "And do take my advice. No. More. Babies."

We are not alone. There are six beds in the ward that smells of bleach and linen: three across from me and one on each side of me. The one on my left is empty, but women and newborns lie in the rest of the beds. The babies cry every so often and their mothers soothe them. I look away but their tiny, helpless cries ring in my ears.

When I can no longer hold my tears back, Dan sits on the edge of the bed next to me and wraps his arms around me.

"Hush, my love. Hush. It will be all right. I promise everything will be all right."

Rubber shoes squeak across the tiled floor and a nurse requests our attention with a cough. She stands at the end of my bed and I can't help but wonder how she keeps her uniform so white in an environment so at odds with that color.

"Excuse me, sir," she says, in a clipped tone, "there is no sitting on the patient's bed."

She doesn't introduce herself, only points toward a sign hanging by the door. BEDS ARE FOR PATIENT USE ONLY.

"Oh." Dan stands up. His cheeks are pink. "I'm sorry, Sister Lillian," he says, assuming. "My wife is upset. We've just lost our son, you see."

"I know," she says. "I'm sorry for your troubles."

I dry my eyes and hold my head as high as I can manage. "I want to go home."

"Oh goodness," she says. "You won't be going anywhere for a while. You've had major surgery, Mrs. McCarthy. You need time to recover."

"I have three girls at home. I need to be with them."

A baby starts to whimper. I want to stick my fingers in my ears and scream.

"I'm afraid not," the nurse says, her clipped tone returning. "You need rest."

"I need my own bed and peace and quiet. I can't be around these babies. Please."

My heart is throbbing. It's not dramatic to say it feels as if it might snap clean in half. The nurse places her hand on Dan's shoulders and turns him toward the door.

"Now, Mr. McCarthy. If you'll be so kind as to be on your way. It's patient quiet time. Visiting hours resume at seven p.m., but Mrs. McCarthy has been through a lot. It might be best if you come back tomorrow."

"Patient quiet time?" I say. "Don't you hear that?"

"Babies cry, Mrs. McCarthy. With three at home already, you should know that."

"My baby doesn't cry. My baby can't. He's dead."

Dan turns back. His eyes are glossy with tears and I want to shovel the words back into my mouth. I reach for his hand and squeeze gently. "Our baby," I correct myself.

"Our baby," Dan whispers.

"Really, Mr. McCarthy," the nurse says, jamming her hands on her hips. "If you could get a wriggle on now, please. As I said, the patients need their rest."

I glare at the nurse. She's an older lady. Close to retirement, perhaps. She's not wearing a wedding ring and I doubt she has any experience giving birth to a baby, let alone losing one.

"Please," I say, holding Dan's hand a little tighter. "Can't he stay? I don't want to be alone. Please."

Her eyebrows pinch. "I'm afraid rules are rules. No husbands on the ward past three p.m. and"—she checks the watch that clips to her pocket—"it's three oh five now."

"To hell with the rules. Who made them anyway?"

"They're hospital rules, Mrs. McCarthy. They're the same for everyone."

All the other mothers sit or lie in bed. They feed or cuddle their babies, or flick through the pages of magazines. Their husbands are all gone. I didn't notice them leave.

"But it's not the same for everyone," I say. "Their babies are all alive and my Philip is gone."

"Mrs. McCarthy, I really am sorry. Perhaps a cup of tea might—"

"I just want my husband."

She shakes her head.

"Damn your rules," I snap.

"I'm just doing my job."

I sob. My whole body shakes. It hurts where they cut me but I can't stop.

"I want my husband. I want my baby. I want to go home."

I think I might be shouting; I can't tell. My voice is coming from a strange place, as if I am submerged underwater and I'm trying to push sound out to reach the surface.

"Mrs. McCarthy, please. You're making a scene."

I feel Dan's hand on my shoulder. I steady myself and look at him. There's so much pain in his eyes. He's looking at the woman in the bed opposite us. I now recognize her as one of Dan's regular customers.

"Congratulations, Mrs. Sweeny," Dan says, his voice crackling like radio static. "A little boy, is it?"

"Yes. Yes. A boy. To take home to his five big brothers."

"He's a fine fella."

"Ten pounds, six ounces."

"A fine fella," Dan repeats.

"I'm sorry," she says, looking away from Dan and toward me. "I'm very sorry for your loss."

"Thank you," Dan says.

"Mr. McCarthy," the nurse calls out, as if she's a school principal and Dan is a naughty pupil. "It is time to leave. Please!"

Dan leans over my bed and kisses me. "Rest, my love. I'll be back this evening."

"Tomorrow would be better," the nurse says.

"This evening," Dan repeats. "I'll bring your scrapbook, love. It might help to look over baby photographs of our girls."

Baby photos are the last thing that will help, but I know my husband means well so I don't say a word. Besides, maybe I can write. Maybe I can write all my thoughts and feelings about beautiful Philip and someday, when I'm ready, it will all be there to share with Dan and my girls, too.

Dan kisses me again before Sister Lillian places her hand on his back and practically pushes him out the door.

Later, the nurse checks my blood pressure and whatnot, and the doctor comes by with a list of questions as long as my arm. The drill is the same for every woman on the ward. Then the nurses gather up the babies and take them to the nursery. A young mother in the bed closest to me, and most likely on her first, requests to keep her baby by her side.

"I'm afraid not," the nurse says. "No babies on the ward after eight p.m. It's the rules."

Those damn rules.

When the nurse leaves and the lights dim, five women sit in bed alone with nothing better to do than stare at the four walls that surround us. Mrs. Sweeny is the first to get out of bed. She's a tiny woman and it takes her some time to shuffle her way toward me. Without a word she hoists herself onto my bed. She points toward the sign hanging by the door and winks.

"They can't give out to me for sitting here. I'm a patient." Then she takes my hand and squeezes. "You'll be all right. Someday."

The woman in the end bed is next to come forward. "I think they should have let him stay. Your husband. None of us would have minded."

The girl in the bed beside me doesn't get up, but she rolls onto her side to face me. She bends her elbow and props her head in her hand. "It's not as if we're getting much rest, with my little lady anyway. You'll hear her any moment kicking up a fuss down in that nursery. They'll come call me and ask me to hush her up. But I've not had a baby before. I don't know the first thing about hushing them."

"You'll learn," Mrs. Sweeny says. "We all do."

"Can't learn if I don't have her here with me. I just want to hold her all the time. I wish they wouldn't take the babies away at night."

"When you've had a few like me, you won't mind so much. You'll appreciate the rest," Mrs. Sweeny says. "It's the shooing the husbands away as if they don't know how the babies got in there in the first place that bothers me. Take my George. He's down the pub wetting the baby's head and he's not had a chance to hold the wee fella yet."

"Will he get drunk?" the young mother asks.

"You can bet on it. He'll have four or five pints at least while I'm here sitting on this bed, stitched from front to back like the hem of a skirt. My sister is looking after my older boys. On top of seven children of her own. It'll be a madhouse."

"I have three daughters," I say.

Mrs. Sweeny squeezes my hand once more; then she slowly lowers herself off my bed and walks back to her own. There's nothing more to say. She has six sons and I have one in heaven.

CHAPTER 35

Maura

By teatime my nerves are frayed. There's no sign of Christy or Dan, and there's no word from the hospital. Every now and then my imagination veers toward the worst and I hate myself for it. I try hard to hide my worries from the girls.

Elizabeth cries for her mother once, but she is distracted with a cuddle and a game of I-spy. Alice sits in her playpen, busying herself with some building blocks. She only fusses when she's hungry or wet. Marie, however, is slightly more difficult to placate. She asks questions I don't have answers to and she's visibly distressed.

"Is Ma gone to the hospital?"

"She is."

"Why didn't she take us? She always takes us."

"Because I'm here today. And I thought it might be fun to play some board games."

She regards me with contempt, but slowly her frown curls upward. "Santy brought Snakes and Ladders. We can play that, if you like?"

"I would like that very much."

The day is long and the flat feels cramped and uncomfortable when the children are restless or hungry. Marie is a great help. She teaches me how to change Alice's cloth nappy, which is surprisingly more difficult than I anticipated. I struggle with the folds and pins as the baby kicks and wriggles. Marie fetches Elizabeth's potty when needed. And when Elizabeth pees successfully in the potty and not on the floor, we all clap. Even baby Alice, who enjoys mimicking most things we do.

Marie tells me, "That's how she learns."

I cook dinner. A stew, and I hope Dan likes it as much as Christy usually does. I feed the children but I can't bring myself to eat. There's no room for anything in my stomach except worry. I set some stew aside for Dan and I spoon some into a bowl and cover it with tinfoil to take home for Christy later. I put Alice and Elizabeth to bed and Marie helps me wash up. She pushes a chair over to the sink, climbs up and dips her small hands in sudsy water, and begins to scrub a pot.

"I can't wait to be a grown-up," she says.

"Oh," I say, thinking back to a time when I had the very same wish.

"I'm going to be a ma, just like Ma."

"Oh," I say again, realizing that Marie and I are quite alike. "You know, you could be anything you want. You're a very clever little girl."

Suddenly, I feel compelled to tell her this. Maybe it's the suds pushing past her little elbows that doesn't sit right with me. Or that she knows how to change a nappy, or fetch a potty. She's just six years old. Her days should be full of coloring and dollies and not much more.

"What could I be?" she asks.

"Oh, I don't know. A teacher, perhaps."

Marie scrunches her face and pokes her tongue between her lips. Clearly school is not her favorite place.

"All right, not a teacher. How about a nurse?"

She shakes her head.

"All right. All right." I search my brain and it's oddly difficult to think of a profession to suggest to this curious little girl. I'm not quite sure why that is, but it makes me want to try even harder to broaden her horizons, certainly wider than mine.

"What about a ballerina?"

She smiles.

"Or an artist. You love drawing, don't you?"

Her smile widens. I see teeth.

I gasp. "I know." I think about all the times people told me I looked just like Doris Day growing up. "What about an actress?"

"What's a mattress?"

I laugh. "An actress. Oh, it's a wonderful job. It's someone who stars in films or on the television. And they play make-believe all the time."

Marie's eyes are wide with delight and she throws her arms in the air, showering us in soapy rain. "I want to be a mattress. I can't wait to be a grown-up and play make-believe."

Marie's happiness fills the air as the door creaks open behind us.

"Da," she squeals, hopping down from the chair and racing toward her father. "Da, I'm going to be a mattress when I grow up. Maura said so."

"That's nice, love," Dan says.

Dan seems years older than when he left this morning. He stands crouched, as if the weight of the day has whittled inches off him. I fear if he doesn't sit down soon, or lean against the doorframe at least, he might topple over completely.

"How about you go and draw me a picture of an actress," I suggest, bending in the middle so I'm face-to-face with Marie.

"Yes. Yes."

Marie scurries into the living area and fetches her coloring pencils and paper and sets to work. I wait for Dan to step farther inside or to close the door behind him. He does neither. I give him time, but when he doesn't budge, I close the door for him and cup his elbow. I don't try words. It's habit, I know. I don't speak when Christy doesn't speak to me first. Dan is a different man. Yet the habit is hard to shake. I guide him to the table and he sits. I heat some stew on the stove and set a bowl down in front of him. He must be hungry after a long day, but he doesn't touch it.

Finally, I bring myself to try words. Words I can't hold in any longer no matter what the consequences. "Is Bernie all right?"

Dan swallows. I can almost see the lump work its way down his throat. "She is."

Relief makes me lightheaded and I have to hold the back of his chair to steady myself. "And the baby?"

Dan doesn't reply. He stares into the bowl of thick, warm stew and I have my answer.

"Oh," I say, deflated. "Oh."

Marie returns with a picture of a rounded person with a blue dress and yellow hair.

"What a lovely actress," I say.

"It's Ma," Marie says. "I drawed Ma. Where is she?"

Dan looks up. His eyes fill with tears as he smiles at his eldest child. He pulls Marie onto his lap and she wraps her arms around his neck.

"Your ma is at the hospital. The doctors and nurses are taking good care of her. You'll see her in a few days."

Marie's eyes narrow and she lets her drawing fall to the floor. "But I want to see her now."

"In a few days, my love."

"Come along," I say, reaching my hand out. "How about a story before bed? Your da needs to eat now."

Marie hops off her father's knee and takes my hand as we walk toward the corner of the living area where her sisters are fast asleep. I fetch the mattress leaning against the wall and lay it flat on the floor and Marie climbs on top. I cover her with a blanket and all the while I'm thinking of Bernie and the baby she'll never bring home. I glance over my shoulder and I can see that Dan is a broken man thinking about the same.

CHAPTER 36

Bernie

The night of Philip's passing, a priest comes to visit me. I already know him as Father Walsh. He touches the rosary beads dangling by his side and places a warm hand on my forehead and mumbles a prayer.

"I'm sorry for your troubles, my child," he says.

"Thank you," I say, as I stare over his shoulder and out the window at the end of the ward. It's dark outside, but I can hear buses passing and a car honks its horn every so often.

"The nurses told me he was too wee and arrived too soon. But the baby is with our Lord now, worry you not."

"Philip. My baby's name is Philip."

He looks at me with empathy. "Philip is a lovely name. I have a cousin called Philip. He lives in England."

We both know there was no time to christen the baby. My son is Philip in my eyes only. To everyone else, he is a baby too fragile for this life. A tiny thing to be forgotten as quickly as he came into the world. I wonder how many other women Father Walsh will visit tonight. This week. This month. Mothers with empty arms and broken hearts. I hope I'm the only one, but of course I know I'm not.

I knew when labor started twelve weeks early that the odds were stacked against us. I'd never heard of a baby so premature surviving. But still, I dared to hope. Foolish of me, I know now.

"We have a wee plot at the back of the hospital," Father Walsh says. "For the little ones who didn't make it. It's a nice spot. A garden, really. With some trees and flowers. The pansies are my pride and joy, if I'm honest. In spring they're very beautiful. Ah, but you'll see for yourself."

I shake my head. I won't ever see.

And that is that. I don't have to sign anything. I don't have to pay a penny. I don't see my little boy ever again.

For nine days more I lie on the flat of my back. The only thing to occupy my racing mind is the window at the end of the hall. *Thank God for that window.* Dan visits when he can. He tells me the girls miss me and my heart hurts.

On the tenth day, Sister Lillian announces proudly that it's time to go home, as if I have served my time and my penance is complete.

I've my case packed and I'm dressed and waiting by the door when Dan arrives. I wait for him to kiss me, but he takes my case and says, "Right, love. Let's get you home. The girls are waiting."

The bus is late and we're cold and wet by the time we hop on. We take our seats and I drop my head onto Dan's shoulder. He smells of sawdust and lavender soap. Familiar. Soothing. But my comfort is lessened when I feel Dan stiffen and pull away.

The flat smells quite different to usual. There's a large bouquet of red roses in a fancy cut glass vase on the kitchen table and when Dan opens the bedroom door the scent of freshly washed linen wafts toward me.

"Where are the girls?"

"Maura took them for a walk," Dan says. "She's been a godsend. And the girls love her. Now, let's get you into bed."

My heart sinks. I wanted nothing more than to cuddle my babies. But I don't say a word, because just looking at my bed with fresh linen, I've never felt more exhausted in my life. Dan tucks me in as if I were one of our girls and he brings me warm chicken soup. I eat, and we talk. About all sorts of things. But not about Philip. I doubt we'll ever talk about him. It's just too hard.

When I'm finished eating, I ask Dan to lie beside me.

"Just until I fall asleep," I say. "I've missed you so much."

"I thought I was going to lose you," Dan says.

I look into the eyes of the man I love so much and wait for him to kiss me. He doesn't and the surprise of it hurts.

"I've moved my things to the living area," he says. "This is your room now. I thought maybe Marie might like to share it with you. And Elizabeth too, perhaps."

I look at the bedside table where his cap should be. It's bare. His spare shoes aren't by the window. His clothes aren't hanging on the back of the door. There's no trace of Dan in our room anymore.

"I don't understand."

"Dr. Davenport said no more babies, Bernie."

"I know, but—"

"You could have died."

There's so much pain and fear in my husband's voice. I reach my arms out to wrap around him, but he steps back.

"But I didn't," I say. "I'm here. I'm here now."

"And that's the way it's going to stay. No more babies. I can't put you at risk."

"Dan . . ."

"This is your room now. I'll sleep in the living area with Alice for the time being. And when she's older she can join you and the other girls in here."

"This is ridiculous. Is this why you won't kiss me? Why you pulled away from me on the bus?"

"I can't kiss you. It's dangerous."

"I don't think kissing ever made a baby, Dan."

"Dammit, Bernie," Dan says gruffly. His frustration is tangible. "Don't you see it's not the kissing I'm worried about, it's what it leads to. I can't kiss you and not want more. I can't share a bed with . . . Jesus, when I think of lying beside you and not being about to touch you . . . well, it damn near drives me insane. This is just how it has to be. I have to keep you safe and this is the only way I know how."

I shake my head. Something inside me is shaking too. My heart. My stomach. All of it.

"This isn't right," I say. "It isn't healthy. This is not a marriage."

"It's our marriage. And it's how it's going to be. I won't hear any more arguments, Bernie. Not about this."

"Fine," I snap. "Then get out of my room."

Dan's heart is breaking as much as mine. I can see it in his rounded shoulders and puffy eyes.

"Get out."

"Bernie, I love you," he says. "You'll see. In time, you'll see this is for the best."

I throw my pillow at him and shout, "Get out. Get out. Get out."

Dan backs out and closes the door behind him. I sit alone with my thoughts for a long time. I think about Philip's tiny body and how much I ache to feel him still inside me. I think about my girls. I miss them more than I can comprehend. And I think about Dr. Davenport. I hate that man. I hate him for what he does to Maura. And I hate him for what he has taken from me.

I find myself writing about it in my beloved sketchbook, the pen pressed so taut against the page that it tears. I keep writing. It's just my son's name at first. *Philip. Philip. Philip.* Over and over. But soon there are other words, too. All my thoughts and emotions spill onto the page, like foam and bubbles when you open a bottle of fizzy pop. I write until my eyes close and the pen falls out of my hand and onto the floor.

Later, I feel Dan take the sketchbook and place it on the bedside table. I feel his warm lips gently kiss my forehead when he thinks I'm sleeping.

"Sweet dreams, my love," he whispers before he slowly walks away from the bed we once shared, and I worry this is the closest I will ever be to my husband again.

CHAPTER 37

Summer 1970

Bernie

"Jaysus, it's warm," I say, not to anyone in particular.

Alice is running around the flat in nothing more than her nappy, and Marie and Elizabeth are wearing white linen dresses that were made from an old tablecloth. I wish I'd had one made for myself too, as I sweat in a long black skirt and blouse. The smell of meat protesting summer temperatures wafts up from the butcher's shop below and every so often my stomach heaves. But it doesn't drag my mood down. Today is a good day. The first in a while, as it so happens.

Maura and I are taking ourselves off to the pictures tonight.

"Christy is working late," she said last week with a wicked grin. "He'll never know."

"What are you going to see?" Dan asks when he finishes work almost an hour early to keep an eye on the girls while I'm out.

"The James Bond film—*On Her Majesty's Secret Service*, or something like that."

"James Bond, if you don't mind," Dan says. "Isn't that a fellas' film?"

"And so what if it is?"

"No matter. Maybe you'll enjoy it."

"Maybe I will," I say. "Maybe I'll find myself a new chap in the cinema. One who actually wants to touch me."

"Maybe you will."

We laugh. But neither of us finds it funny. Dan hasn't laid more than a kiss on my cheek in six whole months. I thought for sure after the first week sleeping on the couch, he'd return to our bed. But one week turned into two. And then a month. Half a year has passed, but I will not accept that Dan and I cannot be intimate ever again. I am, however, running out of ideas to sway him.

Firstly, I tried dressing up. I swallowed my pride and let Maura pay for a flowery, above-the-knee dress in Switzers.

Dan said, "That's nice. Is it new?"

And then he took himself off for a long walk.

Next, I gave one of those wine-and-egg diets a go. But I didn't have the stomach for chardonnay at breakfast and all the eggs gave me gas.

Dan didn't say anything about that, but I could tell he didn't like it. Marie and Elizabeth had plenty to say about it.

I tried straightening my hair. Maura ironed it for me, and Marie said I looked the prettiest ever. I have a small burn on my left ear where the iron tipped off my skin and I wonder if it will heal with a scar. But it was worth it when Dan said, "Holy God, Bernie, I've never seen you looking better."

He took another long walk that night.

Just last week, I cooked his favorite dinner. I borrowed expensive perfume from Maura and I left off my nylons and wore high heels. All throughout dinner I could feel Dan's eyes on me. But when my leg brushed against his under the table, he jumped back as if I'd scalded him with boiling water. Still, I didn't give up. When the girls went to bed, I turned on the radio and danced around the kitchen. I could see Dan's foot tapping for a while before he took me in his arms and we waltzed, carefree, the way we used to.

"You smell wonderful, love," he said.

I pressed my chest into his and said, "I love you, Dan."

"Jesus, Bernie, what are you doing to me? You heard what the doctor said. We can't make any more babies. It could kill you. *I* could kill you. Don't put that on my shoulders."

"Not having a husband is killing me," I said.

"I'm still your husband."

"Not if you won't touch me."

Dan went for such a long walk that night, it was growing bright by the time he got home. I met him in the kitchen, and he took one look at me and knew I hadn't slept either. The irony wasn't wasted on us. The sun might have been rising over Dublin, but it was setting on our marriage.

CHAPTER 38

Bernie

Maura and I meet outside Clerys clock on O'Connell Street. She's wearing cream corduroy slacks. They suit her, I think, and I tell her so. She's not wearing a scarf over her head as she usually does, and her golden hair is longer now than when we first met, pushing past her shoulders. It falls naturally straight and silky. Her brown boots have a block heel, and she has on a jacket made entirely of denim. I wouldn't be exaggerating if I said she was the most beautiful woman I'd ever seen. Men certainly think so. Countless heads turn as we pass. Maura seems oblivious to their admiration, which, if anything, only makes her more alluring. She links my arm and she's giddy tonight. I am too. It's refreshing to be out of the house after dark. I check my watch. The film starts in ten minutes. Thankfully, we're only a couple of hundred meters from the ticket office at the Savoy cinema. But Maura begins to walk in the wrong direction. She's turning away from O'Connell Street and onto Henry Street.

"Where are you going?" I say, coming to a stop.

"You'll see," she says, gripping my arm a little tighter and encouraging me to go with her.

"But the film starts soon. And we still have to queue for tickets yet."

"We're not going to the cinema."

I can't hide my disappointment. I'm no James Bond fan, but I quite fancied an evening in front of the big screen.

"Then where are we going?"

"Trust me."

I trust Maura. She's my best friend in the world, next to Dan, of course. And so, a tad reluctantly, I begin walking again and we leave O'Connell Street and the Savoy cinema behind. Henry Street is sleeping. All the shop shutters are down and we are among very few other pedestrians. Cars pass every so often, their bright lights blinding us, and I curse aloud when I walk into a parking meter and batter my hip.

"Damn thing," I say, rubbing where it throbs.

"There you are," someone says in the distance.

Maura unlinks from me to stretch her arms wide and hug the woman waiting under the glow of lights from Jervis Street Hospital on the corner. I recognize the woman as Maura's friend whom we met last Christmas, but I can't for the life of me remember her name.

Maura unwraps herself from around the woman and says, "You remember Ger, don't you?"

"Yes. Yes, of course," I say. "Hello. How are ya?"

"Hello," Geraldine says, with a wave. "It's nice to see you again."

"Yes. You too. Very nice."

There's a moment of awkward silence before Geraldine says, "Jaysus, Maura, you scrub up well. What the devil are you wearing? Slacks? I like it."

Maura spins on the spot before giggling sheepishly. "Trying something new," she says.

"Well, it suits you. Keep it up," Ger says. "Right. Are we getting a drink or what? My tongue is hanging out. It's been a long day."

I look at Maura, hoping for an explanation about what's happening, but all I get is a nod and a smile before we start walking again, following Geraldine. After a while we turn away from the busier streets of central Dublin and into quieter, more residential areas. I catch Maura by the hand as we veer farther and farther away from familiar areas and whisper, "Where in the blue blazes are we going?"

"No idea," Maura says, "but isn't this fun?"

I shake my head. *I just wanted to go to the pictures.*

Finally, Geraldine stops walking and announces, "Here we are."

I look up at the neon Guinness sign hanging on the wall and I nearly choke on my words. "A pub? What are we doing at a pub?"

"We're going for a drink?"

"Are you mad?" I say. I'm speaking to Geraldine but I'm looking at Maura, waiting for her to back me up.

"Are you sure this is a good idea, Ger?" Maura says. "They're hardly going to welcome us with open arms now, are they?"

"Jaysus, ladies. It's a pub, not a torture chamber." Geraldine steps closer to the door.

"Since when are woman allowed in pubs?" I say.

She shrugs. "My brother is the barman. He'll serve us. Don't worry."

I grab Maura's hand once more and give her a look that asks her to stop this madness. "They'll laugh us out the door," I say, sweating just thinking about it.

"C'mon, Bernie, don't you ever want to bend the rules a little?" Ger says.

I do. Sometimes I want to bend the rules until they snap.

"But a pub . . ."

"There's beer inside. And I want beer."

"Oh Lord."

Maura looks at me, takes a deep breath, and blesses herself. "We're going in," she says, but her voice cracks and I can tell she's as nervous as a skittish kitten.

"It's not too late to go back to the cinema. We'll have missed the start but they might still let us in," I say.

Maura shakes her head. "I'm sick of being a good girl. I'm damn well sick of it."

"Have you ever had a beer in your life?" I ask, knowing the answer.

"No," she says. "And I'm sick of that, too."

"And what if Christy smells it off your breath later, what will you do then?"

Maura shrugs and I've never seen her like this before. Broken. Emotionless. Frivolous with the consequences.

"I might as well be hung for a sheep as a lamb," she says. "I can't win with that man. So I've decided, what's the point in trying?"

"Ah, Maura."

"Are you coming in or what?" Geraldine says. "I'm bleedin' parched."

Maura looks at me once more. This time, I don't see a scared, broken woman. I see a friend begging for support as she takes a bold step. I just wish we were stepping somewhere else.

Geraldine is first through the door. Then Maura. And lastly, I force one jittery leg in front of the other and I step inside. It's dimly lit, and the cigarette smoke is as thick and blinding as fog on a winter's morning. Gray-haired and bald men sit on high stools next to the bar; they're alone, most with a single pint in front of them. Younger men sit in small groups playing cards, smoking, chatting. Their deep voices fill the air and they chuckle every so often. I don't know what I expected to find inside the four walls of a pub, but this is not it. It's all rather unremarkable. Even boring, dare I say.

Geraldine approaches the bar with confidence as Maura and I lag behind, linked arm in arm again.

"Oi," one of the elderly men nearest to Geraldine says in a voice much too loud for indoors. "What you doin' in here? Get out."

"It's all right, Murph. Calm down now. Ger's my sister," the barman says. He approaches with his hands raised above his head as if Murph might take a shot at any moment.

Murph rolls his eyes. "Bloody women, don't know their place no more," he grumbles and then lifts his pint with a shaky hand, dribbling some down his chin as he drinks.

"What are ya having, Ger?" the barman asks.

"Three pints of Guinness, please?"

My stomach heaves just thinking about it.

"Sit yerselves down. I'll bring them pints over to ya." He points toward a booth in the corner. "Might keep this lot happier if yer out of sight, eh?"

Ger huffs, but she pulls some money out of her pocket, passes it to her brother, and then says, "All right, all right, we're going."

"See," she says, turning toward Maura and me with a satisfied grin. "I told ye we'd get served. You just have to be confident."

"The barman is your brother," I say. But deep down I am secretly impressed. I wonder what Dan will say when I tell him I've been inside a pub. His face will be a picture, no doubt.

We slide into the booth and soon there are three pints of black Guinness with frothy cream tops lined in front of us. The barman, who introduces himself as Timmy, passes us three packets of Taytos, too.

"Them crisps are on the house," he says.

He winks at Maura and I doubt he knows she's married.

"Right, first things first," Geraldine says, lifting the pint to her lips and guzzling. "Ah," she gasps, satisfied, as she lowers it back down. "C'mon, you two. What ye waiting for?"

Maura is first to drink. She coughs and splutters and shakes her head. Geraldine laughs. I'm next and I'm surprised by the taste. It's sharp and bitter, and oddly, I think I like it.

"See?" Geraldine says. "It's good stuff."

Soon conversation begins to flow. Geraldine and Maura chat about the latest fashion in Switzers and which of the staff has recently got engaged. I don't have much to say, but I enjoy listening. I don't admit it out loud, but there's something liberating and pleasant about sitting in the pub. When Maura has managed to drink almost half her pint, she sits back with glassy eyes and folds her arms.

"So, did you bring the paper?" she says.

Geraldine's face lights up and she lifts her bottom off the bench seat to pull a newspaper from the waistband of her slacks. "I thought you'd never ask."

She passes Maura the paper, which is rolled up and secured with a brown elastic band. Maura slides a finger under the elastic, ready to slip it off, when Ger grabs her hand and whispers sharply, "Jesus, what are you doing? You can't open that in here. Are you mad?"

"I . . . I . . ."

It may be murky and gray in the room, but I can tell Maura's cheeks are red and glowing.

"Sorry. I'm so sorry. I wasn't thinking," Maura says.

"It's the Guinness," Ger says. "It makes the mind a little looser. But we're pushing our luck enough sitting in a pub of an evening. We don't need getting caught with this. Don't worry, they're in there. Timmy promised."

"How many?" Maura asks.

"Ten. Maybe a few more. I didn't count."

"Oh wow. That many. Wow."

Maura opens her handbag and takes out some money. She stuffs the money into Geraldine's hand and Geraldine's fingers quickly curl tight around it.

"Can he get more?" Maura asks. "If they work. How many can he get?"

Geraldine drains the last of her pint. Then she sits poker-straight and says, "Oh, they work all right. And so long as you don't tell nobody, Timmy can get as many as ye like."

"Get what? What is going on?" I ask, suspecting that whatever it is, it might not be legal.

I glance at Timmy behind the bar. He's drying glasses with a tea towel. He looks like an ordinary man working an ordinary job. Then I turn my attention back to Maura and Geraldine as they sit next to me, huddled in a dark corner of a dark pub where ordinary women are rarely seen and clearly don't belong.

"I think we should go home now," I say, a wobble creeping into my voice.

"What about your Guinness?" Geraldine asks, pointing at the glass I've barely touched. "Don't you like it?"

"I like it plenty. It's this place I'm not sure about. I'm sorry. I mean no offense, but this whole evening has caught me off guard. I thought we were going to the pictures, you see."

Geraldine nods. "None taken. I get it. The first time is always the toughest. But when you bend the rules once, it gets a little easier the next time. Hell, it gets necessary."

I nod as if I know what she's talking about.

Geraldine leans across the table, getting closer to me, and she whispers, "Them French letters are going to change your life, Bernie. You'll see."

My eyes widen and the smoke burns them. I glare at the newspaper rolled up in Maura's hand.

"You do know what a French letter is?" Geraldine asks.

"Of course I know."

At least, I think I know. I've heard mention of them before—accoutrements that cover up a man's nethers and stop a woman from getting pregnant. I've no idea what they look like and even less idea how they work, or even if they work. But I know they are downright illegal.

"If men had to birth babies you can bet your luck French letters would be sold in every shop in Ireland," Geraldine says, forgetting to whisper. "It's nineteen seventy, for fuck's sake. Women are done having countless babies."

Geraldine grows more passionate and louder by the word. I place my finger on my lip to shush her but she ignores me.

"I'm sick of hushing up. I want to shout it from the rooftops." Geraldine gets to her feet and raises one arm in the air. "Women have rights. We deserve better."

I tug her sleeve and pull her back down, almost tumbling her over, but it doesn't shut her up. "Fuck 'em. Fuck 'em all. We want our bodies back."

Murph turns around, wobbling and almost falling off his stool. "Yer no ladies with filthy mouths like that. Shame on you."

Something about the old man with slurred speech, droopy eyes, and a fresh pint waiting in front of him sets a fire in me. I'd ask what gives this drunk the right to judge us but I already know the answer. Maybe Geraldine is right. Maybe bending the rules gets easier over time. If French letters give my husband back to me, then illegal or not, I think I'm prepared to take the risk. I lift my pint and slug the rest until my glass is empty and a loud belch follows from somewhere inside me.

"Whoop!" Geraldine stands and punches the air. "Bernie, you are some rebel."

I'm woozy and wobbly on my feet. But I like it.

Maura stands last. She lifts her jumper and tucks the rolled newspaper under her waistband. Her fingers tremble but her determination never falters. She turns back for her pint. "To rebels," she says. Although she struggles, she drinks the majority of it.

Outside, Maura gets sick. I jump and shriek when a garda car passes with its siren blaring. Geraldine laughs and I've no doubt that Maura and I have lost our rebel badge of honor already. Geraldine leaves us with a hug each and the reassurance that we know where to find her. Maura and I start the long walk home without a word between us. We part ways at Clerys clock and Maura passes me the newspaper like a teammate passing a baton. She helps me hide the newspaper as best I can under my clothes. Nerves make me clammy, and I've no doubt I'll have a face like a tomato by the time I reach my front door.

"Thank you," I say, suddenly overcome with emotion.

Maura smiles. "When we first met, you said we were going to be great friends."

"I did. I did. I remember."

"You were right. This is what friends do. They help. You and Dan are a great couple, Bernie. I want you to be happy. You deserve to be."

I take her hands in mine and I wish I could say something similar to her. But I know her bed is so much harder than mine. Instead, we share a look. A look that says sometimes you go above and beyond for the people who matter to you.

"Now go," she says. "Go on. Surprise that husband of yours."

CHAPTER 39

Bernie

Dan isn't happy. In fact, he's furious. His face is puce and angry saliva sprays from his lips as he marches around the kitchen.

"Shh," I say as I place a finger over my lips and look over my shoulder toward my bedroom, where the door is slightly ajar. "You'll wake the girls."

"Dammit, Bernie, what were you thinking? Can you imagine if my customers found out? Where do you think Father Walsh gets his meat? Mrs. Dunne, his housekeeper, is one of my best customers." Dan claps his hands and presses them down on the top of his head. "Oh, oh, and the Pearsons. Only a few years back they shipped their eldest daughter off to America because she was in the family way without a fella to marry. My God, Bernie, could you imagine what they'd say if they knew we were using those . . . those . . . those whatever they're called."

Dan stops pacing and lowers his hands. He glares at the kitchen table where I've unrolled the *News of the World*, and the contents that look a lot like teabags or lollipop wrappers are scattered around.

"They're French letters, Dan."

"They're contraptions."

"They could be the answers to all our problems."

"Or they could bring us problems. If word got out, people would boycott us. We'd lose the roof over our head."

I gasp. For a moment the thought is so horrific I feel choked. But it passes and I say, "And how will anyone find out? I'm not going to tell a soul. Are you?"

"No." His eyes are wide with torment.

I can tell Dan is as desperate to open one of these little teabags as I am.

"What about Maura? What if she tells Dr. Davenport?"

I snort. "You know as well as I do the type of man Christy Davenport is. It would quite frankly be dangerous for Maura to share this information with her husband."

Dan's shoulders round and I can sense him relax a fraction.

"And this woman, the one who works in Switzers."

"Geraldine. Her brother is the one who organized it all. He's able to get all sorts shipped in from America or England. Don't ask me how. Maybe it comes in with the beer."

"Beer?"

"He's a barman."

"Oh, Bernie, tell me you didn't go to a bar. What if someone saw you? What would they think?"

I exhale and pull a chair out from the table to sit down. I wonder if we will spend our whole lives worried what people think.

"No one saw me. No one will ever find out. Now, are you going to try this or not?"

Dan won't look me in the eye.

"Because I'm telling you, I can't live like this. Some women might be happy never being touched but I'm not one of them. I lie in bed at night and stare at that damn ceiling and it's all I can do not to fall apart. I'm lonely, Dan. I miss you."

"I'm right here," he says.

I look at him, but still there is no eye contact in return. He steps in front of me and crouches. Finally, he looks at me.

"Do you have any idea how hard this is for me? How hard it is to be around you and not be able to hold you, to make love with you? Christ Bernie, I'm losing my mind, I tell you."

"Then try. Try this with me. If you don't like it—"

"I'm not concerned I won't like it. God, Bernie, I know I will. Of course I will. I'm worried about what will happen if it doesn't work."

"It *will* work."

"Oh, Bernie."

I lean forward, and for the first time in longer than my heart can bear I feel his lips on mine. I taste the salty tears that trickle down his cheeks.

"I love you," he whispers in rushed breaths between kisses.

"I love you too."

Dan pulls away and I ache for him instantly. He reaches his hand out, and I take it and let him pull me to my feet. Then he picks up a teabag from the table.

CHAPTER 40

August 1970

Maura

Summer is by far my favorite season. Warm, bright days allow me freedom to wander about the city. An early morning walk in the park. An afternoon visit to my parents. Dinner at Bernie's. A catch-up with Ger over a cigarette. I've even been back to Timmy's pub a couple of times when Christy is working a night shift. Christy's shifts are ever changing and my days mirror his schedule. If his day starts before dawn, so, too, does mine. I make sure to have a hot breakfast waiting for him when he comes downstairs. Evenings are much the same. If he arrives home close to midnight, as he often does, I have a wholesome dinner waiting to be heated on the stove. I do not take my routine for granted and it does not come without its worries and pressures. Chores are ever waiting and they must come first. Cleaning, washing, ironing, baking, cooking. I am the epitome of the dedicated housewife and although he hasn't said it, I can tell Christy is pleased. All things weighed, I enjoy my life. There's just one fly in the ointment: how much Christy wants a baby.

On Friday, 28 August 1970, Elizabeth McCarthy turns four years old.

I've kindly been invited to the McCarthys' flat to celebrate with the family. I change my outfit several times before I find something that will cover all the latest bruises.

I bring homemade apple tart, Elizabeth's favorite, and we nearly lift the roof off Bernie's flat singing "Happy Birthday" as loud as our lungs allow us. Dan pops up from the butcher's shop below for a while to have a slice of tart and a cup of tea, and to tell his daughter that she's the most beautiful four-year-old in the world. Children's laughter fills the flat as they play pin the tail on the donkey.

"Cold. Cold. Turn around, Marie. Warm. Warmer. Go. Go."

I'm watching the children when I feel a hand on my shoulder.

"Is something the matter?" Bernie says.

"Why do you say that?"

"You've a face that would stop a clock and you've been in funny humor all week. Has Christy hurt you again? Maura, if it's getting worse . . ."

"It wasn't Christy this time."

Bernie tells the girls to hush.

"Into the bedroom, girls. Take your playing into the bedroom. The grown-ups are talking."

"But, Ma," Marie protests.

"You heard me," Bernie says, pushing her chair back to stand up and point toward the room at the back of the flat.

Marie, Elizabeth, and Alice sulk away with their arms folded.

"Tell me," Bernie says, sitting back down.

She pours us more tea, although I don't have the stomach for it.

"It was Mother Nature this time," I say.

"Oh, Maura. I'm sorry. How many is that now? Three?"

"Four."

"Oh, Maura."

In the year and two months since Christy and I married, I've experienced four miscarriages. Three because my husband can't control his temper and one because Mother Nature intervened. *Perhaps she's trying to tell me something. Perhaps the Davenport house is not a home for a child.*

"I think it might be for the best," I say, sipping some tea, and to my surprise the warmth soothes me.

"Maura, you don't mean that."

"I do. I think I really do. There are days when I can't keep myself safe in that house. How on God's green earth could I protect a baby?"

"You'd find a way. You're a strong woman, Maura. Stronger than you know."

I sigh and Bernie squeezes my hand and pulls some tissues from her apron pocket to offer to me. I take one, but I'm not going to cry. I'm not sad. I am resigned. And that's a different matter entirely. I've known for some time now that the best way to protect my baby is to make sure he or she is never born.

"Christy Davenport shouldn't be a father," I say.

"Well," Bernie says, folding her arms and nodding, "he does have a very big nose. It wouldn't look good on a baby."

"It is huge, isn't it?" I say. "That's probably why he snores so loud."

Christy's nose is perfectly proportioned. Just as the rest of his face is. But Bernie and I laugh for a long time, nonetheless, until finally she grows serious and says, "Are you sure about this? You would be a wonderful mother. Just look at how much my girls love you."

"I love them too. And I would love my baby. I would love my baby so much that I couldn't bring him or her into my home. Please tell me you understand, Bernie. Please tell me I'm not mad."

"Oh God, you're not mad, Maura. But how? How are you going to avoid it? French letters aren't going to solve your problems, as they have mine. Christy would know, obviously."

"Ger gave me a chart."

"A chart?"

"It keeps note of your monthlies. It tells you what days you can conceive and what days you cannot."

"What do you mean?"

"There's only certain days in the month when you can make a baby. Did you know?"

Bernie eyes me skeptically.

"It's true. Honest. I didn't know either until Ger told me. She said she read it in a magazine Timmy snuck in from America. *Vogue* or something. Anyway, the rest of the days nothing will happen. I only have to keep Christy away from me for three or four days every month."

"And how are you planning to do that?"

I sigh. That part of the plan is certainly trickier. I've learned over time that what my husband wants, my husband gets. Or, more correctly, takes.

"There's a doctor," Bernie says. "A fella in Limerick. He's prescribing the pill for women. He's expensive, but—"

"But I could afford it," I finish for her.

Her face lights up. "You could. If you say your monthlies are wonky he might give it to you. Oh, Maura, this would fix everything."

I shake my head. "A husband has to give his permission for his wife to get the pill. Christy has women ask him for it every day. One poor woman lost two sets of twins. Christy said she cried when she begged for the pill."

"Did he prescribe it?"

"No," I say. "Even if the husband consented Christy would never agree."

"Unbelievable. I worry for my girls' future."

"Me too."

"Could Ger help?" Bernie says.

I shake my head. "Ger says Timmy draws the line after French letters."

Bernie exhales and stands up. I feel her frustration. I share it. She checks on the girls. They've started playing again, a loud game that involves lots of jumping and shouting. Satisfied they can't hear a word, Bernie sits back down and whispers, "I know someone who might be able to help." Her voice sounds strange, as if it belongs to someone else.

My breath catches.

"A woman here in Dublin," Bernie continues. "Her name is Mrs. Stitch and she's a seamstress."

Mrs. Stitch the dressmaker. I smirk because for a moment I think she is trying to lift the mood with a silly joke. But her face remains serious, her eyes focused.

"Listen, listen." She lowers her voice even further, and I have to concentrate to hear her above the sounds of the girls playing in the bedroom.

"She's a sort of jack-of-all-trades, if you will. From noon on she makes coats and dresses and such, but before that, earlier in the day, she has a different line of work."

I listen but I'm not following.

"She takes care of women's problems. The sort of care doctors and nurses don't give, if you know what I mean."

My gut clenches. Suddenly, I worry that I know exactly what she means.

"Oh, Bernie, I—"

"Now look. I'm not saying she could help in your exact situation. But maybe . . ."

"That can't be legal," I say.

"Of course it's not. But neither are French letters and they've changed my life."

I rest my elbows on the table and let my face fall into my hands. I feel Bernie's hand on my back, rubbing circles.

"It's just a suggestion. I owe you so much for helping me. I just . . ." Bernie pauses, maybe to gather her thoughts, or maybe to process the gravity of what she's saying. "I just want you to know she's there. That maybe help is out there."

My thoughts are racing. I try to grab hold of them, but they float inside my head like bubbles and pop before I catch them.

"Would you come with me?" I say.

Bernie stops rubbing my back and I lift my head and meet her concerned eyes.

"Yes. Of course. When?"

"Soon." I swallow hard. "Next week, maybe. Christy is working a long shift on Wednesday, so—"

"Wednesday it is." Bernie glances over her shoulder toward the noise of the girls. "It's not somewhere I want to bring the girls back to, I have to be honest. But don't worry. I'll figure something out. Dan can close the butcher's for an hour or two to watch them."

"You won't tell him, will you?"

Bernie sighs and I know without asking that there are few, if any, secrets between her and Dan.

"Please, Bernie?"

"I'll tell him I'm going to mass and confession. To be honest, it might be no harm to go to confession after this."

I nod, but I don't see the need. Control over your own body isn't a sin.

"Yes, all right," I say.

CHAPTER 41

Bernie

Less than a week later, on Wednesday, Elizabeth starts primary school for the first time. She's a picture in the brown pinafore, a cream blouse, and a brown cardigan that have been passed down from Marie. I had to buy a new uniform for Marie this year. We'll be making do without vegetables for a while to offset the cost.

There is great excitement among the girls as we set out for school. Alice is quickly outgrowing her pram, and pushing her weight over bockety cobbles is no mean feat, so I'm glad St. Anne's, the all-girls primary school, is just around the corner. As the gray building comes into view, I feel Elizabeth's hand slip into mine and she squeezes.

There's a crucifix above the door and a sign proudly declaring that their pupils are YOUNG LADIES LEARNING IN GOD'S LIGHT. I pull Elizabeth close to me, kiss her forehead, and warn her to behave if she doesn't want a wallop of the teacher's stick. Mrs. Plum, Elizabeth's teacher, is kind and gentle, and when Elizabeth cries at my leaving, Mrs. Plum offers her a hug and promises there are lollipops in her classroom for good girls. Marie is green with envy. Her teacher, Sister Sloan, is the principal and not a particularly patient woman. She scares me, not to mention the children.

She yanks Marie by the arm and says, "No crying, Miss McCarthy. You are seven years old. Far too old for such nonsense. Stop it this instant if you don't want to see the back of my hand."

Marie holds in tears as I wave goodbye. I curse Sister Sloan under my breath and decide then to skip confession. Father Walsh might not be ready to hear the things I have to say about Marie's teacher.

The cobblestones on the walk home rock Alice to sleep. I wheel her behind the counter in the butcher's and tell Dan I won't be long.

"And what if she wakes?" he says.

"I'm sure you'll figure it out."

I meet Maura under Clerys clock once more. She's wearing a beautiful lime-and-mustard headscarf and a matching green summer dress, without sleeves. Her pearl earrings match her necklace, and I can't help but think that even on the darkest days, she somehow manages to remain bright.

"I'm nervous," she tells me, but she didn't need to; she wears her unease like a second skin.

I lead the way and we chat for a while but soon allow silence to fall. We're both lost in our own thoughts. My foot hurts, and I think the sole of my shoe might be nearing its end. I begin to limp.

"What is it, what's wrong? Do you need to turn back?" Maura asks.

"I'm fine."

"Maybe we should turn back. We should, shouldn't we?"

I stop walking and place my hands on her shoulders to steady her. "It's normal to be nervous. I nearly passed out when you brought me into that pub last month. But look how well it's all turned out."

Maura smiles and I feel her stiff shoulders relax. "Thank you," she says, and slowly we begin walking again.

It's not long before the red door on the side of an innocent-looking gray building comes into view.

"We're here," I say, and I'm not without my own edginess.

"We're here. Oh God."

I raise my hand and knock three times.

"Just a minute," a woman's voice calls from inside.

Maura and I stand back and wait. The door creaks open and Mrs. Stitch and a young girl appear. This girl looks even younger than the one previously. Her hair is matted and sits in clumps like a bird's nest on her head. I can barely bring myself to look at the glass bottle in her hand. It's full.

"Can't I use your bathroom?" the girl says. "My friend said I could."

"Not today. I've too many patients. Drink it at home. It'll do the trick by the next morning."

"Patients?" Maura whispers.

"Shh," I say.

"And if it doesn't, can I get a refund?"

Mrs. Stitch laughs. "I think money is the least of your problems then, m'dear."

The girl thanks the seamstress, clutches the bottle to her chest, and avoids making eye contact with me or Maura as she passes by and walks away.

"Well, don't stand out there all day," Mrs. Stitch says, opening the door wider. "Mrs. McCarthy, if this is about stitching, I've told you not to call before noon."

"No. No. Not this time."

Mrs. Stitch's lips curl into a wicked smile and she closes the door behind us. She knows without another word why we're here.

"Which of you is it, then?"

Maura taps her chest with her fingertip. "Me."

"Right. And how far along are you, do you know?"

"Oh." Maura stiffens. "I'm not pregnant."

"Then why are you here?"

Maura fidgets with her headscarf as if it's suddenly too tight or itchy. I wait for her to clam up and I prepare myself to speak for her. But she doesn't. She takes a deep breath and says, "I want to make sure I never get pregnant."

Mrs. Stitch laughs. A loud, bellowing belly laugh. "What do you think

I am? A wizard? If I could stop women from getting pregnant, I'd be a millionaire."

"We thought you might be able to get the pill for us," Maura says.

"And how would I do that? I'm hardly a doctor, now, am I?"

"No, but—"

"Look, best I can do is advise you to keep your legs crossed. If that doesn't work, come back to me when there's a bun in the oven. I'll be able to sort you out then, all right?"

Maura's hope deflates. I feel equally as flat. *I never should have gotten her hopes up.*

"I'm sorry," I say.

Silent tears trickle down Maura's cheeks but she holds her head high.

"Thank you anyway," she tells Mrs. Stitch, and then stretches out her hand.

Mrs. Stitch shakes it and says, "You're a strange one, aren't you? But, I suppose, it's always the posh ones who are. Let me tell you something for nothing: babies are babies. Don't matter if you're rich or poor, married or a whore, babies will grow inside you once a man goes near you. It's why I keep away from the feckers. You might best do the same."

"But I'm married," Maura says.

Mrs. Stitch's expression changes. Her eyebrows pinch. "Get out. Get out, the both of you. And don't come back here unless you've got real problems."

CHAPTER 42

Bernie

Maura is as quiet as a church mouse as we begin walking back into town. I don't have many words either. I find myself talking about the weather.

"Bit windy, isn't it?"

The day has taken a turn. What started as a beautiful sunny morning is now cloudy and gray, as if the weather is offering its sympathy. Tiny goose bumps line Maura's arms, and I'm not sure if it's the sudden chill or the experience.

Maura stops walking and turns her attention to a doorway. Someone is curled up under a patchwork blanket.

"Probably a drunk," I say. "It's sad, isn't it? Leave them be. The gardai will move them on soon enough."

I begin walking again but Maura doesn't follow. She's cemented to the spot in front of a blanket that rises and falls with each heavy breath of the poor fella underneath. I guess Maura doesn't get many drunks on her side of town and I give her a moment to gather herself, but she doesn't budge.

"Let go," I say.

Maura points and calls my attention without words. I walk the couple of steps back to stand beside her.

"What? What is it?"

"The shoes," she says. "Look at the shoes."

I drop my gaze to the pair of black patent shoes poking out from under the blanket.

"Huh, a woman." I am shocked.

"Not a woman. A girl. This is the girl we saw leaving Mrs. Stitch's shop. I recognize her shoes."

"Really?"

I don't think I've ever noticed anyone's shoes, ever. And I hope no one notices mine, not with a hole brewing in the sole.

"We used to stock ones just like them in Switzers. I think they still do," Maura says.

"You really think this is her?"

Maura doesn't answer, instead bending down and placing her hand on the mound under the blanket. There's a rustle and someone shoots to their feet. I shriek and jump back. Maura too. But we steady ourselves quickly when we discover Maura is right. Standing, shivering, is the young girl from Mrs. Stitch's shop.

"Don't call the guards. Please don't call them. I'll move. I'll go somewhere else."

The girl smells. I hate myself for noticing, but it's rancid and I wonder when the last time she washed was. Her legs are long and thin like straws, with knees that stick out like doorknobs in the middle. Her fingernails are black underneath and all around. Her clothes are stylish, expensive maybe, but her knitted Aran cardigan is missing a couple of buttons and her pleated maroon skirt is creased and grubby.

"How old are you?" I ask.

"Please don't call the guards."

She shakes like a leaf in the wind.

"We won't. We won't, don't worry," Maura says. She tries placing her hand on the girl's shoulder, but she jerks away.

"How old are you?" I try again.

"Fifteen."

"Jesus."

"Are you pregnant?" Maura asks.

The girl freezes.

"It's all right," Maura says. "You don't have to be scared. We saw you at Mrs. Stitch's a little while ago, remember?"

"Please don't call the guards."

"Listen, please listen," Maura says. "We're not going to call the police. We just want to make sure you're well and safe, that's all."

"I'm well and safe. I'm well and safe. Please don't call the guards, they'll take me away. They'll put me in one of those homes for fallen women. My ma said so."

Her lip trembles and she turns around to gather her blanket and a small rucksack. A glass bottle with the label ripped away is lying in the doorway. It's empty now.

"What was in that?" Maura asks, pointing at the bottle.

The girl shrugs.

"But you drank it anyway?"

"I had to." She places her hand on her stomach.

"Are you going home now, then?" I ask.

The girl begins to cry and I hold her. I think if I don't, she will tumble over. The smell is worse up close and I know the answer to my question is that she has no home to go to.

"What's your name?" I ask.

She swallows hard and says, "Josephine. But my ma calls me Josie."

"Nice to meet you, Josie," I say. "I'm Bernie. And this is Maura."

"You look like a film star," Josie tells Maura, before she looks down at her own clothes and awkwardly tries to hide some of the stains with her rucksack.

"How long have you been out here, Josie?" I ask.

The girl shakes her head as she looks at me and then at Maura.

"We just want to help you," Maura reencourages.

Josie shrugs. "A week, I think. I don't know."

"And where are your parents?" Maura continues.

"At home?"

"But you can't go there?"

Maura is soft-spoken so as not to spook the poor child, and I let her do the talking now because I want to scream. I want to scream and shout, because what kind of parents could leave their fifteen-year-old to sleep in a doorway on the street like a lost dog?

"They don't want me anymore," Josie says, pulling her rucksack closer to her chest. I can hear how the pain of abandonment sticks to her every word.

"Because you're pregnant?" Maura says.

The girl nods. "But if it's gone, then maybe Ma will let me go home. Da says I can never come back, but I think Ma might talk to him. I just need to wait until it's gone."

"Do they know you're here? Sleeping here?"

"No."

"Where do they think you are?"

"America," she says, beginning to cry. "I got an aunt there. She's got a farm and that, and Ma says I can work there. But I didn't get on the boat. They bought my ticket and all, but I didn't go. I couldn't go."

Maura pulls off her head scarf and passes it to Josie. "To dry your eyes," she says.

We give Josie all the time she needs to steady herself before Maura says, "Are you hungry?"

Josie shakes her head. Her pale face matches the gray stonewashed building behind her and her blue eyes have lost their shine. I wonder when the last time she had a decent meal was.

"We need to get some food into her," Maura whispers to me. "Who knows what was in that bottle and if her stomach is empty on top."

The thoughts of food make my stomach turn but I say, "I'm starving. I could murder a hot cross bun. Do you like hot cross buns, Josie? Maura and I love 'em."

"What about Bewley's on Grafton Street?" Maura says. "Do you like Bewley's?"

Josie nods. "Yeah. We used to go there on Sundays after mass. Ma and Da and my brother, Richard."

"Great," Maura says.

Bewley's is busy, as usual. Josie and I take a seat while Maura insists on buying tea and a hot cross bun for each of us. She returns in a jiffy with a tray of goodies. Josie picks all the currants from her bun the way my own girls do and she drinks two cups of tea. I skip mine so she can have another.

"Do you have a chap?" Maura asks, as Josie finishes her bun.

Tears swell in her eyes once more and she shakes her head.

"He's not your boyfriend anymore?" I ask.

She shakes her head again.

"Is he fifteen too?"

She shakes her head.

"Older?"

She nods and gulps down more tea.

Maura places her hands around her cup, warming them. She takes a deep breath and says, "Does he know about the baby?"

Fat tears trickle down Josie's cheeks.

"Does he know?" Maura tries again, almost whispering now.

"No," Josie exhales, and there's anger amid her sadness. It's buried deeper, but nonetheless I hear it. "Da says I'm not allowed to tell him."

"Why not?" I say, loudly, because I just can't hold my frustration in. The couple at the table next to us turns and stares. "Oh, mind your business," I say. They turn back. "Why doesn't he want you to tell him?" I ask again, my voice lower now.

Josie's eyes peer deep into me. I almost feel them cut, as if she's slicing me to see if she can trust what's on the inside.

Finally, she says, "He's my da's friend, that's why not. They play golf on the weekends. And my ma goes shopping with Mrs. Cl—" she cuts herself off before she reveals a name. "My ma goes shopping sometimes with his wife. They're friends too."

"Oh," I say.

"I don't like him, if that's what you're thinking. He smells old. Like Christmas spices. He said it was a secret. He said if I told anyone he'd tell my ma and da I was a slut. And then this happened. And I didn't know for a while. But then I figured it out. And Da says it's all my fault 'cause I wear them short skirts and go out with my friends too much. He says I lead fellas on."

"Oh, Josie," Maura says, peeling her hand away from her cup to place it over Josie's grubby hand. "None of this is your fault. None of it, you hear?"

"What did your ma say?" I ask.

"Nothing, really. She just does what Da says."

Anger boils inside me until it feels like it might bubble out the top of my head. How can this woman call herself a mother? How can she not put her daughter first? I don't know Josie's parents. Or the man who raped her. But I hate them all with such a passion I can hardly breathe with the weight of it.

"Richard said we should tell the guards and then Da smacked him one."

Maura and I are lost for words.

"That's when Da said I had to go to America and Ma said she'd write to me."

"Jesus," Maura and I say at the same time.

Maura turns to me. "What are we going to do?"

"She can't spend another night on the street."

Maura nods. "Josie, would you like to come and stay in my house? I have a spare room."

Josie's back arches like a startled cat's and I'm afraid for a moment that she's going to jump clean off her chair and run away. But slowly she tries on a smile. It doesn't quite come all the way up at the edges, but it's there.

"I have a nice big bath and some warm blankets, and I make a great stew," Maura adds.

"She does," I say. "It's the best."

Josie's smile widens. "I like stew."

"Good. Good. It just so happens I have a pot on the cooker back at my house as we speak."

The missing sparkle in Josie's eyes flashes for a moment, and she's a pretty girl, there's no doubt about that.

"What will you tell Dr. Davenport?" I say.

Discomfort flashes across Maura's face before she inhales sharply through her nose. "I'll say we're cousins. Christy says family is a gift."

"Will he believe you?"

"God, I hope so."

"Maybe Josie should stay with me," I say, my mind racing.

Maura shakes her head. "You don't have any room. And what would you tell the girls? No. This is for the best. Besides, if that potion takes hold, who knows, we might be mighty glad to have a doctor in the house."

Maura is right. We might need Christy before the day is through.

CHAPTER 43

Maura

First things first, I run a warm bath for Josie. I pour in a whole bottle of bubble bath, fetch some fresh towels, and set out some clean clothes. I leave her to it and heat some stew and slice some brown bread. When she appears in the kitchen, my heart skips a beat. She's wearing one of my summer dresses. It's a little too big on the hips, but with a belt it will be fine. The fabric brings out the blue in her eyes and, all cleaned up, with straight black hair that falls almost to her waist, she barely looks her fifteen years.

"Hungry?" I ask.

She nods.

I join her at the table and pick at my stew. I'm still full after Bewley's, but Josie dives in and doesn't look up again until her bowl is empty and her plate is clear.

"Yummy," she says. "It tastes just like my ma's stew."

I hear the turn of a key in the lock and I know Christy is home. Josie looks as nervous as I feel.

"It's just my husband," I say. "You'll like him. He does some amazing card tricks."

"Hello, darling," Christy calls from the hall. "What's for dinner? You wouldn't believe the day I've had. Two sets of twins. Two. I could eat a horse."

The ajar kitchen door swings wider and Christy's head cocks to the side when he spots Josie at the table.

"Oh, hello," he says, ever the perfect gentleman. "And who do we have here?"

"This is my cousin. Josie."

The lie makes my throat feel funny, like it might close over, and my palms are sweating.

"Josie. Josie," Christy says, racking his brain. "Can't say I recall you mentioning a Josie before, sorry, darling."

"We haven't been that close, really. A bit of an age gap. But Josie is here in town and we're getting reacquainted. Aren't we, coz?"

Josie smiles shyly, and she doesn't chance words.

"Well, aren't you a pretty young lady," Christy says. Josie's face scrunches when she hears the compliment and I've a horrible feeling her father's friend may have told her similar. Christy makes her nervous.

"Why don't you go upstairs and freshen up before dinner?" I suggest, desperate to get him out of the kitchen.

Christy examines Josie with his eyes narrowed and she sits as straight as a poker. "Related on your mother's side of the family," he says.

"Mm-hmm."

He claps his hands as if he's delighted with his detective work. "I knew it. She's the spitting image of your ma."

I sigh, beyond relieved.

"Will I make you a drink while you're upstairs?" I say. "Whiskey, maybe? Or a gin and tonic. I got that new gin in town. The one with the red label that you like."

Christy walks over to me, kisses me on the cheek, and leans over my shoulder to fetch a slice of brown bread from the center of the table. "Music to my ears. Gin, darling."

"Gin. All right. Sure."

Christy straightens up and takes a bite of the bread. "Lovely to meet you,

Josie," he says. "I look forward to getting to know you better when I wash the hospital off me."

Josie doesn't make eye contact. She keeps her head down and doesn't lift it again until he leaves the room.

"It's all right," I say. "He's a nice man."

My own words sting. I hate myself for the lie. But Christy *is* a nice man. To everyone else. He will be kind and a good host to Josie and right now, that's all that matters.

Christy eats his stew in front of the television. Josie and I join him in the sitting room. Slowly she finds her voice, and after a while, we chat and laugh. Christy enjoys the banter and good fun of a teenager in the house, and for a split second I wonder if this is what family life might be like for us. But when Christy picks a stray bone out of his bowl and glares at me as if I did it on purpose to try to harm him, I'm painfully reminded that I am fantasizing.

Christy asks how long Josie will be staying and she is unambiguous when she says, "One night."

Her optimism concerns me and I quickly add on a couple of more nights for good measure. "And if she stayed longer, that would be fine, wouldn't it?"

"Of course. Of course," Christy says, without hesitation. "Family is welcome any time."

By 9:30 p.m., tiredness has crept into every part of Josie. I show her to her room, tuck her into bed as if she were my own daughter, and tell her she can stay as long as she likes. Weeks, months, however long she needs to. She can stay. And I dare to hope that she does.

CHAPTER 44

Maura

Five nights pass, and with each new day Josie grows more disheartened. I hear her in the bathroom every morning around the same time Christy leaves for work. She only ever emerges once he's gone, and her eyes are almost always red-rimmed and puffy. Bags hang like purple hammocks beneath them, and despite a warm bed, hot water, and good food, Josie has barely slept since she arrived.

"I don't understand," she says, as we sit at the kitchen table drinking tea. She loves tea. I've never met anyone able to put away as many cups before 10:00 a.m. Sometimes she has a biscuit, but her appetite is slowly fading.

"Mrs. Stitch said it was foolproof. She said I just had to drink it all. I did, I swear. I drank it even though it smelt like toilet cleaner and tasted even worse. I drank every drop. She said I just had to sit back and wait. Things would happen. The baby would shift. How long do you think I'll need to wait? Do you think it didn't work? Should I get more?"

Josie is spiraling. She spills tea on her hand. It's hot and leaves an instant red ring on her flesh but she doesn't flinch or notice.

"I'm sorry," I say, reaching for her hand to check how bad it is. "I know how much you wanted this to work. I know how much you want to go home."

Josie takes her hand back. Thankfully, the burn isn't too bad. I don't think it will blister.

"Should I get more? I have some more money. I think I have enough for another bottle. Or maybe Mrs. Stitch will give me a discount because it's a second try."

I doubt that's how Mrs. Stitch's business model works. But of course I keep my mouth shut. Nothing I can say now will make this any better for Josie. I push my chair back and it screeches against the floor tiles. I check the cupboard where we keep our medicines. The burn cream is buried at the back and I have to roll onto my tiptoes to reach it.

"Wow. That's like a pharmacy in there," Josie says.

I smile and return to the table with the tube of cream. "A perk of being married to a doctor. We have just about every medicine for everything in there."

"Have you something that could help me?"

We both know it's a rhetorical question. "No. I'm afraid not."

Josie shrugs. "Yeah. If only it was that simple."

After breakfast Josie and I walk into town. I have to fetch some shopping and I'm afraid to leave her alone in case she wanders back to Mrs. Stitch, seeking more poison. I hope some fresh air might pick her up, but her problems are much too great for a sunny day to fix. She trails behind me as we visit the greengrocer and the butcher.

"Afternoon, Maura," Dan says when we step inside McCarthy's.

"Hello," I say.

"Be with you in a minute."

Dan finishes serving a nun who seems to set him on edge, and once she leaves, he turns his attention to me.

"That was Sister Sloan. The principal in Marie and Elizabeth's school. God, that woman has a face that would stop a clock. My poor girls."

"Well, I bet your lamb chops can keep her sweet," I say.

"Hope so."

"Got any lambs' hearts or a bit of liver?"

"Sure thing."

Dan hums a tune while he tips my meat onto the scales; then he places it on top of the counter.

"You must be Josie," he says, catching her eye for the first time. "I've heard lots about you. It's a pleasure to meet you."

Josie takes a step back, instantly skittish.

"I'm Bernie's husband," he says. "Dan McCarthy."

"Is it time to go?" Josie asks me, turning her back toward Dan. Her voice is jumpy, as if the ground beneath her is unsteady.

"Yes. Yes. It's time."

I take the bag of meat and Dan mouths a silent "Sorry."

I smile. "Thanks, Dan. See you next week."

We bump into Bernie outside as she returns from school pickup with an exhausted little girl on each side of her pram. She opens the door of her flat as soon as she spots us and tells the girls to hurry upstairs, that there is a surprise waiting for them in the sitting room.

The children race up the steps without a moment's hesitation.

"Hello again," Bernie says.

Josie's face lights up.

"It's so lovely to see you. How are you?"

"It didn't work," Josie says.

"Oh."

Bernie looks at me as if I should have the answer, but I don't know what to say.

"What do we do now?" Bernie says.

"I'm not sure there's much we *can* do. Give it more time, I suppose," I say.

Josie's face fills with sadness. Bernie hugs her. "Don't worry. Sometimes these things just take time."

"I want to go home," Josie says. "I just want to go home."

There's a sudden commotion upstairs and Bernie's girls are laughing and screaming. They come racing down the concrete steps, brimming with joy, and the contrast in mood is almost unbearable.

"A telly, Ma," Marie says, flinging her arms wide to wrap them around her mother. "We really got a telly."

"A telly, a telly, a telly," Elizabeth chirps, fighting her sister for space in her mother's arms.

"It was your da's idea. He's been working so hard. Why don't you go and thank him?"

Marie and Elizabeth disappear into the butcher's shop and there is more laughing and screeches of excitement.

"You have three children," Josie says.

Bernie nods. "I do."

"No more?"

"No more."

"Why not?"

Bernie makes a face. "Erm. I'm blessed with the ones I've got."

"How do you stop it, though? Do you not like your husband?"

It's obvious from the look on Bernie's face that she doesn't know what to say. A French letter could likely have prevented all of Josie's heartache, but what rapist was going to use one, even if he could get his hands on it?

"Don't lose hope, eh?" Bernie says, hugging Josie once more. "Another few days might make all the difference."

Josie sighs. We say our goodbyes and leave the city center behind. Back at the house I offer to make tea and biscuits, but Josie refuses.

"Are you sure? You love tea."

"No, thank you. I'm tired. Is it all right to go for a lie-down?"

It's not yet evening. A girl her age should be full of life and vitality, not exhausted and ready for bed. But I understand. "Of course. It's your bed to take to whenever you choose."

Josie takes herself upstairs and I set about cleaning the house. I work up quite a sweat. Before I hop into the bath, I creak the door of Josie's room open to check on her. She's sleeping, and it's the most peaceful I've seen her look since I've known her.

I wash quickly, hyperaware that I need to get Christy's dinner on soon. I make a fish pie and the smell wafts through the house. Christy arrives home and I serve his dinner within twenty minutes as always.

"Where's Josie?" he asks, not long after we sit to the table.

"Sleeping," I say, spooning some delicious pie into my mouth.

"Sleeping through dinner?" I can see the flash of temper in his eyes.

"She was exhausted. I don't think she's been sleeping all too well—a bit homesick, maybe."

"What happened to staying just one night?" he says.

"Do you mind?" I say. "I quite like the company."

"If she finds her manners and joins her hosts for dinner, then no, I don't mind."

"I'll call her," I say, hating that I have to.

"You do that."

I spot the burn cream on the shelf and open the press to put it away before Christy scolds me for the mess. I gasp when I notice the cupboard is barer than before. Several small brown bottles of pills are missing. I'm not sure which ones, but enough to set my heart racing.

Without another word I charge upstairs. I don't bother to knock and I barge into Josie's room. I freeze in the doorway, hating my eyes for what they see. Josie is lying on the bed. Still. Fragile. Full of youth. Her beautiful face is white like marble. The color is gone from her lips and her arm dangles over the side of the bed as if it's hardly attached to her body at all. Her powder blue eyes are wedged open. I hold my breath and pray for her to blink, but she doesn't flinch. The pill bottles are scattered around the floor. Empty. My scream echoes around me, coming back to hit me like a slap across the face.

"Josie. Oh Jesus, Josie, what have you done?"

I hurry toward her. I drop onto the floor, kneeling, and scoop her small body into my arms. Christy's feet pound up the stairs and he comes to a sudden stop in the doorway behind me.

"Out of the way, out of the way," he says.

His urgency gives me hope. I scarper aside and he stands over her, placing one hand over the other and pressing down on her chest.

"What did she take?"

He's shouting and demanding an answer, but I cannot form words.

"Maura. Listen to me." His voice is breathy and matches the rhythm of his forceful pumping on her chest. "What. Did. She. Take?"

"You're hurting her," I sob. "You're hurting her."

"What did she take?"

There's a fog in my head. My thoughts are hard to see, but I manage something about paracetamol and sleeping tablets.

"Oh Christ," he says. "Oh Christ."

"Should I call an ambulance? The Clancys next door have a phone," I say.

I pick myself up and I'm racing toward the door without waiting for Christy's answer when he calls out to me.

"It's too late," he says. "She's gone."

My knees buckle and I hit the floor.

"She was just fifteen," I cry. "Fifteen. She'd barely begun to live at all."

Christy picks me up and cradles me in his arms.

"I'm sorry, darling," he says. "I know how badly you wanted to build a relationship with her. And your mother. My God, your poor mother. This will break her heart."

I bury my face in his crisp blue shirt. The one Josie had ironed for me this morning.

"Why did she do it? What was troubling her so?" Christy says.

I can feel his deep emotion. It sits in his chest and comes out as heavy, tearless sighs. He, like me, had dared to grow fond of her. If only she had known. *Why didn't I tell her? Why didn't I make sure she knew how much I wanted her to stay?* Forever, if she needed to. She could have been our daughter. We would have loved her like a daughter. And the baby too. I didn't tell her, because I knew that wasn't what she wanted to hear. She was a child, and every child wants to go home.

"Oh, Josie," I cry. "Oh, Josie. Oh, Josie."

I've never known pain like it before. Not when Christy has hit me or when I lost my unborn babies. This pain is great. I think I might die trying to bear it.

After a long time, Christy lets me go and walks toward the door.

"Where are you going?"

"To the Clancys' house. I need to use their phone."

"But you said it's too late."

Christy's voice breaks when he says, "I need to call the police. They'll have questions."

I watch him leave and when he's gone, I drag myself to the bed once more and hold Josie in my arms. Christy will undoubtedly unravel all my lies. Once the police become involved, he will learn that Josie is not my cousin and he will know that I deceived him. I should be scared. I know what's coming, but I am not frightened. There is no room for anything inside me now except sadness. A wound deeper than Christy's hands could ever inflict.

CHAPTER 45

2023

Saoirse

"I can still see her face when I close my eyes. Her skin was like porcelain and her lips like rubies," Maura says. Her eyes are wet.

"She sounds beautiful," I say. My own vision is blurred.

"Unfortunately, she was. And ultimately it cost her her life, through no fault of her own."

"Did her parents care? In the end, I mean. They treated her so wrongly. Were they at least sad when she died?"

"Her mother wore black for the rest of her life," Maura says, and I surmise that she got to know Josie's mother after the tragedy. "Although her life wasn't long after. Just three years. A heart attack, they said. But everyone knew the grief and the guilt killed her."

"If only she'd stood up to her husband. She clearly never wanted Josie to leave home."

"No." Maura sighs. "I don't suppose she did. But it wasn't easy for her to stand up to him then."

"I know. I know. But for the sake of her child."

"I mean no disrespect, but I'm afraid you don't know. Even if she had put her foot down, it would have, most likely, played out in the same way, regardless," Maura says, turning to look out the window.

"Some people shouldn't have kids," I say.

"You're right. They should not."

At Newry a slightly frantic woman boards the train. She's in her late fifties, maybe early sixties, I think, with salt-and-pepper hair. She wears colorful rimmed glasses that remind me of Miles's and her rain mac is almost identical in style and color to Maura's.

"There you are!" she says, hurrying down the aisle and relaxing slightly when she stops next to Maura and me. "You're not answering your phone. Leonardo and I were worried. We thought you might have missed the train or had a fall or something."

She looks at Maura with concern and then she drops her eyes to the scrapbook and the small, empty bottle of wine on the table and she begins to smile. "But I can see you're okay. Enjoying yourself, it seems. Who have you cornered this year, eh?"

The lady's gaze shifts to me, and I'm not sure if I should introduce myself or not. Thankfully, Maura speaks before I overthink it.

"I'm sorry, love. I didn't mean to worry you. My phone is in my bag and half the time I don't hear the blasted thing."

"It's okay. I'm just glad you're okay. Leonardo has the car here at the station, so if you want to hop off we can travel the rest of the way with him. It'll be much faster."

"Oh no." Maura sounds horrified. "I'm not going anywhere. I took this train all the way to Belfast fifty-two years ago, and I'm taking it all the way to Belfast today."

The woman puffs out, defeated. "Okay," she says, with a smile. "I'll tell him." She pulls out her phone and there's a quick conversation to decide they'll meet in Belfast. Then she slips into a seat at the opposite side of the table.

"Are you sure you're all right sitting there? Those seats travel backward.

Won't that make you feel sick?" Maura asks. "It always made you sick when you were younger."

"I'm okay, Aunty Maura. It's just a couple of stations."

I feel the pang of disappointment that soon it will be time we all get off.

"So, is the wine plonk, or am I safe getting a glass?" the lady says.

"It's lovely train wine," Maura says, and I decide that I will call it "train wine" forevermore—even when I'm on a plane or a boat and so on.

The train pulls out of the station and the woman orders a small bottle of wine from the confectionery cart. I buy a KitKat and Maura says she's fine for now.

"This is Marie Russo," Maura says, smiling across the table at the woman.

"Hello," I say, feeling very much like I'm intruding on something personal, and I wonder if I should offer to switch seats.

"Marie is married to a lovely Italian man, Leonardo Russo. But she was a McCarthy before that."

"Oh. Wow. *That* Marie," I say, and I've sudden butterflies in my stomach as if I'm face-to-face with a celebrity.

"I was telling lovely Saoirse all about your ma," Maura says.

Marie blushes and Maura spins the scrapbook around to share it with her. As she does, a piece of paper falls out. Marie picks it up and emotion sweeps over her. The resemblance to a young Bernie in the photograph takes shape instantly. They share a nose and the dimple in their chin. I think Marie might be taller, but that's just a guess.

"I forgot Ma kept this," Marie says, some tears welling in the corners of her eyes.

"Your mother was so proud of your art," Maura says.

"Oh, I'm not sure you could call this art." Marie starts to chuckle and then tilts the paper toward me so I can see a page full of colorful scribbles. "But she definitely encouraged us to enjoy expressing ourselves and following our dreams. I think that's why this scrapbook was so important to her. It was her little piece of self-expression."

"Come now, you and I both know your mother had no trouble speaking her mind. It was keeping her words *in* that she struggled with."

Marie laughs. "That was Ma. Gosh, I miss her."

"Me too," Maura says. "Me too."

There's a moment when both women glance out the window as if they will find Bernie somewhere in the distance, waving back at them from the rolling hills and green fields.

Marie clears her throat and says, "What part of the story are you at?"

Maura's face lights up, and I can tell how eager she is to dive back in. She flicks through the pages of the scrapbook and points to a photograph of a door with a lion's head knocker.

"Mrs. Stitch's place," Marie says knowingly.

"I've just been telling Saoirse about Josie's passing."

"I remember," Marie says. "Ma was cut up for weeks after the funeral. You know, she was convinced she didn't do enough to help her."

"We did our best," Maura says. "It was too late for Josie. But for others . . ."

Marie pours her wine and sighs. "You and Ma did more than your best. But, Saoirse, wait for this next part."

"Is it what the police said?" I guess. "The autopsy would show she was pregnant, wouldn't it?"

"Unfortunately, the police didn't have much to say about any of it," Maura says. "As far as they were concerned, it was suicide. Plain and simple. Josie wasn't the first young girl to take her life in a situation like that."

"Did Mrs. Stitch get in trouble?"

"Hmm," Maura says, pausing for thought. "I think Mrs. Stitch—or Bernadette Brighton, as I would later come to know her—certainly knew how to squeeze a few bob out of a desperate girl or woman. But I don't blame her, not entirely. If contraception had been available she'd have had few, if any, customers. She wasn't the bad guy. But she certainly wasn't a good guy either."

"I can't believe the police didn't do anything. Did they arrest that man? Josie's father's friend?"

Maura shakes her head. "I doubt they ever knew about him."

"Jesus, he got away with it and no one said anything. That's so messed up, isn't it?"

"Actually, people had a lot to say."

"Good. That's good," I say, relieved to hear it. "At least someone shed some light on how shit this was."

"Ah, not quite. Josie was a young woman who took her own life. It was a sin. Families were ashamed. Communities gossiped. It was a dark time."

"But she didn't do anything wrong. It was all that dirty old man's fault. He was the sinner. He was a goddamn criminal."

Maura is quiet. She's thinking of a girl forever fifteen. A young woman who died long before I was born, and yet I feel an intense connection with her—with all the daughters of Ireland lying under the ground because they had no hope and no help.

"Change was on its way," Maura says, cutting into my thoughts. "But let's get another glass of wine, and we'll get to that."

CHAPTER 46

1970

Bernie

I'm in a deep sleep when the banging starts. Alice was cutting back teeth all week. Her cheeks were hot and fiery and she cried with a frustration to match. I've been through the teething terrors with the other two, but neither of my older girls had a temper quite like Alice's. I rubbed some whiskey on her gums and said two Hail Marys that my daughter would sleep through the night. So when the clattering starts, I find it hard to rouse. I drag myself out of bed and, disoriented, make my way toward my daughter. Alice is sleeping soundly. The disturbance is coming from somewhere else. Outside. Goose bumps line my arms and I hurry back to the bed to wake Dan.

"Dan. Dan," I call, shaking his shoulder. "Wake up."

"What? What is it?" Dan says, his voice laced with sleep.

"Something's going on. Someone's outside. They're trying to bang the door down."

Dan sits up, instantly wide awake. He checks the bedside alarm clock. "It's almost midnight."

"I know."

The banging continues. The door sounds as if it might rattle off its hinges.

"Stay here. Watch the girls," Dan says.

He slips on his dressing gown and slippers.

"Be careful," I call after him.

Voices fill the stairwell. And someone is crying, I think. A woman. Maura. I recognize her voice. I leap out of bed, close the bedroom door behind me, and hurry into the kitchen. I come to a sudden stop and my hands press against my cheeks. Maura looks as if she's seen a ghost. Or as if she is one.

"Josie's gone," she says, trembling.

"Gone where? Home?"

Maura doesn't reply. Dan helps her to sit down and I hurry over to put the kettle on. I make three cups of milky tea and Dan is rubbing Maura's back and encouraging her to take some deep breaths when I place a cup in front of each of us and sit down. Dan and I reach for ours, but Maura seems frozen.

"Did it happen?" I say, warming my hands around my cup. "Did Mrs. Stitch's drink work? Was it . . . er . . . erm . . . able to resolve Josie's troubles?"

"No." Maura swallows. "It didn't work."

"Oh."

"She's dead, Bernie. She died."

I gasp, and yet it feels as if no air is making its way inside me.

"She took a whole bunch of pills from the medicine cabinet in the kitchen, I'm not even sure what, and she died."

Tears trickle down my cheeks.

"It's all my fault," Maura says. "If I'd just left her be, she'd still be alive."

"You tried to help. You tried to do your best. Josie's father and that bastard he calls a friend are to blame. No one else."

"She was only fifteen," Maura says. "Still a child herself."

"I know. I know."

"What did the guards say?" Dan asks.

Maura dries her eyes with the sleeve of her cardigan. Her face is red and blotchy and she's clearly been crying for hours.

"Not much. They said things like this happen more often than you would believe. They said runaways are trouble."

"Runaways?" I say.

"They said runaways, especially young girls, break into houses looking for a bed for the night, or some pills for a headache or a cold."

"Surely, they must know—"

Maura shakes her head. "They asked me how I knew her, and when I couldn't answer, Christy spoke for me."

My gut clenches and I push the tea away from me. "Dr. Davenport knows she's not your cousin?"

"He knows. He took one look at me and he knew. He told the guards that we didn't know who she was. Just some kid who helped herself to our spare room and our medicine cabinet."

"And they believed him?"

"Yes."

I realize I don't even know the child's last name. It's all so unnecessary and so wrong that I want to punch something. Dr. Davenport. And Josie's father. And that sick, disgusting creature who stole Josie's innocence.

"What happens now?" I say.

Maura sighs. "I'm not sure. Christy is gone to the station to make a statement. And I came here."

"But if he knows she's not your cousin . . ." I say, my breath catching. "Maura, you can't go home."

Maura's eyes glisten. I search them for fear, but it's not there. All I see is sadness. Unequivocal, all-consuming sadness.

"Dan, say something," I plead.

I'm desperate for my husband to do something to encourage her to stay here with us where we can keep her safe. But Dan is pensive and lost.

"I'll walk you home, Maura," he finally says.

"Jesus, Dan, no. She can't go."

"Thank you," Maura says, standing up.

"Maura. No. Stop. Wait."

Maura walks behind me and places her hands on my shoulders. "I'm all right. I'll be all right."

"But Dr. Davenport—"

"Christy is the most respected man in the community," Maura says, cutting me off. "Everyone knows he's a wonderful man."

"But he's not," I say.

"It doesn't matter. Everyone *knows* he is. It doesn't matter that what they are so certain they know is wrong."

I watch my husband escort my best friend toward the door. I listen as their voices carry when they descend the concrete staircase and walk out onto the street below. I cry. I wrap my arms around myself and let everything inside spill. I cry for a fifteen-year-old girl. I cry for my friend. And I cry for myself, so full of rage at a world in which little matters save for the lives of our husbands, our fathers, our brothers, and our sons.

CHAPTER 47

Maura

I spend one week and two days in hospital. The doctors say I am very lucky to be alive.

"You wouldn't believe how common accidents in the home are," a doctor said, introducing himself as I drifted in and out of consciousness on my first day there.

He has cared for me in the week that's followed but he has not repeated his name. I've taken to thinking of him as Dr. Bow Tie. Today's bow tie is blue with white polka dots. Yesterday's was mustard, and the day before was green. My eyes were too badly swollen to observe the colors before that.

"If only you knew the amount of women I've had slip on a wet floor and break three or four bones. It's odd, really. When a man slips, he breaks a bone. Two at most. But when a woman slips, my golly, it's almost as if that wet floor took her on in a boxing match. If you know what I'm saying."

I allow my eyes to meet his. He's young. Not long finished college, I'd guess. He's tall and thin and his head is slightly too large for his body. When he speaks, it feels as if he is wrapping me in cotton wool.

"If there is anything, anything at all you want to tell me about your . . . erm . . . your fall, I'm here to listen."

I swallow. Suddenly the cotton wool wrapping is crushing me.

"You can trust me. I promise."

I eye him skeptically. Beyond his kind eyes and concerned smile, he is Christy's colleague. And when the truth is on the tip of my tongue, I remind myself of that.

"I can only imagine how hard it is to fall clumsily into a clenched fist when you're late home of an evening. Or what it's like to slip down the stairs because dinner was burnt."

I open my mouth, and Dr. Bow Tie leans closer to my bed, ready to listen. "May I have some water, please?"

He sighs and I can sense his disappointment. "Of course. I'll ask one of the nurses to bring you in a jug of water now."

He pulls the curtain around my bed open and walks away. The heels of his shoes click across the floor and as he reaches the ward door, he turns around.

"I really hope your floors become less slippery soon," he says. "But if they don't . . . or if they become even more slippery, you come back here and ask for me, all right?"

I nod. And I know, without doubt, that if I ever return and ask for the kind and caring Dr. Bow Tie, the nurses would know who I mean.

My time in hospital is a master class in routine. At 6:00 a.m. I am woken by the clatter of cups and the rattle of trays as breakfast is prepared. At 8:00 a.m. my blood pressure is checked and something that burns is injected into my arm. Then it's breakfast. Chitchat with the other patients. Blood pressure. Lunch. Chitchat with the other patients. Dinner. Tea. Lights out. Repeat. The days are long and tiring and I am grateful for every smiling face that walks through the door to visit me.

Ma and Da are first. Ma hugs and kisses me, and Da scolds me for putting the stress of it all on my mother's shoulders.

"She hasn't slept a wink, your ma, so she hasn't," Da says with his hands on his hips and his eyebrows pinched. "How could you be so clumsy, huh?

Broken ribs and a broken leg. Good Lord, Maura. And poor Christy. You've had him climbing the walls with worry."

We talk for some time, and they leave when I tell them I love them and promise to be more careful in the future.

Bernie and Dan stop by too, of course. They have to take it in turns to sit by my bedside because the hospital won't let Marie, Elizabeth, and Alice in.

"No children on the wards," the Sister barks.

"No children on the wards," Bernie mimics as soon as she is out of earshot.

Bernie hangs homemade *Get Well Soon* cards over the metal headboard of my bed. I can tell just by looking at them which card has lovingly been crafted by each child. Alice's card makes me laugh. The artwork consists of a giant green scribble in a continuous circular pattern. Laughing hurts, but I can't help it. Bernie tells me how much the children miss me, and I stop laughing. I miss them too.

Dan is oddly quiet, and although I reassure him countless times that, had he not walked me home that night, my "accident" would have been a lot worse, I suspect he's carrying some degree of guilt.

"Sort me out with a couple of free lamb chops when I get out of here and all will be right again," I say.

"Sure thing." He smiles and tells me he'll leave Bernie to do the visiting from now on.

Geraldine stops by when she gets word.

She eyes me knowingly and says, "Jesus, Maura. I don't give a damn if he *is* a doctor or the president of the country, he needs to learn to keep his damn hands off you."

I place my fingers over my lip and shush her.

"I'll say this and no more," she says. "Something has to change. And soon. I'm worried. This isn't the first time you've landed in a hospital bed. What if next time it's a timber box six feet under?"

I hold my head high but my body feels like it weighs a ton. I'd be lying if I said the thought hadn't crossed my mind.

Geraldine brings the *News of the World*, which I keep firmly hidden under my bedsheets and only read in the bathroom at night after the Sister has done her rounds. When Geraldine asks if there's anything she can do or get for me, she seems surprised when I request a pair of trousers to wear home when I'm discharged.

"I think I'm going to start wearing trousers all the time from now on," I say.

"All right. We've some lovely cords in stock, and rumor has it denim is coming in soon. I can't wait."

"Denim sounds good. Like you said, something has to change."

Geraldine's excitement wanes. "But I didn't mean change your wardrobe."

"I know. But I have to start somewhere. Christy hates trousers on women."

Geraldine's face lights up and she says, "Good for you, Maura. Bloody good for you."

I have plenty of other visitors too. My brothers. My neighbors. Father Walsh. Christy's family keep away and I am grateful for the small mercy. But of all my visitors, I'm most grateful for a particular woman who comes and sits on the end of my bed.

It's not long after lunch one day when she appears at the doors of the ward. She's uncertain about her whereabouts until a nurse appears beside her and points toward my bed. I sit to attention. The woman is neither old nor young. Short nor tall. Heavy nor slim. She's wearing a black dress with a matching headscarf and I don't think I've ever seen a more unremarkable woman in my life. And yet, there is something that draws me to her. A shine in her eyes, or her expression. I can't quite put my finger on it.

She shuffles into the ward, seeming nervous or unsure, and comes to a stop at the end of my bed. She opens her mouth but closes it when no sound comes out. She tries again but the same happens. She's about to repeat for a third time when I realize what it is about her that I'm drawn to. She looks just like her.

"You're Josie's mother," I say.

The woman bends in the middle and a sob escapes. For a moment I'm not sure she's going to be able to straighten back up. But, slowly, she gathers herself.

"Sit. Sit. Please," I say, pointing to the end of my bed.

She lowers herself onto the edge and sits with her knees together and her hands on top. I notice the rosary beads and prayer book peeking out of her pocket.

"I'm Regina Battersby," she says, choking on her words.

"I'm so sorry for your loss."

"I'm here to apologize. They tell me she snuck into your home, but that doesn't sound like my Josie."

There's so much heartbreak etched into Mrs. Battersby's face that it's hard to look at. But I meet her gaze regardless.

"Josie did not sneak into my home," I say. "It's all a little complicated, but she was a very welcome guest."

We talk for a long time. She tells me about Josie's love of Irish dancing. Josie won several feises as a child and Mrs. Battersby still has all the medals. She polished some and placed them in the coffin.

"She got her dancing feet from her da. He was so proud. But that all changed."

"I'm sorry," I say again, and I wish there were better words.

"I was going to pretend the baby was mine. At forty-five I'm a little old, I know, but it happens. People would have believed it. But Tom wouldn't hear of it. Said we'd have no bastard baby in our house."

I look at the woman whose heart is so clearly shattered and I feel her anger. I share it.

"You must think, I'm the worst mother in the world."

"I don't."

"Do you have children?"

She looks at the colorful cards hanging behind me and draws her own conclusion.

"I hope they're all boys," she says. "If Josie was a boy she'd still be here now. She'd still be alive. I miss her so much."

"She was a lovely girl."

"You know, I was sending her to live with my sister in Ohio. She has a farm and Josie loves animals. Tom convinced me she'd be happy there and I was stupid enough to believe him. But Josie was never going to be happy in America, away from her friends and family. So she ran. And I don't blame her. I just wish I would have run with her. I wish I had stuck by her. I wish she knew how much I love her. I wish it was different, that it could be different."

I choke back tears. "I do too."

"Thank you for helping my Josie," she says, standing up.

My tears fall. "It wasn't enough. I couldn't do enough."

"But you tried. You were brave. I was not. And I'll have to go to my grave with that knowledge. I wasn't brave enough to save my own daughter. What kind of mother am I?"

I know there is nothing more I can say. I cannot heal the Josie-shaped hole in Mrs. Battersby's heart. Nothing and no one ever can. Later, when I'm all cried out, I waddle toward the bathroom with the *News of the World* hidden under my nightdress. I'm flicking through the pages when a small piece of paper flies out. It's a struggle to bend and pick it up, and it's even harder to straighten back up. But it's worth the effort when I find a handwritten note.

Maura,

If you really want change, come to Bewley's on Grafton Street next Wednesday at 4:00 p.m.
Ask for Nuala.

Your loving friend,
Ger x

I have no idea what Geraldine's cryptic note means. But I know I'll be there. I think I have to be.

CHAPTER 48

Maura

It's Wednesday before the doctors say I can go home. In truth, Dr. Bow Tie isn't best pleased.

"I'd really like to keep you here a little longer," he said when I pressed the issue of discharge. "Just until you're stronger. Steadier on your feet."

I think Dr. Bow Tie would keep me here until my bones are fully healed and I can walk freely again. Or run, if I need to.

Christy arrives not long after lunch. He's wearing casual gray trousers and a navy jumper that his mother hand-knitted for his birthday. I'm disappointed to find him out of a suit, because I know it means he's taken the entire day off work and he'll want to spend time together.

"Oh, darling, I'm so glad you're coming home." He leans in to kiss my cheek and my skin crawls.

He places a ginormous bouquet of red roses on the bedside locker. It's the third bouquet of roses he's brought this week. He brought jewelry and chocolates and perfume, too. The woman in the bed opposite told me countless times that she wished her husband was more like mine. I told her to be careful what she wished for.

Today, I'm sitting on the edge of my hospital bed, swinging my legs back and forth as if it doesn't hurt. Dr. Bow Tie says I'll be in the cast for another five weeks.

"You won't even know the pins are there," he says, writing something on a chart. "When everything heals up, your knee will feel as good as new."

"As good as new," Christy echoes. "See, darling, it's not so bad."

Dr. Bow Tie's eyes narrow and he looks as if he wants to snap Christy's leg with a kick. I let myself imagine it and a wry smile creeps across my face.

"Do you like my trousers?" I ask.

Christy looks at my blue denim trousers and his face sours. The wide leg does a decent job of covering my cast. My foot peeks out below the flared bottom and Dr. Bow Tie suggests I should wear a sock if I get cold.

"They're very nice," Christy says with a stiff jaw. "I didn't know you had trousers."

"They're new."

"Did a little shopping while you were in here, did you?" Christy jibes, and looks over his shoulder, waiting for Dr. Bow Tie to enjoy the joke at my expense.

But the doctor doesn't laugh. Christy has the good grace to show embarrassment and quickly says, "We'd better hurry. The parking meter runs out soon."

Dr. Bow Tie clicks his pen and drops it into his white coat pocket.

"Maura will be in pain for quite some time," he says. "It was a very nasty break."

"I am aware of the severity of a femur fracture, Doctor. Thank you," Christy says, red-faced.

"Indeed."

Christy slides two fingers under the collar of his jumper and tugs it away from his neck. "Right. We'd better hurry. As I said, the parking meter runs out soon. Thank you, Doctor."

Christy extends his hand, and Dr. Bow Tie exhales audibly before he shakes it.

"Do take care of yourself, Maura. Please."

I nod. If I chance words I might start to cry.

Christy picks up my bag and the bouquet of roses and walks toward the door. I slip my hands into my crutches with the doctor's help and follow my husband. Christy's pace is too fast but I don't ask him to slow as we leave the hospital behind. He throws my bag and the roses into the boot and opens the car door. He places a hand on my head.

"Get in."

His voice is gritty like hail scratching against the window and I'm afraid of him, just as I always am. It's difficult to navigate my way into the car seat and every movement hurts. My ribs ache. My leg aches. My heart aches. Christy loses patience. He snatches my crutches, throws them into the boot, and slams it shut. We leave the carpark and pull onto the main road before I find my voice. And when I do, it's a barely audible whisper.

"Can you drop me off on Grafton Street, please?"

"Excuse me?"

"Grafton Street. Can you let me out there?"

Christy stops at a red light. He lets go of the wheel and shifts in his seat to face me. He snorts. "You can't be serious."

"I am."

"You can hardly walk."

"I can manage with my crutches."

"And what's on Grafton Street?"

"Geraldine. You remember Ger, don't you?" My voice begins to quiver as it does every time his eyes burn this intensely into me.

"The girl from Switzers. What about her?" He folds his arms.

"It's her birthday."

"And?"

"And I have to show my face." My insides are shaking and I wonder if he can tell how frightened I am. "Only for an hour or two. It's her twenty-first. She's a woman now."

The light changes. Christy places his hands on the wheel and we start moving again. I regret eating breakfast now as cornflakes threaten to come back up.

"She's not your cousin, too, is she?" he says with a chuckle.

I hate him. I can't think about anything except how much I despise the man I'm married to.

"I have to go. If I don't, people will ask questions."

Christy slows until we're scarcely crawling forward. It's supposed to intimidate me and it works. It's not long before a car behind us honks their horn.

"Christy, please. People will expect me to be there."

"People can mind their business."

"I am going. I want to," I say, as defiance creeps past my fear.

Christy jams on the brakes. The car behind honks again and swerves around us.

"We are going home," Christy says, as calmly as if he is announcing the sky is blue. But his eyes are cloudy, like a storm ready to unleash rain.

I curl my fingers around the door handle. Christy shakes his head. Determined and wholly terrified, I open the door. A woman pushing a pram on the footpath almost walks into the door and I apologize.

"Be more careful," she scolds.

Christy waits for her to pass before he reaches for my hair. He weaves his fingers through the inches at the back and tugs. My head jerks and fire encapsulates my bruised ribs.

"Let go," I say.

He does not.

"Let go, or I will scream."

"You wouldn't dare."

"I'll scream bloody murder, Christy, just watch me. I'll tell everyone what you do. What you've done."

"No one will believe you."

"They already believe me."

Christy's grip grows tighter. My neck cracks audibly and I yelp.

"What have you been telling people?"

"Nothing," I gulp, as my neck begins to burn from the strain. "I don't have to say anything. People just have to look at me to see what you've done."

He releases me. The sudden freedom is unexpected and possibly more terrifying than his tight grip, because I can't tell what comes next. He gets out, opens the boot, and appears on the path in front of me with my crutches. My heart races as he reaches for me, wrapping his arms lovingly around me and helping me out the door and onto my feet. He offers me one crutch and then the other, and he doesn't let me go until I'm steady.

"There you are now, darling," he says, kissing my cheek.

Two elderly ladies with shopping carts approach. There isn't enough room on the footpath for us all, so Christy steps onto the street, making room for them to pass by.

"Afternoon," he says. "Lovely day."

"Yes. Lovely," one of the ladies says.

"Long may the good weather last," the other adds.

They offer me a sympathetic smile as they walk on. Christy steps back onto the footpath, kisses me once more, and says loudly, "Enjoy the party, darling." Then he lowers his voice and adds, "I'll be waiting up."

He sits into the car and drives away. I can't move at first. But slowly I compose myself and find my bearings. I'm on the wrong side of town. I need to climb the steps of the Ha'penny Bridge and cross the Liffey to reach Bewley's. It's a walk I'd have undertaken effortlessly without a second thought last week, but today it's a mammoth task. I have no money for a taxi and although the city is full of people going about their business, I feel hopelessly alone. I think of Josie and how lonely she must have felt. A child sleeping on the city streets, with nowhere and no one to turn to. I make a promise to her that I will be strong enough for the both of us now. I carry her with me as I carefully place one foot in front of the other.

CHAPTER 49

Maura

What should be a fifteen-minute journey across town takes an hour, maybe more. It begins to rain as I reach Grafton Street. Umbrellas appear to open out of nowhere and the people under them pick up their pace as if they can outwalk the weather. I look up at the sky, grateful for the gentle drops that fall on my face and cool me. My clothes stick to my clammy skin and my palms are blistering from gripping my crutches. I'm disgusted by my grubby toes where my foot peeks out beneath my trousers. Brownish-black blood has dried in the creases of my big toe where I cracked it against a raised cobble-stone on the way.

Finally, Bewley's comes into view, with its stained-glass windows, green-and-cream-striped canopies, and window boxes of emerald-green shrubs. The mosaic tiles at the door are slippery, and a man much better kitted out for the weather in a long tan trench coat comes to help. He cups my elbow and guides me inside. He offers to carry a tray for me, but I tell him I'm meeting friends. And I hope so much that proves to be true.

I make my way toward the counter, and I'm about to ask for Nuala when I feel a hand on my shoulder.

"I knew you'd come," Geraldine says as I turn around. She throws her arms around me and hugs me tight. It hurts, but I don't say a word. "God, you look rough. When did you get out?" she asks, as if I've just broken free from a stint in prison. In many ways it feels as if I have.

"Earlier. Just today."

"I wasn't sure you'd come," she says.

I swallow. I was always coming. Although I'm not quite sure what I've come to.

"Come on," Ger says, placing her hand on the small of my back. "Let me introduce you to everyone."

Several square tables are pushed together to form one long table, and a group of women sit at each side. They look up at Ger and me as we approach, and I am more self-aware than ever.

"You must be Maura," one of the women says. She pushes her chair back and it squeaks against the tiles. She stands up. "I'm Nuala. Nuala Tyrone."

"Hello, Nuala, nice to meet you," I say, as if her name should mean more to me than it does.

Nuala pulls out the empty chair next to her, smiles with kind eyes and a mouth full of crooked teeth, and says, "Have a seat."

I walk around the long table and she takes my crutches and leans them against the wall behind us. I lower myself slowly and awkwardly into the slightly wobbly timber chair as all eyes are on me. There are ten, maybe eleven women at the table. Younger than me, older than me, but none particularly old or young. They sit with teacups and plates of pastries in front of them, and almost everyone has a notebook and a pen. The space next to me is empty until Ger sits down. She tears a page out of her notepad and passes me the pencil that I hadn't noticed tucked above her ear before now.

"Right, ladies, where were we?" Nuala says, and I can tell whatever this is, Nuala is clearly the ringleader.

"The marriage bar," a woman across the table says, before she bites into a scone. "It's got to go."

"Hear, hear," everyone cheers.

Nuala pokes her tongue between her teeth and concentrates as she writes in her notepad. "The. Marriage. Bar. Yes indeed, definitely. Bloody antiquated nonsense. Why should a woman have to become a housewife and quit her job just because she's married?"

"Hear, hear."

There's more cheering and some of the women slap their hands on the table with animated approval.

"Equal education opportunities," another woman, sitting near the end of the table, says. She has to raise her voice to be heard.

"Absolutely." Nuala writes again.

"And protection of the family home," someone else shouts. "My brother-in-law is a gambler. My sister can't sleep at night for worrying that he'll sell the house out from under her and the kids if things get bad enough."

"He wouldn't dare," Nuala says.

The woman stands. She's distressed and I can't tell if she wants to scream or cry. Or both. "He would 'n' all. Things are that bad. And there'd be nothing my sister could do if the mood takes him to up and sell their house. He'd be well within his rights, and she and the children would be out on their ears. She has four children under six."

"Christ," Nuala says, shaking her head before she reaches for her cup to sip some tea. "What is wrong with this country, eh? Well, it's about to change, ladies. We're going to see to that, aren't we? We'll knock on every politician's door. We'll march on every street corner. We won't stop until women's voices are heard. Enough is enough."

There's whooping and cheering and the other patrons of Bewley's stare toward us, rather unimpressed with our voracity and enthusiasm.

"Keep them coming, ladies, keep the ideas coming. Every single word is going in the manifesto. Let's see them keep us quiet then."

I lean toward Ger and whisper, "What is this? What is happening here?"

Ger's face lights up with a smile that would charm the birds from the trees. My question is redundant and we both know it. I know exactly what's happening. Ger has made space for me in the women's rights movement as if

I belong here. Fire burns in my belly. It's both terrifying and exhilarating and I've never felt anything like it before.

"Isn't it amazing?" Ger says. "Most of these women are journalists. Or they're connected to someone who works in radio or TV. Imagine that—they can write about women's problems and actually get it published. In the paper." Ger draws an invisible circle around the table, encapsulating us as a united group. Female warriors. Our weapons are pens and paper and our words are our ammunition. "Imagine old farts like Murph in the pub reading about equal pay for women or married women working. He'd probably choke on his pint. I'd pay good money to see that, if I'm honest."

I laugh. "Me too. But I'm not a journalist, Ger. I'm not sure I should be here."

"You're a woman, Maura. That's enough."

Geraldine stands up, and I catch the sleeve of her cardigan quickly. "Where are you going?" I say, horrified at the notion of her leaving me.

"I'm getting you a cup of tea and a bite to eat. This could be a long day and I don't want you ending up back in the hospital. We need you here."

I fidget nervously. I'm not sure what Geraldine expects from me. What value she's hoping I can bring to the group.

"It's all right, Maura. Them women don't bite."

I look at Nuala once more. She's tall and broad, with thick-rimmed glasses and long, curly hair that's graying at the temples. She carries herself with a confidence most women only dream of. I've no doubt she could bite if she needed to.

"Don't be afraid to speak up," Geraldine says. "I know you have ideas; share them. Be brave."

My stomach is knotted. "I'm not brave."

Geraldine squeezes my hand. "You're here, aren't you?"

"Yes. But I'm still not sure why."

Geraldine takes a deep breath. "You'll figure it out. It's why we're all here. We are women trying to figure out how to live in a man's world."

There's a coolness that whips around me when Geraldine leaves and I feel the eyes of strangers upon me.

"What happened to you?" the woman sitting directly opposite me asks. "You look as if you've been in the wars."

"I . . . eh . . ."

"Your husband?" she asks.

"Um . . ."

The woman's eyes sweep over me as if she's looking for something. The secrets of my marriage revealed on my clothes or in the contours of my face. I don't like her, I decide as I stare back, without blinking.

"Is that why you're here? To get back at your husband?" she asks.

"What? No. Ger invited me."

She snorts. "Ger invited you. You didn't bring a pen or paper. And you show up looking like that. What paper do you write for? I've never seen you before."

"I didn't know this was a press meeting." I glance around, trying to spy Geraldine in the queue gathered at the hot-food counter. My eyes settle on her back and I will her to turn around. She doesn't.

"I'm just a housewife," I say.

"It's not a tea party, love. We take this seriously."

"I . . . I . . . I'm taking this seriously."

"Oh, shut up, Sharon," Nuala says, taking off her glasses to rub her eyes. She slips them back on and shifts her gaze to me. "Don't mind her, Maura. She's just jealous of your perfect hair and fancy clothes. But I'm willing to bet a housewife with a rich husband has her fair share of problems, am I right?"

"Yes," I blurt nervously. "Big ones."

Sharon's eyes burn into me but she's not glaring at me to shut my mouth—she's waiting to hear what I have to say. I know I better make it good.

"I used to work with Ger. In Switzers."

"Lovely," Nuala says.

"Yes. I loved it there. But then I got married and—"

"And that was that," Nuala finishes for me.

I nod. "I'm a housewife now. I should be at home minding the baby. Or babies, I suppose. But that's the problem, actually. I don't want a baby. I did. At first. But not anymore."

"Why did you get married if you don't want children?" Sharon asks, making a face.

Nuala shoots her a look that would hush most people.

"What?" Sharon says, jamming her hands on her hips. "I'm curious. Most housewives want at least a few babies. What else is there to do with your time?"

"That's my business," I say, and I'm glad my knees are hidden under the table where Sharon can't see them shaking. "It's my body. It should be my choice."

My words cut through the air as if I've thrown a samurai sword. Mouths open and eyes widen. Any of the women who hadn't paid attention to me before now suddenly look my way. For a moment I want to rewind. I want to take my words back.

Sharon lights up a cigarette, takes a drag, and puffs a small tuft of smoke out.

"But you're a married woman," she says. "If your husband wants children—"

"Are you joking?" Nuala cuts her off. "If a wife says no and he still goes for it anyway, then it's bloody rape, isn't it?"

"It's not rape if they're married. That's just the way it is."

I'm filled with anger. It bubbles inside me like water boiling on the stove. It's about ready to boil over and I don't know where to put it.

"Look." Sharon turns toward me with round, sympathetic eyes. "It was good of you to come along today, but I think you've missed the point here. We're serious about change and women's rights. We don't have time for marital tiffs."

I wonder if Sharon has ever had a man force himself on top of her. I wonder if she's ever felt his hot skin against her back when her eyes sting with tiredness. Or woken to his cigar breath on her neck. Had a man whisper *I love you* after he has hurt her and will hurt her again. Carried a baby, lost a baby, and known that she was not strong enough to go through it all again but she had no choice. It is all in your husband's control. Your life, your worth, your body. Sharon may write stories for a living, but her own life story must be blank, because were it not, she would be consumed with the knowledge that owning her own body is her greatest right.

Arguing erupts. It's heated and passionate. Voices are raised, language is foul, and hands are banged against tables. I watch as the aftermath of my words ripples across the generations of women. The tide catches me and tries to pull me under, but I hold my head high and refuse to go down with it.

"Do you have friends like you?" Nuala asks, raising her voice so I can hear her above the shouting. "Do you know more housewives who don't want babies? Or any more babies?"

I think of Bernie and her beautiful girls. I think of the little boy she lost and how Dan took himself off to the spare room and it almost broke their marriage. And I nod.

"Look at us," Nuala says, pointing around the table. "We're the Irish Women's Liberation Movement—desperate for change, determined for change. And yet, we're all so conditioned by the rules and regulations that surround us that we've unknowingly allowed them to shape us. The lines of acceptable change are blurred. We might be journalists prepared to pen our woes and print them, but we need women like you, Maura. We need the ordinary housewives of Ireland to stand alongside us. We need every woman in Ireland to fight."

Geraldine returns with a tray. On top are two fresh cups of tea and two Madeira buns with icing.

"Jesus, what did I miss?"

"Um . . . I think I caused this."

Geraldine sets the cups and buns down on the table. When she sits, I stand. It takes me a while to position myself fully upright, and by the time I do, tempers are flaring even brighter.

"I'm sorry if I upset some of you," I say, my words not making a dent above the noise.

Nuala catches my gaze from the corner of her eye. She nods encouragingly. I try again. Louder. "Listen, please."

The arguing continues. Nuala claps her hands. No change. Finally, she shoves two fingers into her mouth and whistles loudly. Heads turn like those of commanded soldiers and all eyes are on their leader.

"Maura wasn't finished speaking," Nuala says.

Sharon groans, and I wish Bernie were here. She'd tell Sharon to fuck off. I'm not as brash or daring with my words, but I am determined to make my point whether Sharon likes it or not.

"As I said, I'm sorry; I'm new here and I didn't mean to upset anyone."

"We're all new here," Sharon jibes. "It's our first meeting."

I think Sharon is expecting laughter. A giggle or two at least, but there is silence until Ger says, "Jesus, Sharon, will you give it a rest? Maura clearly has something to say."

"Go on, Maura," Nuala says. "We're listening."

I swallow and try not to overthink my words as they spill out. "I know sex isn't something any of us like to talk about. But if we never talk about it, nothing will ever change."

"What about sex needs to change?" Sharon asks. "As far as I know, it's worked the same way since the Stone Age."

Geraldine shoots Sharon a look that warns her to pipe down, but I think Sharon's question, although facetious, is a helpful starting point.

"I'm not talking about the mechanics of making love, Sharon, but thank you for your observation. I'm talking about everything that sex encompasses. The different consequences the physical act brings to a man and a woman. For a man, sex ends the moment his body separates from a woman's. For a woman, often, sex is just the beginning. She can fall pregnant whether she wants to or not. She can carry a child for nine long months whether she wants to or not. She can go through the labor and pain of birth whether she wants to or not. The stakes of sex are so much higher for a woman than for a man."

Sharon softens. The dark cloud of anger in her eyes is gone. She is listening. Dare I say it, she's even invested. "What are you saying? You want sex made illegal?"

I roll my eyes. Sharon is an idiot, I decide. "No. Of course not. I want sex made fair."

"And how do you propose to do that? God made sex unfair from day one. We're trying to take on the government here. Not the Lord above."

"Contraception," I say, using a word I'd read in Ger's newspapers. "It's that simple. There are ways and means of preventing pregnancy. The pill, French letters, diaphragms and such, and others that I bet we haven't even heard of. But they're there. Woman all around the world have access to these methods of birth control and yet Irish women are being forced to live in the dark ages."

There is silence. No one dares say a word. Maybe no one knows what to say.

"We deserve to work just as a man does. We deserve a roof over our heads just as a man does. You're right, and it's a tough fight and I will support you every step of the way. But surely we deserve control of our own bodies most of all."

The silence is shattered by whooping and cheering. Feet stomp, hands clap, and my heart races.

"Contraception for women," Nuala says.

"Contraception for women," everyone echoes.

The other patrons stare and not a single woman at our long table lowers her voice or curbs her enthusiasm. Even Sharon claps and chants, "Contraception for women."

Geraldine moves my hair away from my ear and leans in to whisper, "I think you've started something, Maura. Something amazing."

CHAPTER 50

Maura

Nuala drives. Her car is a tangerine Mini with fluffy dice hanging from the rearview mirror and thick gray smoke blowing out the exhaust. Geraldine insists that I sit in the front, next to Nuala.

"It's easier for you with your crutches," she says.

At Geraldine's parents' house, Nuala gets out and lifts her seat so Geraldine can climb out of the back of the two-door car. Geraldine makes a big show of saying goodbye.

"Keep an eye on her," she tells Nuala. "Make sure *he* doesn't touch her." There's so much contempt for Christy in her tone that the words could sour milk.

Nuala nods and says, "I'll take care of her."

Geraldine waves from the porch of her parents' massive detached bungalow in Ballsbridge and I find myself wondering what her father does for a living. I shake my head as if I can spill the thought out and mentally scold myself for turning into my mother.

Nuala sits back into the car and I prepare to make small talk as we pull away from the horseshoe-shaped road of houses and leave Ger, still waving, behind.

"This is the best way to Rathmines, right?" Nuala asks.

"Yes. Take a left at the first set of traffic lights; it'll cut off some of the traffic."

"Grand . . . you're amazing. I hope you know that," Nuala says, and there's a flash of something across her face. Sadness mixed with hope, I think. It's gone before I can grab hold of it to see it clearly. "What you said earlier, your honesty. I can't believe how well that went."

"I don't think Sharon likes me much," I say.

"Sharon doesn't like anybody much. But she's all right when you get to know her. She's just a loudmouth. But we need loudmouths if we're going to get people to listen."

"I suppose."

Nuala flicks on her indicator and we veer left. The ticktock of it soothes me and I close my eyes and lean into the sound.

"I think Sharon fancies herself on the telly. Reading the news, maybe." Nuala snorts as if the very notion of a woman reading the news is farcical, but there's a hint of optimism behind her amusement.

"Wow. That's a big dream," I say.

"She hasn't got the face for it, though. God bless her, she has a face only a mother could love."

I cover my mouth and keep my laughter in. I hadn't noticed anything wrong with Sharon's face. I was too busy trying to make sure her mouth didn't bite me to notice the rest of her features.

"You have it, though," Nuala says. "Your face is practically perfect."

"Oh, erm . . ."

I instinctively touch under my left eye. It's still tender, and no doubt ugly. Nuala takes her eyes off the road for a moment to look at me. She smiles, and although they're as obvious as the nose on my face, she doesn't mention the mottled, yellowing bruises gathered on my cheekbones and temples.

"People used to say I looked like Doris Day when I was younger," I say, and there's a pang of longing, as I miss those carefree days.

"Doris bloody Day, well, my God, you do 'n' all. I see it now. Perfect. It's perfect."

A car cuts us off at the junction and Nuala slams her hand on the horn.

"Typical man," she mutters. "Downright typical."

I pull my hand away from my face and stare out the window. I think of Christy and his temper. I think of Dan and his kind eyes. My da. The nice man who assisted me in Bewley's. My neighbors. The postman, the milkman, the man who sits on the same bench in the Phoenix Park every Sunday after mass and reads his paper while his children play tag. Tall, short, funny, grumpy, happy, sad. All men. All different. There is no such thing as a typical man. Just as there is not, and never should be, such a thing as a typical woman.

We turn onto a less congested road and Nuala drives a little faster, lost in her own thoughts. We don't say another word until I say, "It's just up here, next right."

Nuala turns onto my road. Children are out playing hopscotch that they've drawn on the concrete with colored chalk. Mrs. Keogh in number 17 will complain later and make them wash it away with cold, soapy water. They don't move when they see us coming. Nuala slows and we crawl past them. My next-door neighbor's children are among the giddy group. Two girls and two boys. They wave when they see me passing and I wave in return.

"Jesus, this place is like an advertisement for domestic bliss, isn't it?"

"That's what I thought when I first moved here. Perfect houses, perfect gardens, perfect lives."

"If only," Nuala says.

"If only." I sigh, and then I say, "This is me. Number eleven."

"Wow. Nice. Jesus, those net curtains sparkle."

I smile. It's a compliment. And I should take it as such, but somehow it doesn't quite feel the way praise should. I know Nuala only means to observe the net curtains that my mother-in-law so keenly taught me to keep white. Curtains that I have the time and inclination to hand-wash and dry and hang. Nuala wouldn't have the time. Or Sharon. Or Geraldine. They aren't housewives. They have big, busy lives and I hate that I have to squash the sting of jealousy.

"You know, I grew up in a neighborhood just like this in the fifties," Nuala says, glancing out the window toward the children. "I played hopscotch with my friends and my ma had the whitest net curtains on the road. She died giving birth to my brother, her tenth child. I was fifteen. The curtains went yellow after that."

"Oh, Nuala, I'm sorry."

Nuala tucks her car next to the curb and turns off the engine.

"It was a long time ago. Twenty years ago, next month. And I keep waiting for women's lives to be worth more than keeping house, you know? But here we are, looking at some of the brightest net curtains I've ever seen. Don't you want to let them yellow up? Even just a little bit?"

"I never wanted to keep them white in the first place. In fact, I'd love to rip the damn things down altogether."

Nuala looks at me with wide, almost wild eyes, checking if I understand that we are not talking about curtains. I grin so wide it stings my aching cheeks, but I keep the smile pinned to my face.

"Then let's do it," she says. "Let's tear up every damn curtain in the country."

There's so much fire in Nuala's belly I feel the heat of it. I feel it warm me. I feel it warm the whole car.

"Sharon has some connections in RTÉ. I'm not too sure of the ins and outs of it. But she *might* be able to get an interview on *The Late Late Show*."

Her fire is burning so brightly now it feels as if it might singe me.

"*The Late Late Show*? That's amazing. Oh golly."

"It might only be a ten-minute slot, if even. But there's a lot *you* could say in ten minutes."

I tap my fingers against my chest. "Me?"

"Please, Maura, you have to come on the show with us. Tell the women of Ireland what you told me. Open their eyes to contraception and their right to choose."

"Oh Jesus. I couldn't. I can't. Everyone watches *The Late Late*." My throat closes over just thinking about it. "My parents, my in-laws, my husband, for goodness' sake."

"Good. Let them watch. Maybe we could get them tickets to sit in the audience."

"No. No. God, no. They wouldn't understand. My family aren't like that. They're not looking to fix anything. To be honest, they don't even know it's broken."

"Then show them. Come on the telly and show them."

Something inside me is shaking. Desire. Trepidation. Longing. Fear. I can't tell the difference.

"What about Ger?" I say. "She'd be perfect. She's young and full of ideas—"

"She's also single." Nuala's face is awash in frustration and desperation. "How do you think the people of Ireland would react to an unmarried woman fighting for contraception? We want people on our side."

"But every woman should have the right—"

"Every woman should. I agree. But we'll have our work cut out for us convincing Ireland that women deserve contraception at all. If we bring unmarried women into the argument . . . well, we might as well just shoot ourselves in the foot now and be done with it."

I sigh. Nuala is right. Ireland is not looking to change. If we push too hard too soon, we'll lose.

"That's why we need you, Maura. We need your pretty face and your posh accent and pristine home and suburban life. You're the nearest thing to the perfect woman there is."

"Perfect." I snort.

"Listen. Please listen." Nuala raises her voice. It's too loud for the small space of the car. "If we can show people that it's all a facade, if we can make them see that behind every closed door is a desperate housewife, maybe, just maybe, they'll take our side."

I'm lost for words when Nuala places her hand over mine.

"Say you'll do it? Please?"

"He'd kill me." I swallow. "I think he might actually kill me."

Nuala takes a deep breath. She pulls her shoulders to her ears and holds them there as she looks at me with concern and kindness.

"Then maybe you should tell people that too."

"I'm sorry," I say, disappointment and fear crushing me. "I really am so sorry."

"Yes. Me too."

Nuala's fire has burned down to ashes. I can feel it. She helps me out of the car, and I hobble toward the front door. My body is tired and aching. It's a tiredness I've never known before.

"Hello, Mrs. Davenport," says Tilly Johnson, my next-door neighbor's middle child, turning her attention away from her friends and toward me. She waves. Tilly is about six, maybe seven, and she has a smile that lights up her whole face. But she's not smiling now. She's wearing the concerned expression of an adult. "Did you fall down again?"

"Yes. I did, unfortunately."

"You're a silly billy," she says, twirling the strand of her dolly's hair around her finger. "My ma says if my da ever maked her fall down she'd hit him on the head with the frying pan."

Some of the other children laugh at the idea of frying pan violence. I push on the door handle, relieved to find it's not locked, and step inside. I can't invite Nuala in, and she knows it. We say our goodbyes on the doorstep.

"If you change your mind . . ."

I nod and smile. "I won't. But thank you."

CHAPTER 51

Maura

I make my way into the kitchen and I'm surprised to find it in complete disarray. Dishes are piled in the sink, the good ones that Christy made me buy in Switzers. There's a pot of something on the cooker; the lid is misaligned, and a brownish-yellow stain trickles down the side and gathers in a small puddle around the base. The floor hasn't been swept and it's all so out of sync with the pristine home Christy expects that I keep. I shake my crutches off and lean them against the countertop, then roll up my sleeves and set about washing up. I hum "Paperback Writer," my favorite Beatles song, and I make good headway, but the melody hitches in my throat when I hear my husband creep in behind me like a dark cloud.

"How was the party?" he asks.

He pushes my hair aside to kiss my neck.

"Good. Yes. Very good."

"And her family. Were they there?"

"Yes. I think so."

"You think so?"

"I didn't get chatting to them."

"Any friends? Colleagues from Switzers?"

He continues dotting gentle kisses on my skin. I try to relax, but my body is stiff like a poker.

"There were a lot of people," I say.

"Mm-hmm."

He smells of expensive aftershave. Sandalwood and citrus. He's smelled the same for as long as I've known him. It's funny how a scent can trigger memories. I think now of the early days of our relationship. Strolling around the park, hand in hand. Sunday drives exploring the countryside. Lazy afternoons skipping stones in a lake. All with my head full of dreams of the bright and wonderful future that I was so sure awaited us. I hate his aftershave now. It makes me sick to my stomach.

"How old did you say Ger was again?"

"Twenty-one."

Christy presses his chest closer to my back. I'm sandwiched between my husband and the edge of the sink. The cool stainless steel bites against my flesh and I want to push back. I want to straighten up and stretch my back, but Christy is heavy and he has no intention of moving. I swallow and beads of perspiration gather at the small of my back.

"And is it her birthday today, or just her party?"

"Eh . . . I'm not sure, really."

His questions make me nervous. Tests always make me nervous. My ribs ache. I want to yelp.

"I stopped by Switzers on my way home this afternoon," Christy continues, and I can feel his hot breath glide over the top of my head. "I thought it might be nice to leave some flowers for your friend. Since twenty-one is such a milestone birthday, as you say. But it's funny . . ."

My chest tightens. I know whatever comes next will be far from funny.

". . . that tall chap was there, Dick, I think his name was. The manager. Is that right?"

I can't breathe.

"Anyway, I got chatting to him for a while. Lovely man, I must say. But he tells me Geraldine's birthday is in April. There I stood with a bouquet of roses in my arms for a woman whose birthday it is not."

Silence hangs between us. I wait for him to say more. There is always more.

"I'm sure you can imagine my embarrassment. I thought my wife was at her birthday party. But it so happens her birthday was months ago. So, I found myself asking, *Where is my wife?* And I realized I didn't know."

He pauses and waits for me to speak. I don't say a word. Anything I choose to say will only make it worse.

"Where was my wife?" Christy's voice is light and gentle, as if he's simply inquiring about my day, or asking if I would like some tea and biscuits.

I can't open my mouth. Even if I wanted to. Fear has sealed it shut.

"Where was my wife?"

I catch Christy's arm raise from the corner of my eye. Usually, I close my eyes so I don't see the blow. But not today. I grab a crutch and smack it against him with all my strength. He staggers back. The relief is immense as the weight of his body lifts off me, and I peel myself away from the sink and suck in deep, hurried breaths to fill my aching lungs.

He laughs. He belly laughs as if my efforts to defend myself tickle him. "What was that?" The sound of his chuckling is revolting, like a pig snorting in a pen. "It didn't hurt me. Do you think you can hurt me?"

Christy is right. I am no match for his broad shoulders and strong arms. In the peak of my health, I haven't been able to fight him off. I don't stand a chance with already battered bones. Women are not as strong as men. Not physically. That's just the science. But it does not make us weaker. If anything, it makes us stronger, because we always have to find ways to be smarter. The women's liberation movement is prepared to fight with their words. They will write article after article after article until their words have an impact. A punch. All I have now are my words. And I'm damn well ready to use them.

"Your colleagues know what you are," I say.

Christy slides his hands into his pockets, amused. "Oh, really."

"Yes, really. That doctor, the one with the dickie bow. He knows I didn't fall."

"But you did, darling, you hit your head so hard you don't remember. I told the doctors and nurses all about how awful I felt that I couldn't catch you before you hit the ground. You know, there was one old dear there, Sister something-or-other, and she actually said she'd pray for me. Imagine that, she would pray for me because my wife is so clumsy."

I take a cagey step back, surprised to find the cast cushions my foot and I can stand independently without any pain. Christy takes a matching step forward.

"I don't believe you," I say, daring to take another step back. "People aren't stupid." I take another step.

"Of course people aren't stupid. But they *are* busy. And no one cares, Maura. No one cares about you."

I add another step. I'm in the hall now.

"My parents care about me."

He laughs. "They do. Your poor mother's eyes were full of tears in the hospital. Your father has a bit more smarts about him. He knows when to keep his trap shut. He knows you have it good, Maura. A nice house, a nice car, a nice life. He knows there's nothing more to want."

"I *do* want a nice life, Christy," I say, taking another step. The handle of the front door presses into my back. Slowly I drop my hand behind me and curl my fingers around it. "But I don't have a nice life with you. My life is a nightmare."

The lines of Christy's face seem to deepen and a darkness gathers in his eyes, fiercer and blacker than I've ever witnessed before. I often worry that he might lose his temper so ferociously someday and kill me. Suddenly I am worried that today might be that day. I open the door. My movements are slower and more encumbered than usual and Christy's hands clamp down on my shoulders like a vise as soon as I set foot on the porch step.

I scream. "Tilly! Tilly, call your ma!"

The children stop their playing and look toward our house.

"Tilly, quick, quick. Call your ma. Tell her I've fallen down again. Tell her to bring the frying pan."

The children abandon their game and run. Each and every one of them races toward Mrs. Johnson's house.

"Ma! Ma!" Tilly's voice is big and loud and at odds with her small body. "It's Mrs. Davenport. Dr. Davenport is making her fall down again."

My eyes are on my neighbor's house, willing her door to open, when I feel Christy's hands release me. By the time Mrs. Johnson appears at her door in her slippers and floral apron, Christy is sitting into his car. And as Mrs. Johnson hurries onto the road with her baby on her hip, Christy speeds by her, almost driving clean over her toes.

"Jesus, Mary, and Joseph," she calls out, hurrying toward me. "Are you all right? Are you all right, Maura? Do you need an ambulance again?"

The children of the road follow her. The baby has started to cry and Mrs. Johnson's face is as white as my net curtains.

"I'm all right," I say, my heart beating painfully fast. "I'm sorry. I shouldn't have involved little Tilly, but I didn't know what else to do."

Mrs. Johnson is older than me, sitting somewhere between my ma's age and mine. She's matronly and friendly. She's seen a lot of young, newly married women move onto the road over the years and she makes it her business to make every last one of us feel welcome. She knows every child on the road by name. She knows what time our husbands leave for work and when they return. She knows what family cars we drive, what washing powders we use, what roasts our husbands prefer on a Sunday. She inhales tidbits and snippets of our lives and breathes them back out to anyone who will listen. Everyone listens. Gossip and rumors drive Rathmines, and Mrs. Johnson's stories are fuel for the engine.

"Did you hear Catherine Carpenter is pregnant again? Number six that is now," she said one Sunday as she walked ahead of me into our local church. "Psst, poor Nora Lynch's husband lost his job. That'll be the end of that nice car, that's for sure," she whispered when we bumped into each other in the greengrocers around the corner. In the park last month, she caught my eye and hurried across wet grass to say, "Guess what? Susan and John Banks are moving. Apparently to a bigger house. Well, I say my house is plenty big, thank you very much."

Did you hear? Did you see? Did you know? Mrs. Johnson is never without something to say about someone. But as she stands on my porch, shaking like a leaf, she is lost for words. She doesn't know what to say, because finally, she knows it's all true. All the rumors behind twitching curtains. All the whispers behind closed doors. All the unsavory gossip about the good Dr. Davenport is true. And if Mrs. Johnson knows it, soon, so will all of Rathmines and most of Dublin.

CHAPTER 52

Nine days later

Bernie

Unconsciously, over time, Saturday nights have become an evening of regimental routine. Supper is homemade chunky chips and battered cod, followed by bath time for the children. All three of the girls pile into the tub together with complaints of toes touching and elbows digging into ribs. Afterward, Marie and Elizabeth argue over which Enid Blyton story to choose. Each time, Dan guides them into our bed and selects his personal favorite, *The Famous Five*. I mop the aftermath of their splashing while Dan reads an adventure story complete with character voices, and once the girls are asleep, my husband and I reconvene in the kitchen like two warriors fresh from battle. I brew a pot of tea while Dan opens the biscuit tin and we settle in for a night in front of the television with Gay Byrne, the nation's favorite host. It's the same in every house across the country. The only folks not watching *The Late Late Show* on a Saturday are the single chaps down at the pub.

"Dan, quick, it's starting," I call out as the iconic music plays, and I turn it up a little as if it wasn't loud enough already.

Dan hurries in and I pass him a cup of milky tea, just the way he likes it, and he bites into a chocolate digestive.

"When is she on?" he asks as he sits on the couch next to me.

My stomach flutters.

"I'm not sure. Somewhere in the middle, I think."

We watch as Gay interviews a scraggily bearded chap who has written a book about weather patterns and says the world is going to change catastrophically in the coming years.

Dan calls him a hairy eejit and laughs at his crazy notions about the future. There's a woman from west Cork in a red evening dress with a voice like an angel as she sings something in a different language. And finally, after the second advertisement break, the camera zooms in on three women in a row, sitting behind a long white desk that faces the audience.

I point toward the screen. "Look. Look. There's Maura. Doesn't she look great?"

Maura sits in the middle. Her hair is pinned off her face and she's wearing a knitted cardigan. In real life I know it's egg-yolk yellow, her favorite, but in black and white it appears pale gray.

"Now, folks," Gay says with a clap of his hands. He's standing in the center of the studio floor, facing his audience and staring straight into my sitting room. "We have something very different and—I'm going to go ahead and say it—groundbreaking to discuss with you this evening." He leaves a suitable pause before he cocks his head and says, "Contraception."

There's a collective intake of breath from the audience, amplified by the space of the studio, and Dan and I jump as if the sound might crack our television screen.

"Please welcome Sharon Casey, Maura Davenport, and Nuala Tyrone, who are here to discuss."

There's another pause and I wait for the audience to offer a welcoming round of applause as they do when a new guest or guests are introduced. But there is no clapping in the audience this evening.

"A big word. A big change. A big surprise, I can see from some of your faces," Gay says.

The screen shifts to a view of the audience. An elderly man in a suit and shirt in the front row looks as if he's about to throw his dinner up.

"Would you look at this old fart." I point. "As if he knows anything about women's bodies."

Dan is as quiet as a church mouse. His hands are clasped and resting on his knees, which he bobs up and down. The camera scans the audience. A priest, a young man—younger than me, I'd guess—blesses himself and drops his head into his hands. Another man pulls a face as if he's sniffed farmer's slurry. Older women seem as disgusted as their male counterparts. There are few, if any, smiles. Faces are icy and noses are upturned, and I have a sinking feeling that Maura's already difficult life may become unbearable after this.

The camera returns to the host as he puts a question to the first woman on the panel, whom he introduced as Sharon.

"And can I ask if you want babies?" Gay says with a kind smile.

"You can ask all you like."

His smile falters. "Is that my answer?"

"Take from it what you will."

Gay adjusts his tie and tests a gentle laugh—to lighten the air or to relieve his own discomfort, I can't tell. Sharon folds her arms on the desk in front of her and looks straight into the camera. Straight at me.

"It's my body. My business. It's certainly not the church's or the government's business, that's for sure."

"Some would argue that *it is* the business of the church," Gay says. "Some would say that God blesses us with children."

Sharon is quick to reply. "A fella blesses me with children. If God is there when me and a nice fella are alone, then the Lord above needs to take a long hard look at himself."

Maura smirks and I punch the air.

"Yes," I shout. "You tell 'em."

"Oh my," Gay says as the audience erupts.

There are raised voices. Too many voices. It blurs into one loud, incoherent sound. But one thing is distinctive: objection and rage.

"Now, now, folks, please." Gay raises his hand and leaves it in the air. It takes some time, but the grumbles and shouting dissipate until finally you could hear a pin drop.

"We are not crossing our fingers and hoping contraception falls from the sky," the woman on Maura's opposite side says, cutting through the silence like a sharp blade.

Nuala Tyrone wears thick-rimmed glasses, which she shoves up her nose with her index finger, and somehow, they make her seem smart. I want to listen to this smart woman. The audiences hushes. It's clear, despite their complaints and protesting, they want to listen too.

"If you are not hoping for contraception, would it be fair to say you are asking for it?" Gay says. He strokes his chin with his finger. He's concentrating. "You're asking the government for it, no?"

"No. We are not asking. We are done asking. Women have been asking for years," Nuala says.

"Have they?" Gay says.

"Yes. Of course." There is a flash of temper across Nuala's face and her calm demeanor wobbles.

"Behind closed doors this has certainly been a concern for women for many years," Gay says. "We have families on the breadline with ten and twelve children and it's perceived as perfectly normal. I've no doubt these women have asked, maybe even prayed, for babies to stop. But publicly, I have never heard a woman dare ask aloud for contraception before."

Nuala stands up. Her cheeks are puce and her eyes are wide and bulging.

"Jesus," I say, a little worried she's about to have a heart attack live on air.

"Shh," Dan says, placing his finger on his lips. "I want to hear what she has to say."

"If you've never heard a woman ask for contraception before, then you haven't been listening."

There's more noise among the audience and it takes time to die down. Both Dan and I are sitting on the edge of the couch by the time it does, and Nuala continues.

"Have you heard the cries of young women all over Ireland when they're abandoned at the doors of homes for unmarried mothers? They cry because they don't know if they'll see their families again. They certainly won't see their babies. Ever. Don't you hear them? They've been crying for more than thirty years."

"I think we're getting off track here," Gay says. "We're discussing contraception, not unmarried mothers."

"All right," Sharon says, jumping to her feet as well. "Let's talk about married mothers, if you prefer. Mothers with a clatter load of small children already."

Sharon's hands are flailing about and her expressions are exaggerated and animated. Passion and frustration seem to battle for space inside her. "Them mothers with difficult pregnancies and aching, tired bodies. And them who lost their lives giving birth. Do you hear them crying? Do you hear their lonely children crying out, begging for their mothers back?"

Silence hangs in the air. The audience is lost for words now as they wrestle with their consciences. Dan and I don't budge. We don't breathe. We hope the people of Ireland are listening with equal attention. The bright studio lights are unforgiving, and all three women on the panel wear their emotions on their faces.

Finally, Gay finds words in the shape of a low, somber hum. "There is nothing more tragic than a young mother lost too soon."

"That's why we're not hoping or asking for contraception. We're demanding it," Sharon says, bringing her hand down on the desk with such force it must hurt, but she doesn't flinch. "Here and now we are demanding that no more women are denied methods of birth control that could change their lives. Save their lives."

Finally, Maura gets to her feet. Her pretty face seems a little older and a little more tired than usual. I'm momentarily plagued with worry. What will Dr. Davenport say when he sees his wife on telly? What will her da say? Her ma, too. And the neighbors. All of Maura's posh neighbors will be watching. A small gasp spills out of me, and Dan's hand reaches for mine, squeezing it. He's as concerned for our friend as I am.

"Maura is brave," he says. "She'll be all right."

"She's braver than me," I say. "Look at me. Sitting here with a cup of tea and stuffing my face with bickies while I expect other women to fight my battles."

Dan turns to look at me and sighs. "Bernie, we have to think of the girls. This is not your fight."

"Do you think I should have stopped her?"

"Maura?" he says. "I'm not so sure you could have. Not anymore."

"She blames herself, you know. For Josie's death," I say, placing my hand on my heart.

Dan shakes his head. "A kid on the streets. It's just wrong. So wrong."

I think of my own girls tucked up in bed. If I concentrate, I can hear gentle snoring coming from our bedroom.

Maura's voice calls my attention back to the screen. "What about women who don't want babies at all?"

The camera zooms in on her pretty face, free from the lines and wrinkles that are setting in around my eyes and across my forehead. She doesn't look guilty or scared. She looks confident, determined, fiery. She looks different.

Gay shares the screen. His eyes narrow as he says, "For no reason. They just don't want any babies?"

Maura shrugs. "Not for no reason. But for whatever reason. Any reason."

Gay points toward Maura and, in a gentle whisper, asks, "Are the bruises on your face your reason?"

Maura's eyes glass over and suddenly she looks every bit as tired and scared as I know she is. I hold my breath and wait for her to cry.

"Does it matter?" she says, without tears.

"I think it matters, yes."

"It does not," she says, her confidence returning, even greater than before. "I have my reasons and other women have theirs. That is enough."

"Oh. I see."

The camera focuses on Maura's face for quite some time. Long enough for the audience and the people at home to see she wears her reason in an oval bruise on her left temple. It's healing and someone in makeup has tried hard to cover it up, but it's there. A stamp. The punctuation at the end of Maura's story. And despite her good looks, her right cheek is swollen and puffy, another reason. The audience is forced see the truth in all that Maura hasn't said. They are so silent and invested I almost forget they are there. It's just me and Maura now. She is inside the small box in my sitting room and her damaged face is telling her story.

"Oh deary me." Gay places his hand on his chest as if Maura's truth wounds him. "Oh deary me, indeed."

"Do you understand now?" Nuala asks, as all three women sit back down.

It's evident on all their faces how exhausting it is, fighting to be heard.

Gay's chest puffs out, pushing his suit jacket away from his shirt. "Just to clarify, you are suggesting that some women, for their own personal reasons, do not want to raise a family in any way, shape, or form. At all. Ever."

"We are not suggesting it," Nuala says. "We are simply saying that is *exactly* how it is. Women are not baby-making machines."

"Indeed," Gay says. "Indeed. Indeed. But tell me, ladies. Would you walk into a shop and buy condoms if you could?"

Dan's inhale is so sharp and so loud it makes me jump.

"Jaysus, Dan," I scold. "You put the heart crossways in me."

"Did you hear him?" Dan's eyes are as startled as if an extraterrestrial had just knocked on our front door. "Did you hear what Gay Byrne just said?"

"I heard him."

"He said . . ." Dan gulps, as if the word is too wide for his throat and he has to cough it up. "He said *condom*. On the telly. He just said it as if it was any aul word."

"It is any aul word," I say.

"Ah, here, Bernie. It *is* not."

My mind shifts to the foil wrappers that Dan and I keep hidden in his sock drawer. The French letters that have saved our marriage. The French letters we use but never talk about. Our dirty little secret that sometimes fills us both with such shame that we can't even look at each other afterward.

"Well, they'll certainly be talking about them now," I say. "The whole country will."

Maura, Bernie, and Nuala all agree that if they could, they would be only delighted to buy contraception in any store, in any town, in any county.

"That's something I would very much like to see," Gay says.

"Then watch this space," Nuala says with a confident nod. "Watch this space."

The end credits roll and I stand up, gather the empty teacups, and make my way into the kitchen. I take a deep breath and steady my racing heart. Gay Byrne is not the only one watching this space. I have no doubt every woman in Ireland will be keeping a keen eye on Maura, Sharon, and Nuala from here on out.

CHAPTER 53

Maura

The revolving doors of the dull gray building at RTÉ studios spit us out into the chilly midnight air. Sharon, Nuala, and I stand with our arms folded and our heads bowed, like three convicts on early release from Mountjoy Prison for good behavior. Just like reformed criminals, we are free but forever tainted by our sins.

Gay Byrne and the producers let the open-ended show run over by almost an hour. The debate was heated, and tempers and tantrums no doubt made for good television. After the show, we were guided into a small room in the back and someone handed us a cup of tepid tea each. It wasn't long before Gay came in to shake our hands.

"Good luck, ladies. You have your work cut out for you. But I see no better women for the job. Perhaps you'll revisit us here at RTÉ and let us know how you get on?"

And that was that. It is over. Or it is just beginning. It is overwhelming in every way. A starry sky hangs overhead and my cardigan is no match for the night wind. We look from one to the other and none of us are quite sure how to pick our lives up from here. One thing each of us knows for certain is that nothing will ever be the same again.

The last of the people from the audience are making their way out the main gates of the landscaped studio grounds. Everyone is feeling the chill, with arms wrapped around themselves or hands stuffed in pockets. Heads are down, and the pace is fast. Thoughts are most likely on catching the last bus or getting back to their car before the parking meter runs out.

"Let's go," Nuala says, slipping her arm around mine, taking care not to knock against my crutches. She links Sharon like a crochet hook on the other side. "It's bleedin' freezing."

We begin walking in tandem, leaving the studio and our sins behind us.

"Alley cats," someone shouts, followed by a loud whistle.

"Who said that?" Sharon whispers.

"I don't know," Nuala says.

She seems rattled. I didn't know Nuala could be rattled. But I suppose, despite her clever vocabulary, confident shoulders, and large strides, she is still trying to make her way in a dangerous world.

I spin around, trying to match a body with the sound. The grounds are dimly lit and large. Too large. Darkness and uncertainty hide in the corners where the moon and stars don't shine. I pick up my pace and the others copy.

We're almost at the guest carpark when a group of teenagers appear as if they've been waiting, hiding behind the last remaining cars. They're about eighteen or nineteen, certainly no older than their early twenties. They stride forward and encompass us in a messy circle. I count heads. They outnumber us two to one.

"Shame on you," the tallest of the young men shouts. Angry saliva sprays past his pursed lips. "Your mothers must be ashamed of you."

A shorter man with a nose much too large for his face lunges forward until his giant nose is almost touching mine. "Haven't you ever heard of a disprin? Hold it between your knees. That'll solve your problems."

Nuala seems particularly disgusted by his comment and I have to ask her what he means.

"If you've a disprin pill between your knees, you can't open your legs, can you?"

The image pops into my head and try as I might, I can't shake it out.

The large-nosed chap points at me. "The cripple looks like she enjoys it."

Sharon jams her hands on her hips. "Wash your mouth out."

They laugh. It's loud and ugly.

"Whores, harlots, sluts," they chant.

My heart beats ferociously. It's all I can feel. The pound and the rhythm of it, as if it might beat its way through my chest at any moment.

"Get out of our way," Nuala shouts, louder than any of them.

Their laughing continues, as if there is anything funny about any of this.

"I said move." She tries again, even louder.

"Make us," the tall fella says.

My stomach flips. I see Christy in this young man's eyes. An entitled boy, confident that his value is greater than ours. I place my hand on Nuala's shoulder and try to guide her back, but instead I feel her edging forward.

"Is everything all right here, ladies?" A voice travels through the air to reach us.

We turn around to find a man in a black uniform with a baton in his hand. *Studio security*, I think, never having been so relieved to see a man in uniform before.

"Are these lads giving you trouble?" he asks.

"They were just leaving," Nuala says.

The group doesn't budge. Not until a second security guard appears from the shadows, waving his baton above his head. "Go on. Get," he shouts.

The chaps scarper, almost falling over their own feet. When they run around the barrier, out the gate, and turn the corner, I press my hand against my heart as relief pounds in my chest.

"You all right?" the first security guard asks.

"Yes. Fine," Sharon says.

"Thank you," Nuala adds.

I nod and smile, past words.

"Don't mind them. It's their mothers who should be ashamed, raising a bunch of bullies," he says. "I'm sure your mothers are very proud of you."

I don't like to think what my parents will have to say about all this. I don't like to think about it at all.

"I'm Pat, and this is Gary." He points toward the guard beside him, who has broad shoulders and a round belly.

"Hello," Gary says, catching the peak of his cap and tilting it toward us.

"Hello," all three of us say in unison.

"We watched tonight's show," Pat says, pointing toward a small timber hut next to the entrance barrier. "We always watch the show in there. Gary has a windup telly, you see. It's a bit small, but it does the trick."

Gary nods. "It's portable."

I'm not sure what to say. The windup box appears to be of great importance to them both.

"I'd rather spend me Saturday nights at home with my Nancy than this chap right here." Gary knocks his shoulder against Pat's and they both laugh. "But this work right here pays the bills."

I smile. I think of Pat and Gary in the depths of winter huddled in their hut, keeping up with current affairs.

"You were brilliant tonight, you know. Each and every one of you," Pat says.

There's a brief, awkward silence before Nuala accepts their sincerity and says, "Thank you."

"Nancy and I had no more after our Katie. Five children was as many as Nancy could manage, you see. And our Katie was a big baby. It left Nancy in a bit of a bad way for a while. Now, don't get me wrong, I love the bones of my children. But I miss sharing a bed with my wife. Katie is fifteen now. It's been fifteen years and I still miss my Nancy. Makes me damn well mad when I think about it, if I'm honest. If you ladies can change that for younger chaps coming along behind me, then hats off to you."

My mind wanders toward Bernie and Dan. It's hard to fast-forward to a time when their girls will be teenagers, but I try. And I am so glad that Bernie and Dan don't have to make that journey in separate bedrooms, living separate lives, joined only by the roof over their heads.

"C'mon," Pat then says, tilting his head toward a black car parked next to the hut. "It's late. How about you let this old man give you a lift home?"

"Thank you, but I have my car with me," Nuala says, fishing her keys out of her pocket. They jingle and clank in her hands.

"My, my. Your own car." Pat nods. "You're something else, you are. Something else indeed. I admire you to no end, young lady. And I am keeping my fingers crossed that you can change this backward old country of ours for the better."

"We're going to try our best," Nuala says.

Sharon and I follow Nuala to her car. We sit in and close the doors and Nuala passes each of us a cigarette. Sharon kicks off her white knee-high boots and rests her feet on the dash. There's a hole in her nylons and her big toe peeks out through the gap. She wiggles her toe as she lights up her cigarette, takes a long, hard drag, and says, "Fucccckkk."

I laugh. Not because her profanity is particularly humorous. It's not. In fact, I can't abide swearing. I laugh because right now, there is absolutely nothing more appropriate to say.

CHAPTER 54

Maura

It's an odd thing sharing a house with a stranger. Mrs. Johnson keeps lodgers from time to time. Young men, mostly. Twentysomethings who have moved up from the country to attend university in Dublin or try their hand at their first job in banking or retail. They come and go independently, as young people do, and largely they keep to themselves. Regardless, they change the dynamic of the household, like a jigsaw piece that doesn't quite fit.

Christy and I never fitted together, not the way other couples do, but nonetheless I feel his absence like a missing piece. Christy left our home eleven days ago with nothing more than the clothes on his back. Every morning I wake in fear that today will be the day he returns. And every night I go to bed thankful that another day has passed when he has not. Though my bed is empty, I cannot remember a time my life was fuller.

Nuala Tyrone moved into my house the day we met. She didn't have a bag packed. She didn't have a clean set of clothes, a hairbrush, or a toothbrush. And she didn't have any intention of staying longer than a cup of tea and a chat. She must have circled the block for an hour before she turned around and knocked on my front door. As much as she needed me, she had an inkling I needed her more.

"If you don't come on the telly with me, nothing will ever change," she said. "I know you're scared, but—"

"He's gone. Christy is gone."

Nuala lunged forward and wrapped her arms around me then. Her frizzy hair smelt of lemons and cigarettes and I hugged her tighter and longer than I'd ever hugged anyone in my life. Even my ma or Bernie.

"That's it. I'm staying, then. Let's see him take on the two of us."

Nuala drops Sharon home first. Sharon lives in a flat above a chemist shop in a part of town I'm not familiar with.

"It's a bit small, but it's fine for me on my own," she says, slightly defensively, when Nuala pulls up outside.

Sharon's flat reminds me of Bernie's. There are three narrow windows that don't let in enough daylight across the front and a chimney on top.

"I'd ask you in for a cuppa but the place is on its ear," Sharon says. "The downside to living alone. There's no one to nag me to tidy up."

"It's late," Nuala says. "We should head home anyway."

Home. I would love to go home. To the place where my parents are. To the place where my childhood bedroom remains untouched by time, with the brass headboard and the hand-knitted patchwork blanket on my bed. *Home.* I do not want to go home to number 11 Rathmines.

"Do you think Christy saw *The Late Late* tonight?" I say as we begin driving again.

"Yes," Nuala says with certainty. "And if he didn't, he will hear someone talking about it in the next day or two."

"Oh God, what have I done?"

"Changed everything, that's for sure."

"What now?" I ask, staring out the window as we whiz by dimly lit street-lights.

"We wait."

"And what if no one agrees with us? What if we got this all wrong and the women of Ireland don't want this? What if they're scared?"

"Of course they're scared. You're scared, aren't you?"

"I'm not," I say, my voice quivering.

"Well, I bloody am."

I'm not sure if Nuala's honesty comforts me or terrifies me. Nuala seems so confident, so self-assured and certain in her actions. Something wobbles in my stomach now, with the knowledge that deep down she's as nervous as any of us.

I can barely keep my eyes open as we reach a sleeping Rathmines; curtains are drawn, porch lights are on, and families are tucked away in bed. There is no one waiting to point fingers. No one is out with pitchforks and razor-sharp tongues ready to tear strips off me for shaming our neighborhood. The stillness of a Saturday night on my road is familiar and unremarkable and I almost begin to cry with relief. I suspect wagging fingers and tongues will come, but for now, I look forward to a cup of cocoa and my bed. I have yet to experience a longer day.

"Look," Nuala says, tapping the brakes.

I squint and search through the darkness outside. "What? I don't see anything."

"Look," she says again, louder and with a finger pointed ahead. "Number nine."

I shift my gaze onto the Johnsons' house. The curtains are parted slightly and Mrs. Johnson and little Tilly are standing in the gap. Tilly is tucked against her mother's hip. Up much past her bedtime, the child is rubbing her eyes. Mrs. Johnson is smiling as she offers a thumbs-up. Dazed, I smile back equally as bright and blow her a kiss. She bends, scoops her sleepy daughter into her arms, and lets the curtain fall closed.

"She waited up," Nuala says, letting the car roll forward again. "That's nice."

I close my eyes despite suddenly feeling wide awake. It's so much more than nice. It is everything. There are women who will support us, I realize. They might have to wait until no one is watching. They may hide behind twitching curtains or stay in the shadows. But they believe in us. We *have* to keep believing in ourselves.

Nuala parks the car under the old ash tree and turns off the engine. She helps me out and passes me my crutches. When she's satisfied that I'm steady, she walks ahead and fiddles with a set of keys, trying to find the one to my front door. The keys clang and jangle as she hops from one foot to the other, trying to keep warm.

I'm making my way toward the house when I feel a firm hand on my shoulder. I freeze. Suddenly it's darker and stiller than ever and I am terrified, certain that when I turn around, I will find Christy behind me. I'm about to call out for Nuala and Mrs. Johnson and any and every neighbor on my road when I hear, "I'm so proud of you."

My knees almost buckle, but I manage to stay upright as I turn around and throw my arms around Bernie.

"I'm so proud of you," she repeats.

"Oh God, Bernie," I say, shaking. "I thought you were . . . oh God . . . I thought."

Bernie's face falls as she realizes exactly who I thought was behind me.

"Were you watching?" I ask, redundantly.

Bernie nods and, overwhelmed, I begin to cry.

"Oh, Maura. It's all right." She holds me so tightly I can scarcely breathe. "It will all be all right."

I break away from my best friend and run a shaky hand under my nose. I spy Dan McCarthy's bicycle leaning against the low wall that surrounds my garden. Bernie is red-faced from a cycle across town in the nippy night air. Her long green skirt has a black oil stain down the side where it must have brushed against the bicycle chain. But she is smiling.

"It's late," I say, looking up at the sky. Thick clouds hide the moon and stars. "You shouldn't have cycled all this way. Not at this hour."

Bernie shakes her head. "I have the light on Dan's bike."

"But the girls—"

"Dan is with them."

"Oh. Yes. Of course."

Bernie takes my hands in hers and gives them a reassuring squeeze before she tilts her head toward my house.

"I got it," Nuala announces loudly as my front door finally swings open. "Last key, of course, and I—" Nuala drops the keys and clutches her chest. "Oh Jesus."

A man and a woman emerge from the shadows and make their way toward the porch. They're an older couple, with bodies that are rounded at the shoulders like question marks.

"Hello. Can I help you?" Nuala says. She's over her initial fright and guarding my front door like security.

The man straightens and edges closer. "I doubt that."

I recognize my father's voice immediately and I press down on my crutches and walk as quickly as I can. After a couple of steps, I glance over my shoulder, and Bernie picks up on my cue to follow. As if it has magically appeared from thin air, just now, I spot my father's car parked several houses down and I am kicking myself for not noticing it sooner. *How long have they stood out in the cold waiting? Why are they here at this late hour? Ma doesn't like to stay up past ten thirty; late nights give her a headache.*

She links Da's arm as if she's too tired to stand alone. She's wearing an old headscarf that she's had since I was a child. It's sitting on her head funny, pulled too far forward at the sides, and the front is hanging down over her forehead and almost into her eyes. I have to squint to find her face behind it. Da wears a bollard hat. I balk for a second as the likeness to Christy unnerves me. My parents are hiding under long winter coats and headwear. And I know why. They are ashamed.

"Hello, Ma. Hello, Da," I say, at last.

"Ah. Your folks," Nuala says, relaxing as she drops her guard and bends to pick up the keys. "Did you see the show? Wasn't she great? I'm sure you're very proud. I know my ma would be if she was still with us. Rest her soul."

"Oh, Maura, what have you done?" Ma says, as if Nuala is invisible.

Da unlinks Ma to fold his arms and waits stony-faced for my reply.

"Ah. I see," Nuala says, and I feel heat creep across my cheeks. She shoves her coat sleeve up her arm and checks her watch. "It's way past midnight. I best get to bed." Then she turns toward me and mouths, "Are you okay?" I nod, and she yawns and stretches. "Right, so. Night, night. It was lovely to meet you, Mr. and Mrs. Flynn."

My parents do not speak. Nuala steps inside and hurries up the stairs. Shivering now, I tilt my head toward the house and my parents brush past me to wait in the hall. The unforgiving plastic of my crutch handles digs into my palms and I feel the pop of a blister as I step inside. I want to go to bed. I want nothing more than to bypass my stern-faced parents, climb the stairs, and pull the blankets over my head.

Inside, the ceiling creaks as Nuala walks around her bedroom. Pacing, I can tell. Da grunts, irritated by the sound.

"Who's this?" he asks, his eyes narrowed like glazed almonds as he peers past me to glare at Bernie.

"Erm, this is Bernie McCarthy. Ma knows her husband, Dan. They own the butcher's shop on Talbot Street."

"Hello, Mr. Flynn," Bernie says, extending her hand, but Da doesn't shake it.

"I'll put the kettle on," Ma says, as if life's problems can be solved with tea leaves and boiled water. She walks into the kitchen and Da waits in the hall for me to take his coat and hat. I hang them on the newel post at the bottom of the stairs.

"Are you planning on staying?" Da asks Bernie.

Bernie grimaces and looks at me, unsure. Da is making her uncomfortable, but my eyes are wide and pleading with her to stay.

"Eh. I am. I'm stopping for a while."

Da pulls his pocket watch from the inside of his tweed jacket. "At this hour, you're stopping for a while?"

"I am." She nods.

Da shoves his watch back in his pocket and rolls his eyes. "Well, I think it's best if you get on home now, young lady."

Bernie swallows. She's taken a dislike to my father, and knowing Bernie, she won't try much harder to hide it. "I said, I'm stopping for a while!"

I open the sitting room door and Da takes a seat in Christy's chair next to the fireplace. I don't intend to sit down, but after a drawn-out silence I suspect Da isn't going to open his mouth until I do. I lower myself onto the couch and Bernie sits next to me. It's not long before Ma returns with the silver tray she gave Christy and me as a Christmas present last year. Four cups rattle on top, and she's found the biscuit tin. Ma places the tray on the coffee table and passes Da a cup first, then me and Bernie. Finally, she takes a cup for herself and Bernie shuffles down to make room for her on the couch. Da dips a fig roll into his cup and stuffs it into his mouth, all the while with eyes on me.

"Well, this is a fine mess you've made, Maura," he says at last.

"Da, I—"

My father raises his hand and I shut my mouth. A flare of temper, the color of uncooked bacon, creeps across his face, sweeping in from his cheekbones and gliding over his nose. Da always wears his temper on his face. "The red band of rage," my brothers and I called it when we were children. Oftentimes, the temper band meant one of my brothers would get a leathering with the back of Da's slipper. Da never once hit me.

"How will your ma and I ever face Father Walsh again? You know your ma likes to sit in the front pew at mass. Now she won't be able to show her face in the church. We'll be the laughingstock of Dublin with a tramp for a daughter."

"Da."

My father shakes his head.

"I am not a tramp," I say.

"Going on the television and talking about . . . talking about . . ." Da's eyes drop to the floor. "Well, talking the way you did. That's a tramp in my book, Maura m'girl. A tramp, pure and simple."

I look at Ma, hoping she will say something. Anything. Her eyes don't meet mine as she sips tea that must be too hot.

"You'll fix this, Maura. I don't know how, but you damn well will."

"Fix what, Da?" I say. "I didn't break anything that wasn't already broken."

The redness in my father's face spreads. It creeps up his temples and toward what remains of his hairline. "We know Christy isn't here. He's been staying with his parents. Poor man. Goodness knows the shame this must bring on him. Imagine a doctor with a wife who can't keep her business to herself. Poor, poor man."

"Christy hits her," Bernie blurts.

My mouth gapes. Ma's too.

Bernie looks at me with heavy eyes. "I'm sorry, Maura. But I have to say something."

I inhale sharply. I'm stunned for a split second, but I hold my head high and listen as the dark secrets of my marriage spill past Bernie's lips.

"Her leg." Bernie points at my cast. "He broke it with a kick of his boot. And her face. I can't remember what her face looks like without bruises." She points to the yellow hue of a healing knock on my cheeks. "Your fabulous Dr. Davenport slammed her face into the wall. And it's not the first time. He pushed her down the stairs. He broke her ribs, for God's sake."

I wait for sympathy or understanding to register on Da's face, but he remains expressionless. And then the cold, stark realization hits me. It hits me like the pound of Christy's fist in my gut.

My da already knew.

"Ma," I say. "Did you hear? Did you hear what Bernie said about Christy?"

"I heard her, Maura," Ma says, as a silent tear trickles down her cheek.

Ma's heart might be breaking for me, but that's as far as it will go. She will not raise her voice and speak for me. She will not stand up for me, or even stand with me. She will honor and obey my da no matter what. Even if the cost is her only daughter.

"Oh, Ma," I say, feeling as sorry for her as I often have for myself.

I think of Josie. Beautiful, young, innocent Josie. No one stood up for her and, at just fifteen, it cost her life. I think of Bernie and Dan; of how much they love each other and how dangerous it would be for Bernie to carry another baby. I think of their children. All three McCarthy girls, whom I love as dearly as if they were my own. I can't bear to think of their future filled with the same worries and fears we have today.

"I won't stop." I stand up and place my untouched cup of tea back on the tray. "I won't stop demanding rights for women. I can't. This is who I am now. No one was going to stand up for me, so I had to stand up for myself."

"This behavior will stop!" Da gets to his feet and stomps his foot. Tea sloshes over the edge of his cup and against his fingers. "Dammit," he grumbles, burned. "Dammit to hell, Maura."

"I think you should go home now," Bernie says, on her feet too.

She takes the cup from Da, placing it on the tray, and then walks into the hall to fetch his coat and hat. Ma has begun sobbing. I want to comfort her, but I don't. Da snatches his things from Bernie's hands.

"How dare you," he snarls.

"Please," I say, choking back tears of my own. I don't want my da to see me cry. "Please just go home."

"What will you do?" Ma asks. She's slower than Da at getting to her feet, and she seems shorter than usual, as if the weight of it all has whittled an inch or two off her. "What will you do if Christy doesn't come back? How will you put food on the table? Oh, Maura, can't you see how foolish all this is? There is too much at stake. Too much to lose."

My mind wanders to the biscuit tin under the sink. The one Ma didn't find. I keep it hidden behind bottles of bleach and scrubbing brushes. The small, silver tin was once home to custard cremes, Christy's favorite, but for quite some time now it's been my secret money box. The first time Christy hit me I placed two pounds in the box. Then again, the next time. And the time after. Soon, I was hiding money at every opportunity. The change from the grocery shop. The coins I took from Christy's pants pocket while he was sleeping. I'm not sure why I did. Christy was never mean with money. I could buy beautiful dresses or expensive shoes. But somewhere deep down, I knew that life with a man like Christy couldn't last. I knew someday I would be alone. I just always thought I would be the one to run.

"I'll be all right, Ma," I say. "Don't worry about me."

Ma brushes the back of her hand gently against my cheek, tracing the outline of an old bruise. Her fingers are icy and for a moment I worry that she's ill. The thought hurts me.

"Come along, Maureen," Da says. "We're wasting our breath here."

"Da—"

Da's hand goes up again. "We'll speak to you again when you come to your senses. Not before."

Ma and Da shuffle toward the door, and their bitter disappointment in me exaggerates their age and slow walking. Bernie drapes her arm over my shoulders and we watch together as my parents walk away.

"I'm sorry," she says, placing her hand on the door to close it.

"Leave it open," I say, swaying slightly on the spot as I watch my father open the door of the car for my mother. "I love them, you know."

Bernie nods. "Do you think they'll understand someday?"

I shrug. "Maybe. Maybe not."

Bernie holds me a little closer. "And can you live with 'maybe not'?"

"Yes. I have to."

CHAPTER 55

October 1970

Bernie

It's no surprise that Maura's appearance on *The Late Late Show* is the talk of the country. Dan says the women coming into the butcher's shop are in a tizzy over it all.

"'Did you hear the nonsense on the telly on Saturday night?'" Dan mimics Mrs. Dunne. "'I'll have two pork chops, please? I hope Father Walsh was in bed and didn't see it. That kind of thing could give the poor old man a heart attack.'" Dan's impression of the priest's pious housekeeper has me bent in the middle with laughter. "Does she think if she goes to confession twice a week it'll guarantee her an express pass into heaven?"

Another woman, a new customer whose name Dan doesn't yet know, asked him what he thought about it all and he gave her free liver just to avoid answering. One of his longest-standing customers, Mrs. Burton Shaw, an elderly lady with seventeen grown children—all girls—said, "It's about time something changed." Dan said he gave her free liver, too.

With so much chatter in the shop today it's no surprise that Dan is late upstairs for dinner. The girls have already eaten and are content occupying themselves with the Halloween coloring books that Maura bought them.

Dan washes up, and I plate us up some shepherd's pie. I wait until Dan is almost finished eating before I pull a piece of paper from under my bottom and pass it to him. He reads the handwriting on the front, inhales sharply, and places the paper on the table.

"Oh, Bernie, this doesn't seem . . ." Dan sets his fork down on the edge of his plate so he can adjust the collar of his shirt, which suddenly looks as if it's uncomfortably tight. "This doesn't seem awful appropriate. Getting the girls involved. I mean, they're just children."

"They're just children now. But they will be women someday and I'll be dammed if I'm going to stand back and let an opportunity to better their future pass me by. Life is bloody hard, Dan. I want better for my girls."

Dan picks up his fork again. He doesn't know what to say, I can tell. He wants better for our daughters, too.

I exhale, tired. "Our girls don't understand now. They're too little. It's all going over their heads. But someday they'll look back and see how far the country has come. I really believe that. I have to believe that."

Dan drags a hand around his face. "But what if people find out you're involved?"

"No one will ever know." I place my hand over his and help it back down by his side. "I'm behind the scenes. A faceless flyer maker, that's all. I'll go along to the meetings, stack a few chairs, tidy up after, but I'll keep my mouth shut. I'll stay out of sight."

His eyes glass over. "I'm sorry, Bernie. I know you'd like to do more. I know you'd love nothing more than to speak your piece. But if people recognized you, they'd stop coming to the shop. And what with that new butcher up the way, the one with the fancy fridges, we can barely compete anymore as it is."

"You have my word, Dan. I will put our family first. No matter what. You and the girls come first."

Dan smiles. It's wobbly and nervous. I feel his concerns. I share them. I will be beyond careful. I have to be.

"So, tell me," he says, picking up the flyer again to run his finger over the words. "How many of these did you make?"

The girls and I have spent the entire day making flyers. Each piece of paper is cut neatly into a rectangle about the size of a birthday card. The writing on the front says, *Rights for Women. Contraception meeting at the Mansion House, 14 November at 10:30 a.m.*

The writing on some is more legible than others. Poor Marie complained that her hand hurt after writing for a couple of hours straight and there is certainly the odd spelling mistake in the mix. But none of that matters. The point is made.

"The whole country is invited," I say. "Men too."

Dan almost chokes on a mouthful of mince.

"What? It takes two to make a baby, Daniel McCarthy. Men can come along, too, if they'd like to know more."

"Oh Jesus, Bernie. That's some can of worms you're opening." He sighs. "Has Maura heard anything from Dr. Davenport?"

"No."

"Do you think he'll come back? She made a show of him on the telly."

"He deserved it."

Dan raises his hands above his head as if my words are bullets. "He did. He did. But he can't be too happy about it."

"Maura's happy. At last. That's all that matters."

Dan spoons the last of his dinner into his mouth.

CHAPTER 56

Maura

Nuala and I learn to share a house. I learn that she likes her tea black and leaves her wet towels on the bathroom floor after a wash. She learns that I like to read the morning paper with breakfast, and she cares for me as a master might care for a wounded dog.

"Don't get up, I'll get that," she says when I begin to lift my bottom off the seat to boil some water. "Let your body heal. And your heart."

Nuala means well, and I like her very much. And while she might be right that my leg will heal faster and better if I rest, I have no doubt that my heart may remain forever broken. I don't miss Christy, goodness knows. But I miss the life I once hoped I would have.

The doorbell rings.

As usual, Nuala places her hand on my shoulder and repeats, "Don't get up, I'll get that."

I hear chatter at the door. Nuala returns to the kitchen with a small white sack.

"More post," she says.

She turns the sack upside down and white envelopes scatter like snowflakes in winter.

"More," I say, not quite able to believe it.

In the days and weeks since *The Late Late Show* interview, Nuala and I have been inundated with letters from women all over Ireland. Sharon says she's receiving more letters than she has time to read too. Women post their heartfelt letters to RTÉ studios and someone from the studio delivers sacks full to our door every few days. There aren't enough hours in the day to read them all, but we try our best to get through as many as possible.

Nuala pulls a silver knife from the drawer and creates a makeshift letter opener. She slides the serrated edge under the white flap and tugs a small handwritten letter out. Her eyes sweep the paper.

"Another one signed anonymously," she sighs, somewhat disappointed.

"Did she say where she's from?" I ask.

Nuala shakes her head. "Not this time."

"I wish they weren't ashamed to share their names," I say.

"Me too. But they're scared. I understand."

"Read it?" I say, lifting the china teapot to top up Nuala's waiting cup and then mine.

Dear Ms. Tyrone, Ms. Davenport, and Ms. Casey,

I have watched The Late Late Show every Saturday night since it first aired and I have never been compelled to write in before now. But I just had to tell you how much I admire each and every one of you. I have eight children. I love every hair on each of their heads. They are the best of me and I am very proud of them. I don't understand why, as their mother, I cannot collect the children's allowance for them myself. My husband is a good man. A great man. He collects the allowance every week and brings it straight home. He doesn't spend a single penny on himself. But I know other families who aren't so lucky. I know women whose husbands stop in to the tavern on the way home from the post office. By the time they stagger home there's not one penny left for shoes for the children's feet or a bite of grub for their bellies. If

you continue your fight for women's rights, I'd be mighty grateful if
someday I could collect the allowance all by myself.

> *Yours sincerely,*
> *Mrs. B*

Nuala lowers the letter and shakes her head. "This damn country," she says. I pick up another letter, tear it open and read.

Dear Nuala, Maura, and Sharon,

I watched the show and thought you all look like mighty clever women. I don't want babies. I love my fella but I won't marry him for that very reason. I don't ever want to give birth. I'm scared. Can you help me?

> *Yours sincerely,*
> *Young and scared in*
> *Westmeath*

Nuala rolls her eyes. "Young and scared in Westmeath seems to think we're agony aunts."

"Poor girl," I say. "Imagine being too afraid to experience intimacy. God, it breaks my heart."

"These letters won't stop, you know." Nuala adds some milk and sugar to her tea and stirs. "Even if they stop coming in the post, the words on the page, the problem that forced them to pick up a pen, won't stop."

I curl my hands around my teacup and close my eyes. "Yes, they will," I say with blind determination. "Someday. It will all be different. I really believe that."

CHAPTER 57

Halloween 1970

Bernie

In the weeks since Maura's appearance on *The Late Late Show* she's become somewhat of a reluctant celebrity. People stop her on the street. Some want to shake her hand and tell her how much they admire her.

"You've a lovely speaking voice. And a great face for television. Has anyone ever told you you're a dead ringer for Doris Day? What a great singer she is. Beautiful voice. Just beautiful."

Others want to share their disgust.

"You don't speak for me. Or my daughters. I only hope the Lord can forgive you."

One woman even spat on her shoe. Maura didn't flinch. I said if it was me I'd have taken my shoe off and thrown it at her. Maura laughed and said I wouldn't have. But I damn well would have. People are disgusting. None more so than those who don't support us.

Maura and I are in town today. My girls are with us. People don't tend to approach Maura as often when the children are by our sides. Maura never says as much, but I can tell it's a relief for her.

"So," Maura says, with an enthusiastic clap of her hands. She bends in the middle so she's level height with Marie and Elizabeth. "Let's get some costumes, eh?"

We duck in and out of shops on Henry Street and avoid the cold October rain as best we can. We fetch black sacks, face paint, and colorful ribbon. Back at the flat, I cut head and arm holes in the sacks and pull them over the girls' heads. I tie thick ribbon around their waists. Red for Marie. Blue for Elizabeth. Yellow for Alice. Then Maura carefully paints each of their faces bright green. Alice cries when paint gets in her eyes, and Maura washes it all off and starts over. Maura offered to buy cloth witches' hats in Switzers but I declined and Elizabeth is still sulking. Maura seemed as disappointed as my daughters about the hats, but I couldn't let her spend money she doesn't have anymore. I often worry about how she's getting by financially without Dr. Davenport.

"Nuala pays her way," Maura said, almost insulted when I dared to broach the subject.

I have no doubt Nuala contributes, but it can't be much. Certainly not enough to keep a household running. I haven't mentioned money since. Instead, Dan sends over some chops when he can and I often turn up on her doorstep with a meat loaf or a stew.

"I had leftovers," I say, but I know she sees straight through me.

My girls wait impatiently for night to fall.

"Is it trick-or-treat time?" Elizabeth asks at the first hint of dusk.

I glance at Maura. She's as giddy as the children.

"Yes," I say, passing each of the children an empty plastic bag. Their faces light up as they hope to return with bags full of fruit, monkey nuts, and lollipops. "It's time to go."

"Have you got them?" Maura asks.

I fetch a plastic bag for myself. This one is already full and heavy and I sling it over my shoulder like a rucksack.

"How many flyers are in there?" Maura asks.

I shrug. "Last count ninety-four. But the girls made more since. They've been working on them all week."

"Their fingers must be ready to fall off," Maura says with sympathy. "But imagine the story they'll have to tell when they're older."

"If it works out."

"It'll work out. It has to."

Maura, my girls, and I leave and make our way to the nearby flats. Our teeth chatter from the cold, but the children seem oblivious to the call of winter in the air. They knock on door after door and chirp, "Trick or treat," as sweet as pie.

"Oh my, what do we have here? Three little witches. How nice."

The girls hold their plastic bags open wide and sweetly say, "Thank you," when a treat is placed inside.

"I no like apple," Alice tells a middle-aged lady at the door. I balk when I recognize the woman as Mrs. Dunne, Father Walsh's housekeeper. I had no idea this was her home or I would never have knocked on the door. I take a step back, out of Mrs. Dunne's view, and crumple the flyer in my hand, stuffing my clenched fist into my pocket. Alice reaches into her bag, retrieves the offending fruit, and passes it back to the stunned lady.

When the door closes, Marie bends down and slides a flyer under the door just as she has done for every house previous.

"No, no, no! Not this house," I call out, but it's too late. The flyer is on the far side of Mrs. Dunne's door and we can't retrieve it.

Marie's bottom lip begins to quiver and I dot a quick kiss on the top of her head. "Let's try the next house." I flick my hands to usher the children ahead as briskly as I can. "Hurry, hurry. Maybe they will have oranges."

Marie's smile returns as she takes Alice by the hand and warns her to mind her manners next time. I pull my scarf tighter around my face and cross my fingers that Mrs. Dunne didn't recognize the girls as mine. We are making our way to the next flat when the door reopens.

"Hello, hello," Mrs. Dunne hollers. "Little miss, I found a banana for you."

Alice loves bananas, but they are a rare occurrence in our house, priced outside our budget. She turns, ready to hurry back, when Mrs. Dunne bends and picks up the flyer. My heart skips. I hear Maura gasp.

"What do we have here?" Mrs. Dunne says, straightening up again to read the flyer. "Oh no. Oh my. Oh no."

Alice is next to Mrs. Dunne again. She's standing looking up at the round lady with her bag open wide like a newborn bird with a waiting beak.

"Where's your ma?" Mrs. Dunne asks.

I press myself into the neighbor's door arch, almost falling over my own feet. Maura steps in front of me, trying her best to hide me in her shadow, but it's hopeless. Mrs. Dunne has already seen me.

"Mrs. McCarthy, is that you?"

I step out from behind Maura and pull my scarf down to reveal a smile so wide my face hurts.

"Ah, Mrs. Dunne, how nice to see you. Lovely evening, isn't it?"

Mrs. Dunne wraps one side of her cardigan over the other, emphasizing how cold she is. "Is this yours?" she asks, holding the flyer above her head.

"Oh, eh."

"We maked that," Alice says proudly. "Ma and me. And Marie and 'lizabeth. We maked lots and lots."

Mrs. Dunne's face is a picture. Sitting somewhere between disgust and a need to throw up.

"Disappointing. Very disappointing. Does your husband know what you're up to?"

I should say no. I should tell her I've gone rogue and my poor Dan can't control me. Although the lie is on the tip of my tongue, I just can't seem to push it out.

"And what matter if he does?" I say, jamming my hands on my hips.

"Right, well," Mrs. Dunne says, pulling herself as tall as she can, which brings her just shy of my paltry height. "Consider yourself boycotted. I'll be in to McCarthy's first thing in the morning to settle my tab."

"Ah now, Mrs. Dunne, surely it's not that serious. Dan's meat is the finest in Dublin."

"I wouldn't step foot in the place again for all the tea in China," she says, painfully serious. "And I'll be telling everyone I know with a shred of decency to do the same. That'll teach you."

Mrs. Dunne attempts to close the door, but not before Alice snatches the banana from one hand and the flyer from the other.

"Thank you. Bye-bye," my toddler says as she waddles her way back to me, oblivious. "Look, Ma, a nanna."

I scoop my daughter into my arms and choke back tears.

"Maybe I should hand out the rest of these on my own," Maura says. "The risk is too great for you."

Alice snuggles into me. Her frosty button nose brushes my neck. I hold her a bit tighter, soothed by the warmth of her little body. I can't hold the tears back any longer. Silently, they trickle down my cheeks.

"I want to help," I say. "But the shop."

"I know. I know," Maura says.

I unsling the bag from my shoulder and pass it to Maura. My girls return to knocking on doors as Maura walks in the opposite direction, bending and sliding flyer after flyer under every door.

When the cold burrows its way through my shoes and into the tips of my toes and the girls' fingers are red and raw, I say, "It's time to go home."

Elizabeth grumbles and Alice climbs into my arms again. Marie walks alongside me and says, "Is Maura bad?"

I stop in my tracks and Elizabeth, busy peering into her bag of treats, crashes into my heels.

"Why would you say that?" I ask my eldest daughter, as Elizabeth steadies herself.

Marie shrugs and for a moment she looks as if she might cry. As if she has said something terribly wrong and I am going to scold her.

"It's all right," I say. "You can tell me."

Alice is wriggling and sliding down my hip. I shift her back into place, all the while searching Marie's face for a clue about where this question has come from.

"Sister Sloan said all girls should do God's work and become mas when they grow up. But Maura's a grown-up and she doesn't have any babies. And I heard her tell you she never, ever, ever wants babies. So, she's bad, right? Because she's not doing God's work."

"Oh, Marie, sweetheart, no. That's not it at all. Oh no, no, no."

Marie balls her hand into a fist and rubs her eye as she begins to sob. "But I like Maura. I think she's the best. I don't want her to go to hell with all the other bad people."

An instant headache pinches. I think of Sister Sloan and of the timber ruler she carries in her dress pocket next to her rosary beads. I know she uses it to whack children who are naughty, or make spelling mistakes, or are late for school.

I want to tell my daughter that Sister Sloan is a judgmental aul biddy with too high an opinion of herself. But instead I say, "Well, Sister Sloan won't ever be having babies, and she's not bad, right?"

Marie sucks air through a thin gap between her teeth and then she turns her hand over to show me a pink line across her palm. A shape, the perfect outline of Sister Sloan's wooden ruler.

"She is kind of bad," Marie says, trying not to tear up.

I take Marie's hand in mine and kiss it several times until finally my daughter smiles. I have to agree that, yes, indeed, a woman who hits little girls is bad. Just as a society that hits women down time after time is bad too.

"Sister Sloan is a bully," I say. "And you are right, Marie. Bullies are bad. They are all very, very bad."

Marie's teary eyes brighten.

"But there are people who stand up to bullies. Great people. People who do their best to make the bullying stop. People like Maura."

"Do you stand up to bullies, Ma?"

My heart sinks.

"I want to, sweetheart. I really, really want to."

Marie flings her arms around my waist and whispers, "I love you."

I stroke her head and say, "I love you too. I would change the world for you if I could."

CHAPTER 58

14 November 1970

Maura

Bernie told me once that she would change the world for her daughters if only she could. I used to think I would need to be a mother to understand. But slowly, I am learning that all the daughters of Ireland deserve a better country. A brighter future. And so, when Nuala, Sharon, Geraldine, Bernie, and I set out for our first open-invite meeting, we are full of enthusiasm and hope.

Geraldine's brother knows someone working in The Shelbourne and they offered us a function room to use for an hour, but when the manager finds out the room will be used to host a women's liberation movement meeting, he boots us out. Determined not to lose hope, we gather on the front steps of the hotel and wait. Within twenty minutes there are forty women on the steps. The rain is torrential, and we huddle under umbrellas. Nuala does all the talking.

"We've had enough. We are standing up and standing strong."

Women cheer. Rain pours. Traffic chugs by, throwing up road spray and soaking us all. No one gives up. Not until the guards arrive. The manager stands in the doorway with his arms folded and his foot tapping, watching as Nuala argues with a tall guard, his feet as large as a clown's. The manager doesn't recognize me, but I know him. He shook Christy's hand on our wedding day and wished us a long and happy life together. Then we walked out those very doors and Christy hit me for the first time. The memory is surprisingly easy to push aside when there's a fracas next to me. Sharon has jumped into the argument, and Geraldine too.

"Men like you are the problem," Geraldine shouts, her fiery temper on display. "You don't want women to have any rights."

"I'm just doing my job, ladies," he says. "You're causing an obstruction. You have to move."

"Fine," Sharon says, stepping off the bottom step onto the footpath. "Then we'll move here." She points to a far end corner of St. Stephen's Green. "Or here." She points to the opposite side. "Or here, or here, or here."

"Ah, ladies." The guard sounds genuinely perplexed. "Have you no homes to go to?"

"What do we want?" Nuala shouts.

"Contraception," some voices reply, more timidly than I imagine she was hoping.

"When do we want it?"

"Now."

The voices grow louder. I join them.

"What do we want?"

"Contraception!" I scream, my voice scratching the back of my throat.

"When do we want it?"

"Now!"

The guard warns us that if we don't move on peacefully and quietly, he'll arrest us.

"Haven't you ever heard of the right to free speech?" Geraldine says. She seems more petite than usual next to the policeman.

"Haven't you ever heard of disturbing the peace?" he says, bending his neck so he can glare down at her.

"What do we want?"

The replies are quieter and less enthusiastic as more gardai arrive. Women grab a friend or two and hurry away with heads bowed. All too soon it's Nuala, Sharon, Geraldine, Bernie, and me alone.

"Is there going to be any more trouble, ladies?" the guard asks.

Nuala ignores him and turns toward the rest of us. "Tea? Anyone fancy a cuppa? I'd murder a chockie bickie too."

Confident that our meeting has dissolved, the guards leave.

Sharon shakes her head. "You can't be serious, Nuala. How can you think of biscuits at a time like this? It's a disaster. Everyone left."

Nuala winks. "They did. But they also came. Women showed up. It's a start. A good bloody start."

I feel a smile twinge at the corners of my lips. Women did show up. Not as many as we would have liked, admittedly, but some. Maybe there will be more next time. And more the time after that. Maybe, just maybe, there will be enough that if the guards show up again we won't be scared. We won't budge.

"Right, so, tea?" Nuala says again. "Where will we go?"

"How about in here?" I say, tilting my head toward the beautiful brass door of The Shelbourne. "Let's show everyone we won't be scared away."

"I like it," Nuala says, grinning. "We are ladies who drink tea in The Shelbourne and we are not afraid of anyone."

As we march up the steps, my legs are shaking, but I concentrate on taking slow, even breaths to bury my nerves. Bernie takes my hand. I feel her clammy palms.

"Hello again," Nuala says as we meet the manager at the top step. "We would like a table for five for tea, please."

The manager pushes his shoulders back and I wait for him to ask us to leave. "No funny business," he says as he steps aside, and we walk past.

"No funny business," Nuala says, once we are out of earshot. "That's for damn sure. This business is serious. Pure and simple. Serious."

CHAPTER 59

April 24, 1971

Maura

In many ways it's a pleasure to watch Geraldine and Bernie become good friends. Geraldine encourages Bernie to try new things. Ruby lipstick, trousers, meals that don't include meat—although I have yet to see Bernie actually put any of Geraldine's recipes into practice.

"Imagine serving my Dan a vegetable stir-fry," Bernie had said, laughing. "Sure the poor fella would think his throat was arguing with his stomach."

In other ways their closeness saddens me. Despite their diligence and dedication, my two closest friends in the world sit on the periphery of our group. They retreat to the wings as the halls or function rooms begin to fill with women from all over the country. Their voices are lesser and unheard because one is a mother of three children with a business to protect, and the other is a young single woman who, as such, should have no need for contraception. It serves as a poignant reminder about why we are doing exactly what we are doing, the needless divisions that exist even on our own side.

Over the past six months, word of our meetings has spread like wildfire. Forty women gathered on the steps of The Shelbourne turned into sixty women around the bandstand in the Phoenix Park. One hundred women joined us in an old school hall. Our numbers are ever growing. A message ever stronger.

"People are on our side. They want this," I say.

Bernie seems less convinced. Mrs. Dunne has a big mouth and McCarthy's butcher's has been affected for sure. Some of Dan's longest-standing customers have taken their business elsewhere, and Bernie, Dan, and the girls are feeling the pinch. I can see the worry and strain in Bernie's eyes grow with each passing meeting. And yet she cannot drag herself away. She cannot turn her back.

"For my girls," she says often. "I'm doing it all for Marie, Elizabeth, and Alice."

Bernie and Ger stack chairs, sweep floors, make tea. Last week, at our biggest meeting to date, with over two hundred women in attendance, one woman asked if they were hired help. That was a low point for Bernie, and I thought Geraldine was going to throw the towel in altogether. But to my delight, they are both ready and waiting outside the Mansion House when Nuala, Sharon, and I arrive.

"I think this will be our biggest meeting yet," Nuala says.

"Bloody better be." Sharon sighs. "My blisters have blisters."

Nuala, Sharon, and I have spent the past week driving around the country pinning posters in every city and village. We pin them to phone boxes. Gable ends of shops. The gates of football pitches. Anywhere we find a blank space, we share our message. We keep our words simple: the time, date, and location of our next meeting. We let folks figure the rest out from there. By now, there isn't a corner of Ireland that doesn't know change is coming.

In a small village in Mayo, a man tore down our poster and chased us half a mile down the road.

"Dirty hussies," he shouted. "Don't you dare give my wife ideas."

In another village in West Clare, near the Cliffs of Moher, a woman offered to take some flyers and drop them in the letter boxes of all her neighbors.

The ups and downs of progress are exhausting and my eyes are stinging with tiredness more often than not, but I wouldn't change a thing.

Inside, we get to work. We set out as many chairs as we can reasonably fit. "People will just have to stand," Nuala says.

I do some rough counting. There must be three hundred chairs at least, and I can't imagine anyone will need to remain on their feet. We make tea and skip the biscuits this time.

We place a long table at the top of the room and cover it with a white tablecloth that I fetched from the cupboard in my house. I think it belonged to Christy's grandmother. I wonder what a woman of her generation would make of all this. Nuala, Sharon, and I take our places behind the table. We have water in front of us, and microphones, just as we did on *The Late Late Show*. Bernie and Geraldine stand to the side and we wait with bated breath.

My first thought as people arrive is how very noisy it is. Voices boom and echo around the room. I glance at Bernie and I wonder if she's thinking the same. Numbers grow quickly. Soon all the seats are filled, and, as Nuala predicted, people are standing at the back. I can't quite believe it. There must be hundreds here. And men too. Not many, but some. People file in, brushing past one another and filling up every inch of free floor space.

Beads of perspiration gather around Nuala's hairline. She was hoping for a big crowd, but she certainly wasn't expecting anything so momentously large. "Do you see this?" she gasps. "Oh my God, do you see this?"

Nuala speaks first. It takes her some time to hush the crowd, and even when she does, the room still vibrates.

"Can you really get us condoms?" a woman shouts from somewhere deep in the center.

There is a mass intake of breath as if the mere mention of the word has the power to suck all the air out of the room.

"I'll take ten if you have them," the voice continues.

"Oh," Nuala says, her cheeks flushed. "I'm afraid we don't have any. Not here with us."

Grumbles and moans ripple through the crowd and I worry that there has been a breakdown in communication somewhere along the line.

"Contraception is still illegal," I say.

Countless eyes shift from Nuala onto me. I know I need to say something encouraging that makes all their efforts to be here today worth it.

"That's that then," another voice chimes in. "What a waste of time."

I gaze into the sea of women sitting in front of me. They are all shapes and sizes. All ages. Some, I imagine, left school at fourteen like me and others have university degrees like Nuala. Some are mothers like Bernie or young single women like Geraldine. We are all different and we are all exactly the same.

"Contraception is legal in Northern Ireland," I say. "Did you know that?"

Some of the crowd nod. Some shake their heads. Some don't react at all.

"What good is that?" A man's voice carries over mumbling among the crowd. "My wife died last year giving birth to twins. Our second set in as many years. What good is contraception in the North to women in the South?"

"Belfast is only a train ride away," I say. "We could go there. Our money is as good as anybody's. We could go there and buy condoms and the pill for ourselves."

"Not a chance," the man says. "They'd arrest us on the spot as soon as we stepped foot off the train back home in Dublin."

"Maybe," I say. "Probably, even. But what if more and more women took the trip? What if soon every woman in Ireland was traveling to Belfast for contraception? They couldn't throw all the women of the country in jail."

The crowd hums and haws. My ears ring with the noise of it all.

Nuala leans in her chair. She presses her lips against my ear. "Do you really think we could do this?" she whispers.

I shrug. My heart is beating out of my chest. "Honestly? I have no idea. But I think we should at least try."

"But jail?" Nuala says.

"We should try."

"But the guards. You saw what they were like outside The Shelbourne. Can you imagine how furious they'll be if we enter the country with contraband?"

"Someone has to try," I say. "Why not us?"

Nuala takes a deep breath and puffs out. I feel the heat of it. "You're right, Maura. You're damn well right. Why not us?"

Nuala blesses herself. Then she pushes her chair back and stands up. There is instant silence. I'm not sure what she is doing, but whatever it is excites me. My eyes are on her. I don't dare blink as she places her palm flat against her chest.

"I, Nuala Tyrone, pledge to travel to Belfast, purchase the pill, and return to Dublin with it in my handbag. Who will join me?"

Sharon's chair slides back and she's next to her feet. She stares straight ahead, places her hand on her chest, and says, "Aye."

I hold my breath as I wait for more, but I soon realize no more words are coming. When it is my turn to stand I do not hesitate. When I promise to join my peers on a train to Belfast, it feels less the move of a rebel woman and more a rite of passage. I dare to imagine setting a precedent. I allow myself to dream of a time when women will take contraception for granted, when walking into a pharmacy and purchasing it will be as ordinary as picking up some toothpaste or a loaf of bread.

Slowly but surely, other women in the crowd get to their feet.

A tall woman in a purple hat. "Aye," she says.

A heavyset woman, with a man linking her arm. She looks at him, and he nods and smiles. "Aye," she says.

"Aye. Aye. Aye."

Soon there are almost one hundred women on their feet. Those who remain seated have their reasons, I don't doubt. They praise and admire those willing to take a stand.

"Come, come." Nuala beckons the standing women toward our table. She turns a notepad around and shoves it toward the edge of the desk. She places a pen next to it.

"Sign your name here and you are officially a member of the Irish Women's Liberation Movement."

There is cheering and clapping and an orderly queue forms in front of our table. Nuala shakes the hand of every woman who picks up the pen, and her message to each is the same.

"We'll contact you with details as soon as we can. And thank you. You are going to make history; I just know it."

CHAPTER 60

Early May 1971

Maura

With so much talk of trains, it would be no exaggeration to liken my house to a train station. Letters continue to roll in from women all over the country, more than we have time to read and reply to. Bags of them are stacked under the stairs. Nuala tripped over a bag yesterday and the list of profanity that she strung off dazed me for hours. The hall is equally as crowded. Thick cards lean against the walls; heavy white cardboard sheets with the words IRISH WOMEN'S LIBERATION MOVEMENT written in thick black marker. Dan promised he'd stop by later and attach some timber stakes to the back of the cards for us.

Of the one hundred women who signed up to join us on the train, less than half have remained committed and I panic every day that we will lose more. Their excuses and apologies are reasonable and fair.

My family will never speak to me again. My husband will leave me. My adult children will be ashamed of me. My parents will kick me out.

I hug every single woman who must pull back, and almost all of them cry and promise to support us silently from the sidelines.

"What good is that?" Nuala sulks. "Silence will get us nowhere."

"There are forty-five women here today," I say sternly. "Let's count our blessings and not scare them away too."

In the kitchen, the noise of sewing machines rattles. Women who volunteered to sew are busy creating a cloth banner that we plan to hold over our heads when we return to Dublin victorious. I donated a large green tablecloth. It was Christy's mother's. He didn't notice that I ironed it and draped it across the table last Christmas and on his birthday. I've also parted with some of his expensive tweed suits. There is a moment of release and I almost cry out with satisfaction as his suits are cut and chopped to create letters for our banner. I-R-I-S-H W-O-M-E-N-S. There's disappointment when we run out of material, but I smile widely, showing off my teeth.

"Not to worry, there's plenty more where that came from."

I dash upstairs and gather some of Christy's finest shirts and his favorite pin-striped trousers, then toss the pile of clothes on the table. "There we are. Take what you need."

Teresa, one of the youngest women, picks up a baby blue shirt. She's little more than a grown girl, really, with pigtails in her hair and a shiny new wedding ring on her finger. I don't ask her how old she is, but Bernie thinks she's about twenty or twenty-one at most.

"This looks expensive," Teresa says, turning the shirt back and forth, and I can tell she's reluctant to take her scissors to it.

I shrug and try to offer her an encouraging smile.

Teresa reads the label and shakes her head. "But this is from Switzers. It's beautiful."

"Yes." I nod, catching the end of the soft cotton between my fingertips to stroke it. "This is a very beautiful shirt. The man who wore it was beautiful too—on the outside. Inside, he was ugly to the core."

Teresa nods and snaps her scissors shut, instantly cutting off a sleeve. She laughs and so do I.

"Imagine when he sees this on the news," Nuala says. "Do you think he'll know they're his clothes?"

My heart skips a beat. My rebellion always feels tainted with the mention of Christy's eyes on me in some way. I hadn't thought about Christy seeing me on television again. And I especially hadn't thought about him recognizing his finest clothes spelling out IRISH WOMEN'S LIBERATION MOVEMENT. My palms sweat.

Sharon uses her connections in RTÉ to ensure that our journey is documented.

"There'll be a chap there with a camera. He's a friend of a friend. I can't guarantee it'll actually make the air, but it's worth a shot."

I can see the remaining women's faces change with the mention of television coverage.

"He'll record us getting on the train in Dublin. Come along with us and follow us around Belfast. Then he'll shoot some more back in Dublin. RTÉ will probably bin the whole thing. But say a Hail Mary that we get at least two minutes of news time."

"It's going on the telly?" Teresa says, cutting around an O shape in the sleeve of Christy's shirt. "Oh sweet Lord."

"It's all right," I say.

I'm worried she'll cut herself. Or throw down the scissors altogether and race out the door.

"What will I wear?" she says. "I've nothing to wear. Not for telly."

Sharon laughs. "That's your biggest worry?"

Teresa's cheeks flush. "This is my ma's dress." She tugs at the hem of a full-skirted black dress that was in fashion in the late fifties. "I can't wear something like this."

"I've some nice pieces," I say. "I used to work in Switzers."

Teresa's face lights up at the mention of my previous employment.

"We seem about the same size," I continue, looking her up and down. "Take a peek in my wardrobe. If you see anything you fancy, please help yourself."

Some of the other women ask to borrow clothes too, and soon many of us are upstairs laughing and giggling and trying on dresses and hats and boots as if we're about to make our catwalk debut. I am so busy laughing that I don't hear the doorbell ring, but Bernie calls out to me.

"Maura. Maura. There's a man at the door for you."

I leave my bedroom and peek my head over the banister to catch Bernie's eye. "Who is it?"

She shrugs, and I detect a hint of concern on her face. I come downstairs in a fancy maroon dress that sits above my knees, and my feet are bare.

"Hello?" I say, as I reach the bottom step. "How can I help you?"

The man is dressed head to toe in a black suit as if he's on his way to a funeral. He's made an attempt to brighten his somber ensemble with a blue checked tie and a matching handkerchief tucked in his breast pocket.

"My name is Michael Lloyd," he says, extending his hand. I shake it reluctantly. "I am a solicitor at Lloyd, Lloyd, and Shaw."

I know the solicitors' practice he's speaking about. They have an office on Wicklow Street just a few yards down from the back doors to Switzers. They stick in my mind because they place an oversize Christmas tree in their window every year. It's the most tastefully decorated tree and people often stop to stare open-mouthed at it.

"I am here on behalf of Dr. Christopher Davenport."

"Christy!"

"Yes." Mr. Lloyd nods. "I am the solicitor taking care of the sale of Dr. Davenport's residence."

"This residence," I say, my words catching in my throat.

"This residence. Number eleven The Gardens. Yes."

"But this is my home."

"This is Dr. Davenport's property," Mr. Lloyd says matter-of-factly, and I wonder if he is capable of showing emotion.

"But I live here. I still live here. Where will I go?"

Mr. Lloyd opens his mouth but I continue before he speaks.

"I'm his wife. I'm Christy's wife. This is *our* house."

Mr. Lloyd inhales. The shoulders of his jacket rise and remain up for a moment even after he exhales.

"I'm afraid it is Dr. Davenport's intention to go ahead with the sale.

You have thirty days to vacate the property. I wish you the very best of luck, Mrs. Davenport."

He glances at the placard lying closest to his feet, just inside the door. It proclaims, RIGHTS FOR WOMEN, punctuated with a thick black exclamation mark. Mr. Lloyd tuts and shakes his head before he turns and walks away.

"Oh, Maura," Bernie says as I close the door. "He can't. He just can't."

"He can. And he will. We both know that."

"But this is your home."

I shake my head at the irony. Christy's last punch is not with his fists, and yet it hits the hardest.

"You can stay with us," Bernie says.

Bernie has little enough space for her family as it is.

"I know it's tight, but we'll make it work. We'll think of something."

I listen to the unfamiliar noises in my home. Voices chatting, doors opening and closing, footsteps walking around overhead, sewing machines working.

"Dan won't mind at all, if you're worried about that. Sure, he thinks the world of you."

My feet are firmly on the floor, but inside, I'm swaying as if I'm on a boat deep out to sea during a terrible storm. If I hold on tight, I might be able to weather it, but there's really no way to tell for sure.

"Maura. Oh, Maura, won't you say something?"

"We have more important things to worry about right now," I say, gazing at the placard that offended Mr. Lloyd.

"Maura, I know how much this movement means to you, but this is the roof over your head we're talking about."

I think about the storm hitting my house. I imagine swirling winds ripping the bricks from the walls one by one. "It's bricks and mortar. Nothing more. Houses come and go. But we only get one future." The swirling ocean in me calms, as if the sun is slowly appearing on the horizon. "I'll be damned if Christy Davenport is going to take that from me too."

CHAPTER 61

22 May 1971

Bernie

There is no specific reason we choose 22 May to board the train. It's not an anniversary date or someone's birthday. It's not a bank holiday or a day of remembrance. It's a plain, ordinary Saturday in early Dublin summer. Ordinary like all of us.

It rains in the morning. I wake to the pitter-patter of it against my bedroom window. Not that I've slept much—I haven't. My legs are restless and twitching. I kick Dan in his sleep by accident. He wakes and I apologize. Then he rolls over and holds me.

"Don't fret, love," he says. "Maura knows what she's doing."

I get up. I shiver a little as I pull on my dressing gown and slide my feet into my slippers. Their rubber soles squeak as I make my way across the bedroom, past my sleeping daughters, and into the kitchen to make some tea and fry up some rashers.

I wish I had Dan's confidence, but I'm worried about Maura. It's been three weeks since a man in an ugly suit showed up at her front door and pulled the last remaining pieces of her life apart. In one week, Maura will be out on her ear, and no matter how hard I try, she is refusing to talk about it. I ran the notion of Maura moving in with us past Dan. He was shocked at first, I'll give him that. But he quickly came around. He said we'd make space somehow. I made love with him that night and I told him with my lips and my words that I loved him.

When the girls wake, I dress them in their best dresses, and Elizabeth complains that her tights are itchy.

"Take 'em off," Marie tells her.

"Don't you dare," I say. "It might be summertime but it's fair cold outside."

Elizabeth tugs the thick cream cotton away from her legs and eyes me up, deciding if she's brave enough to defy me or not.

"Jack Frost will bite your bum," I tell her, and she lets her tights go.

Dan drinks his tea standing up and kisses each of our girls on the top of their heads before he kisses me. His lips linger on mine for longer than usual and I realize he's not as confident as I thought he was. The worry I feel for Maura sits in the pit of my stomach like lead and I can't touch my breakfast.

"Bye, love," Dan says, grabbing a rasher sandwich to eat on the go as he makes his way downstairs to the shop. "Give my love to Maura, won't you?"

"I will," I say, watching him leave.

I fetch the girls' coats and they put them on. I help Alice with hers. Elizabeth complains that hers is even scratchier than her tights, and I close my eyes and count backward from five in an effort to hold on to my temper.

"I can't wait," Elizabeth says.

I open my eyes to find my middle daughter with her coat buttoned up and a bright smile on her face.

"Jack Maloney in my class goes on the train all the time," Marie says boastfully. "His goes to Cork to visit his gran every weekend."

"Isn't that nice," I say, wondering how the Maloneys afford train fare for eight children up and back to Cork each week.

"I've never been on a train before," Elizabeth says, catching my eye and nodding as if I wasn't aware of her travel limitations.

"Choo-choo. Choo-choo," Alice says.

"I can't wait," Elizabeth repeats. "I think it's going to be a big blue train."

"Orange and black," Marie says. "Jack said the train is orange and black."

"That's the train to Cork," I say, and I realize I have no idea what a train out of Ireland might look like. Would it be the same color or a special, different color for entering the North?

We leave the flat and begin walking toward Connolly Station. Alice's small hand is curled in mine.

"Choo-choo, choo-choo," she sings on a loop.

The station is little more than a stroll away, and although I pass by it often, I've never been inside. I've not had a need before today. I doubt I'll have a need ever again either.

"I'm going to sit in the front aside the driver," Elizabeth says, skipping alongside me as I walk. I reach for her hand and she comes to a stop.

"We're not getting on the train," I say. "We're there to wave them off. Show our support."

Elizabeth's bottom lip curls.

"If you're very good maybe Maura will bring you something nice back from Belfast."

The idea of a treat seems to settle Elizabeth and she begins skipping again.

When we reach the station, it's busier than I expect. It's bigger, too, and noisy. I feel Alice's grip tighten around my hand. I hoist her onto my hip and take Marie's and Elizabeth's hand so they don't get lost.

"What that smell?" Elizabeth asks.

"Engine oil, I think," I say.

"Trains smell yucky."

"They do."

I search the station for Maura and my breath catches when I find her on platform two with a camera pointed straight at her. I hurry toward her, pushing my way through a large crowd.

"Bernie," Maura squeals, seeing me.

"What's going on?" I say, not quite able to take in what I'm seeing. "I thought Sharon's friend was coming to tape you getting on the train. But this . . . my God, Maura, it looks as if every journalist in Ireland is here."

Maura's face is brimming with delight. "Isn't it amazing? Word must have spread. It's going to be on the news. And all over the papers. Everyone is going to know by tomorrow."

"Oh Jesus," I say.

Elizabeth lets go of my hand to cover her ears. I'm tempted to do the same to drown out some of the bustling noise.

There are cameras everywhere. Five or six, at least. Male journalists shove microphones in front of Nuala and Teresa as they hold the banner made from Maura's tablecloth and Christy's shirts.

"Do you really think you will be able to return with contraception?" a man in a brown tweed suit asks.

"Yes, we do," Nuala says.

"And are you worried what people will say?"

"They can say what they like."

Geraldine appears next to me. "Well, well," she says. "This is a turnout for the books, isn't it?" Geraldine is wearing a beautiful floral dress and a checked coat, all in matching vibrant pink. "I wish telly wasn't black and white," she says. "No one can see my bloody outfit."

I laugh. The priorities of a twenty-one-year-old entertain me to no end.

She leans closer to me and whispers in my ear. "I'm getting on the train."

"What? No. You can't. You're not married. What will people say?"

"Ah, Bernie, you're not still worried about that, are ya?"

"Of course I'm worried about that. Your reputation will be ruined."

"I'm getting on. We need single women on the train. We need single women to stand up and say this is not about men. I don't need a husband to fight for my rights. I am a woman. I am strong."

"You'll have your work cut out for you convincing Nuala," I say.

"It was Nuala's idea."

"Never. No way."

"A few more of the women chickened out once they saw the cameras. Something about their mas losing their tempers if they saw their faces on telly. I volunteered to step in and Nuala was only delighted. I have a womb. I have a say."

A reporter overhears Ger. He shoves a camera under her nose.

"Can you say that again, young lady? Can you look into this camera here and repeat exactly what you just said?"

His colleague with a camera on his shoulder points the lens toward Geraldine and I step aside, careful to remain out of view. The reporter raises three fingers in the air and lowers them one at a time. When his hand is closed, Geraldine speaks. A wave of pride washes over me.

"Da," Elizabeth shouts, pulling my attention away from Geraldine and the reporter. "Da, Da, we're over here."

Dan comes into view. He's red-faced and I can tell he's been running.

"What are you doing here?" I ask when he gets closer.

"Get on the train, Bernie."

"What? No. I can't."

"Do it. Get onboard."

I shake my head. "What about the shop? It could destroy us."

"Look around," he says. "Look how amazing this is. You are a part of this, Bernie. Our daughters' lives will be better because of you and Maura and the rest of these women. So please, my love, get on the train."

Bubbles of excitement pop up inside me. I try hard to squash them. I try hard not to let the hype and thrill of it all carry me away. "But Mrs. Dunne and so many others have already stopped coming to the shop. What if people see me on the telly?"

"Let them see," Dan says. "For every woman who leaves us, there will be more who want to buy their meat from the husband of a hero."

"Ah, stop that now." I giggle. "I'm no hero."

"Get on the train, Bernie, and I guarantee you will be."

"Go on the train, Ma," Marie says, although she's not entirely sure what she's signing me up for.

"Can I go?" Elizabeth asks.

"Choo-choo, choo-choo," Alice sings.

"Excuse me." Someone taps my shoulder. I turn around to find the reporter in the brown tweed suit behind me. "Are you one of the women getting on the train?"

I take a deep breath and look over my shoulder at my husband. Dan nods and smiles. I let my breath out and say, "Yes. I am. I'm Bernie McCarthy and I'm going to Belfast today."

"Good for you, Mrs. McCarthy. Can I get your photograph for the *Times*? Front page, hopefully."

My confidence wavers but I catch Maura out of the corner of my eye. She spots me too and waves.

"Yes," I say. "But could you take my friend's photo too?"

"Is she getting on board?"

"Yes."

He smiles and I race toward Maura and grab her hand. My words are tumbling out like gibberish.

"I'm going. On the train, I mean. With you and the others. And there's a man. A journalist. A reporter. And he has a friend with a camera. And Ger is going to be on the telly. She's going on the train too. Nuala said so. And the man. The reporter. He wants to take our picture for the paper."

"Oh, Bernie," Maura says, and I can tell I've set her head spinning. "You're really coming? Are you sure? What about the shop?"

I shrug. "We'll figure it out. We'll figure it all out. Come quick. The reporter is waiting."

Maura and I stand side by side on platform two with the train to Belfast waiting behind us. Maura drapes her arm around me and I slip mine behind her. She stands tall and proud. Her hair is piled on her head like a small apple tart and she's wearing corduroy slacks that flare over her shoes like the women in magazines. I wish I'd worn my good skirt instead of a black box-pleated skirt and old shoes, but it matters not a diddle now.

The reporter raises his camera and snaps our photo. "Beautiful," he says.

The Polaroid camera spits a couple of photos out. He takes one for himself and passes the other to me. I ask to borrow the pen I see peeking out of his pocket, and when he passes it to me I turn the photograph over, lean it against my thigh, and write on the back. *22 May 1971*. I have a feeling it's a date I'll never forget. I tuck the photo between my hip and the elastic of my skirt. I cannot wait to add it to my scrapbook later.

A whistle blows, and a man's voice shouts, "All aboard for Belfast."

There's a collective shriek of excitement as the women on platform two raise their placards and banners and march down the black-and-white-checked tiles and start to climb onto the train.

I turn toward Dan and he kisses me.

"I'm very proud of you, my love," he says, with teary eyes.

"Bye-bye, Ma," Marie says.

Elizabeth is sulking; she folds her arms across her chest and doesn't utter a word. Alice has fallen asleep on Dan's shoulder despite the noise.

"I love you too," I say. "I love all of you."

"Come on," Maura says, giddy as she grabs my arm. "It's not much good if the train pulls off without us."

"Best of luck, Maura," Dan says.

"Thank you," she says, taking a moment to smile sincerely at my husband despite our rush. Then she begins to run and I have to try hard to keep up. I turn back just as we board and wave at my family. Every one of them waves back.

CHAPTER 62

Belfast, 22 May 1971

Maura

Belfast is similar to Dublin in many ways. The city is a mix of big cars and little cars, buses and bicycles. It's noisy too. Honking horns, engines purring. Someone on the corner shouting, "Fish and chips. Get your fresh fish and chips. Only twenty pence."

"I'm starving," Teresa says, sniffing the air as the smell of hot, greasy food wafts toward us.

"Condoms and the pill first," Nuala says, matronly. "Then you can get whatever you like."

Teresa giggles, as she does every time the word *condom* is mentioned.

"Right," Nuala says. "We should split up. We can't walk around in a group of nearly fifty; we'll be knocking people over in the street. Pair off, maybe groups of four of five. But no more. Call into as many chemists as you can. Everyone needs to return with at least one packet of condoms each and the pill. Do not forget the pill."

"How will we know what they look like?" Teresa asks.

I know she's talking about condoms, although she can't bring herself to say it.

Nuala shrugs. "They say 'Durex' on the box."

"You can come with us," Geraldine says to Teresa, drawing a circle in the air encompassing herself, Bernie, and me.

Teresa's face flushes.

"I'll do all the talking," Geraldine says. "You just have to put the box in your handbag."

Teresa nods. "I can do that. Sure."

As Nuala requested, we break into small groups. A cameraman follows Sharon and Nuala. He's the only reporter who got on the train and, although Sharon never said, I'm guessing he's her contact in RTÉ. I'm relieved that there isn't a camera to follow us as we head in the opposite direction. It will be embarrassing enough to walk brazenly into a chemist shop and ask for contraception without a camera pointed in my face as I do.

The main shopping street is busy. My hopes of dashing in and out of the chemist unseen were fanciful. Geraldine is giddy, like a child on Christmas Eve. She skips instead of walking and she hums the tune of a song I don't recognize.

It's not long before we come to a stop outside a chemist. There's a sign above the door that says PRESCRIPTIONS in thick black lettering, and the man behind the counter is wearing a long white coat that matches his white hair.

Bernie chooses this very moment to discuss the weather. "It's colder up here than at home, isn't it?"

Her nerves are palpable, and there's a jumpy wobble in Teresa's reply. "February weather in May."

Despite the chilly air, I'm hot and sticky. My cheeks are no doubt rosy.

"Are we ready?" Ger asks.

I nod. Bernie closes her eyes and exhales sharply, and Teresa looks as if she might cry.

"You ask for condoms, Bernie," Geraldine suggests.

Bernie taps her chest with her fingertip. "What? Why me?"

"Because you know what the box looks like," Geraldine says.

There's a subtle gasp as Teresa pieces two and two together.

"Have you bought some before?" she asks, and there's a sense of reverence in the way she looks at Bernie.

"Sort of," Bernie says, tugging at the neck of her blouse as if it's suddenly too tight. "But never like this."

"Wow. You're amazing," Teresa says.

"Maura and I will take charge of the pills," Ger says.

"What will I do?" Teresa asks.

Ger smiles kindly. "You can wait out here if it makes you more comfortable."

Teresa thinks about it for a moment. I can almost see the thoughts churning inside her.

"No," she says firmly. "I'm coming in. I've come all this way, I'm going to buy con . . ." She coughs and tries again. "I'm going to buy con . . . Oh Lord."

"It's all right," I say, placing my hand on her shoulder. "Take your time. This is a big step for all of us."

Teresa closes her eyes and I watch a lump work its way down her throat. Then she opens her eyes, stares straight through the shopwindow, and says, "I am going to buy condoms." She squeals like a newborn piglet and jumps for joy on the spot. "I said it. Do you hear me? I said *condom*." A man walks by, oblivious to us, but Teresa steadies and clamps her hand over her mouth. Geraldine laughs.

Inside the chemist, the first thing I notice is the warmth. Then the smell. Cough drops—the hard black kind my ma always had in her pocket that taste like aniseed. I think of Ma now. I wonder what she would think if she could see me. Would she be ashamed? Probably. But I like to think she might feel different if my da wasn't lurking over her shoulder.

Bernie approaches the counter first and the man in the white coat with a name tag that says FRANK comes to her service.

"Hello, how can I help you?" Frank says in a thick accent that I decide sounds beautifully melodic.

Bernie falters, and for a moment I think she will struggle to push the words out. But she forces her shoulders back and with confidence says, "Hello. I would like to buy a packet of condoms, please."

Frank turns around and I hold my breath. I don't say a word, but I'm worried he won't turn back. He bends and picks up a small white box that I recognize straightaway as the same box Geraldine's brother smuggled in for Bernie. Then he passes it to her.

Bernie's hand is shaking as her fingers curl around the box. She doesn't wait for the man to tell her a price before she shoves some British money at him and says, "Thank you." Then she drops her head and runs straight outside.

Teresa repeats the process.

Frank is most entertained by the time I approach the counter.

"Where are you girls from?" he asks.

"Dublin," I say.

"And you've come all the way up here to buy condoms, have you?"

"Yes."

"All right," he says, smiling. "It's a long way to come."

"Two hours on the train."

"And I suppose you want a packet too?"

"No, thank you. I would like the pill, please."

"Can I see your prescription, please?"

"My what?"

"Your prescription from a doctor saying what medication you need."

"I know what a prescription is," I say, jamming my hands on my hips. "But I don't have one. I'm not ill. I just want contraception."

Frank shakes his head and his response catches me off guard. He was perfectly accommodating when Bernie and Teresa asked for contraception. I don't understand why he's taken a dislike to me.

"I'm married," I find myself saying, pointing to my wedding ring as if it justifies all of this. It has come to mean so little, but I know taking it off might be much worse.

"That's fine and dandy, ma'am. But that doesn't change a thing."

"Please?"

"No prescription, no pill, I'm afraid."

"What's wrong?" Geraldine says, stepping forward to stand next to me.

"We can't get the pill."

Geraldine's eyes narrow, confused. "But we were told women in the North can get the pill without problems."

"No prescription, no pill," Frank repeats. "I'm sorry, ladies."

"This is terrible," Geraldine says. Her excitement empties as if someone had turned her upside down and poured her out. "What are we going to do?"

"I can give you condoms, like your friends?" Frank suggests.

"No." Geraldine shakes her head. "We need the pill. We told everyone we would get the pill."

Her panic starts to unravel me as if I am a ball of twine. All our sacrifices will be for nothing if we return to Dublin empty-handed. All of Dan's lost customers. My parents' shame. The women who lost the love and support of their families, friends, and neighbors. It will all have been for nothing.

"Maybe Sharon or Nuala or some of the other women have had better luck in a chemist elsewhere," Geraldine says, clinging to hope that we both know isn't there.

"How can I get it?" I ask.

"It's easy." Frank smiles encouragingly. "Get yourself to a doctor and get a prescription. Everyone does it. I have women coming in here every day with prescriptions. And I've plenty in stock, if you come back then."

"Oh God, no. We don't have time. We need to be back on the train this evening."

Ger is close to tears. It's not like her. I'm once again reminded of how much this means to every woman who set foot on that train this morning. How much of ourselves and our hearts we have given to this fight.

A little bile works its way up the back of my throat before an idea hits me.

"What does it look like? The pill," I say.

"Hmm." Frank folds his arms, thinking. "Like any other tablet, I suppose. Small, round, white."

"Does it look like aspirin?"

Frank flashes a toothy grin. "Yes. Indeed it does."

"Great," I say, instantly feeling a weight lifted off my shoulders. "May I have a box of aspirin, please? Oh, and a small plastic bag."

Frank looks at me as if I've grown a second head, but regardless he passes me the headache medication and a clear plastic bag. I pay for the aspirin, then take the tablets out of the branded bottle and spill them into the small bag.

"There," I say, satisfied. "That'll do just fine."

"That won't stop a pregnancy," Frank says, as if he's worried about my intelligence.

"I know. But no one else will."

"Are you sure you don't want condoms?" he says. "It's important to protect yourself."

"These are just fine. Thank you."

I link Geraldine's arm and leave the shop to rejoin Bernie and Teresa outside.

"Well, did you get the pill?" Bernie asks.

I show her the clear bag with several round white tablets inside.

"Oh my God," she says. "So that's it. A little tablet no bigger than my baby fingernail is the answer to all our problems. Well, I'll be damned."

Later, we regroup. The other women had no trouble purchasing condoms, but they all ran into a dead end accessing the pill without letters from their doctors. When I tell them about my aspirin plan, Nuala hugs me and tells me I am a damn genius. Many of the women dash into more chemists' to buy aspirin of their own. Then we all buy fish and chips and sit at the side of the road to eat it. We must be some sight for passersby. More than forty women dressed in their Sunday best, sitting on the footpath, eating breaded cod and chatting without a care in the world as handbags full of condoms hang off our shoulders.

"We did it," Geraldine says, stuffing her last chip into her mouth. "We damn well did it."

CHAPTER 63

Bernie

Getting back on the train in Belfast is a different matter than boarding in Dublin was. A lot has changed in the space of a few hours. We are not the same women we were when we left our capital city this morning. We departed Dublin as mothers, daughters, sisters, and friends, and we return as lawbreakers. It fills me with anger to think that contraception, so easily accessible for our peers in Northern Ireland, is illegal for us. I'm so full of rage I want to kick something. I lift my leg and draw a swipe at a bright red postbox. My toe throbs instantly and I cry out.

"Are you scared?" Maura asks.

"I'm angry," I say.

"But are you scared?"

I swallow. "Yes."

"Me too."

We climb aboard the train and the banter and excitement that fueled us on the way to Belfast are replaced with silence and nervous anticipation. Almost every woman sits with her handbag on her knees, subconsciously guarding it. I'm no different. Every so often I open my bag and peek inside. Each time I find a box of condoms staring back at me, and it snatches my breath. The train rattles and trundles through scenic countryside. Green fields stretch for miles outside the window like an emerald patchwork quilt. The train seems to move faster on the way home, as if it can't wait to spit us out in Dublin and tell tales of our unsavory behavior in the north.

We're pulling into Drogheda Station before Teresa crumbles and begins to cry.

"Oh Jaysus, not more tears," Geraldine says, rolling her eyes.

"I'm scared," Teresa says.

"We all are," I promise her.

"Speak for yourself," Geraldine says. "I'm not scared. I'm not scared of anyone."

The shrill pitch of her tone contradicts her. There is not a woman among us who isn't worried about the reception we face back home. Teresa has every right to cry. And I have to try mighty hard not to join her.

"Hide in the loo, if you're that worried," Geraldine suggests. "When the train gets into Dublin, hide. No one will notice and you can come out when the guards are gone."

"Oh God. Oh God. Do you really think the gardai will be there? Will they arrest us? I don't want to go to jail."

I want to tell Teresa not to worry, that everything will be all right. But the truth is that maybe the gardai will arrest us. They'd have every right. We've broken the law. It's a stupid, antiquated, disgusting law, but it's a law nonetheless.

There is silence for the rest of the journey. We are all lost in our own thoughts. I worry about my girls. What will life be like for them when their mother is all over the news? Their friends in school, their teachers, our neighbors—they may all treat them differently now. I should regret boarding the train. I should regret the laughs and moments of honest-to-God happiness I felt as I walked the streets of Belfast next to my best friend. But I do not. I do not regret a single moment of this journey. And if I had the chance, I would do it all over again.

Teresa lets out a wail as if she's in physical pain when the train slowly rolls into Connolly Station. The door opens and we all stand up. Time ticks by in slow motion. It's a minute, maybe more, before anyone takes a step forward. Nuala is the first to move. Then Sharon. And soon others follow.

"Let them through. Let them through. Let them through."

Chanting and cheering echo around the station. The noise of it all hits us in the face as soon as we set foot on the platform.

"What's happening?" Teresa says, terrified.

A small number of gardaí are trying to keep a large group of supporters off the platform.

"Stand back," a garda shouts. "Step back."

"Let them through. Let them through. Let them through."

The crowd carries homemade banners and placards, much like the ones we fashioned ourselves. I read as many as I can. CONTRACEPTION IS A HUMAN RIGHT. WELCOME HOME. NO BANNING FAMILY PLANNING.

"What are they saying?" Teresa asks, cupping her ear.

"They're telling the police to let us pass. They're supporting us. Everyone is on our side," I say.

My heart races. I feel a hand around mine. Maura squeezes. "We did it," she says.

"Quick, quick. Take this." Nuala pulls the tablecloth banner from her rucksack. She takes one corner and Sharon takes the other. "Hold it up. Let them see."

The cheering grows even louder as soon as people spot the banner. The gardaí struggle to confine folks to the end of the platform.

Maura, Ger, and I lift it in the middle and all five of us walk behind the long banner. I look over my shoulder to find Teresa behind me. She hasn't run away to hide in the bathroom. She is smiling. The remainder of the women are in a line behind us. We stand together; we walk together. We are brave and we are one.

At the end of the platform, we are guided to one side, where we are told customs are waiting. Uniformed officials stand behind tables, just like the ones from a school classroom, and insist that we open our handbags.

"Fine," Nuala says, shaking off an official who has cupped her elbow. "But you won't like what you see."

The uniformed man with a peaked cap and small, beady eyes shoves his hand into her bag and rummages around. I gasp at the indignity of it all. Nuala doesn't flinch. She stands with her hip jutting out and her arms folded.

The official pulls out the condoms first.

"Are you aware these are illegal?" he asks.

"They shouldn't be," Nuala says.

She reaches into her bag and pulls out the bag of small white tablets.

"I bought these too," she says, with a wide, gummy smile lighting up her whole face.

The man attempts to snatch the plastic bag from her grip but Nuala moves quickly, distancing herself from him. He remains confined behind the table.

"They're mine," Nuala says. "I'm not giving them to you."

The crowd cheers. There's some pushing and shoving. The gardai are losing the battle to hold the people back. I watch a guard hit a man on the head with his baton.

"Now, ladies, take the pill now," Nuala shouts, and her voice sounds as if it could carry for miles.

Every woman on the platform opens her handbag and takes out a single white tablet. Our aspirin. But customs doesn't know that, and the satisfaction I feel is shared by every last one of us.

"One. Two. Three," Nuala says. She opens her mouth wide and tosses the tablet in. All forty-six others of us do the same. Cameras snap. Their flashes blind us. And I've no doubt that we will be on the front cover of every newspaper in Ireland this evening.

We stand and wait. We wait for the gardai to turn their attention away from crowd control and onto us. We wait for customs to instruct that they arrest us. We wait for our fates to be dished out. But no one comes any closer. Customs doesn't open another bag and the gardai don't take a single step toward us.

"Let them through. Let them through. Let them through." The chanting nearly lifts the roof off the station.

"Can we go? Can we leave? Just like that?" Teresa asks.

Nuala nods. She snatches her bag off the table and says, "I'll be taking that," and then she breaks into a run. We all follow.

I spot Dan and the girls in the crowd and I'm racing toward them when I feel a hand on my shoulder. I turn.

"Mrs. Stitch!" I say.

Maura is by my side in an instant. All the noise fades to nothingness and suddenly it is as if we are the only three women standing on the platform, the only three women in the world.

"Well done," Mrs. Stitch says.

"We've put you out of business," Maura says, unable to look at her.

"It's a business I never wanted to be in," she says. "I guess this means contraception must be sort of okay now, doesn't it?"

"Well, Mrs. Stitch, I don't know," I say. "Maybe. Hopefully."

"My name is Bernadette. Bernadette Brighton. I don't think there is any need for Mrs. Stitch anymore," she says. "Thank you."

I hold her gaze for some time. Somehow I am certain Josie is on the platform with us, and both of us can feel it.

By then, Dan has reached us. I fling myself into his arms and hug him as if I have been separated from him for one hundred years. I hug my girls, too, and tell them how much I love them.

Outside the station there are yet more folks gathered. Some are family and friends of the women on the train. Others simply heard about it and have come to offer their support. I spot Maura again to my left. She stands next to Ger and Teresa, and they are blowing up condoms like balloons, tying knots in the ends, and tossing them into the crowd.

Teresa's laughter is youthful and contagious and I wonder if she will remember all of this as the best day of her life. I hope so.

CHAPTER 64

Maura

I'm following the others outside when I feel a firm hand on my shoulder.

"If you wouldn't mind coming with me, Mrs. Davenport," a garda says. He's an older man, with a round belly and a salt-and-pepper moustache.

My body stiffens, instantly guarded, and suddenly I need the bathroom.

"Let her go," Bernie shouts from across the station carpark. "Get your hands off her."

The garda is smiling and there's a kindness in his eyes that throws me. "Mrs. Davenport, please, if you could step this way."

Bernie hurries closer.

"If you arrest her, you'll have to take us all. Do you want to do that? Do you really want to arrest us all?"

The fear in Bernie's eyes stabs me in the chest. I feel it like a blade burrowing into my skin.

"I'm all right," I say, and the lie tastes bitter on my tongue. "Everything will be okay."

I'm not sure if I'm telling Bernie or myself. And it's quite obvious from the look on Bernie's face that she believes it as little as I do. But she backs away.

The garda tilts his head toward a quieter area of the carpark, less congested with celebration. I notice he has a colleague by his side. A younger, silent man.

The two men stand facing me and I feel my insides churn.

"Mrs. Davenport, I'm afraid I have some distressing news."

I don't have words.

"Your husband, Dr. Davenport, passed away this afternoon."

My hand covers my mouth.

"I can imagine this is very hard to hear."

"Where? When? Are you sure it's him?"

"Very sure, I'm afraid. He was discovered in his car outside the hospital by one of his colleagues."

"He works at the hospital; he's a doctor," I say, forgetting that they already introduced Christy as Dr. Davenport.

"I'm sorry. I know this must be terribly upsetting."

I swallow. It is. In spite of everything he did, and my fear that he would one day come home, it is a shock to know my husband is no longer part of this world.

"Your husband had some papers with him at the time of his passing."

"Papers?"

"It seems they are in relation to the sale of your house. Number eleven The Gardens, Rathmines."

"Oh."

"Dr. Davenport passed before he had a chance to sign them, I'm afraid. But I'm sure if you contact your solicitor, they will be able to help with the legal side of that."

"Is the house sold?" I say, struggling to take everything in.

"Not as of this time. But as I said, your solicitor should be able to advise. I'm sorry. I'm sure that is the last thing on your mind right now."

I exhale slowly and sharply, making myself lightheaded.

"Is there anything we can do? Anywhere we can drop you? A lift home, perhaps?" the younger garda says, finding his voice at last.

"I, eh . . ." I glance around at the hustle and bustle. The sounds of triumph reach me now as if I am under water.

"I'm okay," I say. "I will be okay."

And this time, I mean it.

CHAPTER 65

Belfast 2023

Saoirse

"Wow. Just wow. I really had no idea about any of this," I say, slightly embarrassed to admit my poor historical knowledge in front of a woman who indirectly changed my life. Changed all women's lives. "They should teach us this stuff in school."

Maura smiles. "Yes. Maybe someday. We're not great with change in this small island of ours, are we?"

"We're not," I say, and I am reminded of my own struggles, more than fifty years later. "How did he die? Christy, I mean."

Maura shrugs. "Oh, they said a heart attack."

Marie snorts and rolls her eyes, and I guess we're sharing an assumption.

"They put it down to the stress and strain of his high-profile career," Maura adds.

"Really?"

I think of all the doctors I work with. They work long hours and they are almost permanently exhausted, but their hearts are not giving out in their cars. I can't imagine the job was so entirely different back then.

"It's bullshit, I know," Maura says.

I smile. I didn't think Maura had the word *bullshit* in her. How bloody surprising and fabulous, I decide.

Maura sighs. "A fifteen-year-old rape victim could commit suicide. But not a pillar of the community like a doctor. Not Christy Davenport. Nature had to have taken its course. Or so people told themselves, anyway."

"It wasn't considered taking your own life back then," Marie says. "Suicide was a crime. Josie would have been considered someone who committed a crime. Ridiculous, but they had no understanding of mental health. The term wasn't even invented yet."

"Please don't take this the wrong way," I say, choosing my next words carefully. "But I'm so glad I wasn't born until the late eighties."

"It wasn't all bad," Maura says, with a delightful smirk. "It gave me the McCarthys. A family kind enough to open their hearts to me."

"Are you still in touch with Dan?" I ask.

Maura sighs again and her eyes glisten.

"Oh, I'm sorry. Forget I asked. Please."

"Ma passed away in twenty twelve," Marie says. "Cancer. She fought it for five years. But it beat her in the end. She was sixty-nine. Da followed her a year later. Alice, my youngest sister, swears Da died of a broken heart. I think so too."

"Oh absolutely," I say, as if I know Bernie and Dan personally. "He loved her so much."

"Thank you. Yes, he did."

There is a screeching of brakes and I realize with a heavy heart that we have pulled into the station. I glance out the window and find BELFAST clearly signposted.

"It's time, Aunty Maura. Are you ready?"

Marie links Maura's arm and helps her stand. Maura is shaky getting to her feet and I wonder if I should help. I've no doubt Maura's stiffness is the legacy of the broken leg Christy inflicted. And all the lovely train wine added on top.

"The reporters called it the contraceptive train," Maura says, turning back to me. "Or the condom train, for those who like to give all the credit to the penis."

I smile. *Penis* is yet another word I didn't think I'd hear from Maura.

"We didn't mind what they called it once it got the word out. The women of Ireland had had enough. We wanted safe and legal contraception. Even Mrs. Stitch was on board, and that was saying something."

I laugh. Marie does too.

"Come on, Aunty Maura, leave this poor girl be," Marie says, closing the scrapbook carefully before she picks it up and tucks it under her arm.

"No, no, it's okay," I say quickly, trying to hold on to Maura and her story for as long as I can. "I'm just amazed at all of it."

"You know, earlier, in Connolly Station, I spotted a machine in the ladies' loos that will spit out a condom for two euros. What a long way we've come," Maura says.

"Maura, do you know that women under thirty-two have *free* contraception these days? The pill, the coil, the implant. You name it. It's all free."

Maura sighs. "That's great, Saoirse. But, as ever, it would seem birth control is a woman's problem. I suppose we *have* come a long way, but I think there's a lot further to go."

"Yes," I say. "Yes, there bloody is."

Marie curls her arm a little tighter around Maura's. "It was lovely to meet you," she says warmly.

"Yes. You too. Enjoy the city."

"We will," Marie says. "We come up every year. On the anniversary. Covid threw us off for a while, but we're back on track now."

I look at the determined elderly lady linking Marie's arm, and I have no doubt that she will return to Belfast for the rest of her days.

They turn to leave. "Wait, wait," I call out, a little too loudly for the limited space of the carriage. "Can I get a photo of us before you go?"

Maura turns her head over her shoulder.

"I don't have a lovely scrapbook like Bernie, but I'd really like to keep a memory of today on my phone. So when I share this story with my friends I can show them our picture."

"You're going to tell your friends?" Maura's eyes sparkle.

"Yes. Of course. I can't wait to tell them."

"Oh, lovely, Saoirse. You remind me of Bernie so much."

Marie nods and adds, "Ma would have liked you a lot."

I blush. I don't think I've received a nicer compliment before.

I stand up and drape my arm over Maura's shoulders. Then Marie takes my phone and snaps our picture. After, I show it to Maura and she says, "Oh goodness, my hair needs doing. I'll be in to the hairdresser first thing next week."

I smile and suspect that in fifty years Maura hasn't changed a bit.

I watch Marie and Maura disembark and meet other people on the platform. Two women so like Marie—Elizabeth and Alice. There are men and teenagers, and a handful of other adults too, grown-up children, I suspect. There is a baby on someone's hip and I realize that one of the McCarthy girls is now a grandmother. I stay on the train and watch them through the window. They clearly care for one another, and they care for Maura. I suspect that long after Bernie and Dan and Maura, the McCarthy girls, their children, and their children's children will continue to return to the city where a small group of trailblazing women shaped history.

CHAPTER 66

Saoirse

A man in a high-visibility jacket approaches me.

"The train terminates here. You need to get off."

I nod. "I know. It's just that I had the loveliest journey and I needed a minute . . ."

"Are you drunk?"

"No." I take instant offense.

"Okay, good. Then can you please get off? The cleaners need to come on."

I straighten up and my back cracks audibly. "Yeah. Sure. Sorry."

"You're from Dublin?"

I wonder if he recognizes my accent or if he's basing his observation on the train's origin.

"Yeah."

"My girlfriend is from Dublin. Nice place."

"Yes. It is."

As requested, I get off the train. I wander down the platform. The architecture in the station is beautiful and I pull out my phone to take a picture. I send it to Miles.

We need to talk x

Miles texts back instantly.

We do 😗

I walk onto the street and find a bench outside Boots and sit down. I imagine Belfast as a very different place half a century ago. I try to imagine the pharmacies from Maura's story. They seemed like corner stores—like veg shops, or a newsagent. I can't imagine they were anything like the giant chain Boots has become today. I collect the pill in Boots on Grafton Street every month. I will think of it all quite differently the next time I walk inside the door. I scroll through my contacts. I know Miles's number by heart, but I look him up anyway. It's a distraction. I'm buying time, needlessly, because the words are on the tip of my tongue. They are going to spill at some point one way or another. They are words I should have said a long time ago, but I was frightened. I'm still scared. But I'm pushing past it.

I hold my phone to my ear and Miles answers after a single ring.

"Hey," he says. "I was worried."

"I know. I'm sorry."

"So, Belfast?"

"Yeah. I know. Crazy. Nice city, though."

"Are you coming home?"

"Yeah. On the next train."

"Good. Good. I'll wait up."

"Miles?" I swallow hard, and suddenly I don't want to say the next words. They're too big.

"Yeah?"

"It's over, isn't it?"

The line is silent for a moment before Miles sighs. "Yeah," he says. "I think it is."

"You're going to be a great dad someday. I really mean that. Someday you're going to find the perfect woman. With great boobs and a ten for an ass and you are going to make beautiful babies."

There's a pause as the gravity of this settles over both of us. My heart is breaking. It sits in my chest in a million pieces as I give up the man I love.

And yet, in another way, it is whole, and I am full. I give myself permission to let go.

"I want that for you," I say. "I want you to be happy."

"And you? Will you be okay?"

I think for a moment and I look at the train tracks that have led me here, led the women before me here. And I say, "I already am."

ACKNOWLEDGMENTS

This book came about entirely by accident. I was deep in a Wikipedia rabbit hole, researching a different story, when I stumbled upon the events of May 22, 1971. I couldn't believe that a small group of trailblazing women had reshaped Irish history, and yet, to my shame, I knew nothing about it.

I couldn't wait to discuss this tidbit of the past with my wonderful agent, Hannah Todd, at the Madeleine Milburn Agency, over Zoom.

"Oh my God, you have to write a story about this," she said, with an encouraging smile that filled me with joy.

Months later, when Hannah called me, with dodgy reception from a London bus (because the electricity was out in her office—long story), to tell me that some lovely publishers were bidding to acquire the book, I found myself shouting, "*What?!*" Thankfully, the line was bad and Hannah's hearing remains undamaged from my screeching, but it will forever be my favorite ever phone call. I am beyond grateful that this story resonated with people from the very beginning. A million thank-yous, Hannah.

Also, thanks to Hayley Steed for encouraging me to try my hand at historical fiction. And to Elinor Davies for never making me feel like any of my publishing-related questions are too silly—even though we both know they're quite ridiculous.

To my fabulous editor, Hannah Braaten. Thank you for caring about this story so much. And to Sarah Schlick for notes that made editing a pleasure. And to both for keeping me well-informed every little step along the way.

To the wider team at Gallery—I'm so grateful for your time and expertise. Thank you!

Writing a novel set before your own existence means asking a lot of questions, fact-checking endlessly, and quite possibly being a nuisance with too many emails to people in the know.

To my mother, for living through it all and for sharing your memories of life as a young woman living in a country reluctant to change.

Irish rail for swift and fact-filled help—thank you. Especially Orla.

Citizen's Information for not blocking my emails. There were many. And for all the links. You may have unwittingly inspired several further novels.

Angela Gleeson for filling me in on life as a sales assistant in the '60s. And for the lovely tea and scones.

Sophie Keogh. Your knowledge of all things TV and media was invaluable.

To my fellow writer and dear friend Caroline Finnerty for always listening and encouraging me, and insisting that we should celebrate publication with bubbles.

My friends and family, who never get sick of my talking about books. Or, if you do, for doing an excellent job of hiding it. Shout-out to Aisling Ownes Nash, who will bend the ear off anyone about this book given half a chance.

To my husband, Brian, and my kids, Sophie, Ciarán, Aaron, Conor, and Chloe. And for keeping it real with questions like, "What's for dinner?" and "Did you do a food shop?" I love you. And yes, I will continue to feed you.

My dad and my niece. Losing you both in early 2016 was the greatest pain I have ever known. I miss you. It's no exaggeration to say I think of you both every single day. Always such champions of my writing—believing in me, when I didn't believe in myself. I hope this book makes you proud. I am so grateful to borrow your names. Seeing "Laura Anthony" on the cover makes my heart ache and soar in equal measure each time.

Finally, to the women who boarded a Dublin train bound for Belfast with no idea what the future held. Women's autonomy is valued today more than ever because of your actions. Your determination enables my sisters, my friends, my peers, and our daughters to live in a country where control of our choices is at our fingertips. Thank you, thank you!